Deadly Deliverance

Candle Sutton

One

The road had been designed by the devil himself.

Every EMT in the Lincoln City area cringed when a call came from this road. Sharp corners, steep drop-offs, and a high speed limit made for a deadly combination.

Today was no exception.

Dimitrios Lykos eased a brace around the neck of a boy who couldn't be any older than eight. The angle of the boy's leg indicated multiple fractures, but at least the bone hadn't broken through the skin.

A bump the size of a lemon rose on the left side of the child's forehead. Likely concussed.

The kid moaned and his eyelids flickered.

"Hey, buddy." Dimitrios purposely kept an upbeat tone, even though the severity of the scene around him was anything but positive. "What's your name?"

The kid mumbled gibberish.

"I'm Mitri. I'm gonna get you all fixed up, okay? Can you tell me your name?"

"Seth." The word croaked out, barely audible.

"Hi Seth. Hang in there, okay?"

The kid's eyes never opened.

Probably not a bad thing. No kid should ever have to see his mother slumped in a pool of her own blood.

Dimitrios' gaze flicked to the dead woman. Her mouth hung slack in a soundless scream and her eyes stared at what only the dead could see.

He looked away.

Not that it mattered. Her empty eyes were seared across his memory and would haunt his dreams for weeks.

A gurney crunched across glass-littered pavement, coming to a stop behind him.

"What've we got?" Mike leaned in to get a look at the kid.

"Multiple fractures, possible concussion." Dimitrios slid a glance at Mike. Well, he looked okay. Not that anyone would blame him if he wasn't.

"You can stop doing that." Mike bit out the words. "I'm fine."

"It's okay if you're not, you know."

"Just watch out for the patient."

At least the irritation was a step up from the utter lack of emotion Mike had exhibited in the two days since Regan's body had been found. It'd been like hanging out with a zombie.

Frankly, he didn't know how Mike could even work so soon after his girlfriend's murder.

Especially since she'd been killed only one day after Christmas.

They gently strapped Seth to the gurney and rolled it to the back of the waiting ambulance.

Dimitrios hopped in beside the gurney and slammed the doors behind him. Mike slid behind the wheel.

The siren shrilled as Mike put the vehicle into motion.

The ride took only minutes, but may as well have been hours. Between Seth's whimpering and worries about how Mike was really doing, Dimitrios couldn't help feeling like he'd aged five years during the five minute drive.

At least the kid seemed stable.

Mike cut the siren as they glided up to the double doors leading to the emergency room.

Pushing open the back doors, Dimitrios slid the gurney to the end. Mike was already there, grabbing the opposite side.

The legs of the gurney scraped open and dropped to the

ground.

Crack!

The sound bounced off the hospital, reverberating off the pavement. He turned just in time to see Mike collapse.

What…?

"Mike?"

He raced around the gurney.

Mike sprawled on the blacktop, oil puddling around him.

No. Not oil.

Blood.

Coming from a wound on his chest.

He dropped to his knees beside his partner. The crimson on the front of Mike's uniform spread like cancer, as did the lake beneath him.

Likely a through and through judging from the amount of blood.

The blood kept pumping. Way too much of it. If he didn't stop it - fast - Mike was going to bleed out right in front of him.

He ripped back the fabric of Mike's shirt.

Blood flowed from a wound too saturated to see.

"Help!" He jumped up and snatched a package of quick clotting gauze and a handful of regular gauze from the ambulance. "I need help out here!"

Like anyone inside would hear him.

A woman stood frozen on the sidewalk, two teenage boys beside her. He speared them with a look. "Go inside. Tell them I need as many people out here as possible."

The oldest teen responded first, sprinting toward the sliding doors of the ER.

Dimitrios knelt beside Mike, tore open the package of quick clotting gauze, and fed it into the wound.

Too much blood. Not even the clotting agent on the gauze was enough to stem the flow.

But he had to try.

Mike's face had less color than the sheets on the gurney.

Each breath gurgled. A sheen of sweat coated Mike's pasty forehead and his eyes looked glazed as they flicked from side to side.

"Come on, Mike. Stay with me."

Mike's lips moved. Blood leaked from the corner of his mouth.

Dimitrios swore softly. He was losing him.

He glanced at the ER doors. "Come on, hurry!"

"Mitri." Mike's raspy voice captured Dimitrios' attention.

"I'm here, buddy. You're gonna be okay."

He was such a liar.

"Help–"

"Help's coming, man. Just hang in there."

"No!" The word came out with more force than Dimitrios thought Mike could have mustered. "Ari. Help."

"I'll help Ari. So will you." Didn't know what they were helping her with, but he'd say anything to keep Mike calm.

"Fast… track… heaven." The words cost Mike.

"Not a chance, buddy. You don't get to go there just yet." He kept his tone light, even as he saw Mike fading.

"God's… timing…."

"Yeah, well God can't have you. You're needed here."

Wheels rattled toward them, drowning out anything else Mike might have tried to say.

He glanced up to see several orderlies and Margie, the head nurse, rushing toward him.

Good. Margie was the best. Maybe Mike had a chance.

"The kid."

Margie nodded. "We got him, hon."

He looked back at Mike. And knew that this was one battle they were all going to lose.

Unconscious now, each breath rattled through Mike's chest and came out on a wheeze. At least several pints of blood stained the ground around Mike. More oozed from the wound, which had permeated the gauze and now seeped through Dimitrios' fingers.

Mike. His closest friend since the first grade was dying right in front of him and there was nothing he could do to stop it.

But they had to try.

An orderly knelt by Mike's other side.

Dimitrios shifted his gaze up to the other man. "Ready? Lift."

They lifted Mike to the gurney and raced inside. A doctor met them at the door, falling into step beside them and assessing Mike's condition as they wheeled him toward the operating room.

A nurse joined them, pushing Dimitrios out of the way.

They whisked Mike through the operating room doors.

For several long seconds he stood there, unable to move, unable to tear his gaze from the double doors in front of him.

There was nothing more he could do.

It'd been a long time since he'd felt this helpless.

Almost eight years, to be exact.

It was hard to believe it'd been that long since he'd learned his sister Milana was alive, since he'd watched her struggle to survive a gunshot wound.

But Mike had stood beside him then. Now he had no one.

Gunshot wound.

Gunshot.

Reality slammed through him and stole the air from his lungs. Mike had been shot!

Why would anyone shoot Mike?

Milana he could understand since she worked in law enforcement, but Mike? He was just an EMT.

Could it have something to do with Regan's murder? It was pretty coincidental that this happened the same week Regan turned up dead.

Maybe it was random.

Yeah, that had to be it. Mike was a good guy. Everyone liked him.

But if it were random, wouldn't the person responsible

have shot him, too? He'd been an easy target, out there in the open. And the shooter was obviously a good enough shot to have hit him, regardless of how easy or difficult the shot might have been.

Besides, the little town of Lincoln City, Oregon seemed an unlikely place for a sniper to start randomly picking off targets.

He slumped against the wall and leaned his head back.

Mike's ashen face filled his vision. Everywhere he looked, it was all he could see. His friend, struggling to breathe. Struggling to speak.

Wait. Mike had been pretty determined to tell him something.

What was it he'd said? That nonsense about fast track to heaven. And help Ari.

What the heck was that supposed to mean? Ari was Araceli, a friend he'd known almost as long as Mike, but what was he supposed to help her with?

Or was she supposed to help him? Or Mike?

It didn't make sense, but maybe Ari would know.

So would Mike.

Dimitrios clenched his lips together. He'd ask Mike when he woke up. There was no way this would take Mike down. Mike was tough, maybe the toughest guy he knew. He'd beat this, probably faster than anyone thought possible.

Sure, there'd been death written all over Mike's face. Sure, it was a look he'd seen countless times over his career, but never on Mike.

Mike would be fine.

He had to be.

A hand alighted on his arm.

He turned to find Margie standing beside him. Although her head barely reached his shoulder, she had the presence of a giant. Her short white hair was carefully styled and the laugh lines at the corners of her eyes denied the trauma she'd witnessed over the years.

"How you doin', hon?"

The small shrug he offered was a more honest response than he would've given most, but this was Margie.

"The kid's going to be okay. They're doin' surgery on his leg now and he's got a concussion, but he should recover fine. You guys did good work out there."

He'd forgotten all about the kid.

While he was glad the kid would be fine, the only patient he currently cared about was fighting for his life behind the swinging doors in front of him.

Silence descended.

At least Margie wasn't one to offer false promises. None of those empty platitudes like "he'll be fine" or "it could've been worse."

Instead, she stood there, her hand on his arm, offering comfort and strength through the simple gesture.

Time dragged. How long had Mike been in there?

After a few minutes, Margie sighed. "I need to get back. You need anything, you come find me, you hear?"

"Sure." The word scratched through his throat.

Margie's shoes squeaked across the floor, the sound fading as she moved away.

He stood there, alone. The bland walls closed in around him like a crypt.

If only there was something he could do. Anything.

Mike would pray. So would his sister Lana.

But he wasn't one to talk to someone who wasn't there.

The doors swished open. A green-clad doctor, who he recognized but couldn't immediately name, glanced around before approaching. Blood stained the front of the doctor's scrubs and his mouth was fixed in a grim line.

No. It must be a mistake.

Mike was fine.

"How is he?"

But he knew, didn't he? The doctor's expression said it all.

The doctor shook his head slowly. "I'm sorry. We lost

him."

That was wrong.

They couldn't have lost him. Not Mike.

It must be someone else.

"No, Mike Conrad. How is he?"

The doctor placed a heavy hand on Dimitrios' shoulder. "He didn't make it. The bullet…."

Bullet.

The word penetrated Dimitrios' mind as intensely as the projectile had penetrated Mike's flesh.

Who would want Mike dead? And why?

It seemed so impossible. Gangbangers got shot. Cops and FBI and US Marshals like his sister.

But not EMTs.

EMTs saw violence and helped people live through it. They didn't fall victim to it themselves.

The doctor kept talking, something about blood loss and internal damage, but the words jumbled together in a nonsensical fashion.

Sudden silence penetrated the fog in his mind. He blinked.

The doctor's eyes rested on him.

"You're sure?" Stupid question.

The man was a trauma doc. He knew a dead body when he saw one.

Of course he was sure.

The doctor didn't point out any of that, but simply nodded. "There was nothing we could do."

Snow filled his chest. A block of ice wedged in his throat. The chill seeped through his body and froze his tongue.

Not that there was anything left to say.

Mike was dead.

Two

Mike. Dead.

The words rang through his mind, accompanied by images of Mike's death-kissed face.

No! How would he survive without Mike?

One of only two people outside of family that he could go to with anything was now gone. Only Ari was left.

"You need me to call someone for you?" The doctor never took his gaze off Dimitrios' face.

Words failed him. Dimitrios shook his head.

"How about you sit down? You look a little pale."

"I'm fine." The words came out sharp enough to cut.

Sure he was fine. Wasn't that exactly what Mike had said not an hour earlier?

He brushed off the doctor's hand, even as he reminded himself that the man was only trying to help.

"If you're sure…."

He nodded.

The doctor turned toward the swinging doors, shooting one last concerned glance before pushing through.

He was alone. Again.

Only this time he'd been robbed of hope as well.

His vision blurred. He reached a shaking hand toward the wall next to him, the smooth surface feeling warm beneath his icy fingers.

How could Mike be dead?

How!

Short nails grated across the paint as he curled his fingers.

This couldn't be happening.

He wanted to yell. Put his fist through the wall. Point a gun at the person who'd stolen Mike's life.

A hot trail burned down his cheek. Followed by another, and another. He leaned his forehead against the wall and did nothing to try to stem the tide.

He didn't even care if someone saw him. Mike was dead. Nothing else mattered.

Except maybe making sure the person responsible paid for what had happened to Mike.

He sucked in a deep breath.

He had to pull it together.

There were things to do. People to notify.

Except that Mike's parents had died years ago. He had no close family, only a few distant aunts, uncles, and cousins.

None of whom Dimitrios knew how to contact.

Ari.

Mike had been like a brother to her, too. The news would crush her.

As much as he wanted to curl up and shut out the world, he couldn't let her find out about this through normal channels. That was the coward's way out.

He wiped his sleeves across his face.

Red coated his hands, collecting in the cracks and crevasses.

Blood. Mike's blood.

He looked down. It darkened his uniform like a bad dye job.

Ari couldn't see him like this. He'd get cleaned up and then head over there. Before she heard the news from someone else.

Footsteps echoed behind him.

At least he'd regained some control.

He turned.

Detective Jim Whitmire approached, his salt and pepper hair looking as wiry as his frame. Two steps behind was his partner, Courtney Niles, a model-thin woman with cats-eye glasses. While he'd spoken to each of them numerous times at various assaults and domestic violence calls, it'd always been in a professional capacity.

Never as a witness.

"How're you holding up?" Jim's face held a sympathy the man would never put into words.

Dimitrios' eyes strayed down to his blood-stained hands. "Had better days."

Pulling a recorder out of her jacket pocket, Courtney studied him. "You know why we're here?"

Of course he did. He'd been around this kind of thing too long to not know. "Okay if I clean up first?"

"Go for it." Jim nodded. "We'll be right here."

The men's room was only a short distance down the hall. He shouldered through the door, tripping the motion-activated light and banishing the darkness.

He filled his palm with soap and scrubbed.

The suds turned pink, drowning the sink with bubbles that, to him, looked like death.

A glance into the mirror stilled his scrubbing.

Man. He hardly knew the stranger staring back at him.

Puffy, red-webbed dark eyes stared back at him. A streak of blood that didn't belong to him slashed down his right cheek. Thanks to the rain, his hair was no longer spiked, but was plastered to his head like a layer of black skin. Probably had blood in it, not that he could see it.

People talked about living vicariously through others; was it possible to die vicariously as well?

He felt like he'd come to that point. Looked like it, too.

The vise around his heart confirmed he was very much alive.

Rinsing the soap from his hands, he squirted fresh soap into his palm and rubbed some more. Crimson still lined his nails, but he'd probably have to use a brush to get that off.

He splashed his face with water, rubbed the bloody smear, and splashed some more, washing away all evidence of rain, sweat, and tears.

Well, that was probably as good as it was going to get. At least until he got home to take a shower.

Mike was dead and all he could think about was getting clean.

The thought was like a fist to his gut.

The door swished open and a guy in a leather jacket walked in, barely glancing his direction before heading for a urinal.

Life moved on. And he had no choice but to keep moving with it.

He dried his face with the coarse paper towels that could only be found in public restrooms and rejoined Jim and Courtney in the hall.

Time to give his statement. He'd rather do it tomorrow, or the next day.

Or never.

However the sooner he told them what he knew, the sooner they could get to work catching that…

The OR doors swung open and a gurney emerged, draped in a blotchy red and white sheet that used to be only one of those colors.

His stomach plunged.

A buzz filled his head, which felt strangely disconnected from his body. The room spiraled.

"Lykos?" A hand gripped his bicep. "You good?"

He couldn't force his cottony tongue to move or words to work past the block in his throat.

"Hey, grab a doc for me, will ya?"

Jim's words broke through the haze in his mind.

Doc. There was nothing wrong with him.

Dimitrios blinked and gave his head a small shake. The room slowly settled.

"I'm okay. Just…." He drew a breath of antiseptic air. "Need to sit."

He didn't wait for a response. Rubbery legs barely carried him to the waiting room across the hall, where he collapsed into the first chair he encountered.

Man. He needed to pull it together.

It was the least he could do for Mike.

Jim and Courtney settled into chairs across from him.

"We'll give you a minute." Sympathy laced Courtney's words, which did nothing to help Dimitrios' disposition.

Like a minute would change anything. Mike would still be dead. "No. Let's get this over with."

He recapped what had happened. Not that he knew much.

"So you didn't see the shooter? Do you know where the shot came from?" Jim drummed his fingers on his knee.

Dimitrios shook his head. "It happened fast."

Too fast. One minute, Mike was fine. The next, Mike was on the ground, his life spilling out of him.

He swallowed hard, but it did nothing to relieve the pressure in his throat. "I don't know why anyone would want to kill Mike."

"I know this is hard." Courtney leaned closer. "But did Mike have any enemies?"

"Or receive any threats?"

"No. Mike got along with everyone."

Wait. That wasn't exactly true, was it? But was it relevant?

At this point, he'd assume everything was relevant. Besides, it was the police's job to figure that out, anyway.

"Lately Mike had been going off about some guy named Bobby."

Jim's eyes narrowed. "Going off how?"

"Like every bad thing that happened was Bobby's fault. The way Mike talked, you'd think this Bobby guy is the devil himself." It'd really only started up in the last day or two, since Regan's body had turned up. "I thought he was looking for someone to blame for Regan. You know, help him cope. So I didn't give it much weight."

But maybe he'd been wrong.

"You got a last name for this Bobby?"

"Mike never said. I got the feeling Bobby was into gangs or organized crime or something. And that he was connected to Regan's past."

"Regan ever mention him?" Jim studied him.

"No. But she didn't talk about her past. At all."

"What did you think of Regan?" Jim's tone was casual, but Dimitrios wasn't fooled. The detective suspected a connection between Mike's murder and Regan's death. Naturally.

"I didn't know her that well. Like I said, she really kept her guard up. I always felt like she was half a step away from hopping a plane to another country." In fact, she'd really reminded him of some of the domestic violence victims he'd worked with. Secretive and always looking over her shoulder.

"What about that baby from this morning?"

What?

Dimitrios stared at Courtney.

Baby? She had to be talking about the baby who'd disappeared from the hospital earlier, but what did that have to do with Mike's murder? "What about it?"

"Mike said the baby was Regan's. He also said he had paperwork giving him custody in the event that anything happened to her. Could he have taken the baby?"

Mike, a kidnapper? If the idea wasn't so stupid, he might laugh.

"No chance. Mike does..." Dimitrios swallowed, the lump in his throat scraping like a handful of gravel. "...Did everything by the book."

"Yeah, but we all have our limits. Maybe that was his."

No way.

It couldn't have been Mike.

Thoughts flashed through his mind. The nurses had been

talking about the abduction all day. The guy who took the baby had worn baggy clothes, a hat, and managed to avoid having his face get caught on camera.

Mike knew his way around this hospital. Knew where the cameras were.

And he'd been really worked up since the baby had been admitted two days ago. Since then, how many times had Mike ranted about the baby and how the father's story didn't add up?

Too many to count.

Still, Mike breaking the law? Not a chance. "No. Besides, the baby wasn't even his."

"Wasn't his? Whose baby was it?"

"That Bobby guy. Honestly, I'd wondered if Regan was using Mike to have a father for her baby." It sounded pretty horrible out in the open, especially given all that had happened. "But Mike never would have gone outside the law."

Would he?

Mike had been pretty worked up the last few days. He'd gone on and on about how dangerous Bobby was. Could he have thought the baby was in trouble and taken the boy to protect him?

It was possible. Mike would have done what he thought was morally right.

Even if it wasn't the most legal option.

He couldn't voice his doubts. The last thing he wanted was to tarnish Mike's reputation.

"You sure about that? Pretty coincidental that Mike was in our office yesterday trying to get custody of the baby and then today the baby disappears. Don't suppose you were with Mike around five this morning."

"No. But he didn't do it." He couldn't have. Mike would never take a baby from the hospital, no matter what. It'd risk his job, his reputation, his freedom. Heck, Mike would say something about it jeopardizing his witness. He'd heard that line from Mike on more than one occasion about smaller things than this. "Mike's the most honest guy I know."

"I'd get it if he had. Really. I didn't buy the story that guy told when he brought the baby to the ER." Jim laced his fingers together and studied Dimitrios.

None of them had.

The baby had come in with fluid in his lungs and a fractured leg. At-home birth gone wrong according to the father.

Right.

Never mind that Regan was due in three weeks, hadn't been seen in a few days, and had the same blue eyes that the baby had.

When Regan's body turned up the same day, with no sign of the baby, the story had seemed even fishier.

"Don't think we didn't see the evidence." Courtney added, following up on Jim's comment. "Regan gave birth before she died. No one's found any trace of Regan's baby. The baby showed up the day after Regan was last seen."

And the father's name was Robert. Maybe he went by Bobby for short. Maybe the man was the mysterious Bobby that Mike ranted about the last two days of his life.

The problem was that there were too many maybes in this whole mess.

"If you know all that, why didn't you do something?"

Jim shook his head slowly. "It's all circumstantial. You know that."

He did know it. Didn't mean he liked it.

"Besides, the baby looked like the father," Courtney pointed out.

"So? If he had something to do with Regan's murder, does that automatically give him a pass?"

"No. But we have to prove he was involved."

"He had the baby! How'd he get it if he wasn't involved?"

"You know how this works." Jim speared Dimitrios with intense eyes. "Until DNA confirms that baby is Regan's, we have to take the father's word on it. Besides, a woman did come in claiming to be the baby's mother."

What? Dimitrios stared at the detective. He hadn't heard that part before. "When?"

"Yesterday."

The day after the father showed up with the baby, claiming the mother was too weak to get out of bed.

A short, humorless laugh burst from Courtney. "If that woman just had a baby, you can shave my head and call me Carl."

Jim shot his partner a warning look. "Until we can prove it…."

"Wait." Dimitrios stared between the two of them. A simple exam would prove she'd recently given birth. "She wasn't even examined?"

"She refused. Said she was fine. We couldn't force it." Jim leaned in. "Now. Getting back to Mike."

"He didn't take the baby."

"Okay." The tone, if not the expression on Courtney's face, said she remained unconvinced.

Like it mattered. Mike was dead. Nothing would change that.

"I think we've covered it all for now. You'll be around if we have any follow-up questions?" Jim's question was not a request.

Dimitrios nodded. "You know where to find me."

The detectives left and Dimitrios let his head fall into his hands.

He still couldn't believe this was happening. This day had hit him like a Mack truck coming out of nowhere. One minute everything was fine and then BAM! Nothing would be the same.

Part of him wished he'd seen it coming.

But none of them had. No one could have guessed….

Wait. That wasn't true.

Mike *had* seen something like this coming. The key he'd

given Dimitrios yesterday was proof. The key that opened a safety deposit box at Mike's bank. The bank Mike had dragged him to yesterday when he'd insisted upon transferring the box to Dimitrios' name.

Why hadn't he taken Mike seriously? Maybe if he had, Mike would still be alive.

But no. He'd teased Mike about being suicidal.

Mike hadn't laughed. That should've been his first clue something was seriously wrong.

What if he'd handled things differently? Could he have done something to stop Mike from being killed?

Instead, he'd argued with Mike about transferring the box then caved when Mike got more agitated than he'd ever seen him.

He'd planned to give it a week or two then switch the box back to Mike's name.

Except Mike hadn't had a week or two.

A sigh shuddered through him.

If only he hadn't shrugged it all off. Instead, he'd attributed it to Mike's recent bout of paranoia. Paranoia that had turned out to be for legitimate reasons.

He rubbed his face, then forced himself to stand.

He could blame himself later. For now, he needed to get to Araceli's and tell her the news before she heard it from someone else.

Three

Dimitrios slid behind the wheel of his Jeep and closed the door, but didn't start the vehicle.

Because, honestly, this was the last thing he wanted to do. Ever.

Telling Ari what had happened to Mike… how could he even find the words? But she deserved to hear it from him, not on the news or around town.

The three of them had been through a lot together. This would hit hard.

And he would be there for it. For her. No matter what.

He started the Jeep and cranked the heat. Usually the late December cold didn't bother him, but he couldn't shake the chill that had settled into his core when he saw Mike on the ground.

Not even the hot shower he'd taken had helped.

Just like no amount of scrubbing had made him feel clean. He still felt Mike's blood all over him.

The dash clock read 10:03 when he stopped in front of Araceli's older, two-bedroom home.

Knowing her, she was probably getting ready for bed, but would still be up. The light filtering through the curtains confirmed his guess.

He stepped out of the Jeep, the cold enveloping him like the layer of ice around his heart.

What would he say? Every word that came to mind was

inadequate. Was there even a good way to say it?

His shoes felt made of concrete as he forced one foot in front of the other.

It took ages to reach the door. Yet at the same time, he felt like he reached it too soon. The doorbell caved beneath his finger and chimes echoed inside.

He shifted his weight.

Several long seconds passed before he heard movement inside. A few more seconds scraped by before the porch light blinked on.

The deadbolt clicked and the knob rattled, then the door swung open.

And there she was. In faded jeans, a floral print shirt that neither accented nor hid her curves, and bare feet. Deep blue streaked her black hair, which brushed her shoulders in waves that looked made of silk.

Araceli's lips curled into an easy smile.

So unsuspecting. She had no idea the bomb he was about to drop.

Or did she?

Creases marred the skin by her eyes, which darted behind Dimitrios and to the shadows on either side of him.

"Mitri." She cleared her throat and stepped back. "Come on in."

He crossed the threshold without a word. Honestly, he wasn't sure he trusted his voice right now, although he'd have to use it. And soon.

Following her into the living room, he waited until she sat on the sofa before perching on the chair immediately to her left.

"This is..." The smile slid from her face. "What's happened?"

Fire kindled behind his eyes.

No. He would not cry.

Not again. Not here. Not when Ari needed him to be strong.

He'd fallen apart earlier, but he had to hold it together now. Even though he'd lost one of the best people in his life.

"Mitri?" It came out on a breath, as though Ari's lungs refused to function.

The words wouldn't come. His eyes desperately searched the room, landing on an exotic plant on the end table closest to him. "That's new."

No doubt she recognized the cheap distraction for what it was, but she played along. As he knew she would. "It's an African Milk Plant."

"Toxic?"

"Like I'd have anything else?"

Big surprise. Her greenhouse specialized in unusual plants, many of which made their way into her home.

She'd never been a rose kind of girl. Still, the small reddish flowers on this plant were pretty. "So what'll this one do to me if I touch it?"

"Rash. Can even blister the skin, I guess. Not that I've felt like testing that theory." She placed her hand on his arm. "Just tell me."

"I-it's Mike." He fought to get the word past his frozen lips. "There was… He's dead."

Araceli stared at him. Like she was waiting for him to smile and say he was kidding.

But this was no joke.

Her chin shuddered. Lamplight glowed in the tears filling her dark eyes. "Mike? Y-you're sure?"

He nodded.

The first tear escaped down her cheek in a crooked, wet trail.

That one tear was like the crack in a dam. Tears drenched her skin. A harsh sob shattered the quiet.

The pain in his throat was nothing compared to the pain in his heart as she buried her face in her hands, her whole body shaking with the force of her tears.

He pushed up and came to sit beside her, pulling her

against his chest.

The room swirled. A part of him wanted to let go of his control and weep with her, but he pushed the instinct aside.

Tears wouldn't solve anything.

No, the only thing that would make this better was to track down the person responsible and make him pay.

He held her until the shaking stopped and her breathing evened out. He probably wouldn't have released her if she hadn't pulled back to look at him.

"What happened?" Her voice had an unusually gravelly quality to it.

It would be so nice to lie to her. Tell her that there'd been an accident. That Mike had died helping someone.

But he wouldn't lie. Not to her.

Besides, she'd hear the truth somewhere anyway.

"He was shot."

A few more tears leaked out and her eyes slid closed, but she didn't lose control. After several seconds, she focused her eyes on him. "Why?"

"I wish I knew." Should he ask her about the Bobby guy Mike had gone on about? Couldn't hurt, could it? Besides, maybe she'd know more than he did. "Mike ever mention a guy named Bobby to you?"

Ari froze. Her gaze locked on him for a second before darting behind him and back again.

Was someone else here?

He turned around.

No one there. Just the hallway leading back to the bedrooms. Which seemed quiet. He turned back to Ari.

She fidgeted with her hands. Her tongue briefly slid across her lips and she shifted in her seat.

Something wasn't right. "Talk to me, Ari."

"He… he told me not to tell anyone."

The catch in her voice nearly crushed his heart. "Who? Mike?"

A halting nod answered his question.

"Well, he's–" The word *dead* froze in his mouth. "Not here. And it might help."

She stared at him, her brown eyes looking nearly black in the dim light. Several seconds lingered before she pushed up from the sofa. "Come on. Just don't freak out, okay?"

Alarms wailed in his head. What could be so bad that she'd preface it with a warning?

He followed her down the short hallway, stopping outside the spare bedroom.

The door stood open, the dark room stretching in front of him.

Araceli didn't turn on the light, but walked in, pausing by a lump on the bed. As he drew closer, he realized it wasn't a lump at all.

A baby. Just days old, from the looks of him. Wrapped snugly in a blue monkey blanket.

Where did…?

No.

He stared at the sleeping, fair-skinned face. Traces of light blond hair curled on top of the baby's head.

The baby from the hospital? It had to be. Araceli didn't have children.

The cops had been right. Mike *had* taken him.

Worse than that, he'd gotten Ari involved. How could Mike have done that?

"What were you thinking?" His words contained a sharp edge that he did nothing to temper.

"Shhh." Araceli gestured for him to precede her out of the room. Once in the hall, she closed the door, leaving it slightly ajar. "Mike said he needed me to watch him for the day. That's all."

"That's all?" He couldn't be hearing this right. Didn't the word kidnapping mean anything to her? "You could get arrested for having him here!"

"Will you keep your voice down? You'll wake him." She rubbed her forehead. "What do you mean arrested?"

"You're an accomplice! They could convict you and put you in prison."

"Prison?" The word rasped from her, her eyes widening until they dominated her face. "For babysitting for a friend?"

"That's not Mike's baby!"

"No, he's Regan's." The words sounded so logical coming from her. "And Regan had paperwork drawn up giving Mike guardianship in case anything happened to her."

"We don't know for sure that's Regan's baby. Mike...." He couldn't believe they were even having this conversation. "Mike took him from the hospital."

"Took?" Confusion laced the word, but even now, he could see the horrible truth taking root in her mind.

"Yeah. As in kidnapped. The father filed a report with the police earlier today."

If she lost any more color, he'd be picking her up off the floor. "Mike would never do that."

"That's what I said. But," he gestured toward the semi-closed door. "Here we are."

She swayed slightly.

He supported her under her elbow and led her to the living room, not releasing her until she lowered herself onto the sofa.

"So you didn't know?" Not that it would make a difference in the law's eyes.

Ari shook her head. "He told me it was Regan's baby and begged me to stay home from work today. He said there was no one else he could ask." A sob hiccupped out. "He's been through so much this week, I couldn't say no."

"You didn't ask where he found the baby?"

"It didn't even occur to me." She swiped a few tears from her cheeks. "He looked so desperate."

Of course he had. Anyone would look desperate after kidnapping a baby from the hospital. "Did he say anything else? Like what he planned to do tomorrow?"

"I don't think he had a plan. He did tell me that Regan's

ex was looking for the baby and to be careful."

"Why?"

"He said Bobby killed Regan."

Of course he'd said that. But was it the truth? Or nothing more than the crazy ramblings of Mike's paranoia? "And you didn't think that having the baby here was dangerous?"

She shrugged slightly, but avoided his eyes. "The baby had to stay somewhere. Besides, how would they track the baby here?"

It wouldn't be that hard to figure out who Mike's friends were. Dimitrios kept the thought to himself. No point in worrying her tonight, especially since anyone trying to hurt her would have to get past him.

But what to do now? Mike was gone. And they had no legitimate claim to the baby.

"We need to call the police."

"No!" Ari grabbed his hand and squeezed hard, her fingernails poking into his skin. "We can't. Mike asked me to keep the baby safe."

"He's not our baby." Ooh, that didn't come out like he'd intended. "We have to let the police handle this."

"But they'll turn him over to Bobby. And if he killed Regan… we can't give a baby to a murderer. What if he kills him?"

"He wouldn't kill his own son." Would he? Dimitrios tried to squash the doubt. Not an easy task given how many calls he'd responded to over the years where parents had hurt, and on one occasion even killed, their own children.

"You don't know that. You read about this kind of thing online all the time."

Crazy how closely Araceli's words mirrored his own thoughts. Still, it really didn't matter. "It's not our call. We have to do what's right."

"And it's right to hand an innocent baby over to a killer?"

"We don't know that this baby's father killed anyone." No matter how likely it seemed.

"You don't believe that." Araceli's hand squeezed more tightly over his own. "Could you live with yourself? If something happened? We have the chance to save a life."

Man. She knew what to say to cut to his heart, didn't she? "You realize what you're suggesting? That we break the law?"

"Sometimes the law is wrong. Besides, Mike gave me the legal documents granting him custody."

"If," he dropped the word like a hand grenade, "this is Regan's baby. Which we can't prove."

Not until the DNA tests came back, anyway. Which likely wouldn't be anytime soon.

"Well, Bobby can't prove it isn't her baby."

"DNA tests will prove that it's his baby, too. No matter what documentation Regan had drawn up, the courts will probably side with the father."

"But that's not what's best for the baby!"

"Can you prove that?" No matter what Mike had said about Bobby, they couldn't prove anything.

Obviously Mike hadn't been able to prove it either. He wouldn't have taken the baby unless he thought that was his only recourse.

She sighed. "Will you at least think about it? Wait until tomorrow to make your decision?"

Maybe a few more hours wouldn't hurt anything. It'd been a long day for both of them.

And frankly, he didn't have the energy to deal with it right now anyway.

He found himself agreeing before he could give it any more thought.

"Thank you." She tucked her blue-streaked hair behind her ears. "What do we do now?"

"I don't know." But maybe it was time to take the things Mike had said the last few days more seriously. "What did Mike tell you about Bobby?"

"Not much." She paused, her eyes searching the ceiling as though she expected to find the answers written there. "He said Bobby was Regan's ex and that Bobby had killed her. That's it, I think."

It wasn't a lot to go on. Especially since Mike hadn't told him much more. "I got the impression Bobby's in the Mafia or some kind of organized crime. But I didn't take Mike seriously."

A regret he'd carry the rest of his life.

"Okay, I'll try to figure out who this Bobby guy is." He pushed himself to his feet and stared at her. Sitting on the couch with her feet curled up under her, she looked so small. "You gonna be okay here on your own?"

It sounded stupid. She'd been on her own since divorcing her cheating dog of a husband three years ago.

But she'd never had a baby dumped on her before.

Never had a friend murdered.

Never been facing a possible mob threat.

She forced a smile that wobbled like a toddler taking first steps. "I'll be fine. Go. Figure out who killed Mike."

Oh, he would. He didn't know where or how to start, but one way or another, he'd figure it out.

Mike was dead and someone had to pay.

* * * * *

"Is it done?" Bobby held Nicky's gaze with his own.

Nicky's thick neck rippled as he gave a single nod. "No sign of the package, though."

The package was only one of his concerns. "And my son?"

Nicky's silence answered the question.

"You're sure?"

The question came out sharp, but Nicky didn't flinch. "We tore the place apart. Regan's too. Not there."

Bobby swore. They'd already searched Regan's place once, so he hadn't expected they'd find the evidence there, but the whore's boyfriend had seemed a logical choice.

Where else would Regan have put it?

"Got an idea, though."

Bobby waited.

"When I capped him, that EMT said something to his partner. Might be a place to start."

As far as ideas went, it wasn't the worst one.

Bobby rubbed the back of his neck. He wanted nothing more than to put the salt of this ocean town far behind him.

No better ideas presented. Bobby fixed his eyes on Nicky. "Do it. Be as persuasive as you need to be. Just find the package. And my son."

Nicky left the room without another word.

Bobby watched him go but didn't move. He would have what was his. No matter the cost.

Four

The bank's polished tile floor tossed Dimitrios' reflection back up at him with the pristine clarity of a mirror. His shoes squeaked, the sound echoing in the high-ceilinged lobby.

It was as quiet as the morgue. Had about as much life, too. Shouldn't there be more people around?

Shivers raced up his spine.

He rounded an empty seating area and found a single teller behind the counter.

The woman looked up as he approached, a toothy smile engulfing her round face. If she noticed his sunken eyes or drawn features, she was polite enough not to stare. "How may I help you?"

"I need to access a safe deposit box."

Why hadn't he done that before Mike died? When he and Mike had come down here to transfer the box, he should've insisted on looking inside it.

If he had, maybe he would've known just how bad the situation was before Mike had been shot.

Maybe he could've prevented it from happening.

"Of course, sir." She turned to her keyboard. "Let me pull that up on my system."

He answered her questions reflexively and handed over his driver's license, all the while fingering the key in his pocket, the key Mike had given him not two days ago.

"Okay, sir. We're all set. If you'll have a seat, the branch manager will be with you in a moment."

It took the branch manager to access a safe deposit box?

Well, what did he know, anyway?

Dimitrios wandered over to the seating area, but didn't sit. Instead, he stared out the window, watching the traffic move along the street.

Life went on. In spite of the staggering loss in his own life.

It wasn't right.

"Mr. Lykos?"

Dimitrios turned at the sound of his name. A hefty man in a brown suit with a mustard colored tie stood a few feet away. He recognized the man from when Mike had transferred the box. "Yes."

"I heard about Mr. Conrad. Such a shame." He paused momentarily, skimming his face. "I'm sorry for your loss."

His trachea tightened until it felt like steel. All he could do was nod.

"If you'll come with me, I'll see to that box."

Dimitrios fell into step with the man, who didn't seem inclined to fill the silence with empty chatter. His feet felt heavy as he walked down the hallway. They stopped outside a solid steel door, which prevented him from seeing inside the room.

The manager punched in a code and pulled the door open.

Dimitrios followed him inside on legs that felt like they belonged to someone else.

Rows of boxes lined the walls of a room no larger than his kitchen. A table sat dead center in the room.

The manager led him to the far wall and gestured toward box 57 before inserting a key. Dimitrios inserted his key, which turned silently in the lock. When he didn't move, the manager pulled out the narrow box and set it on the table.

"Take as much time as you need." The manager pointed to the phone on the wall. "This will connect you to the front desk. Call if you need anything."

He nodded. Numbness settled across his mind. He barely noticed the manager leaving the room.

A small tremor shook his hand as he reached for the box.

He stared at the box, willing his hands to lift the lid, but couldn't find the strength to make his limbs obey.

The contents might be what got Mike killed. Did he really want to know what was inside?

Yes. No matter what happened. He had to know.

He flipped open the lid.

There was no money inside. No jewels or gold bars or family heirlooms. Instead, a USB drive rested on top of some papers. Next to that sat an envelope with his name printed on the outside. There was no mistaking Mike's sloppy, all caps printing.

A large manila envelope lined the bottom of the box.

He pushed the USB aside and picked up the envelope.

It was thin. Probably no more than a single sheet of paper. A letter from Mike to him.

He slid his finger under the flap and started to rip it open, but stopped before he'd gotten halfway across.

This was neither the time nor the place to read this.

He'd do it later, at home, when he could check out the USB.

He stared at it a second longer before stuffing it in the pocket of his EMS jacket. Scooping up the USB, he slid it into the pocket with the letter.

That left only the manila envelope. He picked it up. Man, it was pretty hefty.

He undid the clasp and slid out a small stack of papers. A *Vegas Today* newspaper sat on top, the headline screaming "Chief Gorley indicted on evidence tampering."

He skimmed the article, but couldn't see how it related to Regan, Mike, or anyone named Bobby.

Maybe that wasn't the article he was supposed to read. He opened the paper, glancing at the headlines as he went. On page five, he paused at a single column article that had been circled in red.

"Police seek leads in shooting."

Okay, well that was one mystery solved. He read the short article about a man with known drug ties whose body had been found at a construction site. There were few details in the article, likely because the police didn't seem to have many details to release.

He set the paper aside and picked up the next item. A ledger? Some vague entries that appeared to be cash amounts, but it didn't make much sense to him.

Weird that it'd be on paper. Didn't everyone use a computer for this kind of thing?

Then again, computers could be hacked. Or subpoenaed. Paper copies could be easily hidden.

And evidently, easily stolen, since he knew the ledger wasn't Mike's.

He looked at the columns more closely. Random seeming letters. Large values, presumably cash. Lots and lots of cash. There was an entry every few days and the numbers all ranged from 6,000 to 9,999.

Keeping it under the IRS' radar of $10,000. Smart. And likely less than legal.

He couldn't tell if the money was coming in or going out, though.

Might be worth having an accountant, or at least someone who knew something about accounting, look it over.

The trick was finding someone he could trust.

He set the ledger aside. The next paper was a list of names, scrawled in a scratchy print.

He examined the handwriting. Not familiar.

Three of the dozen or so names had a single red line going through them.

One name jumped out at him. Lenny Olsen. Now why did that name...

The article.

He shoved the papers aside and flipped to the circled

newspaper article. The murdered man was Lenny Olsen.

Ice tickled down his back. What was this? A hit list?

No. That was crazy. Wasn't it?

His phone vibrated inside his pocket. His hand jerked, knocking the stack of papers to the floor.

He needed to cool it. There was no indication that any of this had anything to do with Mike's murder.

But deep down, he knew it had to be connected. Why else would Mike hide it so securely?

A glance at his phone showed his boss' name. He accepted the call.

"Lykos." He knelt down and pushed the papers into a pile, scooping them up with his free hand.

"Hey, uh, any chance you can pull a double today? I hate to ask, what with, uh, yesterday." His boss cleared his throat. "But I've got a guy out with the flu and another who threw his back out yesterday. We need the help."

Well, it'd keep him busy, anyway. No time to think. There were worse things. "When do you want me there?"

"ASAP."

"Half hour okay?"

"Yeah. Thanks, Lykos."

Dimitrios ended the call and slid the phone back in his pocket. He'd have to study the rest of this another time.

He glanced at the final group of papers in the stack. Some kind of legal… Araceli's name jumped out at him. Then he saw his own.

What?

He skimmed the document, trying to decipher the meaning buried beneath all the legal mumbo-jumbo.

A will.

And Mike had named him and Araceli legal guardians of Regan's son in the event anything happened to him.

Mike had known this was coming. He'd known he would die.

The implication slammed through him.

How? How could Mike possibly know such a thing? And why hadn't he done something more to prevent it?

He didn't have time to think about this now.

Should he take the papers to the police? Let them sort through it? They were trained in this sort of thing, after all. He wasn't.

Even so, he hesitated.

If that was the best course of action, why hadn't Mike taken it?

No, Mike had obviously thought there wasn't enough in here to hang Bobby. Which meant Dimitrios needed to tread carefully, too, or he might end up like Mike and Regan.

He'd keep the papers. For now.

Stacking the papers, he set them on the table and started to close the now-empty box, but paused. There was a lot of sensitive information in this box, information Mike had wanted protected enough to keep it at the bank.

Might be smart to keep it here until he figured out what to do with it.

He replaced the papers, but decided to keep the USB and letter. He couldn't look at them if they were locked up here.

As he closed the box, he paused long enough to grab the custody papers, too. Never knew when those might come in handy. He stuffed them in the pocket with the USB and letter, his fingers brushing the small thumb drive.

Hopefully there would be answers within that would make this whole mess a little clearer.

Mike haunted the garage. And the rec room. The kitchen. The ambulance. Heck, even the bathroom contained reminders of a man who would never again walk through the door.

Dimitrios found himself looking for Mike. Listening for his laugh.

He had to pull himself together.

And staying busy was the first step in doing that.

Dimitrios finished his inventory of the ambulance and went to the supply closet for more gauze and antiseptic.

Laughter drifted out of the rec room down the hall, where a few of the other guys watched the latest superhero movie, but Dimitrios hadn't been able to sit still. Watching a movie left him with too much time to think.

He scooped up the armful of supplies he'd gathered and bumped the light switch with his elbow on his way out the door.

From somewhere in the garage, a door clicked softly.

He glanced around the room, where ambulances stood guard. No sign of movement.

Probably Simpson sneaking out the side door for a smoke. Didn't that guy know those things would kill him?

He crossed to ambulance two and deposited his supplies on the floor of the vehicle so he could put them away one at a time.

A shuffle sounded from nearby.

Footsteps. Furtive.

Tensing, he backed out of the ambulance and looked around. "Anyone there?"

No response.

But he'd heard someone. He knew it.

He waited. Listening for more sounds to confirm that he wasn't alone.

Maybe he should go in and hang around the rest of the guys.

No. He needed to get the ambulance restocked. Before the next call came in.

A minute dragged by. No sounds other than his own breathing.

Okay, he was officially losing it.

He turned back to the ambulance and leaned inside, claiming a few packages of gauze as he did.

Much more of this and he'd have to call the guys in the white jackets.

Take me away. Lock me up and throw away–

A scuff behind him.

The sound barely registered before a vise closed around his neck and slammed his skull against the ambulance's rear door. Pain flashed though his head and light burst into his vision.

His head was jerked back, then slammed again. And again.

Fight!

The command pulsed through his brain in time with the stars erupting in his head.

If he didn't do something, this guy – or guys, there could be more than one – would kill him, just like they had Mike.

He jerked forward, lashing behind him with arms that failed to connect with a target.

Scrape.

His brain told him what the sound was seconds before something cold and hard pressed into his neck.

A gun. The slide had been racked and it was ready to fire.

"Cool it, smart guy." A rough voice half-whispered, sounding more like a ninety-year-old pack-a-day smoker than someone who could take down a strong and healthy EMT. "You ever see what a 9 mil slug does to the throat?"

Dimitrios stilled. He'd never witnessed that particular injury, but it didn't take much imagination to create a clear visual.

Not pretty.

But this was Mike's killer. He knew it. And he wouldn't let the man get away.

All he needed was an opening.

"Where's the package? And the baby?"

Package? What was this guy talking about? "I don't–"

"Don't play dumb! Your partner had 'em and he told you where they were. You're gonna give 'em to me. 'Less you want to end up like him."

Only a fool would ignore the deadly tone.

Then again, he hadn't made the best decisions lately. "He didn't tell me anything."

"Sure you wanna play it that way?" The gun pressed in harder, grinding against his spine.

"I don't know what you're talking about."

"I saw him. Through the scope. After I put a round in him."

Package, package. What was this guy talking about? The baby?

The baby was with Ari. And he'd take a bullet to the throat before he told them about her.

He had to give the man something.

Had to… no!

This man killed Mike! And he had the gall to come in here and threaten him?

Dimitrios jerked to the side and propelled himself backward, his arm sweeping up to knock the gun away.

Or hit the man. Either scenario would work.

His hand hit metal and the gun fell away from his neck.

He caught a glimpse of a solid man with a shaved head. Movement rushing toward his head barely registered before pain exploded in his skull.

Blackness crowded and he felt himself falling.

The cold cement floor slapped his face, shocking his eyes open. Planting his hands, he pushed himself to his knees.

"You got until ten a.m. tomorrow."

"Forget it." The words slurred from his lips like he'd had a few too many drinks.

"I'm gonna do you a favor and forget you said that."

Something slammed into the side of his head, toppling him to the floor. Before the darkness claimed control, words penetrated. "Think on it. You'll be hearing from me soon."

Five

"Lykos."

The sound of his name infiltrated his pain-clouded sleep. Sirens clanged in his head, which felt about ready to explode.

"Hey, man. Wake up."

Someone was messing with him. Touching his head, wiping at him.

He forced his eyes open and feebly tried to swat the offender away.

A face swam into view.

Simpson. Smelling like smoke.

"Ugh." The sound broke loose and Dimitrios reached a hand up to his throbbing head.

"Dude." Simpson rocked back on his heels and stared at Dimitrios, blood-soaked gauze still pinched between his fingers. "What happened to you?"

What? Dimitrios searched his mind, but it was like trying to penetrate the thick fog rolling off the ocean. What *had* happened?

A memory sliced through the fog. A rough voice. A gun. Questions and threats.

Ten a.m.

He sat up, the room tilting dangerously, and closed his eyes until his stomach stopped churning.

"Lykos?"

Simpson stared at him, obviously still awaiting an answer.

But he couldn't tell Simpson what had happened. It was too dangerous. Which meant a believable cover story. "Some guy jumped me. Think he was looking for needles or drugs or something."

"You let some punk get the drop on you?"

Dimitrios couldn't tell if Simpson believed him or not. And at the moment, he didn't really care. He cradled his head in his hands and tried to keep from spewing his lunch across the floor. Warmth oozed through his fingers, coating them with a sticky liquid that he didn't need to see to identify. "I don't feel so hot."

"No fooling. Looks like you took a good hit to the noggin'."

More than one. He didn't respond as he waited for the nausea to pass.

"How 'bout we get you patched up?"

Simpson rose and moved toward the ambulance, grabbing some of the supplies Dimitrios had just stocked.

Leaning back against the still-open rear doors of the ambulance, Dimitrios closed his eyes as Simpson began swabbing the gash on his temple.

Several minutes passed as Simpson worked silently.

Dimitrios' stomach settled marginally. He licked his dry lips. "Might wanna check the back of my head, too."

Simpson rose, tilting Dimitrios' head forward, and let out a low whistle. "Nice gash. Dude, it's a good thing you've got such a hard head."

Not hard enough, evidently.

What was he going to do? He couldn't give those guys what they wanted. They'd probably take it and kill him anyway. He was a liability.

And they obviously had no problem with killing.

He couldn't even go to Jim and Courtney. Not unless he wanted to admit Mike had taken the baby. Plus, he'd have to hand over all the evidence Mike had left him.

No, his survival depended upon no one else. He was on

his own.

ꟷ ꟷ ꟷ ꟷ ꟷ

"Dimitrios."

The word, written in Mike's familiar scratch, sent a tremor through Dimitrios' hand. He set the letter on the table and closed his eyes against the sudden pressure building behind them.

His head still hurt from the attack several hours earlier, but he needed to read this letter. He only hoped it would give him direction on what to do next. About Ari, the baby, the evidence, and the threats.

So far, he'd said nothing to Jim or Courtney about the baby. After the attack earlier, he wasn't sure he should.

Maybe everyone would be safer if he gave these guys what they wanted.

Ari's question haunted him. Could he really live with himself if he turned a helpless baby over to a group of killers?

Maybe. It was better than the alternative of not living at all.

He pushed the thought aside.

First, the letter. Then he'd figure out the rest.

He reread his name before moving further down the letter.

"If you're reading this, then Bobby got to me. I'm sorry, man. I shoulda told you more about what was going on, but didn't want to put you in danger.

"But if I'm gone, someone's gotta stand up against this guy and you're the only one I can trust with that task.

"The man responsible for Regan's death, and presumably mine, is Bobby. I don't know his last name. Regan refused to say, but he's the head of a mafia family in Vegas. He's got connections everywhere, man, so don't trust anyone. Not even the cops. Regan saw him with senators, cops, feds, you name it. I don't know how far his reach goes, but it's high.

"You've got all the evidence you should need to get him indicted, if you can get it to someone legit. If you haven't looked at it all yet, do it. I hope it'll all make sense. Remember our most challenging climb. I know you'll figure it out."

Challenging climb?

It was when he and Mike spent almost a week on Mount Rainier, he knew that for a fact. But what did that have to do with Bobby?

Well, he could figure that out later, too.

He returned his attention to the letter.

"Regan stumbled across the video on the drive. That's why she ran. Didn't matter that she was carrying his kid, she knew Bobby would kill her. And he did.

"You need to get this evidence to someone who will see it through. No one in Vegas, that's for sure. Maybe that sister of yours? I don't know. I've been trying to figure something out for a while and keep comin' up empty.

"Sorry to dump this on you, man. It's not your fight, but you're my only option. Do what you want with it. And watch your back. Unless you've made your peace with God since we last talked, you're not ready to die."

The letter wasn't signed, just had a sloppy MC scrawled at the bottom.

Aww, Mike.

Of all the chicks in the world, why'd he have to get mixed up with one on the run from the mob?

Well, he couldn't change anything about it now.

The pounding in his head had intensified as he'd read Mike's last words. His body ached. All he wanted was to crawl into bed and forget everything bad that had happened.

Too bad that wasn't a realistic option.

He had decisions to make.

Could this Bobby guy really be that well connected? It seemed impossible. The stuff of movies, not real life.

But Mike wasn't one to jump to conclusions or believe conspiracy theories.

He'd do some research on this Bobby guy. See what he could come up with. If the man was that well connected, there should be a heavy digital trail to find.

Tomorrow. For now, his body needed rest.

Assuming he *could* sleep.

ꟷ ꟷ ꟷ ꟷ ꟷ

"You got what I want?"

Dimitrios' mouth was suddenly as dry as the tumbleweeds that blew across central Oregon. He'd known this call was coming, had rehearsed his response. But now that the gritty voice rasped through the speaker on his phone, he blanked.

"How did you get this number?"

The voice laughed, an unpleasant sound that made his hand shake. "I can get a lot more than that. Like maybe your brother. You already lost your sister. How'd you like to be an only child? Or an orphan?"

The words crashed through his mind, just like the man on the phone knew they would.

This man knew about his family.

"Leave them out of this."

"You got what I want?" Challenge laced the man's words.

He had to comply, didn't he? He couldn't risk his family's safety.

Maybe the guy was bluffing. Learning about his family was one thing. Going after them was something else altogether.

Still, it was his family. He couldn't take the risk. In spite of Mike's last wishes.

But he couldn't give them what they wanted either.

As long as he had the baby and the evidence, he had leverage. Although that theory hadn't worked out so well for Mike.

"No." He forced the word through lips as stiff as the

backboard in his ambulance.

Silence.

"No?" The word contained more warning than question.

"You've got the wrong guy. I don't know anything about any evidence. Or a baby."

"You know the bad thing about having a twin? It's easy to mistake one for the other."

That was a direct threat against Cyrano!

His tongue felt too big for his mouth, choking any words he might have said.

When he remained silent, the voice on the other end made a small clucking sound. "Remember you asked for it."

The line went dead.

As Dimitrios slowly lowered the phone, he couldn't shake the feeling that he may have placed a target on his family's backs.

He replayed the conversation.

The man had mentioned Dimitrios losing his sister, so he must not know Lana was still alive.

At least she would be safe from these killers.

But there were still several members of his family who - because of him - were now in a killer's crosshairs.

Dad's truck pinged in the driveway. Sounded like he hadn't been home for long.

Dimitrios walked past the cooling vehicle, his strides eating up the front walk. Hopefully both his parents were home.

He reached the front door and knocked once before trying the knob.

Unlocked.

Naturally. Maybe they should hang a sign that read "Welcome criminals!" Why didn't they take more precautions?

He poked his head inside. "Hello?"

His mother's voice drifted from the kitchen. "In here, Mitri."

Amazing how she could always distinguish his voice from Cy's. Even from only one word.

He walked down the hallway and stepped into the kitchen. Dirty gray light streamed in from the sliding glass doors and filtered down from the twin skylights above his head.

Ah, winter in Oregon. Lots of clouds and gloomy days.

His mother glanced at him from the island in the center of the room, offering a quick smile that faded as she took in his face.

Maybe he should've left the bandage on.

No, that would've brought more concern. At least this way she could see the cut for herself instead of leaving it up to the imagination.

Hair more white than brown brushed her slight shoulders. She finished with the celery stalks in front of her before setting the paring knife aside and coming to give him a hug. "What happened?"

His throat clogged. What was it about his mom that made him want to let go of all control?

"Mitri? Are you okay?"

Was he okay? Definitely not. Not that he could get into all that with her. "Just a little accident at work. I'm alright."

She studied him. Skepticism was evident, but she didn't push. Probably because she knew it wouldn't do any good. "How are you doing? With Mike?"

Such a loaded question.

"Still processing." Time for a change of topic. "Is dad here, too?"

She nodded. "He should be coming in any time. You know how he gets around lunch."

Yeah. Dad's stomach was more accurate than any timepiece. "Good. I need to talk to both of you."

Now if only he could convince them to leave town for a while.

"Well, since you're here you can join us for lunch." She turned and started gathering lunch supplies. Peanut butter joined the celery, as did bread, lunch meat, mayonnaise, and mustard.

A typical Lykos family lunch.

Except he wasn't the least bit hungry.

Still, not ten minutes later he found himself sitting across from his mother at the dining room table, his father to his left, a sandwich and veggies on the plate in front of him. He ate on autopilot, his mind still scrambling for the words he'd need to convince them to leave without giving them a solid reason.

Because he sure couldn't tell them the truth.

"You going to tell me how you got that cut or do I need to get the story from Mi..." His father's voice trailed off and his Adam's apple bobbed. "Sorry. Have they set the funeral yet?"

They? He strongly suspected that he'd be the one making the funeral arrangements.

He'd have to check with Jim or Courtney to see if they'd managed to track down any of Mike's aunts or uncles. "Not yet. Still waiting for the police to release the..." The word *body* stuck in his throat.

"I'm sorry, son." His father's firm hand landed on his shoulder. "What can we do?"

"Leave." The word popped out before he could properly phrase it.

His father pulled back. "What was that?"

Dimitrios pushed his plate aside and leaned on the table. "Get out of town for a while. Please. Just until–" He pressed his lips together. He couldn't tell them how long they needed to be gone. He didn't even know how long.

As if sensing his fear, his mother leaned in. "What's going on?"

"I need to know you're safe."

"And we aren't here?"

His father didn't give him a chance to reply to her question before asking, "Are you in some kind of trouble?"

"I can't talk about it." Dimitrios gingerly touched his scabbed forehead. "But this wasn't an accident. Mike, well, he was trying to do the right thing and some people didn't like it."

They absorbed that in silence.

"And now these people expect me to help them and they threatened you and Cy." Shut up! He clenched his fist as if the action would stem the words bleeding from his mouth.

"Cy?" His mother's face paled a shade.

"I'm headed there next."

"What did the police say about this?"

If he told them the police didn't know, they'd want to know why. And that would require telling them more than he wanted them to know. "Please. Get away from here. For a week, maybe two. I'll even buy your plane tickets. Anywhere you want to go."

Not that he could really afford it, but he'd make it work. Even if it took him a few months to pay off the credit card bill.

"You haven't told the police?" His mother stared at him. "Honey, that's their job! Let them do it."

"I can't. There's too much… I can't."

They were looking at him like he'd lost his mind. And rightly so. The whole thing sounded nuts.

But it wasn't. It was deadly serious.

How could he make them understand?

"Mitri, you've been through a lot." His dad slid a glance at his mom before returning his attention to Dimitrios. "I think maybe you're making this a bigger deal than it is."

"Dad." He pulled his firmest tone, the one he used with obstinate patients like his sister when they tried to refuse the treatment he knew was best for them. "These guys shot Mike out in the open. I watched him bleed out in front of me. Then they attacked me inside the garage and managed to avoid being caught on camera. They got my cell number and they knew all about you and mom and Cy. Besides, have I ever been one to blow things out of proportion?"

They didn't even have to answer that. Cyrano had always been the more melodramatic of the two of them, and even he was pretty logical about things.

His dad sighed. "Still. Leave? That's pretty crazy, you gotta admit."

"But it's what I need you to do." If he couldn't get them to agree for their own safety, maybe he could get them to do it for his. "I can't watch my own back and take care of all this if I'm worrying about you, too. Please. You'll be safer, I'll be safer. We both win."

"We can't just up and leave."

"Wasn't that why you retired? So you could travel?"

His dad looked ready to argue, but his mom put a hand on his arm. "I think we should do what he says."

Yes! If his mom was on board, it was only a matter of time before his dad caved. "Come on. When was the last time you guys had a real vacation?"

"You've been promising me we'd get away for quite some time now."

His dad stared at his mom for several seconds before returning his attention to Dimitrios. "You win. But you're not paying for it."

Fine by him. He really couldn't afford it anyway. "And you'll leave today?"

"Yes." His mom said before his dad could reply. "I've always wanted to go to–"

"Don't tell me. It's safer if I don't know." Now he officially sounded crazy. But he didn't care. He'd gotten what he wanted.

"You should come with us. We'll bring Cy, Donna, and the girls, too. Like a big family vacation."

He shook his head. "I gotta deal with this head-on. If I run, it'll still be waiting for me when we get back."

But taking Cy and his family was a good plan.

"I was headed to Cy's next. Lemme talk to him. The girls would love it."

And since school had released for Christmas break, both Cy and Donna should have extra time on their hands.

He pushed away from the table. "Okay, I'm going there now. You guys start packing. You need to get out of town today."

His dad offered a stiff salute. "Yes, sir."

Fine. Let them mock him. He didn't care. Just as long as they did what he said.

No one else would end up like Mike. He'd see to it personally.

Six

"So what's so important you had to kidnap me from a game of Candy Land? I think I was winning."

Dimitrios glanced briefly at Cyrano before turning his attention back to the road. "Sounds like the girls will thank me later."

Or not. His two young nieces had begged him to stay and join the game but instead he'd taken their father away from it.

It was for their own good. Even if there was no way they could understand that now.

"Sooo?"

"What? I can't have coffee with my own brother?" No way was he going to get into this while he was driving. When they got to the coffee shop, maybe, but not now.

He felt Cyrano's scrutiny, but kept his eyes on the road. He knew what was coming, not just because it was Cy, but because it was the question everyone had been asking him for the last day and a half.

"How're you doing? You know, with Mike and all?"

Yep, Cy didn't disappoint.

His fingers tightened on the wheel. No point trying to hide anything from Cyrano. "Getting by. It's been rough."

"I bet. Anything I can do?"

He forced a tight smile. "Not unless you can raise the dead."

The pause felt heavy. Like Cyrano was waiting to say

something, but holding back. A few seconds passed before Cyrano spoke, his voice slightly thick. "Yeah, well, there was uh, only one Man who could do that and He, uh, lived two thousand years ago."

"A two thousand year old dead guy who can raise the dead? Sounds like a fraud to me."

"Nah. He's the real deal."

What was Cyrano talking about? And why bring it up in the first place? "You all right, bro? I'm supposed to be the one suffering PTSD here."

Cyrano's chuckle sounded forced. "I'm good. But I've been wanting to talk to you about something."

Weird. They never had trouble talking to each other.

This must be big. Or bad. Maybe both.

"Just say it, bro. Whatever it is, you know I got your back."

"So, uh, Donna and I have been going to church."

Seriously? Was that all? "Yeah, I know. Mom tells me about it every chance she gets." Probably hoping he'd cave to the pressure.

Not gonna happen.

"Yeah, well, I gave my life to Christ last Sunday."

The words echoed in his head, weighing the silence that suddenly fell between them.

"What? Like the whole 'Jesus come into my heart' thing?" Dimitrios swung the Jeep into the parking lot of the coffee house and pulled into an end space.

"There's a little more to it than that, but yeah."

Was he the only one in his family with a brain? It'd been bad enough when he'd been getting the religious mumbo-jumbo from his parents, Mike, Ari, and Lana, but Cyrano had always been right there with him. They'd always had each other's backs.

Now he was on his own.

It felt like a betrayal. Even though it shouldn't.

He turned off the engine and looked at Cyrano, but made

no move to get out of the vehicle. "What changed?"

"The things the pastor said really made sense. And I felt it here." Cyrano's fist lightly bumped his chest. "I knew it was true. All of it."

"Whatever works for you." Worse than the words was his tone. If Cyrano was happy, he was happy. It was that simple. So why couldn't he feel it?

He needed air. He unlatched his seat belt and pushed open the door.

Cyrano scrambled from the other side. "Come on, man, give it a shot. I'm tellin' you, there's something to it."

Sure there was. And he could nicely ask Bobbie's goons to back off, too.

"Gettin' the usual?"

Cyrano followed, his face stating he wasn't done with this conversation. "Yeah."

Approaching the counter, Dimitrios ordered Cy's caramel latte and black coffee for himself. He picked a table tucked in the corner and sat with his back to the wall. If anyone got too close for his comfort, they'd take their coffees and finish the conversation in the Jeep.

"I need to ask a favor."

Cyrano paused with his drink inches from his mouth, then slowly lowered the cup. "Shoot."

"I need you to take your family and leave town for a while. That's what winter break is for, right? Go somewhere." Preferably far away.

"Winter break's only another week."

"Plenty of time." He hoped. "I bet Donna would love to get away to someplace warm. Southern Cal is probably nice right now."

Cyrano's eyes narrowed. "Why are you trying to get rid of me?"

After sliding his gaze around the room, Dimitrios focused in on his brother again. "For your safety. Mom and dad are going away and suggested you go with them."

"What about you?"

"I have to stay and take care of this."

Cyrano leaned on the table and dropped his voice. "And what is *this*?"

"The less you know, the better."

"Does this have to do with Mike?" Cyrano shook his head. "Of course it does. What's going on?"

"I can't tell you. But Mike died trying to do the right thing and now I have to handle it."

A man stepped away from the counter, his gaze travelling across them. Casual or intentional?

He couldn't be too careful. Dimitrios dropped his voice. "Threats have been made. You guys need to leave. Today."

"And leave you here? No way." Cyrano picked up his cup. "I'll send Donna and the girls, but there's no way I'm leaving you to face this alone."

He watched Cyrano take a swig of the caramel concoction. "You don't get it. These guys killed Mike. They've threatened all of you. What if they go after you by mistake?"

It didn't matter that Cyrano wore his hair a little longer and didn't have the muscle toning that Dimitrios had formed from his hours at the gym. They were still identical and could easily be mistaken. Had been mistaken. By their own sister, who was a trained US Marshal, no less.

"You have to go. Your family needs you."

"And you don't?"

"I need you safe." He had to get through to Cy somehow. "Look, even if you stayed, what would you do? You're a teacher. You handle rebellious kids, not criminals."

Cyrano stared at him for several long seconds. "Then call Lana. She does handle criminals."

Not a chance.

By all accounts, these guys didn't know she existed and he intended to keep it that way. She'd had too many brushes with death as it was.

But maybe Cy would agree if he thought Lana was

coming to help. "I'll call her. Now, will you go?"

"I'll talk to Donna. See what she thinks."

The man at the counter collected his drink, then meandered to a table a short distance from them. Too close. It'd be too easy for that guy to listen in.

Okay, he'd crossed from worried to paranoid.

But what if he wasn't paranoid? What if that was Bobby? He didn't know what Bobby looked like. It was possible.

It could also be someone who worked for him. It wasn't the guy who'd attacked him last night, but Bobby likely had other thugs.

Was it worth the risk?

He didn't even have to think that one through. Time to go.

"Let's finish this in the Jeep."

Cyrano arched an eyebrow. "We just got here."

Dimitrios stared at Cyrano for a second, hoping his look conveyed an urgency he didn't dare put into words.

With a sigh, Cyrano pushed back his chair and collected his drink.

They exited in silence, which continued until they were both in the car.

He hit the automatic locks and kept an eye on the entrance. So far, no one was following. But that didn't mean there wasn't someone else out in the lot watching them.

Maybe they should've talked at Cy's house, but the last thing he'd wanted was for Donna and the girls to overhear their conversation.

"So what was that about?" Cyrano's voice jerked him back.

"There was a guy in there. I think he was trying to listen in on our conversation."

"Listen in?" Cyrano jerked around to look at the coffee shop. "You're serious, aren't you?"

"Mike was killed right in front of me! Did you think I wasn't serious?"

"No, but I..." Cyrano set his coffee in the cup holder and

ran his hands down his face, something he only did when he was upset.

Good. He should be upset. Another push ought to do it.

The man exited the coffee shop, cup in hand, and sauntered toward a white SUV with dark tinted windows parked on the opposite end of the lot.

"That's why you have to leave. Now." Dimitrios lowered his voice. Which was stupid. It wasn't like that guy could hear him from this far away, especially since they were inside an enclosed vehicle. "If anything happened to you or Donna, or Iris or Lillie…"

An image of his two curly haired nieces, lying on the ground, soaked in blood, seared his mind. His breath failed. Pain pricked his eyes and his heart felt like it was being ripped in half.

He couldn't let that happen.

Cyrano's hand landed on his shoulder. "Okay. You convinced me. Let me talk to Donna."

Pull it together. He forced in a deep breath, followed by another. In and out, until the panic passed.

The SUV had disappeared.

Maybe that guy hadn't been watching them after all. Or maybe he'd simply moved the vehicle to throw off suspicion.

Either way, he had to get Cy home so he could get his family to safety.

He started the Jeep.

As he backed out of the parking spot, Dimitrios said, "Don't ask Donna. Tell her. You guys need to leave town and you need to do it today."

"I wish you'd come with us." Worry colored Cyrano's words.

"I can't." Dimitrios pulled onto the road and punched the accelerator. "I have to take care of this or we'll never stop running."

"But you'll call Lana, right? Let her help?"

"Sure."

"You're not just saying that to get me to agree?"

Of course he was. Deep down, Cyrano probably knew it, too. They'd never been good at keeping secrets from each other. Still, this was one time that he had to try. "I said I'd call her, didn't I?"

And he would call her. That way he hadn't outright lied to Cy.

Not that he'd tell her what was going on. Knowing her, she'd hop the next flight, stick herself in the middle of this mess, and get shot or stabbed or something.

Nope. Better for everyone if she remained in the dark.

For now, anyway.

"Fine. Donna and I were talking about taking the girls to Anaheim this summer, anyway. We'll just push it up."

Perfect. That should be sufficient distance to keep them safe.

Dimitrios turned onto the winding two-lane road that led to Cyrano's neighborhood. "Thanks, man. This takes a load off me."

"Well, I wish you weren't carrying this load alone."

"I got it." He hoped. At least with his family out of the way, he could focus on a solution.

A white van turned onto the road behind him. A work van. Like the kind a plumber or electrician might drive. Except there were no markings.

He forced his gaze back to the road. An unmarked van was hardly suspicious.

Or was it?

His eyes strayed back to the rearview mirror.

He hadn't seen that vehicle in the parking lot at the coffee shop, but that didn't mean it wasn't connected to Bobby. Maybe the guy from the white SUV had sent the driver of the van after he'd been discovered.

Or maybe he was much too suspicious of everything and everyone.

The van gained.

Too fast.

The thought had barely registered before a crunch filled the Jeep's interior.

Thrown forward, the only thing that stopped Dimitrios from meeting the windshield was the seat belt digging into his chest. He gripped the wheel and wrestled the Wrangler back into his lane.

A hat covered the driver's head, aviator sunglasses obscuring much of the man's face. In fact, all Dimitrios could see was a dark goatee.

Dimitrios pressed the accelerator.

"Mitri? What're you doing?" Cyrano looked behind them. "Pull over."

Dimitrios tried to keep his eyes on both the van behind him and the road in front of him. "That guy's not interested in exchanging insurance information."

The van surged forward.

Dimitrios pushed the pedal further. The speedometer shot up.

He couldn't keep this up for long. He'd have to slow for that sharp right corner ahead. Failing to make that turn guaranteed a dangerous ride down a steep drop off.

He'd responded to too many calls on this corner to want to join those numbers.

The van was nearly on his bumper now.

He jerked the wheel to the left and slammed the brakes. The Jeep skidded easily into a hundred and eighty degree turn, fishtailing into the oncoming traffic's lane.

At least there *was* no oncoming traffic. One thing working in his favor.

A screech echoed in the Jeep as the van scraped the bumper when it shot past.

With any luck, that van would fail to navigate the corner and go over the edge. Then he'd have them.

Dimitrios straightened out and accelerated down the road.

Brake lights glowed in his rearview mirror. The van

whipped in a u-turn he would've thought impossible for a vehicle that size. Smoke drifted from the squealing tires as the van straightened in the lane behind him.

That guy knew how to drive, he'd give him that.

The van bore down on him again.

He barely took his eyes from the rearview mirror. "Call 911."

Cyrano dug his phone from his pocket.

No license plate, not that he thought that would have helped the police catch these guys anyway. The van was probably stolen.

What if he pulled off the road and got out? What would that guy do then?

Probably run him down. Or shoot him.

Either way, he'd put Cyrano at greater risk.

No, their best chance was to stay a step ahead of the van until the police could arrive.

He half listened to Cyrano relaying their situation. The van closed in. He braced himself.

Crunch!

The impact threw him forward.

His tires edged onto the gravel shoulder.

Another jolt.

He slammed his brakes. The van's engine roared behind him.

Another hit.

His tires left the pavement, skidding across the gravel. Toward the edge.

He fought the wheel.

The van rammed him again.

Time suspended as the Jeep's tires left the ground. The weightlessness lasted a fraction of a second before they went down.

A giant tree filled his vision. Glass shattered. Then everything went black.

Seven

"Ugh."

The groan rumbled through Dimitrios' chest as if it had a life of its own. He couldn't see, couldn't move. Pain radiated through his torso.

Man. What happened?

Memories flashed through his mind. The van. The wreck. The trees.

He pushed himself back.

The airbag filled his vision. Powder coated his face, his hands.

With awkward movements, he shoved the airbag down.

Cy! Was he okay?

Dimitrios turned to look at the passenger side, only to scrape his cheek on a large branch. The branch stretched between the driver's and passenger's seats, obliterating his view of the other side of the vehicle.

"Cy?" The word croaked from his throat.

No response.

In fact, no sign of any life at all.

What if he was impaled? Or had been crushed? "Cy!"

A raspy cough answered. "Mitri?"

He was alive! "You good?"

"I think so." A pause. "Hurts to breathe."

Which could be something as simple as a strain or something as serious as a punctured lung. "Don't move. I'm coming over."

He fumbled for his seat belt.

A vise closed around his neck and slammed his head into the deflating airbag.

"We got your attention now?"

That voice! The same one from the attack at work. The same one from the phone call. "I'm gonna kill you!"

"You ain't in no position to make threats, tough guy. Next time someone dies. The evidence and the baby. We'll be in touch."

The grip vanished.

The man was getting away!

Dimitrios thrashed against the seat belt. His hand closed around the door release. The door didn't budge. He threw his shoulder against the door. It creaked, but didn't open. He slammed it again. It groaned with an agony he felt and slowly gave beneath his weight.

He fell out of the vehicle, landing hard on the rocky, weed covered ground.

Pushing himself up, he caught a glimpse of a man running around the front of the white van.

He had to stop that guy!

Before he'd made it two steps the van thundered to life, spitting gravel as it spun from the shoulder.

His curse echoed in the sudden silence.

The man was gone.

But Cy still needed his help.

Pain shot up his spine as he forced his legs to move around the back of his mangled Jeep. He approached the passenger door, his breath coming in short bursts.

Blood trickled down the side of Cyrano's head. Not a huge amount, though. Hopefully just a small cut from flying glass.

He didn't know if he could handle anything more serious.

He wrestled the door open and punched the airbag away from his brother's face. "Cy? Hey, man. Talk to me."

"Who was that guy?"

Cyrano's voice was alert. The words crisp.

That was good. It didn't sound like he'd gone into shock, which likely meant any injuries he'd sustained were minor.

More than that, the words made sense. Cy probably didn't have a serious head injury, not if he could think so clearly.

"He's the reason you're leaving town. Where are you hurt?"

"I'm fine." Cyrano's gaze was sharp, his dark eyes almost black, as they locked on Dimitrios. "What did that guy want from you?"

Sirens sounded in the distance. Hopefully coming for them.

"Something I can't give him." Dimitrios leaned back. "We need to talk about what we're gonna tell the cops, though."

"What we're going to tell them?"

"Yeah. Some crazy guy, probably on drugs, ran us off the road. Hit and run."

Cyrano stared at him. "You want me to lie to the cops? Last I heard, that was illegal."

"It's close enough to the truth."

"Not really."

Yeah, not really. But what choice did he have? The sirens were almost on top of them now. They had maybe a minute, tops, before help arrived. "Look, I need you to roll with me on this one, okay?"

"Bro, this is serious. You need to tell the cops what happened."

Dimitrios glanced around. No sign of anyone. Unless the trees had ears, no one else would hear what he was about to say. "I can't. Mike stumbled onto something big. Organized crime big. He said not to trust anyone, that these guys have connections everywhere. I don't know that I can trust the cops."

"But you've worked with these guys for years. Heck, we grew up with half of them."

"Yeah, and Mike did, too. But he didn't trust them. There's gotta be a reason."

The sirens burped off. A glance at the road found two squad cars pulling to a stop.

"You gotta trust me on this one. Let me handle it."

Cyrano pressed his lips together, but said nothing.

It was a look Dimitrios knew well. Cy wasn't happy about it, but he'd go along with the plan.

Dimitrios' attention shifted to the tree trunk just inches from Cyrano's head. Tremors attacked him. That'd been close. If the Jeep hadn't hit where it did, he would've lost Cy.

He locked his knees and leaned heavily on the side of the Jeep.

"You look about as bad as I feel. You sure you should be moving?"

He rolled his head around to look at Cyrano. "Adrenaline dump is fading, but I'm alright."

"Oh yeah? 'Cause from where I stand, you look like a man without a plan."

"Trust me. I have a plan."

Kind of. Too bad his plan was little more than a disjointed skeleton.

* * * * *

"Okay, Lykos. We've been doing this way too much lately."

Dimitrios managed a smile he didn't feel at Courtney's light tone. "You're telling me."

They sat in the hospital cafeteria, the detectives on one side of the table and him on the other. Jim nursed a cup of black coffee.

Did he know that coffee was made out of road sludge?

"How's Cyrano?" Courtney asked, stirring some sugar into her tea.

"A cracked rib and some minor cuts, but he'll be okay."

"Looks like you got about the same diagnosis."

"Minus the cracked rib." All in all, they'd both been pretty lucky. Cy had already told him that God must've been watching out for them.

Yeah, right.

If God was watching, why had it happened in first place? Why had Regan been murdered? Why was Mike dead?

"How about you walk us through what happened."

Dimitrios zeroed in on Jim. It was likely he'd already heard a lot of the story from the responding officers. "I was taking Cy home when this van came out of nowhere. He hit my Jeep and I lost control."

A beat. "If you were taking him home, why were you headed away from his house?"

Crud. He hadn't thought about that angle. "I was trying to get away from the van. When he came up on me the first time, I swerved out of the way. He clipped my bumper and spun me. I thought getting away from him was the best option, even if it meant going the opposite direction."

"So you're telling me that the van pulled a u-turn and came after you again?"

Deny it?

There would be evidence at the scene that would show the truth. Skid marks, at the very least.

Better to be honest. At least partially. "Yeah. I don't know what his deal was, but he made a u-turn and rammed me a few times until I lost control of the wheel."

"Who was it?" Courtney asked, her fingers lightly tapping the table.

"What?" What kind of question was that?

"Who was driving the van?"

"How should I know?" Huh. It was even an honest answer. While he knew it was one of Bobby's goons, he had no idea who.

"Come on, Lykos. You can't really expect us to believe that some van randomly decides it would be fun to run you off the road. Especially in light of the last few days."

Yeah, that was exactly what he expected them to believe. Too bad they didn't. "I don't know what else to tell you. Maybe the guy was crazy and has a problem with black Jeeps or something. Maybe he was on drugs. Maybe I cut him off in traffic. I don't know."

"You trying to tell me that you don't suspect any connection to what happened to Mike?"

Pain rippled across his shoulders as he managed a slight shrug. "Of course I thought about it, but I don't know what kind of connection there could be. Unless, of course, you know why Mike was killed."

Jim clamped his lips together. As expected.

Courtney was much smoother. "We're still investigating. But right now, your safety is our greater concern."

Sure it was. Only because they thought he could help them solve their case. Or maybe his death would just bring too much extra paperwork.

Okay, that wasn't fair. Nor accurate. He'd always gotten along with the detectives.

"Well, I don't know anything more than what I've told you."

"Anyone you can think of with a grudge against you? Or maybe against your brother?"

He snorted. "Cy? You're kidding, right? Everyone likes him."

"That brings us back to you, then."

"I've probably got some enemies. You know, families of people I couldn't save. But running me off the road is a pretty extreme reaction, don't you think?" He had to get them to drop this. For now, anyway. "Really, you track that guy down, I think you'll find he was on something. He was all over the road."

"Why were you giving Cyrano a ride, anyway?"

He stared at Courtney, who looked at him with an innocence he wasn't buying. Why was she asking?

"Something wrong with that?"

"Not at all. I just thought it was strange. Was something wrong with his car?"

"We went for coffee. I said I'd pick him up. No point having two vehicles down there, right?"

"Makes sense." Her tone said exactly the opposite.

Fine. Let her think it was weird. Let her be suspicious. At least he was clearly the victim here.

A few more mundane questions and then they rose. "Well, we'll get Cyrano's statement, then we'll get out of here. You'll be around the next few days if we have any more questions, right?"

"Sure." Didn't take a genius to read between the lines. Don't leave town.

He was pretty sure they didn't think he had done anything wrong, but they knew he wasn't telling them everything. He'd bank his career on it.

Well, he'd settle everything as soon as he could. For now, the secrecy was necessary.

He followed the detectives out of the cafeteria and watched as they headed toward the ER, where Cyrano was probably still waiting to see a doctor. A trauma case had come in, bumping Cyrano down the list since his injuries weren't life threatening.

Man, he hoped Cyrano's story matched his. And that Cy didn't say anything about their conversation.

A bank of chairs sat opposite the nurse's station. He sank into one on the end and leaned his head back against the wall.

How'd he get to this point? Lying to the cops, fighting mob guys, running for his life?

More importantly, what did he do next? His family was leaving town, that was good. At least he'd know they were safe.

But if these guys were watching him, they'd find out about Ari. If they didn't know about her already.

He had to get her out of town. And the baby, since he

doubted she'd give him up.

Besides, as long as they had the baby, they had some leverage.

He rubbed his head. He was a jerk. What kind of lowlife thought of a baby as leverage?

At least he was a jerk who was trying to do the right thing. But where could he take her?

Florida.

There was no one he trusted to keep her safe more than Lana. Not that he could tell Lana what was going on, but Lana would spot trouble before it hit.

Besides, these guys didn't seem to know Lana was alive. A definite benefit.

He straightened as Jim and Courtney approached. This was it. Either Cy had covered for him or he hadn't, but he'd know soon enough.

The detectives stopped a few feet from him. Courtney broke the silence. "He's pretty worried about you, you know?"

What did that mean? Had Cy told them or not? "Oh yeah?"

"He's afraid Mike's killer might go after you next."

Cy sold him out? How could he? He'd really thought Cy had his back. "Why would they do that?"

"He didn't know. Just said that between Mike's murder and the hit and run earlier, it seemed like someone was targeting EMTs and you might be next."

That was pretty generic. Besides, they called it a hit and run. No mention of the man or the threat. "Come on. Targeting EMTs? Sounds like something from a bad movie."

Jim stuffed his hands into his pockets and jangled his keys. "After today, it's not sounding so far-fetched."

"Seriously. I'm fine."

Jim looked at Courtney. "You buying that? 'Cause I'm not." Turning back to Dimitrios, he speared him with his eyes. "Cut the crap, okay? We know you're holding out. We can't do our job unless we have all the facts so how about you level with us?"

He could deny it, but he knew it wouldn't convince them. Instead, he returned the stare until Jim looked away.

"Fine. But don't expect us to bail you out when you're in over your head."

Courtney pressed a card into his palm. "Call us when you're ready to talk."

The detectives walked away without a backward glance.

A slight tremor shook Dimitrios' hand as he slid the card into his pocket. They'd be watching now.

Another reason to get Ari and the baby out of town. Sooner rather than later.

The plan started to form. First, he'd call his boss and tell him he needed a little time off. It had been offered after Mike was shot, but he'd turned it down. All he had to tell them was that he'd changed his mind and could use a little time to recoup from the trauma.

Then he'd arrange to get Ari out of town.

But he couldn't send her away on her own.

Sure, he'd done it with his family, but they all had each other. She had no one.

Then again, he may not be the safest of company. Still, he couldn't stand the thought of her being out there alone.

One way or another, he'd keep her safe. Or die trying.

Eight

Everything looked quiet.

But then it had looked quiet before the attack inside the ambulance, too.

Dimitrios let the slat of the mini blind fall back into place. He'd turned out the lights over an hour ago and had sat in the dark, watching the street. No sign of anyone lingering.

He crossed his darkened duplex, stopping at each window to peek through the blinds. No sign of anyone on the west side of the unit, either.

The backyard was also clear.

Time to throw some things into a duffel and get out of town.

He'd called Araceli from the hospital and told her his plan. He couldn't use his cell phone. They might be monitoring it.

A glance at the clock showed it was nearly midnight. Almost time to meet Araceli.

At least she hadn't accused him of being as paranoid as he felt. In fact, she'd gone along with his plan. Almost too willingly.

Then again, she'd been pretty shaken when he told her about the car accident. And the threat.

Fear had a way of killing a stubborn spirit.

He quickly copied down a few key numbers from the contact list in his phone, then removed the battery.

Okay, time to officially file himself in the same category as those guys who wore tinfoil hats.

Dropping both the phone and battery into his dresser drawer, he took one last look outside before heading for the sliding glass door leading to the back patio.

The night embraced him like an old friend. At least his black hair and dark clothes should provide some camouflage.

He cut across the back yard and down the alley, sticking to the shadows as much as possible.

At the end of the alley, he paused.

He skimmed the shadows. No sign of movement. Anywhere.

Half a dozen cars parked on the street. They looked empty, but it was nearly impossible to tell in the dark.

In the distance, a dog barked, setting off a mini chain reaction across the neighborhood.

Well, the longer he stood here, the more likely it was that someone would notice him.

He jogged across the street and stole down another alley.

Reaching another cross street, he paused to survey the area. Still no sign of anyone following him.

Evidently if anyone had been watching him, they'd only monitored the front of the house.

He turned down the street and attempted to walk casually. His body ached with every step. That car accident earlier hadn't done him any favors.

It took another ten minutes to reach the rendezvous spot – a public parking lot for beach access.

One car sat in the corner of the lot. The little white sedan was almost as familiar as the silhouette he could make out inside.

The engine purred to life as he approached.

He tossed his duffel on the floor of the backseat and glanced at the sleeping baby in the car seat before opening the passenger door.

Araceli put the car in motion, although she didn't speak

until she'd pulled out of the parking lot. "So what's your plan?"

"Get out of town." He adjusted the side mirror so he could keep an eye on the road behind them. So far, so good.

The pause, weighted with anticipation, put him on edge. "And then?"

What did she want? He was making this up as he went. "I'll figure it out. Think your car can make it to Florida?"

"*Florida*?" He sensed her gaze on him. "You're kidding, right?"

"Nope. Well, maybe about driving there." Man, was he tired. He'd love to slouch in the seat and steal a nap, but he couldn't. Not when he needed to keep his eyes open for trouble.

"Mitri." Frustration lined the word. "I can't just leave. I have my business–"

"You have Celeste."

"Who is my business *partner*. Meaning she didn't sign on to cover everything while I go jetting around the country."

"She covered things fine today, didn't she?"

"Exactly. I can't ask her to keep doing it for… I don't even know how long." Her sigh sounded loud in the small vehicle.

He had to get through to her. "These guys aren't playing around. The only other option is to hand over the baby."

She pressed her lips together.

Good. Exactly the response he'd expected.

Of course, even if she gave them the baby, they'd still want the files he had, but she didn't seem to make that connection.

"Why Florida?" Defeat laced the question.

"My sister lives there. She's a good person to have watching your back."

"How so?"

"She's a US Marshal." He slanted a glance at her in time to see her eyes widen.

"Really? Well, that's convenient."

Not really. Her career choice had put her life in jeopardy a few too many times for his liking.

"So what's she like?"

Headlights appeared in the side mirror. Off in the distance, but gaining. Too quickly?

Without removing his attention from the lights, he tried to form an answer. "Uh, her name's Milana. She's a lot like me. Well, a female me. Who's shorter. And a lot smaller."

A soft laugh, oblivious of the potential danger approaching from the rear, filled the car. "So in other words, she's not that much like you. Besides, I don't care what she looks like. What is she like?"

The headlights turned left down a side street.

His breath came a little easier. "She's not as talkative as Cy, but talks more than me."

"I could've guessed that last one."

He rotated his head to look at her. "Oh yeah?"

Even in the darkness, he caught the amused curve to her lips. "Yeah. It took you thirty years to even tell me you had a sister."

"We thought she was dead."

"Still, the fact that you're a triplet and not just a twin is pretty significant, don't you think?"

"We didn't talk about it growing up." He rubbed his bruised jaw, which hurt significantly less than the pain from the past. "It was easier. Especially for dad."

"He took it the hardest?"

"Given that the guy who took her was trying to get back at him, yeah. He blamed himself for years." Probably still did, even though Milana wasn't dead and had turned out okay.

"What happened?"

"A little girl died in a fire. My dad retrieved the body. The girl's father went berserk, then started a fire in Milana's bedroom one night to get even. The accelerant caused an explosion, so we didn't know he'd taken Milana with him. He took her to some pastor's house in Colorado, then drove back and turned himself in. He told everyone he'd killed her."

The familiar ache settled into his gut. All those years with his sister living across the country. All those years they'd never known. How his family could believe in God was beyond him. If God was there, shouldn't He have stopped this from happening?

"Oh, Mitri. I'm sorry. You should've told me before. I wish I'd known."

"It's not like you could've done anything."

"Still, it's one of those things friends should know." She maneuvered the windy, forested roads like a pro. "So. She's a US Marshal who lives in Florida. What else? Is she married? Does she have kids?"

"No and no. But maybe soon. She's been seeing this guy Paul for a while now and it sounds like things are moving that way."

The guy would have to be crazy to let Milana get away.

Then again, he'd let Araceli get away before. And if he didn't say something soon, it'd probably happen again.

But if he said something and she didn't feel the same way, he'd ruin the easy camaraderie they had.

After losing Mike, he couldn't lose her, too.

He had to keep his feelings hidden, at least for now.

Why couldn't these things be easier?

"You know, if you don't talk to me to keep me awake, you might be pushing my car out of a ditch."

He shook his head as if that would clear the thoughts away. "Sorry. Been a long day." Reclining the seat slightly, he sighed. "Okay, Milana. Let's see. Adopted by a pastor, so she's pretty religious. You guys will probably get along."

It came out sounding more like a dig than he'd intended.

"There's a big difference between being religious and having a relationship with God, Mitri." Araceli's tone was light.

At least she didn't sound offended. He angled his head so he could see her profile in the moonlit car. "That sounds like something she would say."

"Well, I look forward to meeting her." She grinned and glanced over at him. "But aren't you worried about the two of us brainwashing you or something?"

A yawn popped his jaw. "Nah. I brought my anti-brainwashing shampoo."

Lame. Was that the best comeback he could make?

Evidently. He'd blame the trauma and sleep deprivation for that one.

"So am I headed to Portland? The airport?"

That's right. He hadn't planned much beyond the get-out-of-town phase. "Yeah. Can I use your phone to try to book our flights?"

"Sure. It's in my purse.

He spotted her purse on the floor behind her seat. Snagging it, he fished her phone from an exterior pocket and navigated to the airline's website.

Man, did he hate leaving such an obvious trail.

If Bobby had the connections Mike suspected, tracking their movements would be easy. Especially since he had to book the flights under their legal names and using a credit card.

Okay. Think.

Not easy to do, especially given how wiped he felt.

Maybe the best thing would be to fly into another city, rent a car, and drive to Jacksonville. That'd be harder to track, wouldn't it?

Atlanta. Or Miami. Either one should be far enough away to mask their movements.

He searched flights for both locations.

Then booked the cheapest option. Atlanta.

The red-eye wouldn't leave until ten twenty five tomorrow night. He looked at the clock.

That gave them roughly twenty one hours to kill.

Or sleep through. They needed to find a place to catch some rest or they'd never make it to Milana's house.

Well, they'd reach McMinnville soon enough.

He navigated back to the travel website and brought up hotels, picking the one with the best rate that didn't look like it'd be more popular with the city's local druggies than with tourists. It also had a late check-out option. He booked two rooms, partly because he knew Ari would insist, but also because he didn't want to be woken up by the baby.

One of them needed to be well rested and since she was the baby's caregiver, that left him.

Lastly, he arranged for a rental car in Atlanta and booked it for a week.

Dang. This would put a dent in his bank account.

At least Ari would be safe. Money could be replaced, but Araceli was all too valuable.

ꟷ ꟷ ꟷ ꟷ ꟷ

A muggy breeze carried the salty scent of the Atlantic as Dimitrios pushed open the door of his rental car. The sun felt nice on his face and arms and for a second he wished he and Araceli were really vacationing instead of running from the mob.

As he followed Araceli to a nearby picnic table, he punched Lana's number into Araceli's phone.

Setting the car seat on the picnic table, Araceli pointed at the nearby restrooms before heading that direction. He glanced down at the carrier. At least the baby was asleep.

"This is Lana." Milana's voice drifted into his ear. Papers rustled in the background.

She sounded distracted. He glanced at his watch. A little after ten a.m. She was probably at work. "You're staying out of ambulances, right?"

A pause. "Mitri?"

"Who else?" He was probably the only one who greeted her by asking if she was avoiding ambulance rides. Given that his first interaction with her as an adult had occurred when he bandaged her up in the back of his ambulance, it shouldn't be a surprise.

"Sorry. I didn't recognize the number."

"I'm using a friend's phone. Mine's out of commission at the moment." No point in telling her he'd taken it out of commission himself.

"Is everything okay?"

Leave it to her to know something was up. "Sure. Why wouldn't it be?"

"Well, you're using a friend's phone and you're calling, not texting, for starters."

Man, maybe he should call more often. "Actually, I'm sitting at a rest stop outside Jacksonville."

"You're what?"

Araceli exited the building and crossed the lawn to where he and the baby waited in the shade. "Yeah. Thought I should finally see where my baby sister lives."

"Who're you calling baby?"

He figured that would distract her, at least for a moment or two. "You're the youngest."

"By five minutes. It hardly counts."

"Younger is younger." He tried to ignore the way Araceli studied him, her face radiating disapproval. "So you up for a few houseguests or should I book a hotel?"

"No, no. Stay with me." This time the pause was more pregnant than Regan had been when she'd been killed. "You said a few. Who's with you?"

"A friend. You'll like her."

"Mitri, what's going on?"

"What do you–?"

"Come on. You fly all the way across the country, dragging a *friend* with you, for no reason at all? You can't really expect me to believe everything's okay."

Continue to play innocent?

What was the point? She already knew something was up.

He swallowed. "A friend of ours died this week. We really

needed to get away for a few days."

Silence.

Man, if this was how Lana did her job, she was darn good at it. He wanted to spill it all, right now, on the phone.

And he wasn't usually one to spill his guts.

"Okay, we'll talk about this later." A sigh filled his ear. "I'm neck deep in work right now. I can't get away."

"That's fine. It was a red-eye flight so all I want is a nap anyway."

"Okay. You have my new address?"

New? "Uh, the one on Casa Verde Lane?"

"That's the old one."

"When did you move?"

A pause. "A few months ago. I had to after… well, let's just say I had to."

Hmmm. Sounded like he wasn't the only one with some explaining to do. "What happened?"

She waited so long he wasn't sure she was going to answer. Finally, she cleared her throat. "There was an incident." Her voice sounded strained and slightly hoarse. "Someone tried to kill me."

She called that an incident?

Sounded more like a crisis to him. Then again, maybe it was becoming familiar ground to her.

He wished he could say that was the first time someone had tried to kill her, but he knew better. But what did that have to do with moving?

A thought pummeled his mind. "Wait, in your home?"

"So are you ready for that address?"

A diversion. He'd have to get the story later. When they were face to face and she couldn't dodge him. "Yeah."

"It's ninety-nine Hidden Palm Court, unit thirty-three."

An apartment?

Uh-oh. Did she even have room for them to stay with her? "How big is your apartment?"

"It's a condo and it's three bedroom. You'll need my code

to get in the front gate."

"Okay, hold on. Let me get something to write with."

Araceli dug into her purse and produced a pen and sticky note pad.

"Okay, go ahead." He jotted down the eight digit code Lana gave him. "Got it. You have a hide-a-key around?"

"Are you kidding? That's one step away from leaving the door unlocked."

What, because a gated community with an eight digit code wasn't secure enough? Law enforcement people were so paranoid sometimes. "Soooo, you want us to wait on the porch?"

"Of course not. Let me call Paul. He can probably meet you there."

Whoa. Things with Paul may be more serious than he'd originally thought. "I can't believe you gave him a key."

"Rein that in right now. He only uses it in emergencies or to check on the place when I'm gone. You know me better than that."

So Paul wasn't living there.

Or staying over, evidently. That made more sense, given what Lana believed.

"Living together isn't a crime, you know. This isn't 1850."

"God's standards haven't changed between then and now, so neither have mine." A voice, muffled, sounded in the background and he heard her say something muffled in return before coming back on the line. "Look, I need to go. Let me call Paul. If there's a problem, I'll call you back. Otherwise, he should be at my place in about thirty minutes."

"Sounds good. And thanks."

"It'll be good to see you. But you're not off the hook about that explanation."

Neither was she.

They ended the call. He looked up to find Araceli, hands on her hips. "You didn't ask her if we could come?"

"I knew it would invite too many questions." And maybe

a refusal, which he couldn't have afforded. But he knew that once they were here she wouldn't say no. "Besides, she doesn't mind."

"No woman likes having people drop in unannounced to stay for a few days. Trust me."

Yeah, well Lana wasn't most women. Besides, if she had a problem with it, she'd get over it.

Now all he had to do was figure out what to tell her.

He could do that after he'd had some sleep. If he didn't get moving soon, he'd be lucky to get them to her place alive.

Fifty-two minutes later, he pulled up in front of a massive, gated complex. Palm trees flanked the entry, obscuring but not obliterating his view of the six foot stone fence surrounding the complex. A wrought-iron gate blocked the driveway going in, with a keypad situated in front of it.

A few well-shaded parking spots sat vacant to the left of the gate. They practically screamed "You're not special enough to get in!"

Good thing he had a code.

He pulled up to the keypad and punched in the code Lana had given him. The gates slid open.

The driveway immediately curved to the left. He followed it, noting the numbers on the buildings as he passed.

The white stucco buildings appeared to be clustered in groups of four: two buildings with two units each. The units were duplex style; two-story townhouses with a one-car garage and small lawn in front. Some lawns had low fences, but most were open.

The drive wove around the buildings. When he came to a split, he paused. Which way?

Well, the branch to the left would take them back toward the main road. If he knew his sister, she wouldn't have chosen that location. He stayed right and was rewarded with units in the twenties.

Should be almost…

There!

The decorative sign by the driveway ahead said thirty through thirty-three.

He turned into the shared driveway. The two units facing the road were thirty and thirty-one. Following the drive around to the back, he found unit thirty-three at the end.

About as far from the road and entrance as possible. Yeah, that sounded like Lana all right.

A nineties model pickup sat in front of the garage.

Paul's?

He'd find out soon enough.

He pulled into the paved parking space adjacent to the garage and killed the engine. The rental pinged in the suddenly silent afternoon.

The baby cried.

Dimitrios glanced in the rearview mirror, but couldn't see anything more than the back of the car seat.

It was remarkable how quiet he'd been through most of their travels. Almost as if he knew his life was a gift and didn't want to waste time on self-pity.

Okay, that was ridiculous. Man, he must be more tired than he thought.

It was a baby, after all.

Baby. Poor kid deserved a name.

Maybe he had one. Why hadn't he thought to ask before?

Araceli had opened the door and was unhooking the car seat. He stepped from the vehicle, the muggy Florida air wrapping him like a latex glove. The temperature was probably in the seventies, but heavy cloud cover and the threat of rain put a damp chill in the air.

"Did Mike tell you his name?" His voice sounded loud in the almost unnatural stillness.

"No. I've been calling him Joseph." She hefted the car seat from the vehicle and stared at the baby's face. "Seemed only fitting since violence took him from his family."

What did violence have to do with the name Joseph? Did they know someone named Joseph who had lost his family?

"I'm not tracking."

She hip-bumped the door closed. "It's in the Bible. Joseph was his father's favorite and his brothers were jealous, so they sold him into slavery and made up a story about him being killed by animals."

A Bible story? Figured. "Harsh."

She ran a finger down the baby's cheek. "But God had big plans for Joseph, in spite of the evil done to him. God used him to save countless people, including his brothers."

Right. Like that was anything more than a story in an outdated book.

Whatever. One name was as good as another.

He retrieved their luggage from the trunk and led the way up the sidewalk. The door opened before he reached it.

He didn't know what he'd expected a man who'd devoted his life to helping troubled kids to look like, but the tall, solidly-built man with slightly unkempt brown hair didn't fit. Neither did it fit his image of the kind of guy Lana would be interested in.

Although he didn't really know much about that. Not being around her for most of their lives had left him somewhat stunted in many areas.

"Paul?" He offered his hand.

The other man shook it, an easy smile creasing his face. "Dimitrios. It's good to see you again."

Again? Dimitrios stared. "We've met?"

"A lifetime ago." Paul jerked his head toward the house. "Come inside and I'll fill you in."

Dimitrios motioned Araceli to precede him. "This is Araceli. A friend."

Lame. Why couldn't he simply let it hang and leave Paul to his own assumptions?

"Nice to meet you." He glanced at the carrier. "And who's this?"

"Joseph." Araceli shifted the baby's weight. "I'm his legal guardian."

Paul closed the door behind them and turned, his eyebrow arching. "Where are his parents?"

"They died." The word came out on a whisper and tears glowed in her eyes.

"I'm sorry." Paul gestured to the living room. "Go ahead and have a seat. Need anything? Something to eat or drink?"

While he was too tired to eat, his sandpaper throat screamed for something wet and cold. "Don't suppose she has any pop? I could use the caffeine."

"Not usually, but let me check." Paul skirted the wet bar and entered the kitchen. "Nope. Just sweet tea or milk."

"Water's good."

Short cries came from the car seat. Removing Joseph from the device, Araceli cradled him for a second before digging one-handed in the diaper bag. "I need to get a bottle ready for Joseph."

Paul gestured to the kitchen. "Do what you need to do."

While Paul moved around the kitchen like it was his own, Dimitrios checked out what he could see of the condo. High ceilings, hardwood floors, open floor plan. A staircase lined the wall to his left, leading to what appeared to be a loft, where he suspected they'd find the bedrooms. The lightweight curtains lent a soothing blue glow to the room.

His baby sister had chosen well.

As Paul returned to the living room with two glasses of ice water, Dimitrios had a feeling she'd chosen well in more ways than one. "Sorry to mess up your day."

Paul waved off the concern. "I'm usually pretty flexible. The couple who run the group home were both around and we didn't have anything major going on, so I was able to get away."

"Why was I thinking that you ran the group home?"

Paul's smile dimmed a shade, his eyes showing… regret?

"I used to, but I signed it over to the Webbers. Now I'm on staff." He studied Dimitrios. "I get why you don't remember me, but Lana never mentioned any of this?"

Dimitrios snorted. "Do you know my sister? Getting anything from her is like performing surgery with a plastic knife."

Paul laughed. "Still, I'm surprised she never mentioned it."

And on that note, now was a good time to find out when their paths had crossed before. "So when did we meet?"

"Years ago. Right after Lana was shot."

Impossible. Lana hadn't met Paul until several years after that. Plus, he remembered that night vividly. From the smell of blood to the look of death. He'd been certain they would lose her, but her injuries turned out to be less severe than they'd first appeared.

Araceli returned to the living room, bottle in hand, and sat on the sofa. The fussing ceased as Joseph sucked at the bottle.

Although he watched, Dimitrios' thoughts were centered on things from years ago.

Paul hadn't been there. No one had been there that night except his family, Lana's adoptive family, and a friend of hers that'd been on scene when the shooting went down.

"You probably remember me as Nate. I was the guy in the parking lot."

Dimitrios turned back, studying the man sitting across from him. "I remember *that* guy."

In fact, he could still picture him. He'd been smaller, and his facial features were different. Not as angular.

"I had plastic surgery after that. To hide my identity."

"Why?"

"Because I was a thief and an accessory to murder and your sister could identify me." Paul's tone was matter-of-fact, like he was telling them what he wanted on his pizza rather than disclosing his own criminal history.

Maybe his sister hadn't chosen so well after all.

None of this made sense.

Lana, with a criminal?

Not a chance.

"Sounds like there's a lot she hasn't told you." Paul rubbed the back of his neck. "The short version is that my brother was an assassin. I knew what he did, but didn't ever try to stop him. I also helped him break into places, then turned a blind eye to whatever he did once he was in. Before all that, I was a pretty good thief."

"Why are you telling me this?"

"Because you're Lana's family. Besides, it's been pardoned. I signed the home over to the Webbers, turned myself in, spent a few years in prison, then made a deal with the FBI to help them bring down a militia group. In exchange, they scrubbed my old life and let me officially become Paul Van Horn."

"And Lana's good with this?"

"I know, right? It took her a while, but yeah." He leaned forward. "But I need you to keep this to yourselves. I've still got enemies out there and if they find out I'm alive, it could bring trouble."

Which would spill over into Lana's life. Paul didn't have to say it. "No one will hear it from us."

"Thanks."

There was still a lot that didn't make sense, though.

"So after the plastic surgery, you what? Called her up?"

"No. I had no intention of ever seeing her again. I started a new life. I found God. But then my brother died in an accident." He shrugged. "I don't know how to explain it. I didn't think it out, I just packed up everything and moved here. And ended up at her dad's church. She felt sorry for the loner sitting alone, talked to me, and well, things went from there."

"So you changed your identity and stalked my sister."

Paul had the decency to wince. "It sounds bad when you say it like that."

"How should I say it?"

"A work of God? In His timing?" Paul held up his hands. "I swear. Coming down here was more instinctive than anything else. Call it a knee-jerk reflex of losing my brother. Lana was the only other person who'd ever really understood what I'd gone through as a kid. I wanted to be near, even if it could never amount to anything. Or so I thought."

Huh. The guy seemed sincere enough.

More than that, Lana trusted him and she didn't trust easily.

Unlikely as the whole story sounded, maybe it was true. Besides, it was Lana's life, not his. He needed to let it go.

He forced a smile he wasn't sure he felt yet. "Sorry about the interrogation. Just watching out for my sister, you know?"

"Believe me, I'm glad. Someone's got to do it, right?" Paul looked back and forth between them. "You guys look beat. How about I show you where you can stay so you can get some rest."

Arguing would have taken strength Dimitrios lacked. Besides, Paul was right.

Sometime during the conversation Joseph had fallen asleep. Araceli placed him back in the carrier, then followed Paul to the stairs.

The stairs spilled into an open space that would've made a good rec room or office, but there wasn't a single piece of furniture in sight. Skylights dumped sunshine into the area. A waist high wall bordered the edge of the loft so no one would fall down into the living room below.

Two doors occupied the wall straight ahead of them. Another two were on the wall bordering the stairs. All stood open.

Paul crossed the empty space, leading them to the far wall. He stepped into the one on the right. "This is the guest room."

Singular. Meaning she only had one guest room set up.

Dimitrios nodded at Ari. "Take it."

Araceli stepped inside, then hesitated. "What about you?"

"I'll be good on the sofa. Tired as I am, I could sleep anywhere."

"Actually, Lana suggested that one of you take her room."

Dimitrios slid a glance at Paul. "I'm not kicking her out of her room."

Holding his hands up, Paul shook his head. "Hey, I'm just the messenger. You can take that up with her."

He would. As soon as she got home.

Although for now, it wouldn't hurt to stretch out across the bed and get some sleep. He wouldn't use her room tonight, but there was no harm in using it now. Especially since she was still at work.

"This one's the office." Paul gestured to the door on their left. "Lana's room is back there, next to the bathroom. " He jerked his thumb behind his back.

Dimitrios looked across the loft area to the rooms on the other side. Through the open doorway, he could see the corner of a bed, decorated in shades of yellow, blue, and green.

"Make yourselves at home. Lana said she probably wouldn't be home until after six, but to help yourself to anything in the kitchen."

"Thanks." Araceli offered a smile before entering the bedroom and closing the door behind her.

Dimitrios assessed Paul, Araceli's earlier words running through his mind. "Was she mad? That we dropped in like this?"

A brief hesitation marked Paul's response. "Not mad. But she's worried."

Of course she was. But she wasn't the only one. Her earlier comment about an incident at her old house, not to mention the security of this one, brought more questions than answers. Combine that with the stalker-not-stalker boyfriend of hers, to whom she'd entrusted a key, and a serious conversation was pending.

"So why'd she move?"

Paul crossed his arms over his chest. "Sorry, man, can't help you. It's her story to tell, not mine."

Fair enough.

While he still questioned Paul's motives, at least the man had his sister's back.

"I'm headed back to work." Paul clapped a hand on Dimitrios' shoulder. "Look, I don't need to know what's going on, but talk to her, okay? I don't like to see her upset."

Yeah, well what if what he told her upset her even more? He simply nodded. "Thanks again."

"I'll see you guys around. I'll leave my number on the counter downstairs. You know, in case you need anything. Don't hesitate to call."

Colorful past aside, Paul seemed like an okay guy. "Will do."

Dimitrios watched the other man walk toward the stairs before heading for his sister's bedroom.

He kicked off his shoes and dropped onto the bed. Sleep couldn't come fast enough.

Especially now that he and everyone he loved was finally safe.

⁂

"Well?" Bobby narrowed his eyes on the two men in front of him. Anthony squirmed, but Nicky never moved.

"He's, uh, he's gone."

Bobby's attention riveted on Anthony. "What do you mean, gone?

Shooting Anthony a disdainful glare, Nicky smoothly interjected, "He slipped the detail we had on him. We tracked him on a flight to Atlanta. He rented a car, but the trail goes cold after that."

Idiots! Must he do everything himself? "Rentals have GPS. Find him."

A smug smile crossed Nicky's face. "Already on it. There is one other thing you should know."

A pause. He hated it when Nicky did that.

"He wasn't traveling alone."

Really.

Not that he cared who Lykos traveled with, but the fact that a single man in full-flight mode would take someone with him was significant. He'd bet money that the travel companion was someone important.

"I take it you wouldn't waste my time if you didn't have a name."

"Araceli Lopez. Single, no children. But get this. They were traveling with an infant."

His son! So Lykos had known more than he'd let on. Surprise, surprise. "Tear his life apart. Hers, too. If they know anyone on the East Coast, I want to know who."

"I already got someone checking phone records."

"Do *not* disappoint me again. Find them. Whatever it takes."

Anthony darted out of the luxury hotel suite like a jackrabbit, but Nicky sauntered out as though time was of little importance.

Bobby ground his teeth. If Nicky wasn't so good at what he did, he'd put the man into retirement. But it'd be too hard to replace Nicky. So he'd have to put up with Nicky's arrogance.

For now, anyway.

But if he failed on this task no amount of skill would save him

Every minute that passed gave Lykos more time to cover his tracks. He needed to be found. Soon.

Might be time to call in some favors. Who was his best resource?

Craig Allen.

He snatched up his phone and scrolled through the contacts until he found Craig.

Ringing filled his ear. He pushed up from the too-hard armchair and paced to the windows overlooking the ocean.

"Allen." Craig's baritone sounded distracted. Keys

clacked in the background, evidencing that Craig was still at work.

"I need a favor."

"Bobby." The clacking stopped.

Good. He had Craig's full attention.

"What can I do?" Craig's tone was all business.

"Phone records for the last six months." He gave Craig Lykos' number. "I'm looking for an East Coast connection."

"Got it. Anything else?"

Too bad he didn't have Araceli Lopez's number, too. Although he'd bet Lykos was the mastermind behind this, not the woman. "If this turns out dry, then there may be an additional number, but let's start there."

"You got it."

"And Craig? This is personal. The sooner the better."

"Top of my list. I'll call you soon."

Bobby ended the call and stared at the churning waves. Unlike Nicky and Anthony, he had no doubt that he would hear from Craig soon.

And that Craig would come through. With any luck, he'd have a location by the end of the day.

Nine

Ugh. Had his muscles ever been this stiff?

Yeah. Probably when he and Mike had climbed their last mountain. Something they'd never do again.

There was a lot they'd never do again.

He pushed the thoughts aside and jogged a few laps up and down the stairs to limber up.

Better. Though not great.

His stomach rumbled.

Man, he was hungry. Maybe Lana had something to munch on.

He wandered into the kitchen and opened the fridge.

Huh. Milk, juice, yogurt, cottage cheese. Didn't the woman believe in lunchmeat?

Evidently not.

He checked the time on the stove. Nearly six. He'd taken a decent nap. Then again, he'd also been pretty tired.

As quiet as it was in the house, he didn't appear to be the only one.

A whirring noise came from somewhere in the house. What was that?

Several seconds passed before a door opened and closed. Lana? Or had Bobby's guys tracked them here?

Ridiculous. Wasn't it?

"Mitri?"

As crazy as his paranoid thoughts were, hearing his

sister's voice was a relief. "In here."

She came into the kitchen, looking exactly as he remembered her. Almost a foot shorter than him, a petite frame reminiscent of their mom, and long dark hair.

Crossing the kitchen, she gave him a hug. "It's good to see you."

"You, too. You look good."

She stepped back and studied him. "Wish I could say the same. What happened?"

What hadn't happened? "Accident at work."

"Really." Skepticism lined the word. "Looks like a pretty serious accident. What'd you do?"

"I got careless. It happens." Dang. He sounded as defensive as he felt.

"I can't believe you'd lie to me." There was no condemnation in her words. In fact, they sounded as casual as if she'd told him the daily forecast was warm and sunny. "You combine that with your unexpected visit and you can see why I'm not buying it, right?"

It would've been smart to create a believable cover story before she got home. Too bad he hadn't thought about it.

There were times when it was better to simply say nothing at all. This was one of those times.

"I knew it." She straightened. "How can I help?"

Something in his expression must've given him away. "By leaving it alone. I'm dealing with it."

"By running away."

"It was the best option."

"In my experience, secrets that can do that," she nodded at his head injury, "only get worse. Does this have anything to do with the friend you mentioned on the phone? The one who died?"

He didn't owe her an explanation. It was his life and if he wanted to keep secrets, that was his right.

Then again, he'd been the one to barge into her home.

Fine. He owed her.

But where did he even begin? And how much did he want to tell her? It seemed that everyone who knew anything about this ended up being hunted down.

"Is everyone okay?" The hesitation in her voice speared him.

"Yes." The word slipped out automatically. Time to correct course. "I mean, Cy's recovering, but he's going to be fine."

"What happened to Cy?" Alarm rang in her words.

Dang. He hadn't mentioned the car accident earlier, but now he had to tell her. "We were in a little fender bender. No big deal, but we both got a little banged up."

She crossed her arms over her chest. "You told me it was a work accident."

This was why he shouldn't lie. It was too hard to keep his stories straight. "It was. Work accident one day, car accident the next. Too bad Cy was with me for the second one."

"Two accidents in two days, then you skip town and come here. And you really expect me to believe nothing's going on?"

Okay. Time to give her some version of the truth. Maybe if he offered a generic one it wouldn't put her in too much danger. "You remember Mike?"

She stared at him. Trying to process, no doubt, but it didn't look like she was making the right connection.

No wonder. She'd met him maybe two times. Each meeting had lasted all of a few minutes, if that.

"EMT? My partner?"

Recognition dawned. "Okay. What about him?"

"He was murdered this week."

The words ripped open the hollowness in his chest. Would it ever not hurt to say it?

"I–I had no idea." Lana stared at him, eyes and lips curled down slightly.

Man. If she started crying, he was done for. He pressed his lips together to keep them from shaking.

"I'm sorry." Her words conveyed both sympathy and a knowledge of the pain of that kind of loss. "I know you guys were close."

"Yeah." He stared down at his hands, still seeing the blood that he'd long since scrubbed away.

Lana waited.

He didn't want to talk about this, though. Not now. Or ever.

In fact, all he wanted to do was pretend it had never happened. For all the good that would do.

"I thought I heard voices." Araceli's voice came from the doorway.

Ari to the rescue. Maybe he oughta buy her a cape.

She stood inside the kitchen, thumbs hooked in the pockets of her faded jeans, a lace trimmed pink sweater hugging her curves.

No sign of Joseph though, so he must be sleeping.

"That might not be something you want to admit out loud." Lana smiled at Araceli before turning to him with raised eyebrows.

He may not be able to read her as well as he did Cy, but he had no trouble interpreting the question in that expression.

Araceli laughed. "It didn't sound like that in my mind."

Well, let's see if he could botch this introduction as badly has he had earlier with Paul. "Lana, this is my friend Araceli. Ari, my sister, Lana."

Much better.

"It's nice to finally meet one of his friends. I was beginning to think he didn't have any."

Strain edged Araceli's smile. "Well, he is down one these days. We both are."

Lana's smile slipped. "He told me about Mike. I'm sorry."

"It's been a bad week." Araceli leaned against the doorframe. "So Mitri tells me you're a US Marshal. That must be exciting."

"It's not as glamorous as the media makes it out to be and

you'd be surprised at the amount of paperwork, but I like it." Lana's stance was relaxed, even though he knew she had a million questions colliding in her mind. "So are you an EMT, too?"

A laugh burst from Araceli. "Heavens, no! I can't stand blood. I own a nursery back home. Plants, not babies."

"She's also a pretty good botanist, too. She's always working on some new hybrid. Her specialty is poisonous plants." Keeping Lana focused on Araceli was a good way to dodge the questions she had for him.

Lana arched an eyebrow. "Really? Like what?"

"I'm currently working with Peruvian Violets. I actually recently made a breakthrough on a serum that causes temporary paralysis with minimal risk of side effects."

He straightened. "You didn't tell me that."

"It's been a busy week."

"What would the applications be for something like that?" Lana's question drew Araceli's attention away from him.

"There are lots of them. It could be used by animal control officers to catch aggressive strays, by fish and wildlife officers to sedate wild animals who get too close to the human population, even as a nonlethal option for law enforcement."

"I'm always up for more nonlethal options." Lana tucked her hair behind her ears. "Has it been tested?"

"Only once, but it was highly successful. I'm actually in negotiations with a private lab right now. If I can get the proper backing, we can do more testing and maybe get it on the market."

"That's amazing." Lana tilted her head. "Why have I never heard of the Peruvian Violet before?"

"Well, it's pretty rare. In our country anyway. Although I've had good success growing them in my greenhouse so if this pans out, they would be easy to mass produce. I think they'd sell well as a rare plant, too. They're toxic, but have these amazing multi-hued purple blooms. It's beautiful."

Not as beautiful as her.

He didn't have to see the Peruvian Violet to know it was true.

Not that he'd ever say it out loud.

He watched Ari interact with Lana. Man, he knew Ari was tall, but seeing her standing close to Lana really accentuated her height.

Or maybe just showed how small his sister was.

Either way, her height was yet another thing he liked about her.

A cry came from upstairs. Araceli's eyes rolled up toward the ceiling. "Sounds like I'm being beckoned. See you guys later."

Silence enveloped them as she left the room.

It was coming. If he knew Lana, she was only waiting until Ari was out of earshot.

Footsteps sounded above their heads.

Lana's gaze zeroed in on him. "So. Araceli?"

"Just a friend."

"And the baby? Is she hiding from the father?"

"The baby's not hers." Dang. That didn't sound good at all. And with Lana's personal experience, not to mention her job, that wasn't going to sit well. "I mean, she's taking care of him. It's all legal–"

"Mitri. Whose baby is he?" Her tone was even, her words measured.

Deep breath. Dangerous ground to tread here. "Mike was his guardian. He left Joseph in Ari's care before…."

A knot lodged in his throat. Would he ever be able to talk about Mike without choking up?

"It's all legal?"

"Yeah. I've got the paperwork and everything."

Narrowed eyes examined him. "Mike had paperwork drawn up putting the infant in her care? Did he know trouble was coming?"

Footsteps sounded on the stairs. Joseph's cries drew closer.

"Look, can we talk about this later?" It wouldn't stop the questions, but it would buy him time to decide how to answer them.

"Later. Count on it."

✥ ✥ ✥ ✥ ✥

"How long will you be able to stay?"

Dimitrios didn't move from where he leaned against the counter, watching as Lana put the leftover hamburgers from dinner into the fridge. He'd known the interrogation would come, but she'd saved it for when Araceli went upstairs to put Joseph to bed.

"Until we wear out our welcome?"

"Which might be sooner rather than later if I don't get some answers." She sighed. "You know you're always welcome here, but I need the truth. What's going on?"

"Why did you move?" He injected a challenge in the words. "Answer mine and I'll answer yours."

"I told you. Someone broke into my home and tried to kill me."

"So you're telling me it was random."

"No." She pulled out a barstool and sat down. "I know Paul told you about his past. Well, you know that case he helped the FBI with? He infiltrated a white supremacist group. They thought they could use me to control Paul. You can imagine how I took that. I hurt one of the guys, his pride more than anything, and he decided to come after me."

Her throat worked. A tremulous hand raked through her hair. "He nearly got me. After that, I… my house wasn't the same, you know? I felt threats everywhere. I tried to get over it, but finally decided to move."

Not only move. Move into a gated, secure facility.

Although with as much danger as she put herself in, it was probably a good thing.

Still, the fact that this incident was Paul's fault was a problem. A big one. A frown pulled at his lips. "If that's the kind of trouble you get when you're with Paul–"

"It wasn't his fault. Besides, that's all in the past. And, before you ask," she speared him with a small frown. "Paul is not a stalker. I'd appreciate it if you trusted my judgment and gave him a chance."

He deserved that. "Sorry. He seems like a nice guy. The story, well, it isn't what I expected to hear."

"It's unconventional, but Paul's one of the most genuine guys I know. Living proof of what the grace of God can do in a man's life. Now. Back to my question." Lines edged her eyes, which suddenly had more red than white. Her face had lightened a shade and the smile she usually wore was nowhere to be found.

The story had cost her. Frankly, he was surprised she'd shared it.

But she had. And now he owed her more than the cursory explanation he'd offered earlier.

"It ties back to Mike." His throat tightened. He stamped down the emotions and moved on. "Or, more specifically, his girlfriend. She was also murdered. Days before Mike. Joseph is her baby." He held up a hand as she opened her mouth. "Don't worry. She made Mike Joseph's legal guardian and Mike drew up similar paperwork granting both Araceli and me legal guardianship. It's all legit."

At least he hoped it was.

No point in mentioning that Mike had taken the baby out of the hospital. Or that they hadn't conclusively proven the baby to be Regan's.

"Okay, but that still doesn't answer why you brought them here."

"Mike's killers have been threatening me."

"And the police? They're on board with this plan?"

Crud. He knew how she'd feel about this one. He pressed his lips together, as if not answering would make this easier.

"You didn't tell them." A statement, not a question.

"I couldn't. Mike didn't tell them. Until I know what's going on, I'm going to follow his lead."

"Mike also ended up dead."

He flinched. Did she have to be so blunt about it?

"You need to tell them." She stared at him. "If those bruises and cuts are any indication, they did more than just make threats."

"Yeah. They attacked me at work, then ran me and Cy off the road."

Her eyebrows lowered. "So neither of those accidents were really accidental. Is he as bad as you?"

"A cracked rib, but he'll be fine. I convinced him to take his family and leave town for a while. Mom and dad, too. Ari was the last on the short list to get to safety."

She nodded slowly, absorbing details in that detached way that he was pretty sure was taught to all law enforcement in basic training. "Why are they threatening you?"

No way. He'd already told her more than he'd intended. "I have something they want."

"Something worth your life? Or theirs?" She gestured above her to where Ari and Joseph were.

"Maybe." Okay, definitely not true. Not even close. "Right now I'm buying time to figure it all out."

She rested her elbows on the bar. "How much does Araceli know?"

"Enough to be scared."

"So what's your plan? You can't hide out indefinitely."

Stuffing his hands in his pockets, he leaned his hip against the counter and studied her. "I'm going back to Lincoln City to figure it all out. I needed to get them somewhere safe first and I knew you'd watch out for them."

"I can't stay here all day and cover them. You need to tell the police."

"I'm telling you." The words hung for a weighty second. "You're the only one I know I can trust."

A sigh leaked from her. "Usually *I'm* the most paranoid person in the room."

"With good reason." He studied her face, so similar to Cy's. Set lips, lowered eyebrows, pinched eyes. If it were Cy, he'd know exactly what she was thinking. But a lifetime apart had robbed him of the familiarity he would need to do that. "All I need is a little time."

Somewhere in the house, a clock hand scraped. After what felt like hours, she nodded. "Fine. But this conversation isn't over."

As expected. He may not know her as well as he should, but he knew enough to know that she'd bring this up again.

ᘎ ᘎ ᘎ ᘎ ᘎ

"Bobby." Craig's crisp voice crackled through the phone. "Sorry for the early call."

Bobby put the last of his clothes in his suitcase. "What did you find?"

"Not as much as I should have. Which is telling."

Papers shuffled. Bobby waited.

"There are multiple calls to a Florida cell number. Registered to M. Tanner. Now here's where it gets weird."

Weird how? Bobby narrowed his eyes but remained silent.

"I tried to track the phone but it doesn't come up. So it's either really old, off, or someone removed GPS functionality."

Interesting. "If you had to guess?"

"I'd say the last one. The first initial could indicate a privacy nut or someone with something to hide. Especially since it's on official records, not just a public listing."

"Did you find anything else?"

"The address tied to the account is a P.O. Box in Jacksonville. No physical address, which is also unusual. Most phone companies want that on file. Tells me this person likely has some kind of connections."

Just what he needed. "So you're saying you can't help me."

"No, no, no." Craig drew a deep breath. "I'm sure I can get what you need, but it's going to take a little longer than usual. I'm still working on it."

The rental car's GPS might be a faster method of tracking them after all. "I'm going to have my guys chase down another lead. Get me everything you can find on this M. Tanner. I need to know who we're up against here."

"On it."

Bobby ended the call and texted Nicky, who entered the suite a few seconds later. "Anything on that GPS?"

"Anthony's still hacking."

Naturally. When it was important, the man seemed to have only one speed.

It might be time to recruit a better hacker. "Lykos has been talking to someone named M. Tanner in Jacksonville. Find out who he is."

Nicky nodded and made his exit.

Another fine mess Regan had created. Now he not only had to contend with Lykos and the Lopez woman, there was this M. Tanner variable.

It didn't matter who this Tanner guy was, his men would find Lykos and take out anyone who got in the way.

The password you have entered is incorrect.

Dimitrios stared at Lana's laptop. It shouldn't be this hard to access a USB drive. What would Regan have used?

He didn't know Regan well enough to know the answer to that.

"How's it going?"

Dimitrios started at Araceli's voice behind him. She wasn't holding Joseph, which meant he must be sleeping.

Seemed all that kid did was sleep.

"I can't get this password." Hmmm. Araceli had been a little closer to Regan than he had. "Any idea what Regan would have used?"

Araceli thought for a second. "Not offhand."

"Do you know what she planned to name the baby?"

"Every time I asked, she said she wasn't sure." Araceli paused. "Almost like she expected that she wouldn't be giving him a name."

Weird. Then again, as scared as she had been, maybe not so weird after all.

"What I don't understand is how Regan password protected the USB." Araceli's blue curls bounced as she slowly shook her head. "She really wasn't good with computers at all. Mike was the genius."

Mike.

He was such an idiot! *Mike* would have set up the password, not Regan. "You're right. Now all I have to do is figure out what password Mike would have used and we're golden."

The note.

It had said to think about their most challenging climb.

That was easy. It was on Rainier. He typed that in.

Incorrect.

Okay, too obvious.

Maybe Kautz Glacier? That was the climb they'd chosen. It could also be Kautz ice chutes or Kautz ice cliffs or even Camp Hazard. All of those were memorable parts of that climb.

He punched in each of those options. Incorrect. Incorrect. Incorrect. Incorrect.

Come on, Mike. What did you use?

A soft floral scent assailed his sinuses as Araceli eased onto the sofa beside him. "Did Mike leave you a clue?"

"Yeah. Our most difficult climb."

"Okay, so was there anything weird that happened? Or a

running joke?"

That was an idea. Mike was always cracking jokes.

He rifled through his memory.

Nothing stood out. In fact, the thing that stuck the most was the near-tragedy at the crevasse.

Mike had lost his footing on the ice and almost gone over the edge. If they hadn't been tethered together and Dimitrios hadn't had his ice cleats firmly planted, he'd have been planning Mike's funeral a lot sooner.

He could still see the shaky smile on Mike's snowy face. *"Dude, I almost took the fast track to heaven."*

They'd had a good laugh about the phrase "fast track to heaven," although it had probably been due to the adrenaline dump rather than because it was actually funny.

Wait.

Mike had said that just after being shot. Maybe to point him toward the right password?

It was worth a try. He punched in *fast track to heaven* and hit enter.

A file popped open.

Finally.

Araceli leaned in, her hair brushing his bicep. He fought the urge to touch her, instead focusing in on the laptop screen.

Two files. One video, the other text.

He opened the video file.

A low resolution image of a construction site filled the screen. A dark SUV drove into the frame, parking outside the fence.

Several seconds passed before a man who resembled a scarecrow approached the SUV, his movements as steady as a jackrabbit. After glancing around, he stopped by the back of the vehicle. The dome light came on inside the SUV and two men joined the scarecrow at the back.

Dimitrios squinted at the too-small picture. It was hard to say for certain, but he didn't think any of the men looked familiar.

The scarecrow gestured, waving his arms as though shooing birds away, his movements stiff and agitated.

Too bad there wasn't sound.

The larger of the two men moved slightly. Something appeared in his hand.

Two flashes. The scarecrow jerked, then dropped.

Araceli gasped. The sharp intake of breath right next to his ear made him jump.

On the screen, the smaller man looked around, his face a stoic mask of indifference. The shooter knelt next to the body, searching the dead man's pockets.

After stuffing something in his own pockets, the shooter rose and walked to the driver's side of the SUV. The smaller man disappeared down the passenger side. A few seconds later, reverse lights flashed and the SUV rolled over the corpse.

He could almost hear the crunch of pulverized bones.

The video ended.

They'd witnessed a murder. Not the trumped-up, melodramatic Hollywood style where people didn't really die but the real call-the-cops-and-open-an-investigation kind.

The eggs he'd had for breakfast scrambled in his gut.

"Is that – is that real?" Araceli's voice had a breathless quality he hadn't heard since the night Mike died.

"I think so." Actually, he was sure of it. "Let's see what the other file is."

He opened the text document. A few lines appeared on the screen.

This could bury you.
30 grand or it hits the news.
I'll call you.

Blackmail. But who was the target?

It had to be Bobby, right? Maybe he was one of the men in the video.

Although from the little he knew about the man, Bobby didn't seem like the type to get his hands dirty.

No, more likely, the men on the video worked for Bobby. Or were at least known associates of his.

"Why would Mike have this?" A wobble rocked Araceli's voice.

"It has to tie back to Regan."

"You think she was blackmailing Bobby?"

"It would explain her murder, right?" But it didn't fit. While the evidence pointed that way, the woman he'd known had been too scared to blackmail anyone.

"I don't know. She didn't seem the type."

Not that either of them knew what blackmailers were really like. "So maybe she kept this as some kind of insurance?"

If so, that hadn't really worked out so well for her. Or Mike.

A tear slipped down Araceli's cheek. "I wish Mike was here so we could ask him."

He took her hand and squeezed. "Me, too."

"Did Mike leave you anything else?"

"Yeah, but I couldn't bring it with me. There were some ledgers and a newspaper, that's it." Wait a second. The article had mentioned a murder at a construction site.

It couldn't be coincidence.

"There was a newspaper article about this murder. And a hit list. That guy was on the list."

"What was in the ledgers?"

He shrugged. "Numbers. I don't know. It's not really my thing. I'd thought about having an accountant look them over, but never got that far."

"Take them to the police. They can figure it out. Then we can get back to our lives."

Her eyes pleaded with him to agree. But he couldn't. "Why didn't Mike do that? If that was the best solution, wouldn't he have done it?"

"I don't know, but we can't stay like this forever. You have a job. I have my business. Celeste can cover for me for a few days, but I have to get back."

She was right. Her greenhouse wasn't the only thing at stake. His whole family was in danger because of him.

But if Mike didn't trust Jim and Courtney enough to give them the evidence, why should he?

"Let me talk to Lana. Maybe she can help."

"Got something."

Bobby looked up to find Anthony grinning like an idiot. "Well?"

"It's–"

The private jet hit a spot of turbulence, jostling the ice in Bobby's scotch and sending Anthony's tablet sliding toward the edge of the table in front of him. Anthony caught it before it left the ledge.

The plane smoothed out a few seconds later and Bobby nodded at Anthony.

Anthony held up the tablet. "GPS tracking on that rental puts it at an address in Jacksonville. It's been there for the last twenty-four hours. Address is for a condo. Owner is M. Tanner."

So. All roads led to the mysterious M. Tanner. "What have we found out about Tanner?"

Anthony slid his gaze to Nicky.

"Still working it. There's lots of M. Tanners out there."

Idiot. With any luck Craig would do better.

"Keep searching. And be ready to fly to Florida. You'll leave as soon as we get to Vegas."

"Aren't you going?"

Bobby arched an eyebrow. "Do I need to?"

"No, no, 'course not." Nicky held up his hands. "But with your kid involved, I thought maybe you'd wanna be there."

"Just bring him home. And don't forget the evidence."

Nicky nodded before turning his attention to his phone.

Bobby picked up his own phone. It'd been a few hours since he'd heard from Craig. It wouldn't hurt to call for an update.

Craig answered on the first ring. "Bobby. I was about to call you."

Swirling his scotch, Bobby took a sip while waiting for Craig to continue.

Papers rustled in the background. "Took some doing, but I think M. Tanner is Milana Tanner."

So M. Tanner was a woman. "How does she connect to Lykos?"

"Still working on that. Let me tell you, just getting her name was hard enough. The only reason I got that was because I backtracked a phone number that she calls a lot. Led me to some guy named Paul Van Horn. Now this guy could be a relative, friend, or significant other, but the number of calls, length, and times tells me it's personal. And Van Horn's much easier to trace. Works for a group home for troubled kids in Jacksonville. I also found some news articles from a few years back when he witnessed a murder by some serial killer. Tanner's name came up in connection with that whole thing when the killer almost ended her."

Interesting. Although none of that told him how Tanner connected to Lykos.

"And her address?" He'd trust Craig's hacking a heck of a lot more than Anthony's.

"Working on that, too. But I've got an address for that group home. And copies of the news articles. I'll send it to you straight away."

Bobby ended the call. If more of his guys were like Craig, he wouldn't be in this mess right now.

His thoughts turned to Milana Tanner.

It wasn't easy to make yourself as invisible as Milana Tanner had. Why the effort?

Who cared? His guys could handle one woman, even if she was an unknown variable in this game.

Although unknown variables always made him uncomfortable.

It might be worth having Nicky and Anthony pay Van Horn a visit to see what they could find out. From what Craig said, Van Horn would be able to answer all his questions.

All they had to do was persuade him to talk, which wouldn't be hard for Nicky and Anthony.

Pain could be very persuasive.

Ten

"Of course I remember you, dear." The sweet, wobbly little voice reminded Dimitrios of his grandmother. "Regan always spoke so highly of you."

Hmmm. Not sure he bought that, but if it'd help his cause, he'd roll with it. "Thank you, Mrs. Evans. I'm sorry for your loss."

The spunky, silver-haired woman may not have been related to Regan, but from what he'd witnessed when he and Mike would visit the gift shop where Regan had worked, Mrs. Evans had nearly made Regan family.

"That's sweet of you to say." The woman's voice faltered. "I–I can't believe…"

Evans' voice broke. Labored breathing drifted through the phone.

Dimitrios waited. He understood her pain all too well.

"I miss her so much." Evans sniffled, then cleared her throat. "You didn't call to listen to me carry on. What can I do for you?"

"I'm trying to make sense of all this and wondered if you could give me some information. Like maybe the name of Regan's previous employer? Or personal references she might have listed on her application?"

"Dear, shouldn't you leave the investigating to the police? Especially after what happened to Regan and Mike?" Concern laced the words.

"I will." Yet another lie, but worth it if it helped him catch Bobby. "I'm just trying to help them out. You know, get as much information as I can so they can follow up on whatever's relevant."

The pause spoke volumes.

Would she go for it? It was probably against the law or something for her to give out that kind of information.

He didn't know. He'd never dealt with it before.

Finally, she sighed. "I suppose there's no harm. Seeing as you're a friend of hers and she's…" Her breath hitched. "Not around."

Yes! "Whatever you can tell me would help out tremendously."

"Give me a minute here." Footsteps sounded in the background, followed by a drawer scraping open. "Okay, here it is. Previous employer is listed as Artistic Expressions in Las Vegas. But there was a six month gap in her employment between that and here. Probably after she met that abusive boyfriend she was running from."

Huh. Maybe Mrs. Evans knew a lot more than he'd expected. "She talked about that?"

Evans made a disgusted sound. "Didn't have to. Anyone with eyes could see the poor girl was terrified of the baby's father."

So it was all supposition. Possibly true, but Regan hadn't told Evans anything.

Which was good. The less Mrs. Evans knew, the safer she was.

"Did Regan list any references?"

"Nope. And I didn't ask about them, either."

Well, at least this Artistic Expressions place was a start. "Thank you, Mrs. Evans. That's very helpful."

He ended the call and accessed Lana's laptop, punching "Artistic Expressions Las Vegas" into the search bar.

A website popped up. The home page showed a variety of pictures, mostly of beautiful women in colorful costumes.

Some costumes covered more than others, but many of the pictures left little to the imagination.

Had Regan been a stripper?

His mind rebelled, mostly at the thought of Mike falling in love with a stripper.

Then again, his sister loved an ex-con. Anything was possible.

"*What* are you looking at?"

He whipped around at Araceli's voice. Part of him wanted to close the laptop, which was stupid because he wasn't doing anything wrong. Even if he had been, he didn't answer to Araceli. "This is where Regan worked. Before leaving Vegas."

His gaze dropped to the blue-eyed infant in her arms.

Had she gotten pregnant while working for Artistic Expressions? If she had, the gap in employment would've made sense. Most of these costumes left no room for a baby bump.

But she'd only been about three months pregnant when she arrived in Lincoln City.

No, she'd quit Artistic Expression prior to becoming pregnant, for reasons he might or might not be able to find out.

Araceli drew closer, her attention on the screen. "You know, I remember Regan mentioning dancing. Although I guess I always assumed it was a hobby, not a career."

He clicked on some of the links. "Looks like this is some kind of agency. Helps dancers connect with producers or something."

The contact link offered a phone number.

"I'm gonna give them a call."

"Artistic Expressions." The male voice was smooth, but he couldn't tell how old. The man could've been as young as twenty or as old as eighty.

"Dimitrios Lykos, FBI." Araceli swatted his arm, but he ignored her. "I'm working on a missing persons case for a former employee of yours. Regan Cox."

"Regan's missing?" The man sounded genuinely concerned.

"Trying to get as much background as I can so we can find her and bring her home safe." He was such a liar. Regan wouldn't be coming home safe. She was gone. Just like Mike. "Are you the manager?"

"Yes. She's such a sweet girl. I do hope she's all right."

If you called dead all right, then sure. "I understand she worked for you. How long was she there?"

"Almost three years. Excellent dancer. She had a natural grace and rhythm that most girls would kill for."

He winced at the man's choice of words. "And, the nature of your business is, uh…"

Was there a tactful way to ask the guy if he was a pimp?

"Dancing. Strictly hands-off." The man paused. "Although what the girls choose to do in their free time is up to them, but Regan had class. I don't think she ever sold herself on the side."

That made him feel a little better. Not that Mike was around to care any longer, but he hated to think of Mike with someone like that. "Why'd she leave your company?"

"She didn't say and I didn't ask. I offered her more money, but she turned it down."

"And you didn't think that was odd?" Money was usually a pretty strong motivator.

"Not really. You gotta understand, there's a lotta turn in this industry. Frankly, she stuck around longer than most."

"What can you tell me about her personal life? Was she seeing anyone?"

"I stay out of my employees' personal lives."

Hmmm. The man's tone had changed. No longer open. He now sounded guarded.

This man couldn't be Bobby, could he?

Unlikely. From what little he knew, Bobby was higher up the food chain. He likely wouldn't be answering phones.

Which meant he might've said something wrong. Had he

somehow tipped the guy off to the fact that he wasn't FBI? "Can you think of someone who might know? One of your employees that she was especially close to, maybe?"

"What agency did you say you were calling from?"

Yep, definitely suspicious. "FBI."

"I don't think I have anything else to say."

Time to do some serious damage control. "My only goal is to find out who might want to hurt Regan. Her fiancé is very concerned and mentioned an abusive ex-boyfriend in Vegas, but didn't know his name. I'm trying to track him down to see if he knows anything about Regan's disappearance."

Silence.

Had the man hung up?

No, he could hear background noises. After what felt like minutes, the man sighed. "Yeah, there was this one girl. She and Regan roomed together for a while, if I remember correctly. Sorry. I gotta be really careful. You'd be surprised how many freaks try to stalk my employees."

"Actually, I wouldn't be that surprised." Now to make the guy trust him enough to give him the information. Maybe if he suggested Regan's friend initiate the contact it would ease the man's suspicions. "In fact, if it would make you more comfortable, I can give you my contact information so she can call me."

The pause lingered for the space of several heartbeats. "Yeah, I could do that."

Dimitrios repeated his name and gave the man Araceli's cell phone number. Ending the call, he set the phone aside.

How long would it take for a call back? Would she even call back?

"I can't believe you passed yourself off as a federal agent!" Joseph jerked in Araceli's arms and she lowered her voice. "Isn't that a crime?"

Probably. He shrugged. "No one will know. Unless you plan to report me."

She huffed. "I should. It'd serve you right."

Yeah, sure. He knew an empty threat when he heard one.

"Did you at least learn anything?"

He recapped the conversation, which hadn't revealed much. Certainly not anything that helped them locate the elusive Bobby.

If Regan's friend didn't call them back, this whole thing had been for nothing.

ꟷ ꟷ ꟷ ꟷ ꟷ

"The bad man is back."

Paul paused with one hand on the doorknob and looked back at Maria, who stood barely inside the kitchen, arms crossed over her stomach.

Bad man.

Those two simple words brought an assault of memories. The last time he'd heard her say that had been three years ago, before prison, when he'd witnessed a serial killer in action and almost lost Lana to that same murderer.

But that was all in the past. The killer wasn't going anywhere. Ever.

"I saw him." Maria rocked slightly on her feet.

He set down the bag of garbage and crossed the kitchen to kneel in front of her. "What bad man?"

At nine, she was still tiny for her age, but her self-confidence had grown by bounds. Small hands clutched one of his as she leaned in, her eyes wide and anxious. "From before you went away. Remember?"

"I remember, but he's in jail. The police locked him up."

She studied him. "Maybe he got away."

"He didn't get away. He's still there." At least he hoped the killer was still behind bars. There'd been no word of a jailbreak and a criminal that high profile would have definitely made the news.

"He's in the car."

"I'm sure it's not him."

So why couldn't he convince himself?

Could there be someone lurking, someone who would cause trouble for one of the kids? From anyone else, he would have shrugged it off as an overactive imagination. But not Maria. Years of abuse had made her more observant and cautious than children twice her age. "Can you show me?"

She led him to the front of the house and surveyed the street. "I don't see him."

A chill skated up his spine.

The conversation was eerily familiar. They'd had a similar one when the Jacksonville Ripper had been watching him several years ago.

She'd been right then; why not now?

Because no one should be interested in him now, that's why. He hadn't seen anything he shouldn't have.

Sure he had enemies from his past, but the FBI had done a good job at faking his death. Only a handful of people knew Nate Miller was still alive and living under the name Paul Van Horn.

She had to be imagining this one, right?

Turning her to face him, he looked in her eyes. "I'm sure it's not anything to be afraid of, okay? If you see the car again, I want you to tell me right away so I can take care of it."

She nodded, her lower lip caught between her teeth.

"Now I'm going to take the garbage out, then maybe we can play a game, okay?"

A small smile freed her lip and she nodded slowly.

Retracing his steps, he grabbed the plastic bag and opened the back door. He passed the swing set and basketball court and let himself out the gate at the rear of the property. The alley smelled faintly of spoiled food, thanks to the dumpsters and garbage cans awaiting tomorrow morning's pickup.

He looked up and down the alley. Nothing jumped out as suspicious.

What if Maria was right? What if someone was watching?

It would have to be about him, wouldn't it? No one else at

the home would attract the wrong kind of attention.

They didn't even have any kids mixed up in gangs at the moment, so that left the option of a gang connection out of the mix, too.

What if his true identity had somehow leaked?

With the exception of Lana, all the people most important to him lived in that house. Could he be putting all of them in danger?

No. There was no reason to think someone was after him.

Nate Miller was dead. No one would be looking.

He lifted the top of the dumpster and deposited the bag inside.

Movement flashed in his peripheral. Pain exploded across his face.

He stumbled, his head smacking against the dumpster. His knee scraped the ground as he fell on it, shards of broken glass slicing into the ball of the hand he'd put down to break his fall.

Bells rang.

He didn't know if they were in his head or outside. He blinked the alley back into focus.

A shoe scuffed the asphalt of the alley behind him.

His attacker was still here!

The truth propelled him to his feet and into a defensive stance, knees slightly bent, fists raised.

If there was one thing he'd learned through the rough times in his life, it was how to fight.

Two men, both with ski masks covering their faces, stood a few feet away. One of the men rivaled him for height. The other stood several inches shorter.

A gun hung from the taller man's hand, extended to an unnatural length by the silencer screwed to the end.

Both men were solidly built. He doubted they'd need the gun to take him down.

Hired muscle.

It was the first thought to flash into his mind and

although it made no sense, it stuck there.

"Tell us about Milana Tanner." The demand, low and cold, came from the thin lips of the taller man.

Lana?

He stared at the taller man.

He didn't know why these men were asking about her, but one thing was certain. If they thought they could get information from him, they had no idea who he really was.

"Who?"

The man stepped forward and swung the pistol like a bat.

He threw his arms up, his left forearm taking the brunt of the blow, and swung his right arm around. His knuckles collided with the guy's jaw, the impact sending shockwaves through his body.

The man staggered backward.

Paul didn't wait for him to recover before diving forward, his fist already aiming for the man's solar plexus.

The man doubled over as his fist connected. He drew back for another blow.

Something slammed into his side, tossing him like he'd tossed the bag of garbage before all this madness started.

Curling into the fall, he rolled and pushed back to his feet.

The second man approached, his dark eyes wary, his lips curled in a sneer. Behind him, the taller man staggered and slowly straightened, leveling the gun at Paul.

Paul froze.

The shorter man stole the opportunity and swung, his fist crashing into Paul's jaw.

He almost went down again, but managed to keep his feet under him. Warmth trickled down his chin and filled his mouth with a metallic taste. The world spun and he could hardly hear over the ringing between his ears.

"Milana Tanner. Tell us who she is." The terse command broke through the cathedral in his head.

"Milana who?" He spit blood on the ground. Great. Felt like a split lip.

"Don't play dumb. There're calls between you."

"Insurance agent?" He couldn't overpower both of these guys. Especially not when they had a gun.

He had to get to the house. Call 911 before one of the kids came outside and these guys zeroed in on them.

"You don't talk to an insurance agent that often. Who. Is. She?"

He had to give them something. At least stall long enough to come up with a plan. "Sponsor. AA."

A pause. The shorter man glanced at the gun-toting giant who never removed his icy eyes from Paul. "And her connection to Dimitrios Lykos?"

Dimitrios. What did her brother have to do with this? "Who?"

The gun shifted. A muffled explosion echoed. Pain sliced through his leg, which gave out beneath him.

A half-cry, half-groan slid from him as the pain dulled into a burning throb.

This psycho had shot him!

"Lykos. How does she know him?"

Lana would kill him if he said anything about her brother. "Look, man, I don't know. She's my sponsor, that's all."

"Hey!" Dale's voice came from the direction of the house.

Part of him wanted Dale to come help. Even the odds a bit. But these guys had a gun and wouldn't hesitate to use it.

"Call the cops!" he yelled, praying Dale had already done it.

The shorter man glanced toward the house, then smacked his partner's arm.

Sirens wailed. Distant, but they'd likely be here in under two minutes.

This was it. Either the man would kill him or retreat. Maybe both.

The tall man shoved the silencer into his cheek and dropped something on the ground. "No cops. Tell Lykos to answer that when it rings or next time someone dies."

The man shoved him over, then followed his partner down the alley.

A groan escaped as Paul pushed himself off the ground. In front of him, a phone rested next to a small pool of blood.

His blood.

"Paul?"

He pocketed the phone as the gate creaked and Dale pushed through.

"Hey, you alright?"

Glancing up, he tried to smile, but his face refused to cooperate. "Been better. At least I'm alive."

Dale's attention shifted to the oozing wound on Paul's leg. "Is it bad?"

"Hurts like heck, but that's a good thing."

Dale knelt beside him. "How is pain a good thing?"

"It means I haven't gone into shock. Which means the wound isn't too bad." He looked at the wound.

Not centered on his thigh. In fact, it was close to the outside edge. Should've mostly impacted muscle. The exit wound on the back indicated a through and through.

Lights flashed down the alley and the siren pounded in his head as the sound drew closer, then chirped one last time before going silent. An ambulance and a patrol car descended on him from opposite sides.

"What'd they want?" Dale's question seemed loud in the ensuing silence.

How much should he tell Dale? He wouldn't lie, but until he talked to Dimitrios, and Lana, he didn't want to say too much.

Besides, this might be one of those times where not knowing the truth could be safer.

"Tell you later. Call Lana, okay?"

A gurney rattled toward them, saving him from any further probing. Dale stepped back and pulled out his cell phone as emergency personnel descended.

He recapped the attack, but said nothing about the

questions or the cell phone.

That part would be reserved for Lana. She could decide what to do with it.

Pain coursed through his veins as the paramedics situated him on the gurney and wheeled him toward the back of the ambulance.

His stomach lurched. Nausea roiled.

He forced it back.

A jackhammer rattled inside him. His white fingers clutched the edge of the gurney like it was a life preserver in the hurricane-churned Atlantic.

Those guys were dangerous and they were asking about Lana.

And Dimitrios.

He knew something was fishy about her brother's sudden visit. Why hadn't he pushed for more information?

It didn't matter if he was Lana's brother. If he'd brought danger to Lana's doorstep, Dimitrios would have to answer to him.

Eleven

The phone rang.

Dimitrios looked at it. Not a number in Araceli's contact list. Also not a familiar area code. Could it be Regan's former roommate?

"Lykos."

"Agent Lykos?" The woman's voice, containing a sultry quality often found on the other end of 900 numbers, sounded hesitant.

"Yes. Are you Regan's friend?"

"Annabelle." Some of the hesitation dropped away. "Oscar told me she's missing?"

"She is. I'm trying to find out what happened to her." How should he approach this?

"I'll do whatever I can to help. She's like a sister to me. We roomed together for two years, until she moved in with Bobby."

How convenient of her to bring Bobby up right away. "Bobby?"

"Yeah. Isn't she… I mean, Oscar mentioned a fiancé. That's… that's not Bobby?"

"No. She moved to Oregon about six months ago."

A gasp. "I can't believe she left Bobby. She was crazy about him!"

Interesting. Obviously finding out her boyfriend was a killer had cooled her emotions. "What can you tell me about

Bobby?"

"What can't I tell you? He's rich and handsome and all the girls dream of catching his eye, but only Regan really did." She paused. "But now that I think about it, he's been catching shows again. I've even seen him talking with some of the girls, but I never connected it all."

Frankly, he wasn't connecting it all either. "How about you start from the beginning? When did Regan meet Bobby?"

"It was after a show. Cats, I think. Or maybe Phantom of the Opera. They all run together, you know? Anyhow, Regan and I were just doin' backup for the show and he walked right up to her afterwards and asked her for drinks."

"Isn't there security for these shows?"

"Sure there is, but it doesn't apply to Bobby. He does whatever he wants."

Whatever he wants? Like kill with no consequences? Ice trickled down his back. "How come?"

She laughed. "Because he's Bobby Carpelli."

Carpelli. He jotted down the name. "So?"

"So? The man is like a trillionaire. He owns one of the largest resort casinos in Vegas and comes from old money. Rules don't apply to people like that."

Obviously. "What else do you know about him?"

She dropped her voice to a conspiratorial whisper. "Rumor has it that his family was tied to the mob or something. I don't think it's true, but that's what people say. It makes him more exciting, don't you think?"

Made him more something all right. Exciting wasn't the word he would choose. "So he invited her for drinks, and then?"

"And she turned him down! Can you believe it? All the girls hope to catch his eye. Some do and he invites them back to his suite. Always only for the one night, but a girl can dream that he'll settle down, right? Anyhow, Regan turns him down flat. I just about fell over."

If she turned him down, how'd she end up with him? "He

must not have taken no for an answer."

"He was persistent. Bobby came to the next show. With roses. Asked her again." Annabelle laughed, a deep throaty sound. "I'll never forget the look on his face when she smiled sweetly and said she wasn't interested in being anyone's one-night stand. He was a player. We all knew it. Most girls didn't care, but Regan was different."

Maybe Regan had the class that her employer said she did. "But at some point she caved?"

"No caving. He countered by asking her to dinner. Just dinner. She agreed. It was so romantic."

Yeah. Until he killed her. He swallowed the sour thought. "So dinner turned into…"

"More dates. Then he proposed. You shoulda seen the rock. It was amaz–" She cut the word off and drew in a breath. "Anyway. She quit her job and moved in. We kinda fell outta touch after that."

"So was he still a player? After Regan moved in?"

"No. We didn't see him at any of the shows and I never heard about any of the girls going back to his room. Well, until recently. That's why I said I shoulda known that Regan wasn't with him anymore."

Was there anything else he should know? He had Bobby's last name, so he could follow up on that now. And knew more about how Regan had ended up pregnant and on the run.

Although he still didn't know much about her background.

"Did she ever mention her life before Vegas?"

"Not much. I know she grew up back East somewhere. Maybe New Hampshire or Maine? Someplace cold. Oh, and she was raised Catholic. Like super strict. I guess her parents freaked when she said she wanted to dance professionally. They were okay with ballet as a hobby, but doing it professionally? Not cool. I don't remember her ever calling her parents."

"Not at all?"

"Nope. I think maybe her parents disowned her or something."

Not that any of that was relevant to Bobby or Regan's murder.

Time to end the call. "I think that covers most of my questions. Thank you, Annabelle. You've been most helpful."

"Anything for Regan." The hesitation was back. "I hope you find her."

"Me, too." Probably not the most authentic of responses for an FBI agent, but what the heck. He wasn't FBI anyway. He ended the call and set the phone aside.

"Well?" Araceli looked up from the bottle she had in Joseph's mouth.

"We have a name. Now to see who we're up against."

And if Bobby Carpelli was as much trouble as Regan and Mike had led him to believe.

Man, did he ever hope they were wrong.

₪ ₪ ₪ ₪ ₪

"Paul?"

Paul looked up as Lana approached his bed. His head felt like it'd been steamrolled and his leg throbbed in tandem with his pulse, but at least seeing her helped his heart. Especially since he'd spent the hour since arriving at the hospital worrying about whether or not those guys had gone after her once they'd left his place.

Her eyes narrowed as they moved across his face. Although he hadn't looked in a mirror, he suspected a split lip and significant bruising.

Good thing she couldn't see the damage to his leg.

Although from the way her eyes lingered on his elevated leg, Dale must've told her about the gunshot wound.

"Are you okay?"

"Nothing a few stitches didn't fix. I don't think they'll need to keep me overnight." Ooh, did his lip hurt. Too bad not talking wasn't an option. "Least I got in a few good hits."

She ran light fingers across his temple, down his cheek, and over his lip. "I don't care if you fought back. What happened?"

"Two guys jumped me. Where's Dimitrios?"

Black eyebrows arched over her dark eyes. "What does he have to do…?"

She stared at him for a few seconds. Understanding, then dread, lit her eyes.

"Please tell me he didn't have something to do with this."

"They gave me a message for him." The words scratched his sand-filled throat and he reached for the glass of water beside his bed. After pulling in a painful drink, he set the cup aside. "They asked about you. Your connection to him. Then told me to give him a message."

"What message?"

Her eyes narrowed into slits as he relayed the conversation.

Good. Her anger and concern would make her more cautious.

He pointed to the bag containing the jeans the EMTs had cut off him. "They gave me a phone and said he'd better answer it or someone would die. I don't think they were joking."

"I don't either." She caressed his swelling jaw. "I'm sorry. This is my fault."

She must be out of her mind. He caught her hand. "How do you figure?"

"I knew he was in trouble. I knew it was bad. But I didn't press him."

"You couldn't have known."

"I should have." She shook her head. "He told me about his partner's murder. I didn't think they'd follow him across the country. I was wrong."

Her voice cracked. So did his heart.

Dang. Gunshot wound aside, if he wasn't nearly naked

under the sheet covering him, he'd stand up and hold her.

For now, he'd have to settle for rubbing her hand. "Hey, I'm okay."

She made a short, abrupt swipe at her eyes. "But it could've gone differently. You could've been killed. Or one of the kids could've gotten hurt."

The air froze in his lungs.

She was right. What if Maria had gone out to the dumpster with him?

The next time he saw Dimitrios…

He didn't know what he'd do. Maybe punch him for putting Lana and his kids in the line of fire.

Might be better if Lana dealt with him first.

"It's all right. It's a flesh wound and no one else got hurt." This time. "I can't believe I'm telling *you* this, but you gotta trust God to cover us."

A smile tweaked the corners of her mouth. "When did you get so wise?"

"Must be the company I'm keeping."

A nurse with a sumo-wrestler's build pulled aside the curtain and penguin-walked toward the bed. "Good news for you, my man. Doc says you get to be our guest tonight."

That was good news?

"He's not being released?" Lana's eyebrows knit together.

The nurse shook his shaved head. "Not with a concussion and the risk of infection in that wound. Observation and all that. You know."

Yeah, he knew. He eased out a pent-up sigh.

Well, at least the kids should be safer if he wasn't around. He hoped.

The nurse waved in a few orderlies. "Don't sweat it. We got a deluxe suite with your name on it upstairs."

The orderlies unlocked the wheels on his bed. "Better have a view."

A grin slid across the nurse's face. "Finest view of the east parking lot. Guaranteed."

As much as he wanted Lana to stay with him all night, there were more important matters she needed to address. He nodded at the bag with his clothes. "Can you take care of that for me? And maybe bring me some clean clothes tomorrow morning?"

Assuming he'd be getting out of here tomorrow.

As Lana grabbed the bag, he swiveled his attention to the nurse. "I am leaving tomorrow, right?"

"Long as there're no complications, sure."

So he'd pray for no complications. Staying in this place too long wasn't an option, not as long as there was an active threat against Lana.

Aside from that, he had a bone to pick with Dimitrios.

While he had no doubt Lana was going to grill Dimitrios tonight, he had a few questions of his own.

⁂

"I would've thought Lana would be home by now." Dimitrios glanced at the clock as it changed to 7:50.

Leftover taco fixings cooled on the stove. When they'd eaten a half hour ago, he'd expected the door to open any minute.

Could she have run into trouble?

"Relax. I'm sure she got caught up at work." Araceli offered a wry grin as she patted Joseph's back. "Surely you can understand that one."

She was probably right. Still, what would it hurt to call and make sure?

The garage door whirred as if on cue.

Finally.

She entered the house, dropping her keys on the counter before unclipping her holster and setting it beside the keys. Only then did she look at him.

Her lips were set in a tight line. Black eyebrows lowered over her dark eyes. A plastic bag emblazoned with St.

Elizabeth's Jacksonville General dangled from a clenched hand.

A hospital?

At least she looked okay. No obvious sign of injury. Nor was she pale.

And she'd driven herself home. So obviously the hospital trip hadn't been for her.

Although if the look on her face was any indication, he might be needing one himself soon.

"We need to talk." Her words were measured, but there was no missing the fury beneath them.

"I, uh, think it's time for Joseph to go to bed." Araceli shot him a sympathetic glance as she rose and practically ran from the room.

He watched her retreat. *Thanks for nothing.*

Not that he blamed her.

"What's going on?" He kept his tone light in hopes that she'd relax a little.

No such luck. "You tell me."

"Uh, there's leftover tacos. You know, if you're hungry."

She threw the bag at him. "What do you see?"

He opened the bag. A black t-shirt and worn jeans. With a large, rust colored stain that was all-too familiar. Blood.

Did he even want to know?

Didn't matter what he wanted. He needed to know. And he had no doubt she'd tell him anyway.

"Well?"

It felt like a whole taco was lodged in his throat. He swallowed as he shoved the bag across the table. "Blood. Whose is it?"

"Paul's." She crossed her arms over her chest. "He was jumped by two men who gave him a message. For you."

They'd found him. But how? And how did they connect Paul to all of this?

"Now I want to know what kind of trouble you've brought with you. The whole story. Right now."

Heat rippled through his body, followed by a wave of ice. The truth was dangerous. He couldn't tell her. "You're safer if you don't know."

She pulled the bloodstained jeans from the bag and shoved them against his chest. "You call this safe? Whoever you're running from has already found us. I need to know what's going on so I can assess the threat and neutralize it."

"Is he okay?"

"He has a concussion and a gunshot wound to the leg, but he'll recover. We may not be so lucky next time. Now spill."

"We'll be out of here first thing in the morning." Not that he had any idea where they would go.

Both her anger and her energy seemed to evaporate. She fell heavily into the closest chair. "Mitri. You can't keep running from this. Let me help. It's what I do."

"You also get hurt. I won't let that happen."

"It's too late for that. You really think they'll leave me alone just because you aren't here any longer? They'll come after me next. Paul said they were asking him about me. It's only a matter of time before they track me down."

Why hadn't he thought about this before coming to see Lana? How could he have been so naïve as to think that if he didn't say anything, they wouldn't find him?

Now Paul was hurt and a bunch of killers were hunting Lana.

Again.

He rested his head in his hands. What should he do?

"You can't handle this on your own."

Lana's voice cut through his thoughts.

He lifted his head to meet her eyes.

"I lost Mike." The words scratched from his throat. It felt like they scraped part of his soul with them. "I can't lose you, too."

"Then tell me what's going on. You know what they say about the best offense."

Is a good defense.

She was right. About all of it.

He did need help and, like he'd told her earlier, she was the only one he knew for certain he could trust. "It all goes back to Mike's girlfriend, Regan."

The story flowed from him like a swollen river, disjointed at times and raging at others, until the words dried up.

Lana didn't interrupt once, not even to ask questions or clarify. Instead, she listened and nodded occasionally. When he finished, she was silent for several seconds. "I think the first thing we need to do is learn more about this Bobby guy. Do you have a last name?"

"Carpelli. From what I've gathered, he's got some pretty big connections everywhere."

She arched an eyebrow. "I find that hard to believe."

"Yeah, well how do you find out who you can and can't trust, huh? Mike didn't even trust the local PD, guys we've worked with for years. And Mike was a pretty trusting guy."

"After losing Regan, that's understandable. But we're on the opposite side of the country from Vegas. If we get the local FBI involved–"

"They'll hand it off to the Vegas FBI, who might be in bed with Bobby."

She stared at him, her dark eyes so like Cy's. "They wouldn't all be in on it."

"Maybe. Maybe not. Either way, how do we know that it'd get put on the desk of someone honest?"

"Do you hear yourself? You sound like one of those conspiracy nuts."

"Yeah, well, after what I've been through this last week, I feel like them, too." His fingers curled into a fist. "Besides, they found you, didn't they? I'm betting you've made that pretty hard to do."

She didn't deny it. "Assuming you're right, I guess our first step will be figuring out if Bobby is really as well connected as Mike thought he was."

"How do you plan to do that? It's not like they'll confess

to being on the take."

"True, but maybe we can find out through alternative channels." She paused. "But we'd need some idea where to start. We can't investigate every member of law enforcement in Vegas."

"I ran an online search on him earlier. All I found were links to his casino, some business connections, and social gossip junk."

She tilted her head. "Don't discount that social gossip. What'd you see?"

"Mostly pictures at local events. But who he's with is a lot more important than where he's at. Some of the highlights from those pictures included the mayor, police chief, and a senator."

"It doesn't mean that they're privy to his illegal activities."

"Doesn't mean they aren't either."

She nodded. "Agreed. Well, at least we can start by running down those names. See if anything suspicious pops."

The ledger. Could some of the names in there be law enforcement? He didn't have any better leads. "Mike left a ledger. There are a lot of names in there."

"It's worth looking at. Is it upstairs?"

He shook his head. "It's back in Oregon. Mike left it in a safe deposit box and that seemed like the best place to store it."

She stared at him, her face a blank mask. He could tell she was processing, but her face gave nothing away.

If only he'd thought to take pictures of that ledger. Then it would've still been secured but he'd have the information on his phone.

Not that he'd brought that with him.

It seemed like minutes passed before she blinked. "We'll need to look at that. Could you send someone to get it and maybe have them scan it to us?"

"I doubt it. The bank's pretty firm about who can access those boxes. Besides, I don't want to involve anyone else.

You've seen what happens when people get too close."

"So we'll need to make a trip out there, then."

Hadn't she been listening? "There's no we here. It's my mess and I'll take care of it."

The look she leveled told him he'd already lost the battle. "So you know what you're looking at? And have access to databases to cross reference the names on the ledger?"

"I can't have you getting hurt."

"Like it or not, I'm involved. You need help and I can provide it." Her lips curled in a small smile. "Besides, I have a gun and know how to use it."

He hoped it wouldn't come to that. "When do you want to go?"

"This weekend? We could leave Friday, go to the bank Saturday, and come back Sunday. There's too much going on at work right now for me to miss very much time."

Work. He'd barely given a thought to his job since telling his boss that he needed to take some time to cope with Mike's death. While he hadn't set a return date, he knew he couldn't be gone long.

Then there was the matter of Mike's funeral. Without any close family, planning that would fall to him.

All the more reason to get this wrapped up as quickly as possible. "Sounds good."

Silence lingered for a few seconds. He cleared his throat. "I'm sorry about Paul. I never thought they'd go after him."

He didn't know what else to say. He should've known that Bobby and his goons would go after anyone and everyone to get what they wanted. Hadn't they already proven that murder was no big deal to them?

"It could've been worse. If one of the kids had gotten hurt, well, I think Paul would flatten you."

And he'd deserve it.

He was done talking about this.

Time for a new subject, one that would be big enough to distract her from what had happened tonight.

"Cy's part of the whole religious thing now." Dang it. Why had he said that? It wasn't much better than the previous topic.

"Really?" Surprise tinged her tone, but her lips curled in a genuine smile. "I'll have to give him a call soon. Thanks for telling me."

He shrugged, wanting nothing more than for this conversation to die, too.

Maybe he could beg exhaustion and head to bed.

"How are you doing with that?"

Figures she couldn't let it go. She'd made no secret of her desire to see him and Cy join her in the whole God thing. "It's his life."

"Right. And the fact that he's your brother means you don't care what he does."

"Okay, fine. You want the truth? I'm an outcast in my own family, okay?"

"Oh, Mitri. That's not true and you know it."

"I guess I don't understand what was so wrong before. I mean, Cy's a good person, better than me. Doesn't that count for something?"

She studied him for a second. "Have you ever lost a patient? Despite your best efforts, there was nothing you could do to save them?"

What? Where was she going with this? "Yeah. Sometimes the trauma's too great or we can't get them to the hospital fast enough. It's part of the job."

Not a part he enjoyed, but one he'd had to learn to accept.

Even though it ate him up every time.

"It's kind of the same with God. No matter how hard we try, we can't be good enough. Jesus is our EMT. He comes to us when we're literally dying because of our sin and offers to save our lives. He takes our place on the gurney, so to speak, and gives us His goodness to compensate for our own lacking."

He pushed up from the table so fast that the chair rattled

against the tile. "See, that's what I don't get! Why would you want to try to please a God who tells you you're never good enough?"

"But He does say we're good enough. He said it at the cross when Jesus took our sin and gave us His righteousness. We're good enough because of Him."

"Yeah? Well, I don't wanna follow someone's list of rules just to be accepted. I want to do my own thing and if that's not good enough, tough."

"You've got it all wrong. Following God isn't about keeping a list of rules. It's freedom. Knowing that He loves me, no matter what I do, and that He forgives all my sin gives me a freedom I couldn't have otherwise. I don't have to live under a burden of guilt because Christ took that guilt away."

Guilt. Like the guilt eating at him for failing Mike. For Cy's injuries. For Paul. For getting Ari and Lana involved in all this.

It'd be nice to get rid of that guilt.

But he couldn't. It was on him.

"I am the Lord your God, who teaches you what is *good* for you and leads you along the paths you should follow. Oh, that you had listened to My commands. Then you would have had peace flowing like a gentle river and righteousness rolling over you like waves in the sea." Lana's words, softly spoken, echoed in the room.

He stared at her. It was almost like she could read his thoughts. What wouldn't he give for peace right now? "What was that?"

"A verse from Isaiah 48. It's God's promise to His people. When we do things His way, it's not only good for us, but He gives us peace, in spite of whatever is happening around us."

In spite of a group of killers tracking his every step? In spite of everyone he loved being in danger?

It'd be nice to believe that.

He'd believe if he could. The thought stopped in his mind. Did he want to believe?

He did. But he couldn't. Too many things argued against the existence of a powerful, loving God.

"I'd offer a penny for your thoughts, but I have a feeling they're worth quite a bit more."

He blinked her into focus. "Maybe."

She stared at him. Not pushy or probing, but waiting. Probably hoping he'd open up.

Why not? If there was one thing he'd learned about her the last few years, it was that she didn't force her beliefs on others.

"I wish I could believe."

There. It was out there.

She nodded slowly. "Sometimes belief is a choice."

A choice? How the heck did she figure? You either believed in God or you didn't. No choice involved.

It was like believing the earth was flat. Or that there was no such thing as gravity. You could believe it, but that wouldn't make it true.

"Well, if God really wants me, He's going to have to convince me."

"Be careful what you wish for." She grinned. "Because now I'm going to be praying that He does just that."

"Tell me you learned something valuable."

The silence on the other end told Bobby all he needed to know. He clenched his hand as a curse spilled from his lips.

"If you have nothing to report, why are you wasting my time?" The words came out taut, tension oozing from each one.

"We put the squeeze on that Van Horn dude who says Milana Tanner's his sponsor. Not sure I believe him."

"That's a lie. Craig said her name cropped up in connection with some serial killer a few years ago." He should've told Nicky everything he'd learned from Craig.

Maybe Nicky could have altered his questioning to be more effective.

"Yeah, well, that's the story he stuck with." Nicky sucked in a breath. "The dude didn't budge, not even when I shot him. So he's either tougher than he looks or tellin' the truth."

"You *shot* him?" Great. Just what he needed. Another trail to cover up.

Who did he have in Florida?

No one.

"Just in the leg. Dead men don't deliver messages."

A message. Well, maybe Nicky hadn't totally botched this after all. "Did he give you anything on Tanner's connection to Lykos?"

"Claimed he didn't know. I gave him a burner and told him Lykos better answer when I call. Figured I'd give him 'til tomorrow since the dude's likely all doped up at the hospital tonight."

"Keep me posted. And do not screw this up."

Bobby terminated the call, his mind anchored on what he'd learned.

Interesting. And concerning.

A bullet to the leg would make most people talk. Yet it hadn't worked with Van Horn.

That left three options that he could see. Maybe Nicky was right and Van Horn didn't know anything. Maybe Tanner was more important to Van Horn than his own life. Or maybe it wasn't Van Horn's first time staring down a gun.

The first two options didn't concern him too much. That last one could derail everything.

What had Craig told him about Van Horn? Not much. The guy worked at a kids' home, had witnessed a murder, and had helped the cops apprehend the killer.

Could that have toughened him enough to not be phased by being shot?

Not likely.

Maybe the guy was ex-military. Or had some connection

to law enforcement. Or had been on the opposite side of the law himself. Any of those things might have given him the gumption to stand up to Nicky and Anthony.

Speculation wasn't going to ease the gnawing in his gut.

He picked up the phone. Since Craig seemed to be the only guy on his team who was worth anything, it was time to have Craig do some more digging. He needed every little skeleton that Van Horn had hidden.

There could be no more surprises.

Twelve

Dimitrios glanced up as Araceli entered the room, hair still damp from her shower. He hadn't seen her since her hasty exit from the kitchen the night before. She settled on the sofa across from him.

"Joseph asleep?"

She nodded. "He went down about an hour ago."

Which meant he probably wouldn't sleep too much longer.

"So Lana didn't kick us out. I take it you two worked out whatever was going on."

His mouth dried at the memory of last night's conversation. "Yeah. Paul was shot yesterday."

Araceli's gasp seemed loud in the silence of the room. "Is he okay?"

"He will be. But he was given a message for me."

Her eyes widened and her lips trembled. "Mike's killers?"

"Probably." Scratch that. It was definitely Bobby's guys.

"Did you tell Lana? Is she going to help?"

"Whether I want her to or not." He shook his head slowly. "We're planning to fly home to retrieve some files Mike left for me. Maybe between us we can put it all together."

Relief washed her. "Good. I really need to get back to the shop."

"I, uh, think you should stay here."

She stared at him. "Here. When we know those guys are

in town?"

"I'll leave a trail when I fly. They'll follow me back." He hoped. But how could he know for certain? "Maybe you should go see your family for a while."

"And risk bringing this to them? No way." She glanced at the ceiling. "Besides, it'd be hard to explain Joseph without telling them what's going on. And they're a pretty nosy bunch."

"Maybe you should give Joseph up."

Fire sparked in her eyes. "I told you. I'm not giving him over to a man who can kill his own son's mother!"

"What about Regan's family? Do you know how they'd feel about taking in her son?"

"No. She never talked about her family. Besides, if they were estranged, they might not welcome Joseph."

"Maybe she fixed things with them before she died." Man. How horrible would it be for them if she hadn't?

"I don't know. If she had, wouldn't she have gone there after leaving Bobby?"

"Maybe she didn't want Bobby to go after them. Or she knew it was the first place he'd look for her."

Araceli's hand came to her lips. "Do you think they even know she's dead?"

"The police would've told them." But did they know they had a grandson?

A ringing echoed in the living room. Not Ari's ringtone. And Lana didn't have a landline.

That only left one other phone in the house.

The one that'd been given to Paul last night.

He jumped to his feet and crossed to the dining room table. The phone was exactly where Lana had dropped it the night before.

The caller ID simply said "private number."

Not answering was not an option. He accepted the call. "What."

"Think yesterday was bad, hotshot? You got until one to

meet us with the kid and the papers."

He glanced at the clock. Just under two hours. Impossible. Heat flashed through his blood. "I don't have them."

"You wanna play tough? Maybe I oughta pay a visit to your buddy Milana Tanner, huh?"

Buddy. Not sister.

They didn't know the connection. They also likely didn't know much about Lana or they wouldn't make such a glib threat.

Still, there were several of them and only one Lana. He couldn't take the risk.

"I'm not lying! I don't have them. I left them in Oregon."

A pause. Then the voice returned, gruffer than before. "One o'clock. Atlantic Park. I see anyone but you, the chick, and the baby and I do some target practice."

"I told you–"

The line went dead.

Dimitrios gripped the phone. This wasn't good. Not good at all.

Now what? Call Lana?

And have her get involved? Not a chance. He wouldn't be responsible for her getting shot. Again.

But without her, there was greater risk to Araceli.

How could he choose which one to put at risk?

He couldn't. And he wouldn't.

He'd go alone.

⁂

"Absolutely not." Araceli put her hands on her hips. "He said he'd be looking for all three of us or he'd start shooting. You aren't going alone."

"He said that to keep me from calling the cops."

"I'm going."

Did she have any idea how hot she looked? He'd never had this fiery streak directed at him. If her life weren't on the line here, he'd kinda like it.

Instead, he crossed his arms over his chest. "You really think you can force this?"

She stepped closer and looked him in the eye. "You really think you can stop me?"

He couldn't muffle a small chuckle. "Oh, I know I can."

"And how are you going to do that, huh? Lock me in my room?"

"If I have to." Right. Like he'd ever use force with her. It was a lame bluff and they both knew it. "Look, it's safer if you stay here. With Joseph. You know they're after him."

She deflated a little. "It feels like I'm choosing him over you."

"I can take care of myself. He can't. He needs you more."

Silence fell for a brief second before she smiled. "I'll ask Paul to watch him for a few hours. That way I can help you."

"Paul was shot, remember?"

"Oh. Then someone in his home. I can't let you do this alone or you'll end up like Mike."

She broke eye contact and looked away, a tear leaking from the corner of her eye. He brushed it away, his gaze moving down the curve of her high cheekbones and resting on her lips.

Close enough to kiss.

A flowery scent enveloped her, enticing him to act on the impulse. Whether it was perfume, shampoo, or lotion, he didn't know. Didn't care. It was exotic and beautiful and suited her.

When his hand lingered on her cheek, she turned back to him.

Pooled tears glowed in her eyes.

He didn't stop to think, just leaned in until his lips found hers.

It was perfect, sweet, and over too soon.

With a sigh, he pulled back. "I'm not going anywhere."

If the kiss had surprised her, she didn't show it. "When do

we leave?"

"Not until we have a plan." A good one. One that would keep her far away from Bobby and his men.

₪ ₪ ₪ ₪ ₪

"Hello?" Cyrano's voice sounded normal. Not scared or worried or alarmed.

Dimitrios eased out a breath he hadn't realized he'd been holding. "Hey."

"Mitri? Thank God you called. Why haven't you been answering your phone?"

"I don't have it with me. I didn't want them to be able to track me through it." Man, that sounded paranoid. Beyond paranoid, actually. Had he really been reduced to this?

At least Cyrano didn't point it out. "Whose number is this?"

"Araceli's. I thought those guys might go after her, too, so we skipped town."

"You okay? Where are you?"

"Lana's." Yikes. Maybe he shouldn't have said that. The less Cy knew, the better. Although if Bobby's guys did go after Cy and tried to get a location from him, he'd rather Cy know so he could tell them. Something told him these guys weren't above torturing someone to gain information.

"How's she doing?"

"Alright. How are you guys? Everything cool?"

"No sign of trouble."

Phew. At least it didn't appear Bobby's goons were actually hunting down members of his family.

No, they were only coming after him.

But better him than his parents, Cy or Donna, or the girls.

"Are mom and dad with you guys?"

"Yeah. The girls are having a blast. I can tell dad's keeping a close eye out, but so far everything's cool."

That sounded like dad. "Good. I need to get going, but I

wanted to touch base."

"I'm glad you did. I've been concerned. Especially since you didn't answer your phone."

"Sorry. I shoulda let you know that I wouldn't have it. Things happened pretty fast." That was sure an understatement, but he didn't want Cy to know that he was winging this with every step. Better if everyone thought he had a plan.

"Well, be sure to let Lana help you. And listen to her. This is her world, remember?"

Right. Like he was going to drag Lana into this any more than she already was. "Sure thing."

"Uh-huh. I know that tone, Mitri."

Araceli walked into the room, Joseph pressed against her chest, a diaper bag over one shoulder. Funny how natural that looked for her.

"Look, Cy. I gotta go. Have fun and be careful."

"You, too. We're all praying for you."

Yeah. Good luck with that one.

He ended the call and met Araceli's eyes. "You ready to go?"

She nodded. "Everything okay with your family?"

"Yeah. It'd been a few days so I thought I should check in." He grabbed the keys to the rental car and opened the front door for Araceli to precede him out.

The clenching of his gut reminded him that they weren't headed out for lunch.

No. They were headed to meet a group of killers.

Araceli shouldn't be a part of this. How the heck had she convinced him to let her come along?

Maybe he could leave her at Paul's group home when they dropped off Joseph. What were the odds he could ditch her and pick her up later?

Slim to none. No, he'd made a mess of this and now she was right in the middle of it.

She buckled Joseph into the car seat, then settled into the

passenger seat.

As Dimitrios navigated the curving roads of Lana's neighborhood, his gaze kept straying to Araceli.

She hadn't mentioned the kiss.

Then again, neither had he.

But thoughts of it consumed him. Probably not a good thing when they were headed to meet killers.

Yet it refused to be shaken.

They'd have to talk about it sometime.

Man, he hoped he hadn't royally screwed up their friendship.

"So." Araceli's voice broke the quiet.

Uh-oh. He wasn't going to like this.

"I'm going to text Lana and let her know what's going on."

"No way. She'll come in and get herself shot." Again.

"No, she'll provide needed backup in case things get ugly."

He glanced over. She already had her phone out and was tapping the screen.

There was really no way to stop her.

And maybe, just maybe, she was right.

"Okay. Let her know. But make sure she knows not to call in the FBI or something." That was all they needed.

He rolled to a stop, put down his window, and hit the button for the gate. The two sides parted…

A man appeared from the right, darted through the opening, and raced toward the driver's side.

What the…?

A long, black cylinder extended from the man's right hand. Gun!

Get the window up!

He punched the button.

The window rose. Slowly. Almost there.

Crash!

Glass showered him. A scream pierced the car.

The barrel of a gun filled his vision.

More glass shattered behind him. Araceli screamed again.

He whipped around. A man stood outside the passenger door, fingers wrapped in Araceli's hair as he jerked her head out the window.

Joseph's cries filled the sudden silence.

Movement from the front! A white van approached, blocking him in.

Not that he could go anywhere as long as that goon had a hold on Araceli.

A voice came from behind the gun outside his window. "Unlock the doors."

No! He couldn't give in.

But if he didn't, these guys would shoot him. Maybe shoot all three of them. Unlocking the doors at least bought him some time to figure things out.

He hit the button.

The gun didn't move. The dome light blinked on and a door slammed.

"My partner's got a gun on your chick's head. You try anything and she'll be splattered on the windshield. Got it?"

He gave a taut nod.

The gun disappeared, the door behind him opened, and the gunman slid in. "Now turn the car around and head back to the house."

They knew he was staying with Lana. What else did they know?

The drive back to Lana's was too short for him to come up with a plan.

Even though it might put her in danger, he wished Lana would come home early. She'd know what to do.

It was the middle of the day. She wouldn't be home for hours.

He was on his own.

He pulled into her driveway and shifted into park. The van pulled in behind him.

"Outta the car. We're gonna walk inside nice and calm now or your girl's gonna pay the price."

As he reached for the door handle, he looked at Araceli. She had one hand on the handle, the other reaching under the seat. What was she doing?

No time to figure it out now.

He stepped out of the vehicle. Maybe one of the neighbors would look outside, think something looked off, and call the cops.

He could hope.

"Lead on, smart guy."

His jaw clenched tighter than his hands. If Ari wasn't a factor…

But she was. He couldn't do anything to endanger her.

He led the way inside.

The guy holding the gun followed him.

Wait. Maybe he could turn this.

So far he'd only seen two weapons. No doubt the others were armed, but they'd have to get their guns out.

Besides, Bobby wanted his son. As long as Araceli was holding him, she should be safe.

And as long as he was the only one who knew where to find the evidence, they couldn't kill him either.

He walked into the kitchen, stopping next to the stove. And the knife block.

Two guys about his size followed. Araceli clutched Joseph a few feet behind them and two more guys trailed her.

Four against one. Not great odds, but he was personally motivated.

"Keep movin'." One of the men placed a meaty hand between Araceli's shoulder blades, propelling her into the room.

She stumbled into the island, knocking a vase of flowers to the floor. The glass shattered on the tile.

Joseph wailed.

The men glanced at her.

It was now or never. He slid a knife out of the block and slashed through the air.

The blade arced toward the hand holding the gun.

The man jerked aside, but not fast enough. The knife sliced skin, not deep enough to do any real damage, but enough to draw blood.

The man bellowed, his left hand going around the cut bleeding from his right hand.

The gun clattered to the tile.

Dimitrios kicked it aside as he charged the man, burying his shoulder in the man's gut.

The impact propelled them into the man behind him, a kid who didn't look old enough to shave. Both men went down.

He whipped around.

One of the two men still standing came at him, a scowl pulling down the long scar tracing his cheek. The other man held Araceli with a beefy arm wrapped around her neck.

The man holding Araceli howled.

Whatever she'd done, it caused his grip to loosen. She turned and drove her knee up. With a groan, the man doubled over.

Good for her.

The scarred man paused at his accomplice's outburst.

No way was that guy going to get his hands on Araceli. Dimitrios lunged at the scarred man while yelling at Araceli. "Go!"

She hesitated, then pushed past the doubled-over man and bolted through the living room.

He jabbed at the scarred man, but the man sidestepped the blow, then brought a fist down on Dimitrios' forearm.

A spasm shot through his hand and the knife fell from his fingers.

He brought his fist around. The man parried, then delivered a roundhouse that rattled Dimitrios' teeth.

Something crashed into the back of his head. Pain

exploded, stars invaded, and his world tipped.

He didn't even feel himself hit the floor, but cold tile beneath his cheek evidenced that he was down.

Another blow landed by his temple.

Something struck his core, forcing his breath out in a whoosh.

"Let go!" Araceli's scream sounded far away.

Ari! They must have her!

Two more strikes to his midsection left him gasping. Hands gripped his biceps and hauled him up, but his vision wouldn't clear enough for him to see what they were doing with him. He felt himself being dragged, his uncooperative feet trailing behind him.

He'd failed. And Ari would pay the price.

Thirteen

"Hi, you've reached Araceli–"

Lana terminated the call for the fifth time without leaving a message and pressed the accelerator harder.

A glance at the clock proved that it had been twenty minutes since she'd received Araceli's text.

Home 911.

That was all it had said. Yet it had driven icicles into her gut.

She looked at the display on her car's dash. No new text messages, so Araceli still hadn't replied to her text. And Araceli wasn't answering her phone.

Given what she knew about the situation they were in, it all added up to trouble.

Almost there.

She pulled up to the gate and keyed in her code. The gate chugged open.

Seriously. Was it always this slow?

Ahead of her, glass sparkled on the pavement.

Her eyes narrowed. How long had that been there? She didn't remember seeing glass earlier.

The sight of it only added to her unease.

The gate finally opened enough for her to edge in. She took the quiet drive much faster than she usually would as she wound her way back to her unit.

As her building came into view, she forced her mind to

slow down.

If she was interpreting the text correctly, something bad was going on at her house. Someone there, maybe? Someone who meant them harm?

If so, she needed to maintain the element of surprise.

She parked down the block on the opposite side of the street, silenced her phone, and stepped out of the car. Shoving the phone into the back pocket of her jeans, she kept her hand on her Glock but didn't pull it from the holster.

Not yet, anyway.

The last thing she wanted was for her neighbors to see her running down the street with a gun in her hand.

No sign of trouble from the front.

But that didn't mean too much, not with the location of her unit.

She jogged up the driveway. Frequent backward glances confirmed no one followed her.

At the end of the building, she crossed the grass and moved to put her back against the neighbor's house.

She peeked around the corner.

Dimitrios' rental car sat in front of her garage.

Blocking it was a white panel van. No windows on the sides or back, only on the driver and passenger doors.

It looked perfectly normal. Like the kind employed by any number of private plumbers or electricians.

Except she hadn't called any service techs to her house.

No, this was something else. Definitely trouble.

The front of the van faced her, giving her a clear view of the driver's and passenger's seats. Both empty.

No one stood out front. Her curtains were drawn so she couldn't see inside.

On the upside, no one inside would be able to see her, either.

She raced toward the van.

She expected shouts. Or gunshots.

The silence was almost scarier than either one.

She peered in the passenger window. Fast food wrappers on the floor, plastic cups in the cup holders. Nothing to identify the passengers or their business here. She tried to see in the back, but the darkness prevented her from seeing much.

Probably empty. If someone had been inside, they would have already come after her. Or at least moved. But everything was still.

Like a graveyard at midnight.

Except no one was dying today. Not if she could help it.

She edged down the side of the van and tried the back door. It opened easily.

Huh. She would've expected it to be locked.

The interior was mostly empty. A few duffel bags sat against the walls. She snagged the closest one and looked inside. Clothing.

She didn't have time to go through them all, but one thing was clear. This van didn't contain any plumbing equipment.

She gently closed the door, snapped a picture of the license plate, and darted past Dimitrios' rental.

Now what?

She could let herself in the front door, but without knowing what was going on inside, such a move might very well be her last.

Maybe she could see something through one of the other windows.

She pulled her gun, keeping it low but ready, and sidled down the exterior of the garage. Past the solid steel-core door Paul had installed on the side of her garage. Not much to look at, but much more secure than the cheap door the previous owner had put in.

The lock system she'd chosen made entry that way impossible. Short of some C4, anyway.

She reached the dining room window.

The curtains were mostly closed, but a narrow gap between the two panels provided limited line of sight to the interior. She squinted through the space.

Dining room table and chairs, but no people.

Moving on.

She peered around the corner. The shared back lawn was empty, except for some unoccupied patio furniture outside unit thirty-one.

She eased down the back wall.

Curtains blocked the other dining room window. But just because she couldn't see inside didn't mean they couldn't see her shadow.

Ducking beneath the window, she crept forward.

She stopped at the edge of the French doors, the one not-so-secure extravagance she'd allowed herself. The doors had decorative ironwork throughout the glass, as well as a series of bolts and locks that would make breaking in difficult, but not impossible.

At least she didn't have blinds or full curtains on the doors. Semi-sheers filtered her vision as she looked inside.

Nothing seemed wrong at first glance.

Then movement caught her attention.

She strained to see the source.

There! On the other side of the island.

Shapes moved.

As her eyes adjusted, she could make out three distinct figures, all congregated around something. Two had their backs to her but the third faced her direction.

She would have a better view from the kitchen window, but she'd have to cross the patio to get there.

Too risky. That one guy might see the movement and–

The man turned away.

She didn't stop to think, just ran across the patio and plastered herself against the wall on the other side of the door.

Her heart battered her ribs and her breath came in short bursts.

Had they seen her?

If so, she'd find out soon enough. Nothing back here would provide any kind of cover. Why hadn't she planted some large bushes or something?

Right.

Because if it would provide cover for her now, it would also provide cover for other people at other times.

She forced deep breaths into her lungs.

And kept her gun ready, just in case that door opened.

Seconds passed.

No movement at the curtains. No scraping of the locks. No gunshots or shouts or footsteps.

Looked like she was in the clear. For now.

She slid toward the kitchen window and risked a look inside.

The lightweight sheers provided a much clearer view than she'd gotten at the doors. The three figures she'd seen turned out to be two large men and one scrawny one. One of the large guys held an intimidating looking handgun. Possibly a .357 Magnum, although it was hard to be certain from this distance.

Still, knowing a gun was present changed things.

And it was likely the others were all packing, even though she couldn't see their weapons.

One of the men swung his arm. Something jerked.

Mitri!

Though she only caught a glimpse of his face, the image imbedded in her mind. There'd been blood.

He hadn't fought back, which probably meant he couldn't.

That, combined with the height at which his head had been, told her he was likely restrained to one of her dining room chairs.

She pulled her phone out of her pocket and called for backup.

How long would it take them to get here? Five minutes? More?

Where was Araceli? And Joseph?

She ducked under the window and went to the other side

before looking in again.

There!

Araceli sat in one of the chairs in the living room, her face turned toward the kitchen, Joseph in her arms. Another large man stood a few feet away from her, a gun cradled in his hands.

Joseph's tiny wails reached her through the glass. The men didn't seem too concerned about the distraught baby.

No surprise. They probably kicked puppies, too.

One of the men backhanded Dimitrios again.

Backup or no backup, she had to get in there and put a stop to this. Whatever this was. But how?

While Joseph's cries might mask the sound of her breaking in, what she really needed was a diversion, something to divide the men so they weren't all in the same room.

She could ring the doorbell, but she'd likely end up captured herself.

If it wouldn't put them in danger, she'd get one of the neighbors to do it while she came in the back, but that was too risky. It was bad enough that Mitri and Araceli were in the middle of this. She wasn't going to get any other non-law enforcement personnel involved.

Think, think. There must be a way.

Her garage door. Not foolproof, but it might work.

She sent one final glance in the kitchen. The men were doing something….

Dimitrios hollered.

She couldn't wait any longer.

She crossed the property line and sprinted across the lawn between her neighbors' units. The seconds it took to reach her car felt like hours.

She grabbed the garage door remote and raced back up the driveway.

"Everything okay?"

She whirled, aiming her gun at the deep voice before

recognizing Bert Marlin, her neighbor, who didn't seem bothered to have the weapon pointed his direction.

Then again, he was former military. Retired after forty years in the service.

It wasn't like he'd never been around guns before.

He leaned against the window sill, assessing her silently through the screen. Behind him, his wife Martha wrung her hands.

"Intruders in my house. I'm dealing with it."

"I saw them." Martha's soft voice piped up behind her husband.

She shifted her attention to Martha. "You saw them arrive? How many were there?"

"Four men. Plus the couple that's been staying with you." Martha lightly punched her husband's arm. "I told you they looked like trouble."

"Yeah, yeah." He waved her off, his narrow eyes still on Lana. "Need a hand?"

She shook her head. "Please stay inside and away from the windows. The police are on the way."

He nodded. "Don't do anything foolish."

She wished she could say she wouldn't.

Instead, she offered a tight smile and hurried around the front corner of the house.

Now to draw them out. The trick was to not be too obvious.

She opened one of the back doors on the van, then closed it most of the way so that it was only slightly ajar.

Next, she stopped by Dimitrios' car and opened the driver's door, leaving it wide open.

Finally, she took up position at the side of her house, around the corner from the garage door.

Please, Lord.

If her plan worked, the men would come outside, see the open driver's door and recognize it as a trap, then see the slightly ajar van door and think she was hiding in there.

If it didn't work, they'd turn the corner and find her.

Then the only contest would be who could get a shot off first.

Chance of failure was higher than she'd ideally like, but she didn't have time to come up with anything better. Dimitrios' life might depend on her actions right now.

She hit the button on the remote.

The garage door whirred open.

She only hoped the men could hear it. Joseph's crying might block the noise.

Well, if it did, she'd simply go in that way. She'd still have the element of surprise.

She waited.

Please, Lord. Make this work.

Seconds dragged.

They hadn't heard it.

She released a slow breath. Okay, then. Time to go in–

A noise. Joseph's cries grew crisper, then muffled again.

Someone had opened the door. Which meant that someone was likely in the garage.

A scuff.

She tightened her right hand on the grip of the Glock, her left hand resting loosely on the slide. As much as she wanted to have the weapon ready, she needed the man to hear her rack the slide.

A shadow stretched toward Dimitrios' car.

Barely daring to breathe, she watched it stretch longer until the man came into view. His back was to her as he took one tentative step after another toward the rental car.

It was the scrawny man she'd seen from the kitchen window. Only him.

That meant that the other two were still inside, likely beating Mitri more.

Plus there was still the man guarding Ari. Even after she subdued this guy, she was outnumbered three to one.

Well, hopefully her backup would arrive by then.

The man paused by the trunk of the rental.

Time to move.

She glanced inside the garage. Empty. The interior door was closed, too.

Good enough.

Stepping forward, she racked the slide, the noise echoing inside the garage behind her. "U.S. Marshal. Drop your weapon."

The man whirled, his eyes widening as he stared at the gun in her hand before looking at her.

Time slowed.

She saw his eyes travel down her body and return to her face. Saw them narrow. Saw his eyebrows drop and his lips harden.

Bringing her left hand around the grip, she sighted the gun on him. "I will not ask again."

His jaw clenched and unclenched. Fingers whitened around the Ruger clutched in his hand.

Her finger rested on the trigger.

Please don't make me do this.

A scowl twisted his mouth as his arm swung up.

She squeezed. The boom registered as the recoil traveled down her arm.

The man dropped.

She didn't have to check him to know he was gone. The bloody hole in his forehead confirmed the fatal shot.

Aside from that, she didn't have time. That gunshot would bring more trouble.

She raced down the side of the house to the French doors, pulling out her key as she ran. A glance inside confirmed Dimitrios was alone in the kitchen. She inserted the key and twisted the deadbolt, then repeated the process with the main lock.

It took forever.

She would've simply broken the glass and stepped inside, but the ironwork would've prevented entry and the shattering glass would have drawn even more attention.

Any second those other two men would reappear and start shooting.

She pushed the door open and stepped inside, panning left, then right, watching for any sign of movement.

Dimitrios watched her through swollen eyes. A split lip painted his teeth and chin red.

Man, they'd done a number on him.

The dining room was clear. She sidestepped through the kitchen, barely looking at Dimitrios as she passed.

She jerked back as a gunshot blasted, the bullet splintering the cabinet by her head.

"Let me go!" Araceli's voice contained a hysterical note, meshing with Joseph's rising cries.

It might mean a bullet in the face, but she couldn't let them hurt Ari. Leveling her gun, she whipped around the corner in time to see movement at the open front door.

The living room was empty.

She dashed for the door.

The doorframe splintered as she approached. She dropped to a crouch but continued forward.

Sirens wailed in the distance.

Not close enough.

She stepped outside as the van doors slammed. Hurdling the steps, she tore across the lawn, stopping halfway to aim at the tires.

Rubber squealed. She squeezed off a shot as the vehicle lurched forward.

Missed.

She aimed again, but the erratic pattern prevented her from getting a clear shot. The van careened around the corner.

They were getting away!

Maybe the police would block them in.

She ran down the drive, reaching the road as the van disappeared from sight.

There was nothing more she could do here.

Jerking her phone from her pocket, she checked the license number. Maybe if she got the APB out there right away, someone would see the van fleeing the neighborhood.

It was the only play she had.

After issuing the APB, she approached her unit, her attention going to the body sprawled on the driveway.

Blood pooled under the man's head and painted rivers across his face.

Eyes stared at the blue sky he would never again see.

She'd killed a man.

Hollowness settled in her stomach.

He looked young. Maybe early twenties. He should have had a lot more years ahead of him, but now he was dead.

Tremors attacked her hands, vibrating up her body. Her stomach lunged.

She swallowed the bile backing up her throat.

It wasn't the first time she'd shot someone, but it was the first time she'd had to look at the man she'd shot. A man who was someone's son. Someone's friend. Maybe even someone's father.

Don't think about it.

Besides, she'd given him more than enough time to drop his weapon. He'd made his decision.

She went back inside.

"Ari?" The word came out slurred as Dimitrios watched her approach.

"They took her. I just issued an APB on the van so hopefully someone will stop them before they get too far."

She dodged a bloody knife on the floor, grabbed a clean one from the block, and sliced the ropes around Dimitrios' hands.

"Are you okay?"

Her question seemed to fall on deaf ears. He rubbed his wrists. "I can't believe I let them take her."

"Mitri!" Her harsh tone brought his head up. "Are. You. Okay?"

"No, I'm not okay! Not as long as they have Ari." The words slashed through the air.

They'd have to deal with that one later. "Are you hurt? Shot or stabbed?"

"No." He followed her gaze to the bloody knife on the floor. "I used that on them."

"And Ari? Did they hurt her?"

"Not that I saw. But who knows by now."

"They wouldn't take her if they intended to kill her." She hoped. Besides, they probably needed someone to take care of the baby.

"We have to go after them!" He pushed up from the chair. "Let's go!"

"We'd never find them by now. The APB is our best bet."

He collapsed back in the chair and cradled his head in his hands. "This is all my fault."

No argument formed on her tongue.

She could still hear Araceli crying as the men dragged her away. Joseph's wails echoed in her memory.

She'd failed them.

They'd come to her to keep them safe and she'd failed. Now they were at the mercy of a group of killers.

As if her failure wasn't enough, she'd also killed a man.

Her mind flashed to the body on her driveway. The memory engulfed her. She felt the recoil traveling down her arm again. Saw the man drop. Everywhere she looked, all she could see was the blood pooled on her driveway. The lifeless eyes staring up.

Her legs wobbled. They wouldn't support her much longer.

Better keep an eye on the crime scene. The last thing she needed was for it to be contaminated.

She needed to talk to someone. Someone who would tell her it was okay.

Paul.

She needed to hear his voice. He was the one person

outside of work who wouldn't be horrified by what she'd done.

Not with his past.

Sinking onto the front step, she stared at the lump on her driveway and pulled out her phone.

Uncooperative fingers fumbled through the contact list. It took a few tries, but she managed to find Paul's name and touch the green phone button.

"Hey." Paul's voice, warm and casual, did little to soothe her.

Ice seeped into her bones, freezing her blood, numbing her mind.

Say something.

Words failed her.

"Lana?" Concern edged his voice. "Is everything okay?"

"I killed someone."

A sharp intake of breath indicated she'd said the words out loud. "What?"

"A man. He had a gun. And Mitri, Ari." Words jolted past her disjointed and rigid lips.

"Where are you?"

The concern in his voice flooded her eyes. The lump on the driveway swirled.

"Home."

"I'm on my way." A pause. "And Lana? This wasn't your fault."

If only she could believe that was true.

Fourteen

"I killed someone."

Dimitrios lifted his head. Lana's voice sounded raw. And heartbreakingly vulnerable.

She'd killed one of the men? He'd heard the gunshot, but had never imagined....

And it was because of him.

Ari was gone and Lana had shot someone. Because of him.

He pushed up from the chair.

The front door stood open. Lana sat on the step outside the door, her phone clutched in her hand.

Whoever she'd been talking to was obviously no longer on the phone.

His attention shifted to the body sprawled by his rental car. Blood pooled beneath it. A gun rested a few feet away from a lifeless hand.

Looked like the shooting was self-defense.

So why was she taking it so hard?

Because it was still a life. No matter how bad that man might have been, she'd taken his life.

Pain pulsated through his ribcage and his head pounded as he lowered himself beside her. "Who was that?"

There wouldn't likely be many people she would talk to about something like this. Maybe her boss or a coworker. Or Paul. He doubted she'd even tell her parents about killing someone, at least not until she'd had time to process it and could talk about it in professional terms.

She didn't look over. Her gaze was fixed on the lump on the driveway. "Paul."

No surprise there. He stared at the body. "I'm sorry."

"I told him to drop it." Her voice had a mechanical edge, like he was listening to a robot rather than his sister. "Waited longer than I should have. He raised his gun. I didn't have a choice."

"I know." She never would have killed the man if she'd had any other option.

She turned to him. "Are you okay?"

Normally he'd put on a brave face, but frankly, he hurt too much to pull it off. "Been better. Do you think Ari's alive?"

Part of him wasn't sure he wanted to hear the answer. If anything happened to her, it would be on him.

He'd really screwed this whole thing up.

"I think they need her. Not only to take care of Joseph, but also to use her against you."

He absorbed Lana's words. Man, did he hope she was right. "As soon as the cops get my statement, I'm outta here. I've gotta get to Oregon, get that file, and save Ari."

"You know the police are going to expect you to stick around."

"Ari's life's on the line here. They told me I only have forty-eight hours to get them the files."

Sirens drew nearer. They'd probably be here any second.

"They said no cops." He held her gaze with his own. "We can't tell them what's going on."

"I won't lie."

"No lying. Just don't tell them everything."

Her arm flew out, pointer finger extended. "I've got a dead body in my driveway! What do you propose I tell them?"

"Tell them some guys broke in. Just leave Ari, Joseph,

Mike, and all that stuff out of it. Please. Ari's life depends on it."

"It's too late for that. I already put out an APB. With the baby involved, I bet it's been escalated to an Amber Alert. Besides, the more we tell them, the more they can help us. Roadblocks, watching the airport, that kind of thing."

She had a point. But was it worth the risk?

If it helped Ari, definitely.

Police cars pulled into the driveway, followed by an unmarked vehicle. Police officers spilled out, weapons raised.

Lana stood, hands in the air. "Deputy Milana Tanner, US Marshals. I phoned this in."

One officer, a beanpole with a sparse mustache, approached, weapon still drawn. "ID."

She reached for her pocket, then dropped her hand.

"It's in my car. I must've forgotten it with everything else going on." She nodded toward the unmarked vehicle that was pulling to a stop behind the patrol car. "But that's my boss. He can vouch for me."

The officer stared at her but didn't lower his weapon. "Scene secure?"

"Yes. One casualty."

They both turned to look at the body, where another officer was already feeling for a pulse.

"Tanner!" An African-American man with a build that would make most linebackers jealous burst from the unmarked car, followed closely by a woman with short-cropped blonde hair.

Dimitrios vaguely remembered her from several years ago. One of Lana's coworkers, if he recalled correctly.

The man strode across the lawn, badge held up as he approached Lana and the officer. "What the blazes is going on around here?"

"Men in my home, sir." Lana's tone was composed. In spite of the man's apparent ire, she didn't seem concerned. "He and his cohorts attacked my brother–"

All eyes turned toward him.

Yeah, go ahead and stare. He couldn't look any worse than he felt.

"I drew him outside, identified myself and told him to drop his weapon, but he pointed his gun at me. I had no choice."

"Where are the others?"

"They got away." She clenched her fingers. "With two hostages. I put out an APB. Any sightings?"

"I'll check."

A door closed nearby. He turned to see a silver-haired man with ramrod posture crossing the lawn from the adjacent unit.

The man approached the group.

One of the cops held up a hand. "Sir, this is a crime scene. I'll need you to–"

"Bert Marlin." His words came out clipped, with a slightly severe edge. "Happened just like she said. I watched the whole thing from that window."

"Mr. Marlin." Lana's voice held a scolding tone. "You could've been hurt."

Bert snorted. "I faced worse punks in the Gulf war. 'Sides, someone had to make sure you didn't get in over your head."

"We'll need to talk to you, sir." The lanky officer nodded toward Bert's house. "How about you wait inside and we'll get to you shortly."

At least Bert could back up Lana's version of the story.

It had been a necessary kill, but he hated that Lana would be placed on administrative leave and investigated because of him.

Another police car pulled into the driveway, stopping behind the unmarked vehicle. They killed the siren, but not before its shrilling drilled into his head.

He'd pay good money for a few aspirin. Maybe kill for something stronger.

Dimitrios closed his eyes against the harsh sunlight,

wishing he could block the throbbing in his body as easily.

Then again, he deserved the pain.

He'd failed Ari. Put her and everyone else he loved in danger.

Put Lana in a hard spot.

"Sir?"

He opened his eyes to find the lanky officer in front of him.

"Deputy Tanner says you can tell me more about what went on here?"

Dang. He should've used the time to come up with a cover story. "Uh, yeah. What do you want to know?"

"How about you walk me through what happened."

This was it. Tell them everything or condense the story?

Lana approached, arms crossed over her chest. He knew which option she'd advocate.

And she was right. If the cops could stop these guys from leaving town with Araceli, it was worth the risk. "A friend and I were headed out and these guys jumped us at the gate. They put a gun to her head, forced me to drive back here, then beat me up and took her and the baby."

The cop jotted down Araceli's name. "Where were you headed?"

"Atlantic Park. It seemed like a nice day to get out." Okay, so not exactly how it happened, but he still wasn't comfortable bringing up Bobby's name, the phone calls, or the threats.

"What did they want?"

"Some file. I don't know. They kept going on and on about a file."

A frown pulled the cop's lips down. "But you don't know what they were talking about?"

"Can't say that I do."

"Could it be something that Ms. Lopez has? Maybe that's why they took her?"

If he wanted to believe that, so be it. "Maybe. Like I said, they kept hitting me and asking about some file like I should know."

"Deputy?" The officer turned to look at Lana. "Anything to add? Could this file be connected to your work?"

Moment of truth. Would Lana rat him out?

She shook her head. "Unlikely. If someone wanted something connected to my work, they'd come after me, not my family."

An ambulance glided to a stop.

Yeah, that'd be for him. If he could've stopped Lana from calling them, he would have.

Sure, he was bleeding, but head wounds did that. Yeah, he had a monster headache, but it'd fade.

Lana waved them over.

Swell.

Two EMTs approached, guiding a gurney between them.

Yeah, not gonna happen. There was no chance that he'd get on a gurney and let them wheel him away like an invalid.

The EMT closest to him, a solidly built Jamaican man with dreadlocks tied back from his face, inspected the wound. The name on his uniform identified him as Ris. He let out a low whistle.

The other EMT, a stout man who was only slightly taller than Lana, leaned down to get a look. "That's pretty gnarly."

Yeah, dude. Gnarly. He bit back the words. "I'm fine."

His eyes locked on the stitching on the second man's uniform. Abe. Now if only Abe and Ris would go away and leave him alone, he could get back to the more serious issues at hand.

His injuries would heal. A bullet to Araceli's heart would not.

"Howsabout you hop on the gurney so we can get a look at it, mon." A hint of an accent colored Ris' words.

"I'll take care of it myself later. I have the same training."

"Mitri. Let the man do his job."

Man, Lana was cranky.

Then again, she'd killed someone and had her house shot

up. She had good reason to be cranky.

"I'm okay."

"I said the same thing after I was shot and you know how that came out. Now get on that gurney so they can make sure you're alright."

She had a point.

Although a blow to the head was a heck of a lot different than a hemorrhaging gunshot wound.

Ris guided him to the gurney and gave a not-so-gentle push downward. Dimitrios dropped onto the sheet, but didn't lay down.

One of the cops said something to Lana, too low for Dimitrios to hear. Questioning his account of the attack, perhaps? He'd have to ask her later. He couldn't afford to be under suspicion, especially not when he had to leave town as soon as possible to save Ari.

"So that your sister?" Ris' question dragged Dimitrios' attention away from Lana.

"How'd you guess." Not really a question, given their physical similarities.

Ris chuckled. "It's pretty obvious, mon. 'Sides, I figure only wives, moms, and sisters get away with being so bossy. She woulda thrown you down if you'd given her much more lip."

The man might've just met Lana, but he'd pegged her pretty accurately. "She's small but you don't mess with her."

Lana, still talking with the police officer a few feet away, scowled at him.

So she'd heard him, huh? Good.

"Where does it hurt?"

Where didn't it? The question unleashed fresh waves of pain, almost as if giving his body permission to acknowledge it.

The pounding in his head intensified, but it was the shooting pains in his core that concerned him most.

Hopefully there were no broken ribs.

"Ribs are the worst. I took a pretty good blow there." Mentioning how many would guarantee a ride to the hospital.

Although, honestly, he was probably headed there anyway. It's the call he'd make if their positions were reversed.

A commotion drew his attention to the driveway, where a police officer tried to block a determined-looking Paul from approaching. Lana waved him through and Paul went straight to her, glancing down at her face briefly before pulling her close.

In spite of the fact that Paul probably wanted to kill him right about now, he was glad Lana had someone like that in her life.

Paul was tough enough to handle his sister.

Abe spoke up from beside him. "Let's finish up in the ambulance. Better than stripping down outside, right?"

"Unless you like putting on a show. Been brushing up on your striptease, mon?" Ris laughed, a hearty sound that shook his whole body.

In spite of the circumstances, a smile worked the corners of his mouth. He pushed off the gurney and stood unsteadily on papery legs. "My stripper name could be defib."

That earned him a laugh from both EMTs.

Abe shook his head. "Your catchphrase could be that you put all the ladies into cardiac arrest."

That'd be the day. Especially since there was only one woman whose heart he wanted to affect and she might not live to see the sunset.

No. She'd live. And he'd get her back.

His legs steadied and he fell into step beside Ris while Abe pushed the gurney behind them.

They were halfway there when his world tipped slightly.

He stopped, waiting for the world to right itself. Maybe he shouldn't have been so stubborn about the gurney.

Well, he wouldn't give in now. Besides, they were almost there.

"You okay, mon?"

Ris' face swirled in front of him, then came into focus. "Yeah. Just got a little lightheaded."

He started moving again, his gaze locked on the ambulance. Almost there.

Stopping by the rear doors, he waited for Abe and Ris to load the gurney inside before following Ris in and sitting on the gurney.

"You know the drill, mon. Let's get that shirt off."

At least they weren't cutting it off him. He didn't have much in the way of clothing here.

Pain shot up his right side as he pulled the shirt over his head.

Ugh. He was gonna be sick.

He clenched his jaw and jerked the shirt the rest of the way, dumping it on the gurney beside him.

Ris listened to his breathing, then probed his side. Each touch slapped him with fresh agony.

Maybe he was worse than he'd originally thought.

"Aagh!" The cry slipped out when Ris pushed beneath his ribs on his right side.

"Mitri?"

Figured Lana would pick that moment to walk up. He didn't turn to her. "I'm fine."

"Doesn't sound like it."

He looked over to find that she'd shifted her attention to Ris. "How is he?"

Ris leaned back. "I don't think anything's broken, but I'd recommend some x-rays to be sure."

As much as he wanted to argue, he couldn't. It was the right call. The roar in his head swelled like the sea, nearly drowning out Lana, Ris and Abe, and the chaos beyond. Maybe the doc could give him something for the headache, too, although it'd have to be something that didn't impair his thinking.

"Mon?" Ris' voice penetrated. "You cool with that?"

He nodded. He'd be of no use to Ari if he had a broken rib, it punctured a lung, and he couldn't breathe.

In the background, he heard Lana's voice and Ris responding, but he tuned them out. Right now, he needed to get patched up and on his way. Ari was counting on him.

Ari. What was happening to her right now?

ꟾ ꟾ ꟾ ꟾ ꟾ

Joseph wailed as the private jet lifted from the runway. One of the men shot a glare her way and she cradled Joseph closer to her chest, making small shushing noises in his ear.

Tremors shook her so violently that her teeth rattled.

What could these men possibly want with her?

Maybe she was the temporary nanny. None of them looked like the type to take care of a baby. Maybe once they landed, they'd let her go.

But she'd seen their faces.

In every movie she'd ever watched, that was always a bad sign.

"Can't you shut him up?" one of the men, a young guy with a shaved head, snapped.

"He-he..." She gulped a breath. "I think he's hungry."

The kid looked at her like she was incompetent. "You're a chick. Nurse him or something."

Heat flashed through her. Seriously? Sure, he was young, but hadn't he ever taken health class? "It doesn't work like that."

But Joseph did need something to eat.

"I don't suppose you have a bottle and formula."

A large guy with a scar tracing down one cheek stood and moved to a cabinet, grabbing a box. He pulled out a bottle and mixed the formula, stuck it in the microwave, and removed it a few seconds later.

All without saying a word.

She checked the temperature. Perfect.

Huh. So not everyone on Bobby's crew was clueless.

Joseph settled as she offered him the bottle.

"What's Bobby gonna do with her?" The kid had lowered his voice, but she had no trouble deciphering his words.

Scarred face shrugged. "Not my business."

Ice numbed her limbs.

They were headed to see Bobby. The Bobby. The man Regan had been hiding from. The man who had turned Mike into a paranoid person she'd hardly recognized. The man who had ordered Mike's death.

She'd suspected as much, but somehow hearing it out loud made it real.

A shiver worked up her body.

They didn't need her. They'd probably only grabbed her so they'd have someone to take care of the baby. Once they reached Bobby, she was expendable.

Oh, God. God, please. Help me.

Fifteen

The sun hung low in the sky by the time the last member of law enforcement drove away from Lana's house.

Paul pushed up from the lawn chair Lana's neighbor had set out for him earlier, folded it up, and leaned it against the side of the neighbor's house.

His left leg throbbed with every movement.

Probably shouldn't have sat so long.

Although the gunshot wound would hurt no matter how much or little he moved around.

Thoughts of the gunshot brought to mind the man responsible for it all.

Dimitrios.

He still hadn't had a chance to talk to the man who had caused all this trouble. The dude might be Lana's brother, but he didn't care. Dimitrios had brought a lot of pain down on Lana these last few days, something for which he owed more than an explanation.

Paul hobbled across the lawn, his gaze locked on Lana. She stood outside the crime scene tape stretched around her driveway, her gaze locked on the rust-colored stain on the pavement.

Man. He needed to get her away from this place.

Aside from that, it was a crime scene. He didn't know how long until they'd release it, but surely she couldn't stay here tonight.

Reaching her, he put an arm across her shoulders and gently steered her away. "Looking at it isn't going to help."

"Did I do the right thing?" She looked at him. "I mean, really. There must've been some other option, right? I could have shot him in the shoulder or something. I didn't have to kill him."

Her voice broke on the last word and with it, a bit of his heart.

He could remind her that her training instilled the need to neutralize the threat. Or that the thug she'd shot wouldn't have been shooting to wound. None of that would help her right now.

Instead, he pulled her against his chest.

Sobs ripped from her, the sound muffling into his shirt, which was drenched within seconds.

Speaking to her right now wouldn't do any good. Besides, he suspected that what she needed more than anything was to let all the pent up emotions out.

So he held her. Said nothing. And let her cry until the tears ran dry.

His injured leg ached, the muscles quivering under the strain of standing so long. He had to tough it out. Lana needed him. He shifted his weight slightly to his uninjured leg and the pain lessened.

As her breathing evened out, he finally spoke, his words drifting above her head. "I'm glad you didn't shoot to wound."

She jerked back. "What?"

"I remember a certain woman who was shot in the shoulder." Man, did he ever remember. He wished he could forget the look of death that had covered Lana that night, the way her blood had saturated her clothes, his shirt, and everything around them. "If you had only wounded this guy, he might have killed you. As hard as this is, I'm glad you didn't give him that chance."

"Someone loved him, too."

"And he should have thought of that person before he broke into your house, threatened your brother, and pointed a gun at a law enforcement official. He made his choices, Lana."

A stray tear meandered down her cheek. "I know. But it doesn't make it any easier."

"I'd be concerned about you if it was easy." And he'd spent enough of his life around a killer to recognize the signs of a callous heart. His thoughts drifted to Matt Stevens who, in spite of being a gun for hire, had also been a brother to him.

"Did Stevens ever regret killing?"

No surprise Lana's thoughts followed his own.

Matt wasn't a topic they discussed. Ever. Too many bad memories for both of them.

But if it took her mind off of what happened today, he'd welcome the diversion. "If he did, he never showed it. We didn't talk about his work. Mostly because I didn't want to know."

"It's easier to pretend when you aren't confronted with it." There was no judgment in her words. In fact, he got the impression that she was speaking from personal experience.

"I get the feeling you're not talking about Matt."

"I did a lot of pretending as a kid. It was easier than believing I hadn't been good enough to keep." The sigh shook her whole body. "So I pretended I was really part of the Tanner family. By birth. And didn't spend much time thinking about my biological family."

He had no words for that, but it didn't seem like she needed any.

In his own way, he could relate.

"I wish you could've known Matt like I did." But she hadn't. And she never would. To her, Matt would always be Stevens the hitman.

"Me, too."

His stomach gurgled, the sound like an alarm in the quiet early evening air.

A light laugh escaped her. "Hungry?"

"Hey, you called just before lunchtime. Heck, yeah, I'm hungry."

She studied his face, her eyebrows lowering over her cocoa eyes. "And pale. Are you supposed to be on your feet like this?"

Without waiting for a reply, she put an arm around his waist and led him toward the front step. He could have made it without her help, but if it made her feel better, he'd do most anything.

Easing down on the step, he gingerly stretched his leg out in front of him before looking up at her. "How about we stop for pizza on the way to the hospital?"

Hopefully he could even get her to eat a slice or two.

"Let me run inside and pack a bag for me and Mitri. I'd invite you in, but it's a crime scene now."

"I'm good here. Just don't take too long or I might mistake your shrubs for a salad bar."

⁂

"What do you have?" Bobby pressed the phone against his ear and waited. Craig had to have found something on Van Horn.

"Van Horn is almost as mysterious as Milana Tanner. He keeps a low profile for the most part. Lots of information on him when he witnessed that murder a few years ago, then nothing. But what's really interesting is that his history only goes back about seven years."

"What do you mean?"

Papers rustled. "I mean that there's nothing. A birth record, but after that he disappears for thirty years. No credit, tax returns, utilities, nothing. Until seven years ago when he pops up in Montana, buys and sells some property there, then moves to Jacksonville where he started a group home."

Another intangible.

Pain shot through his head. Could this thing get any

worse? "How can that be?"

"You ask me, our guy either spent his youth and most of his adult life behind bars or, more likely, Van Horn is an assumed identity."

Swell. It was bad enough when Tanner was an unknown variable. Now they had a second one in Van Horn.

Given that Van Horn had taken a bullet without giving up anything of value, he'd place money on Van Horn being the bigger threat.

He rubbed his head. "Keep digging. Let me know the second you learn anything useful."

Dimitrios watched as Paul pulled Lana's car up to the curb. Lana opened the back door and stepped aside so the orderly could help him out of the wheelchair.

Ugh. He hated being in the wheelchair.

But it was standard procedure for the hospital.

Besides, his head felt a little funny from whatever pain meds the doc had given him earlier.

He settled in the backseat and leaned his head back against the headrest.

"We're not going anywhere until you tell us everything." Lana twisted in the passenger's seat and speared him with narrowed eyes. Paul watched from the front.

"You're in a loading zone."

Paul drove fifty feet to the closest open parking spot and shifted into park.

Dimitrios sighed. The simple movement sent pain vibrating down his body, but nothing like what he'd experienced earlier.

The ER doc had given him some good meds. "I'm fine, just so you know."

"I know. Now I want to know everything that's not in the police report."

He recapped the attack from earlier, leaving nothing out.

Paul let out a low whistle when he was done. "They kicked you how many times and didn't bust anything?"

"These guys are obviously good at inflicting pain with maximum control." Very, very good at it. He didn't think there was a single place on his body that wasn't sore.

"Tell me about it." Paul's jaw locked.

Dimitrios met his eyes in the mirror. "Yeah. Sorry about that, man. I didn't think–"

"You didn't think! Forget about me. You have any idea the danger you put Lana in?"

Paul was right. But had Paul forgotten all Lana had gone through because of *him*? "Me? What about–"

"Guys." Lana's voice was calm. "What's done is done. Let's move on."

"Take me to my rental car and I'll get out of here. Then I'll be out of your hair, okay?" Not that he felt like driving, much less catching a cross country flight. But Araceli's life was at stake. What other choice did he have?

"You're not getting rid of me that easy." Lana held his gaze. "What's your plan?"

"Next flight to Oregon. I'll get to the bank in the morning, retrieve those files, and wait for their call."

"We need to get the police involved. Let me bring Barker in. He can pull some strings–"

"No cops. They said they'd kill her."

"That's a standard line. Right now, she's leverage. Once you give them what they want, she's expendable. You both are. We need the support the police can give."

"No, we need to do what they say so we can get Ari back in one piece." The fight drained him even more than his injuries. "Come on, Lana. Drop me at the airport and let me do this my way, okay?"

"I'm going with you."

"You're. Not. Coming." Paul was right about one thing. He was toxic to his sister right now.

"You think you're in any condition to stop me?"

"I think between me and Paul you don't stand a chance."

"And I think I'm the one who's carrying. Look, you need backup. You won't involve the police, so you've got me."

"If it's about the gun thing, just give me yours."

"Right. Because guns are something you hand out like candy. Besides, do you even know how to use it?"

"Point and shoot. It's not that complicated." Even as the words left his mouth, he knew they were a lie.

She stared at him. "I shouldn't even dignify that with a response. Do you have any idea how many hours of practice I put in with my weapon? Because of it, my aim is excellent. Yours wouldn't be. You need me."

Dang. He hated that she was right. A gun in his hands would be about as useful as a syringe in hers.

Still. He'd already put her in enough danger, and caused her enough trouble.

It would be better all the way around if she'd stay here.

He didn't have the energy for this kind of argument right now. "Come on, Paul. Talk some sense into her, will you?"

Paul gave a light shrug. "Have you met your sister? You really think I can change her mind?"

"You're stuck with me, Mitri."

"Both of us."

Lana jerked around to look at Paul. "Not a chance."

"If you're going, I'm going. It's that simple."

Good. Maybe that'd be enough to convince her to stay here. Or at the very least, it put someone else around to keep an eye on her. He couldn't be worrying about Lana when Ari needed to be his focus.

"Fine." Lana faced out the front. "Let's get a good night's sleep and start fresh first thing in the morning."

As much as he wanted to argue, Dimitrios found that he didn't have the strength.

His body and his mind had completely different agendas and his mind was clearly losing.

In the background, he heard Lana and Paul discussing where to stay for the night and settling on some hotel, just in case his attackers hadn't left town and decided to come back for more.

Not that it seemed likely. They'd made their point quite visibly earlier.

Yet it was better to play it safe. No one else needed to be put in harm's way.

ᘎ ᘎ ᘎ ᘎ ᘎ

A hand planted between her shoulder blades and pushed her forward.

Araceli stumbled from the black SUV, her gaze transfixed on the estate in front of her.

Wide stone steps led up to ornately carved double doors that looked like solid mahogany. The house was constructed of stone that screamed old money.

Standing at the top of the stairs, staring at her like a lion might look at a mouse, stood a lean man with wavy brown hair. Casually dressed in jeans and a polo shirt, he hardly fit the image of Bobby she'd created in her mind. She wasn't sure what she'd been expecting exactly, but he looked too… ordinary. Not like the tough gangster she'd thought he'd be.

"Take her up to Regan's old room."

Even his voice was softer than she'd expected.

His eyes narrowed on the infant in her arms, but he said nothing.

A hand closed around her left bicep and jerked her forward. She kept her eyes on the ground in front of her, not wanting to see the man who could kill the mother of his own child.

The bitter winter air cut through her lightweight sweater. A shiver rocked her, one that might not be entirely from the cold.

As she stepped through the massive front doors, her

sneakers squeaked on the polished tile. Light sparkled from a cut crystal chandelier above her head and a wide stairway swept up in front of her. A formal living room, cloaked in the darkness of early twilight, yawned to her right and a set of closed double doors denied access to whatever was to her left.

The man gripping her arm guided her toward the stairs, pulling her up with him. At the top of the stairs, they went left, passing two doors before stopping at the last one. He pushed the door open and released her arm.

"In."

Her legs moved of their own volition. She'd barely cleared the door before it slammed behind her. Joseph jerked in her arms, made a little noise, then settled back to sleep.

It'd be nice to be so peaceful.

She felt for the light switch and flicked it up. Light flooded the room, revealing a king sized bed covered with an abstract floral print comforter in shades of deep blue. Coordinating pictures accented the walls and blue curtains closed off the outside world.

An antique blue chair and wood table sat to the side of the window.

She was in the house of a murderous mobster. Alone. With no help or way of escape.

Quivering legs barely carried her to the chair. She sank onto the firm surface.

What was she going to do?

She looked at the ceiling.

Did God see her? Did He even care?

⁂

"Who is she?" Bobby slanted a look at Nicky.

"Araceli Lopez. Friend of Lykos'. She's been carin' for the baby."

"And you brought her here because…?"

"Lykos didn't have the file with him."

Idiots. "I suppose he told you that, didn't he? And you believed him."

"We searched." Defensiveness lined Nicky's words. " 'Sides, if he'd had it, he woulda told us. Trust me."

Knowing Nicky's persuasive tactics, he had little doubt.

"But, uh, there was a… thing." Nicky rubbed the back of his neck and shifted his weight.

This didn't sound good. "What thing?"

Movement on the driveway drew his attention. Anthony approached from the direction of the garage, where he'd just finished parking the SUV.

A blood-soaked bandage wrapped Anthony's arm.

"What happened?"

Nicky hesitated. "Lykos fought back. Got a few good jabs in before I stopped him."

So they'd left blood evidence. His jaw clenched. Sloppy. Amateur. His men knew better. Should *be* better, for the amount he paid them.

He could make it all go away, but it would be more money down the drain.

Regan had cost him more than he'd ever imagined.

He whirled and headed inside, knowing his men would follow him. Crossing the entry hall, he pushed open the double doors to the left of the stairs. Light glowed from the lamp on his desk, illuminating the room. He headed straight to the bar, poured a glass of scotch, and turned to look at Nicky, who'd stopped inside the door.

"What other evidence did you leave behind?"

The hesitation was longer this time.

He speared Nicky with a look he usually reserved for his lowest lackeys.

"Smitty's dead."

Dead.

He stared at Nicky, wondering if he'd heard correctly, and slowly realized he hadn't seen the kid get out of the SUV.

Great. So not only did they leave blood evidence, they left

a whole body!

"Can he be traced back to us?"

"Don't think so. He'd done some stuff for us before, but it was all off the books." Nicky hesitated. "But he was Colt's nephew. Colt's not happy."

Naturally, but he really didn't care what Colt thought.

This was a nightmare.

He downed the scotch in the glass and poured another. "What happened?"

"This chick showed up. She drew him outside and shot him."

"Who was she?"

"I'm guessin' that Tanner chick. Didn't stick around to check her ID, but it was her house."

He fought the urge to shoot Nicky himself. For the failure or his insubordination, Bobby wasn't sure.

Frankly, he really wanted to shoot someone right now.

"Explain. Every little detail."

The mystery surrounding Tanner deepened as Nicky recounted the events from earlier. What kind of woman took on four large, armed men all by herself?

He knew he should've investigated her more thoroughly. This was why he never allowed intangibles in his work.

"Did you find anything at her house that might explain who she is? Why she had a gun?"

"Nah. But we weren't lookin' for nothing on her. Just the file."

Fools! When this was over, he'd bury them all. "Then I think it's time we had a conversation with Ms. Lopez."

He set his glass down and strode across the room, leading the way upstairs and to the bedroom that had once housed the woman he loved.

Loved?

What a joke.

Lopez startled as he entered the room.

Good. She was afraid. As she should be.

"Anthony, take my son to the maid. Tell her he's her primary responsibility until I can hire a suitable nanny."

Anthony hesitated only a second before crossing the room. Lopez held the baby closer, shielding him with her body.

"Now, Ms. Lopez. Hand my son over or Anthony might get most unpleasant."

"Y-you know my name?"

What a naïve woman. This would be cake. "I know quite a bit. About both you and Dimitrios Lykos. My son. Now."

She stared at him but made no move to comply.

Smack!

The sound of Anthony backhanding her echoed in the room. She gasped as Anthony pried the baby from her arms.

"Please!" The word sounded strangled coming from Lopez's lips. "I-I took care of him. He's just a baby!"

What did she expect? A thank you? These people had stolen his son from him!

Although the baby did seem to like her. Maybe he should have her take care of his son until he found a nanny.

No. She wouldn't be here that long anyway.

His son would be fine with someone else. Someone on his payroll. Someone whose loyalty sided with him.

"I want to know about Milana Tanner."

"M-Milana?"

What was she? A freakin' parrot?

"Yes. Who is she?"

"Sh-she's his sister?"

Sister? Lykos' sister was supposed to be dead.

Lopez must be lying. But why? What was her endgame? "His sister is dead. The truth this time."

"That is the truth!" Lopez's breath shuddered through her chest. "They thought she died but she didn't. They only found out a few years ago."

As far as stories went, that was a pretty poor one. How could the family not know she was alive?

If she wanted to stick with that story, fine. There were more important issues. "Who is she?"

"I don't really know her that well." Her tongue flicked over her lips and words spilled out. "I only met her a few days ago. She didn't grow up with them because she'd been kidnapped as–"

"I don't care about her past! I want to know who she is now. How she was able to kill one of my men with a single bullet."

"She killed one of your men?"

Was he stuttering? "Yes. Now tell me what you know about her."

Lopez shot to her feet, arms crossed over her chest. "I'm not telling you anything."

So she had a little fire in her after all, huh?

Good.

Made crushing her all the more enjoyable.

"I think you will. Nicky is quite good at convincing people to talk." He nodded at Nicky, who simply flexed his hands.

Her eyes widened slightly, but she clamped her lips together.

Nicky pulled a knife from the sheath at his hip and reached her in two steps. Gripping her arm in one hand, he pressed the blade against her cheek with the other.

"Now, one more time. Why did Milana Tanner have a gun on her? I won't ask again."

"She's a US Marshal! I think she always has a gun."

US Marshal.

The words reverberated inside his head.

His curse echoed in the quiet room. Lykos' sister, if that's who she really was, was in law enforcement! He wanted to grab that knife and bury it in Lopez's chest, just to spite Lykos, but with a cop involved he needed the hostage more now than ever.

"What did Lykos tell her?"

"I–I don't know. Honestly! I wanted him to tell her everything, but he didn't want her involved. She confronted him after Paul was shot," Lopez's eyes strayed to Nicky, "but I don't know what he said. I left the room to give them some privacy."

Even if Lykos hadn't told her before, after today's events she probably knew everything.

Did he have a contact in the Marshal's office? He ran through the list in his head.

No. He'd never needed one. Until now.

He met Nicky's eyes and gave a small shake of his head.

A sob broke from Lopez as Nicky pushed her away. She darted behind the chair, watching them with wide, wary eyes.

Not even her fear satisfied him this time.

A Marshal! Could this day get any worse?

He strode from the room. Nicky joined him in the hallway, pulling the door to the bedroom closed behind him.

"No one goes in or out of this room. I'll send someone to relieve you."

He stalked away, his mind running through options.

A US Marshal. They were probably already coming for him.

How could he slow them down? Or at least cast doubt on anything Lykos or Tanner might say?

While his contacts in the FBI could create some false reports, Tanner's connection to the Marshal's office would make stopping her most difficult.

Then again, she'd likely go through official channels. And those could take considerable time, especially if he had people on the inside running interference.

He headed toward his office. He had calls to make.

But first he needed to calm down.

He poured another scotch, leaned against his desk, and sipped the cool liquid.

So this was a setback.

It wouldn't stop him, though. He was untouchable. He'd

find Lykos, and Tanner, and make them both disappear.

Sixteen

"There's something you should know."

Dimitrios looked at Lana. Serious tone. Even more serious face. He wasn't going to like this, was he?

The airport bustled around them. Somewhere out there, Paul had gone in search of coffee and breakfast, leaving him and Lana alone. Knowing Lana, she'd probably asked him to go so she could have this conversation, whatever it was.

"I told Barker."

Barker, Barker. Should he know that name?

His face must've revealed his lack of recognition for she leaned closer and dropped her voice. "My boss. I told him everything."

Everything. The word settled like a mountain in his mind. "That wasn't your call to make."

"I had a dead body in my driveway. I didn't have much choice."

"You always have a choice. And yours might kill Ari."

Her eyes narrowed. "I might have just saved her life. Barker agreed to hold off on taking action until we get that file. Once we have it, we'll send it to him and reevaluate."

"You don't understand–"

"No, *you* don't understand!" She pulled in a steady breath and continued in a lower tone. "I shot a man. I'm on administrative leave until this mess is cleared up. I had to turn in my gun. I should've turned in my badge, but I dropped it in the car in all the chaos and Barker said he'd get it later."

"Really?"

"Yeah. He shouldn't have, but he was cutting me a little slack in case I needed it in Oregon."

And it was his fault. She wasn't saying it, but she didn't have to. They both knew it. "They'll clear you. You'll get it all back."

"I know I will. That's not the point. The point is that I'm under investigation. If I hadn't told them everything, it would've made things even worse for me when the truth came out."

"But Bobby has contacts everywhere. If he hears about this, he'll kill her."

If anything happened to her, he didn't think he'd survive.

He wouldn't want to survive.

"Mitri. I trust Barker with my life. He's saved my life. If he says he's going to keep this quiet, he will. And we desperately need the help and resources he can provide."

Man, did he hope she was right. At any rate, there was little he could do about it now. "So your plan is to get those files and fax them to him?"

"Yes. I don't know enough about accounting to be much help, but one of our deputies has a background in accounting. Barker will have him look at the ledgers while someone else runs the names to see who we're dealing with."

It was a good plan.

Too bad he didn't know if he could trust the people at her office.

But he did trust her. And if she trusted them, that would have to be good enough.

It wasn't like he had any other choice now, anyway.

"You know, your whole argument for coming with me was that you'd have your gun." If he'd known she'd turned it over, he would have fought harder to keep her out of it.

She shook her head slowly. "I turned in my service weapon. I still have my backup, which is a personal weapon."

Naturally. Man, he really did not think like a cop, did he?

Silence hovered for a few seconds before she spoke, her tone neutral. "Can I ask you something?"

Hmmm. If she had to ask, it was probably a sensitive topic. "Go for it. I won't promise to answer, though."

"You said you wished you could believe in God. What's stopping you?"

How long had that question rattled around inside her mind? Well, it was safe enough to answer. "Proof. I don't see anything that supports the existence of God, but plenty that supports the idea He isn't there."

"So what qualifies as proof?" The words held a hint of challenge, but no condemnation.

"I don't know. Seeing, touching, hearing, those kinds of things."

She nodded. "So you must not believe in other solar systems, right? I mean, you can't see them, touch them, or hear them, so how can you possibly know they exist?"

"They've been documented by experts. Nice try, though."

A slow grin curled her lips.

Why did he feel like he'd played right into her hand?

"Funny thing. God's been documented by experts, too. The Bible records accounts from people who did see Him. People who heard Him. People who touched Him and were touched by Him and walked alongside Him."

Maybe the pain meds were clouding his mind more than he thought. He should've seen that one coming. "That's not proof. They could've made all that stuff up."

"So could the experts who've documented the solar systems. Are you saying you'll only take the word of people who hold a degree?"

"Well, no, but you gotta admit that they're more credible than a bunch of guys who've been dead for thousands of years."

"Actually, the Bible is very credible. Historical accounts support the facts stated in it. And if you stop and think about the unlikeliness of so many authors over so many years fabricating stories that support one other, well, it becomes pretty unreasonable to think that it's all a hoax."

Were they really having this conversation here, now, when Araceli's life hung on the line?

Then again, Ari would applaud Lana for getting him talking about God.

"How do you know it was created by all those authors? Maybe some people used those historical accounts to create it."

Lana arched an eyebrow. "Do you realize what you're suggesting? That a group of people had nothing better to do than waste a lot of time creating a massive document full of lies? Not to mention the expense of producing and distributing all those copies. What would be their motivation? They sure wouldn't see a payoff in their lifetime."

When she put it that way, it did sound pretty ridiculous.

Still, he couldn't agree with all this. Could he?

No. No matter how nice it'd be to believe that there was Someone bigger involved, Someone who loved Araceli and was watching out for her, he couldn't buy it. "Let's drop it, okay?"

"Sure." She hesitated. "Just one more thing. Take your doubts to God. He's big enough to handle them. Give Him a chance to prove Himself."

Like it was really so simple.

He nodded, his gaze wandering the people milling about the airport while his mind rehashed Lana's words.

Take the doubts to God, huh?

Well, what did he have to lose?

Okay, God. Not sure You're there, but if You are, then You know where my head's at. If You're real and You care, help me save Ari.

₪ ₪ ₪ ₪ ₪

The drizzling rain matched his mood.

The flight to Oregon had felt especially long and if one more person looked at his face and did a double-take, he might punch someone.

Yes, he looked bad. He got it.

But didn't people have anything better to do than stare at the human punching bag?

The only consolation was that Paul didn't look much better.

How sick was it that he found that consoling?

Dimitrios adjusted his duffel bag and led the way to long-term parking. Good thing Lana had thought to bring Araceli's belongings with them. Even better that he'd been able to find Araceli's keys without digging all the way through her luggage.

Hopefully she wouldn't mind him borrowing her car.

Now where had she parked it?

He hit the lock button and heard a blip from a few rows over.

Finally her white Honda came into view. The engine turned over smoothly and he looked at the clock.

After four.

He could thank the two long layovers for that.

It was at least a two hour drive back to Lincoln City. If traffic was good.

Looked like they wouldn't be making it to the bank today. But he'd be there when they opened the doors in the morning.

"Have you heard from Bobby yet?" Lana's question mingled with the rain tinging off the top of the car.

"Not yet. If they hold to the forty-eight hour mark, they'll call sometime tomorrow afternoon." And something told him they'd stick to it.

"When he calls, be sure you speak to Araceli."

He didn't ask why. He didn't have to. They both knew there was a chance that Araceli had already outlived her usefulness.

He couldn't dwell on that now.

"You said Bobby's from Vegas?"

"Yeah. Some big casino hotshot."

"He'll arrange the meet there."

He slid a glance her direction. "He might still be in Lincoln City."

She shook her head. "No, he'd want to get back on familiar ground. And if he's as well connected as you seem to think he is, he'll want to do this in a place where he has people on his side. That won't be here."

Made sense. Looked like he'd be catching another flight soon.

"Anything else I need to do when he calls?"

She paused. "Try to set up the meet in a public place. And buy us as much time as you can so we can scout out the location before the meet. I'd like to maybe have Paul stationed at a good vantage point where he can call for help if things start to turn south."

"Or take a shot if I have to."

Dimitrios met Paul's eyes in the rearview mirror. "You know how to shoot?"

A terse nod answered. "I picked it up pretty naturally when I was younger. Haven't had as much practice lately so I'm definitely rusty, but I could serve as a diversion if nothing else."

"I hope it won't come to that." Lana twisted around in the passenger's seat to look at Paul. "Besides, you don't have a weapon."

"I could get my hands on one if I needed to."

She shook her head. "Do I even want to know how you'd do that?"

"Probably not. Let's just say I learned a few things from Matt over the years."

Matt?

Oh yeah. The assassin. Sometimes it was hard to remember that Paul used to be tight with a killer.

Well, at least this situation wasn't likely to freak Paul out.

"Besides," Paul shot a pointed grin at Lana. "I bet you brought two guns anyway."

"Asking a woman to surrender her backup weapon is almost as bad as asking her weight or age." Lana feigned indignation, but the hint of smile touching her lips betrayed her.

"Yeah, well I think I have a pretty good idea on both of those, too."

"That better be a secret you plan to keep."

Their banter eased his tension, if only a little. It felt so normal that he could almost pretend everything was okay.

Too bad pretending didn't change the facts.

Araceli was at the mercy of a killer and he was not even close to being able to save her.

⁂

"So we've got a few options." Dimitrios glanced at Lana, who had not closed her eyes once during the drive to the coast.

In the backseat, Paul stirred, stretched, and blinked a few times.

"My duplex is a two bedroom. I can give you guys the rooms and take the couch. Or, Lana, you could crash at Ari's place. She's about ten minutes from my house so it's not too far. Or we could invade mom and dad's."

This would be much simpler if his sister and Paul didn't have their religious beliefs holding them back. Then they could share his spare room like a normal couple.

Whatever. Their choice.

Lana was silent for a few seconds. Probably weighing the pros and cons of each idea.

Paul spoke first. "I don't like the idea of splitting up. Not with everything that's going on."

"I agree." Lana's words were firm.

He waited for her to say more, but she didn't. Okay. Looked like the decision was up to him. "My place it is, then."

"One change, though." Paul looked at him in the rearview mirror. "I'm not putting you out of your room. I'll take the couch."

"You say that now, but you haven't spent a night on that couch. Trust me. You'll want the bed." Truer words had never been spoken. That couch was fine for watching football, but sleeping? Ugh.

"Dude, I spent over two years on a prison cot. Anything is a step up from that."

"Neither of you is taking the couch." Lana glanced over at him. "I don't think we should stay at your place. Any of us. I'm guessing the police told you not to leave town, right?"

Ooh. He hadn't thought of that. "Yeah. They might be looking for me."

"Running makes you look guilty."

Naturally. Not like he'd had much choice, though.

He'd have to worry about that later. There was too much going on right now for him to concern himself with that.

"Even mom and dad's house is risky, but I think it's our best bet. You said they were out of town?"

"Yeah. They'll be sorry they missed you, though." And sorry they'd missed meeting Paul. If the way Paul looked at Lana was any indication, his parents would want to meet their future son-in-law.

"I'll have to make it back out this way soon. It's been too long."

About thirty years too long. His family had been robbed of so much time with her.

Another reason he couldn't believe in God. If God was really there, how could He have let that happen?

The past had made each of them who they were today.

The thought shafted through his mind like the sunlight piercing the dark clouds overhead.

It was true. The past had shaped each one of them.

If Lana hadn't been taken from his family, she might not have become a US Marshal, something she obviously loved. She certainly wouldn't have met Paul.

Maybe he never would have become an EMT. Or met Mike and Araceli. Maybe his whole circle of friends would have been different.

Maybe decisions would have been made that would have led to tragedy. Maybe he would have lost someone in his family in an accident or something.

What if everything that had happened all those years ago had brought each of them to where they were today? Would he really wish that any of that had been reversed, just so his family might have had Lana with them all those years?

The possibilities made his head hurt.

Really, it didn't matter anyway. There was no undoing the past.

There might not even be any changing of the future.

He navigated to his parents' house, a drive he could make in his sleep. Good thing, too, since he felt half dead right now.

Darkness stretched from the house like an ominous presence.

He stopped the car outside the garage, climbed out, and punched a code in the digital box mounted by the garage door. The door whirred open, the sound echoing in the stillness of the early evening.

The empty space next to his dad's truck highlighted the fact that his parents weren't home. He pulled into the space and closed the door, then gathered his bag and led the way inside.

Even though he'd been here by himself plenty of times when he was a kid, it now felt weird to be in his parents' house without them.

He led Paul to the guest room, gave Lana his parents' room, then dumped his stuff in the office with the oh-so-comfortable sofa bed.

At least it pulled out into a bed. That was a small step

above his own sofa.

Honestly, though, he was tired enough he could probably sleep on most anything.

His stomach rumbled. First things first. Order some pizza, then off to bed.

Stepping into the hallway, he almost ran into Lana, who carried an armload of sheets. "What are you doing?"

"Washing the bedding. I found spare sheets in the closet, but I want to put clean sheets back on the bed for them when they return."

Huh. Okay, so he wouldn't have thought of that. Must be a woman thing.

He walked into the kitchen, pulled the phone book out of the drawer in which his parents had kept them for the last thirty years, and flipped to the pizza pages.

While he'd ribbed his parents for keeping their landline, he was suddenly glad they had one.

Although if they hadn't, he always could've used Araceli's phone, since he had that in his possession.

He dialed Mario's Gourmet Pizzeria, placed an order for delivery, then returned the handset to the cradle.

Lana came into the room, tennis shoes in one hand, a small gun in the other. "How long until the pizza arrives?"

Did she hear everything that went on? "About forty minutes. You going somewhere?"

"I'm going to take a quick run. After all that time sitting today, I need to burn off some energy."

Paul came into the room behind her, wrapped an arm around her waist, and pressed a kiss into her hair. "Be careful, okay?"

"I'm not on anyone's radar." She pressed the gun into his hand. "Hang onto this, though. Just in case."

Paul clipped the holster to his waistband as Lana slipped her feet into her shoes and knelt to tie them.

What? Wasn't Paul even going to argue with her about leaving her gun behind?

Maybe the man wasn't as good for Lana as he thought.

"I think you should keep that with you." Dimitrios crossed his arms over his chest. "Bobby's guys could be anywhere and you'll be an easy target out there on your own."

"Dude, she's got a piece clipped to her back. You really think she goes anywhere without it?" Amusement tinged Paul's words.

Okay, that made him feel better.

"I'll be back soon." Lana disappeared from sight and a second later, he heard the front door open and close.

Dimitrios looked at Paul. "I wish she would've stayed here."

For all he knew, Bobby had goons following them. He'd lost too many people to Bobby.

"Trust me, I get it." Paul stuffed his hands into his pockets. "But one thing I've learned is that smothering her only makes her mad and, frankly, more determined to do things her way."

Yeah, that sounded like his stubborn sister.

On the upside, now he could talk to Paul without Lana around to interfere. "I have a favor to ask."

"Shoot." The smile on Paul's face likely wouldn't be so easygoing if the man knew what he planned to ask.

"Teach me how to break into a place."

The smile slipped and Paul stared at him. "What's in your head?"

"We both know Bobby isn't going to set up the meet in a neutral location. It'll be at someplace he owns, with a bunch of his guys around. I need to be able to get in some way other than through the front door."

Paul moved stiffly toward the table, still favoring his injured leg. "I gave that life up a long time ago."

Dimitrios watched Paul ease into a chair.

Yeah, that too was his fault. Would he ever not feel guilty again?

Jesus can take the guilt.

The words shot through his head, spoken in his sister's voice.

Yeah, yeah. Back off already.

Focus. Saving Ari was his primary objective now and this man could tell him how to do it.

He pulled out a chair across from Paul. "But you still possess the knowledge to break into secure places."

"Lana would kill me. Are you trying to break up me and your sister?"

"She'll get over it." Yes, Lana would be mad. There was a reason he'd waited until she left to bring this up.

"Maybe eventually."

Okay, he needed another line of attack here. Maybe even a brief diversion. "So what're your plans where my sister is concerned, anyway?"

Paul studied him for a few seconds. "I've been carrying the ring in my pocket for weeks. Just haven't found the right time to ask."

"You know, if there's one thing I've learned from all this, it's that there is no better time than the present." You never knew if you'd have the future.

Raking his fingers through his sandy hair, Paul released a breath. "It's a tough thing. I mean, what if she says no?"

Seriously? Did this guy not see how his sister softened every single time he was around? "She's not gonna say no."

"It needs to be something memorable. She deserves that much."

"You really think she cares about some fancy proposal?"

Paul nodded slowly. "I know you're right but there's still a lot of pressure. You get it. I mean, seriously, have you told Araceli how you feel?"

Were they really sitting here talking about their feelings?

Man, he must be even more tired than he thought. "That's why I need your help, man. I mean, really. What if it was Lana? Wouldn't you do whatever it took to save her?"

He had Paul with that one. They both knew it.

Paul would do anything, had already done crazy things, to help Lana.

Paul's sigh deflated his entire body. "God help me. What do you need to know?"

"How would you break into a place?"

"Depends on the place. Usually, I'd spend days, if not weeks, studying everything about the place. Blueprints, all the entrances and exits, their security system, the number of people who would be there at any given time of the day and how formidable those people would be in a fight, the surrounding neighborhood, everything I would need to know to plan for things that might come up."

That was a luxury he didn't have. "If you didn't have that kind of time, what would you do? Like when Lana was taken by that killer."

Paul's lips tightened.

Yeah, not a good memory, for sure.

"I watched the place for a few minutes, then acted. But that was different. There was a wicked storm for cover. And it was a shack in the middle of a swamp with one guy inside, not what you're likely to be up against."

"What do you think I'll be up against?"

"Trained, armed guards. A handful of them at the very least." Paul rested his elbows on the table and leaned in. "If I were in Bobby's shoes, I'd choose a place I owned. If I had a business that would be deserted at night, I'd go with that. If not, I'd choose my house or an out of the way place in an environment I could monitor and control."

"The guy owns casinos. Think he'll set the meet there?"

"Unlikely. Too many cameras and potential witnesses. If he's planning to kill you both, he wouldn't want any evidence tying you to him."

And Bobby surely planned to kill both of them. Evidence or no evidence, they knew too much.

None of this was working in his favor. "What would you

do in my place?"

"Get there as early as you can. Assess the situation. Find an alternate way to get inside, maybe through a side door, roof access, or window. Alarms are a concern, but sometimes you can use that to your advantage. Once you're inside, anyway."

Easy for him to say. "Can you show me how to pick a lock?"

Silence.

In fact, Paul stared at him without blinking. Thinking about it? Or thinking he needed to tell Lana about it?

Paul rubbed the back of his neck. "You're not trying to ruin my relationship with your sister, you're trying to make her kill me. What'd I ever do to you?"

It sounded like he was kidding, but it was hard to be sure. "No break ups or murder. This can be our secret."

He snorted. "Right. Because that works."

"I'm doing this with or without your help. If you help me, I stand a better chance of surviving it."

More silence. Finally, Paul sighed. "I have a feeling I'm going to regret this, but if we want to do this before Lana gets back, we'd better hurry."

Dimitrios rose as Paul slowly pushed himself up from the table. Yeah, they'd better hurry. Because if Lana saw Paul teaching him to pick a lock, they were both going to be in big trouble.

Seventeen

Lana strode through the emergency room entrance of the hospital and headed straight for the desk.

Stopping by the hospital hadn't been on her radar, but Dimitrios had left the key for the safe deposit box with a friend. Margie. And since he was well known around the hospital, Lana had opted to come in his place.

A young guy in scrubs straightened as she stopped by the counter.

"Hi, I'm looking for Margie. Is she around?"

The guy nodded. "You just missed her. She ran up to the third floor for something. Bet you could catch her at the nurse's station."

"Thanks." Lana headed for the elevator.

The door opened on the third floor with a quiet ding. Stepping out, she saw the nurse's station a few feet to her left.

As she approached, her gaze locked on a woman standing toward the back of the work area. She ran through Dimitrios' description. White hair with a little bit of blond, short, carrying a few extra pounds, glasses on a chain around her neck.

That looked like Margie.

She approached the counter. The woman looked up, offered a smile, and approached. "Hey, hon. You need something?"

"Margie?"

A nurse nearby glanced their direction, but made no move toward them.

"You found me."

Lana pulled out her badge and showed it to the woman. "Is there someplace we might speak in private?"

Curiosity lit the woman's eyes. "Sure thing, hon. The waiting room's probably free this time of day."

Lana followed her down the hallway and into the waiting room. Sure enough, empty.

Evidently not many people hung out in waiting rooms at ten in the morning.

Margie settled in a chair and folded her hands in her lap. "What law enforcement agency did you say you're from?"

"US Marshals." Lana passed her badge for Margie to inspect. "Milana Tanner, uh, Lykos." It felt weird rolling off her tongue.

Margie's eyes widened and she looked like she was about to say something, but nothing came out.

"Dimitrios is my brother."

"I can see the resemblance. I didn't know he had a sister."

Lana smiled gently. "For a lot of years, he didn't know it either. You should ask him about it sometime. It's quite a story. In fact, it was almost the story of my death."

Blue eyes traveled her face. "I remember you now. Gunshot wound, right?"

"That was eight years ago."

Margie tapped her temple with her pointer finger. "It's all right here. We don't get a lot of gunshot victims here. Even fewer that has one of my boys camped outside the OR all night. Leaves an impression."

Obviously.

Enough small talk. Time to get down to business. "He sent me for the key."

A beat. "Key? I can't say that I know anything about a key."

"He also said to tell you that your nephew made it

through the surgery." She paused, watching recognition flicker across Margie's face. "It doesn't make any sense to me, but I'm guessing it means something to you. You know Mitri. He doesn't really explain a lot."

Margie laughed, a hearty sound that came from deep inside. "Isn't that the truth?"

"Mitri needs that key. Can you help me?"

"Sure, hon, I can help. Follow me."

Lana rose, following Margie out of the room and down the hall. After stopping briefly at the nurses' station to let the nurse know she needed to get something from another floor, Margie led her into the elevator.

"I'm surprised the Marshal's office is interested in an EMT's murder."

Sharp woman. Lana smiled. "I'm actually not here officially. Mitri needed help and I was the one best qualified to provide it."

With a cluck of her tongue, Margie shook her white curls. "That boy needs more help than he'd like to admit some days."

"Most days."

Margie laughed with her. "He doin' okay?"

Lana hesitated. She wouldn't endanger this woman, but Margie really seemed to care about Dimitrios. She deserved a decent answer. "He's struggling. If you're a praying woman, he could use some prayer."

"Hon, I see too much to believe there's anyone up there." Margie appraised her with narrowed eyes. "Honestly, I'm surprised you can believe that with all you've seen in your line of work."

"It's because of what I've seen, and experienced, that I can tell you for a fact that God is there and He cares."

"Huh. If you say so. But he's okay?"

Explaining Dimitrios' physical condition would invite too many questions. Besides, Margie was likely more concerned with his heart. "He's hurting and not dealing with it very well, but he's surrounded by people who love him. He'll bounce back. It's just going to take some time."

The elevator dinged and Lana looked at the display.

Basement.

Where'd Margie hide that key? The morgue?

"Well, you tell that brother of yours to get his butt back here in one piece or I'll come after him myself."

"Yes, ma'am." Lana gave a mock solute. Even though Margie was only half Mitri's size, Lana wouldn't mess with this woman.

Margie led her down the hallway, around a few corners, and into a narrow room lined with lockers.

Lana looked away as Margie spun the dial on the padlock, only turning back when Margie swung the locker door open. Ducking her head, Margie looked under the locker's sole shelf, then reached up and peeled a key off the bottom.

Margie handed her the key, but didn't release it right away. "You watch out for him, you hear me? I already lost one of my boys. I can't lose another."

So Margie was the resident mom around here.

That explained a lot, including Dimitrios' decision to trust her.

"I don't intend to lose him." Lana held her gaze for a heartbeat. "Although he's not making it easy."

"They never do. Stubborn, every one of them."

Funny. People had said the same thing about her. Maybe it ran in the family.

The thought chilled her.

Oh, Lord. Please don't let his stubborn streak lead him down the same road I walked.

Because if it did, he may not survive.

ᘯ ᘯ ᘯ ᘯ ᘯ

"So what do you think?" Dimitrios cringed at how loud his voice sounded in the small room.

Lana looked up from the ledger. "I think I don't know enough about this kind of thing to know if there's anything suspicious here."

"Look at the amount of the transactions."

"I see them, but just because there are large transactions doesn't mean that it's illegal activity." Her dark eyes roamed the page. "We need to have Barker run these names. See if anything pops."

"Then let's get them sent over. Mom and dad have one of those printer/scanner combos at the house."

Lana cleaned out the box and put everything into the oversized handbag she'd brought with her. Her phone rang as she dropped the last ledger inside.

Glancing at the display, she froze. "It's Paul."

Which could be very bad news. Paul had opted to wait in the car and watch for any sign of trouble.

She accepted the call and put it on speaker. "What do you see?"

"Cops. Plainclothes, but they're cops, no question. Probably detectives."

Great. Just what they needed. What were the odds that they weren't here for him?

"How many?" Lana flicked her eyes up at him.

"Two. Male and female."

Jim and Courtney. It had to be. Well, there was one way to find out. "Small guy with gray hair and a thin woman?"

"You got it. Friends of yours?"

"Try the detectives running Mike's investigation." He swore, then shifted his attention to Lana. "Now what?"

"Paul, when you see us, start the car and pull toward us. Be ready to get out of here in a hurry." She terminated the call and slid the phone into her bag.

"How'd they know?" Dimitrios blew out a deep breath.

"They must've been watching the place." She reached for the door handle. "Let's see what we're dealing with here."

This was bad. If Jim and Courtney found him, they'd

likely detain him, wouldn't they? After all, they'd told him not to leave town.

Even if they didn't detain him, the questions would slow him down.

And if that happened, Ari was dead.

He had to get out of here. Now.

Lana poked her head out the door. "It's clear. Come on."

They stepped into the short hallway. The lobby - and the exit - was around the corner ahead.

Maybe they should go out the emergency exit. Yeah, it'd trip the alarms, but the chaos should give them enough cover to get away.

Maybe.

He really didn't like maybes. Absolutes were much more comforting.

Lana hurried down the hallway and looked around the corner.

As he stopped a few feet behind her, he heard Jim's baritone voice rumbling from the lobby. The words were indecipherable, but it was definitely him.

Lana stepped back. "Here's the plan. I saw the restroom right around the corner. Wait there and I'll call you when it's clear. You have Araceli's phone on you, right?"

"Yeah. You got the number?"

She nodded. "Go. Wait inside and when I tell you to move, move fast."

"What about you? What if they question or detain you?"

"They have no grounds to do so. Besides, they aren't looking for me so they probably won't even notice me."

"What about one of the employees? They might tell the detectives you were with me."

She paused, then removed the clip from her hair and ran her fingers through the loose waves that fell down her back. "Problem solved."

Man, did he hope so. If she was recognized, this whole thing would be over.

She looked around the corner again. "They've got their backs to us. Go now."

He didn't stop to think. He slid past her and pushed into the men's room.

His heart hammered his ribs.

Any second now, Jim would throw that door open, slap on handcuffs, and haul him away.

He locked the door.

Seconds ticked.

No pounding footsteps. No shouting voices. Nothing.

Certainly no handcuffs.

He leaned against the door. Hopefully no one needed the bathroom for a few minutes. Single occupancy had its drawbacks.

Although right now he couldn't see any.

He pulled the phone from his pocket and stared at it, as though somehow that would magically make it ring.

Come on, Lana. Call already.

What was going on out there, anyway?

ʘ ʘ ʘ ʘ ʘ

Lana sauntered into the lobby, her eyes wandering in a well-practiced nonchalance. Yep, two detectives over at the manager's desk. If they'd come for Mitri - and it seemed likely that they had - how'd they know he was here?

She moved closer, stopping at the table in the middle of the room and grabbing a deposit slip.

Now, as long as no one made a lot of noise, she should be able to hear at least part of the conversation.

"How long ago was that?" A woman's voice. Courtney, if she remembered correctly.

"I-I don't know. Maybe ten minutes. I called right after my assistant took him back." She recognized the branch manager's voice from when Dimitrios had spoken to him earlier.

"And he's still here?" A man's voice. Must be the other detective. Jim, was it?

"I haven't seen him come out."

"Take us back there." Something about Jim's voice nagged at her. It seemed familiar, but that was impossible. Wasn't it?

Unless he was one of the detectives she'd worked with eight years ago.

That could complicate things.

Law enforcement had uncannily good memories when it came to faces. If he remembered her, it might raise unnecessary questions.

One problem at a time. She'd deal with that when, and if, it became an issue.

A cleared throat. "Um, he has the right to privacy while he's looking at the box. Do you have a warrant for that?"

Silence.

She let her eyes flick up.

The detectives' backs were to her. The manager shifted, his face a shade lighter than it had been when they'd arrived. He was facing her, although not looking at her.

Good thing, too, because he might remember her from earlier.

He hadn't been the one helping them access the box, so that should work in her favor, but there was still a chance that he'd remember.

"Look, we're not asking for him to hand over the box. We only need to ask him some questions and he's been ducking us. We can wait outside while you go in and get him." Courtney's voice adopted a persuasive tone.

Lana refocused on the paper in front of her.

Couldn't seem too interested or it would draw undue attention.

Heck, she was likely drawing attention now by how long she'd been standing here. It didn't take that long to fill out a deposit slip for crying out loud.

"Weeell…" The manager's voice wavered.

"This is a murder investigation. You wouldn't want it to go on record that you were uncooperative." Jim's voice held nothing but warning.

Please.

Good cop, bad cop? Could they be any more predictable?

"I suppose it wouldn't hurt anything as long as you waited outside. I have to consider the privacy of my patrons. You understand?"

"Of course." Courtney's tone was like butter.

"This way."

She caught movement in her peripheral but kept her head down.

Keep on walking.

Two people passed, but the third slowed as he approached the island.

Why was he slowing?

She was the only one standing here. This couldn't be good.

"Excuse me."

She looked up. Yep, definitely the same detective from eight years ago. "Yes?"

Hands buried in the pockets of his khakis, he stared at her. "I know you from somewhere."

Realizing that Jim wasn't right behind them, the manager and Courtney stopped a few feet away. Lana felt the weight of their curiosity.

Play dumb?

No, it was always better to play it straight.

She examined him. "You know, I think we worked together when I was in town some years back. Milana Tanner, US Marshal's office?"

Recognition lit his eyes. His lips curled down. "That's right. Multiple shootings, two dead bodies, almost three, counting you. Did I leave anything out?"

Plenty, but he wasn't aware of most of those details. "I think that about covers it."

His eyes narrowed. "I also recall that you don't live in this area. What brings you back to town?"

"I'm afraid I can't discuss that. You understand."

The tightening of his lips said he did. "Why are you at this bank? Right now?"

"I'm afraid I can't discuss that either."

"Naturally." He planted both hands on the counter and leaned toward her. "You know, you remind me of someone. Dimitrios Lykos. We're actually here to talk to him now."

Figured he'd see the family resemblance. "Then I shouldn't keep you any longer."

He didn't move. "Are you muscling in on my case?"

"No." She held his gaze. "I'm not after this Lykos guy, nor investigating him. I'm here on another matter."

Kind of. It was a half-truth, at best, but it was all she could offer right now.

"But you can't tell me what."

She pressed her lips together and smiled. "Sorry."

"Well, deputy, if there's anything *weee* can do to help with your investigation, you'll be sure to let us know, won't you?" Sarcasm dripped off the words.

"Of course. Good luck with your interrogation."

Jim pushed off the counter and strode toward his partner and the branch manager, muttering things she had no desire to hear.

Phew. Dodged that bullet.

For now, anyway. She didn't want to be anywhere around when they came back out, though.

She counted to five, then glanced back. The three of them were just passing the bathroom.

Whipping out her phone, she brought up Araceli's number. Dimitrios answered on the first ring.

"Get out of there. Now." She dropped the phone back in her pocket and turned for the door.

Dimitrios caught up with her outside, his long strides easily outpacing her. Paul jerked to a stop in front of them and she climbed into the back seat while Dimitrios circled around to the front.

"Here." Paul tossed a baseball cap at Dimitrios.

Pulling the cap low over his eyes, Dimitrios slouched in the passenger seat and released a shaky sigh as Paul turned out of the parking lot. "Man. That was close."

Understatement of the year.

Paul turned onto the main road. "How'd they know you were there?"

"The bank manager called them." Lana looked behind them, half expecting to see flashing lights, but saw nothing. "If I had to guess, I'd say that they'd already come to the bank with a warrant, learned about the safe deposit box but couldn't access it, and left instructions to call immediately if Mitri showed up."

"But you got what you came for?"

Her hand went to her bag. "Yeah. We got it."

"Soooo, back to the house?"

"We can't go back." She looked at Dimitrios. "Now that they know you're in town, that'll be one of the first places they look for us."

Paul appraised her in the rearview. "So where to?"

Dimitrios twisted in his seat. "All our stuff is there. Including the burner phone that Bobby's supposed to call on. We have to go back."

Crud. Why hadn't Mitri brought that with him?

"Fine. Five minutes, tops. Then we make tracks out of here. We'll get a hotel room in McMinnville and send the documents from there."

Another hotel. And definitely another flight. Probably two, since she'd have to fly to Vegas and then back home.

Times two. She couldn't – and wouldn't – ask Paul to cover any of this with his own limited resources.

She was going to have to do some serious damage control with her finances to recover from this adventure.

But it was family. What other choice did she have?

Eighteen

"We need to make one other stop."

A scowl twisted Lana's face.

Yeah, that was pretty much how he'd imagined that would go over. Paul wisely kept his eyes on the road.

"Mitri. The police are looking for you. Probably me, too, after that incident at the bank. We need to get as far from here as possible."

"It's on our way out of town."

"What's so important that you're willing to risk blowing this whole thing?"

"Peruvian Violet." The idea had come to him as he was throwing his stuff in a bag back at his parents' house. Araceli's latest serum might be the key to saving her without having to kill anyone.

"You want Araceli's serum?" The scowl softened as she studied him. "That's actually not a bad idea."

She sounded so surprised. While he should be offended, he was glad she was coming around. With Paul behind the wheel, he would've had zero shot at this if she'd disagreed.

"Do you have a key to her shop? Or know where she keeps this serum?"

"No, but Celeste will."

"Celeste?"

"Ari's business partner. She brings the business smarts while Araceli knows the product."

Lana didn't reply for a second, but a sigh finally broke free. "Fine. But we need to hurry. That could potentially make it on the short list of places they might look for you."

Phew. She'd agreed. He hadn't wanted to jump from a moving vehicle to get his way.

He directed Paul to Araceli's shop and greenhouse on the outskirts of town. The open sign sent a red glow through the window, which was filled with an array of plants. Four cars sat in the Exotic Blooms' parking lot, one of which was Celeste's.

Three customers. Hopefully none of them cops.

He studied the cars as Paul parked. Not law enforcement plates, that was a good sign. He ruled out the Corvette and the cherry red Beetle, but the sedan was a possibility.

Unlikely, though. The vanity plate read "W8 4 IT" and he had yet to see a department issued vehicle with vanity plates.

He led the way inside, passing a middle-aged man with thin wisps of hair, who walked out with a pink flowered plant in hand.

While Celeste patiently answered a woman's questions, he wandered the shop.

She'd gotten a lot of new options since the last time he'd been in, including some brightly colored planters and fancy watering cans.

A few minutes later, the bell above the door dinged as the customer made her way out. The final customer browsed the cut flower arrangements.

Celeste crossed to them and pulled Dimitrios into a hug.

"Ah, Mitri. It is good to see you." The rich accent of the deep south weighted her words. Gray streaked her curly black hair, which was a mass around her round chocolate face.

"Hi Celeste. This is my sister Lana and her boyfriend Paul."

The whites of Celeste's eyes glowed in her dark face as she took in Lana. "You have a sister? And you didn't tell me until now?"

Laughter lingered in her outrage. "For what it's worth, I didn't tell Ari until recently either."

Celeste looked around. "Speaking of Ari, where is that woman?"

Did he tell her?

It might put her in danger.

But he needed her help and if telling her gained him the compliance he needed, then that was what he'd have to do.

"That's why we're here." He glanced over at the customer, who had pulled a red vase filled with red, yellow, and blue flowers from the refrigerated case. "Maybe we can talk in the back?"

Celeste nodded. "You head on back there. I'll be along shortly."

The humidity of the greenhouse smothered him like a blanket as he stepped through the door.

He pulled off his sweatshirt. Tender ribs protested the move and he gasped as pain shot up his torso.

The pain receded to a throb. Not sure it'd been worth it, but at least he was cooler. Good thing he'd put on a short sleeve shirt this morning.

"Wow."

He turned to Lana, who stood inside the doorway, absorbing the scene. "I forget how striking it is the first time you see it."

The greenhouse was the size of a football field. A decorative stone walkway curved down the center, weaving around trees and foliage that provided an almost jungle-like atmosphere. Small pathways shot off the main walk, paths that he knew from past experience led to rows and rows of start-up plants.

Straight ahead, a fountain bubbled. The noise was usually soothing, but right now only served to remind him who should be here but wasn't.

"This is not what I expected." Lana gently fingered a feathery leaf to her left. "I guess I thought it would be a lot smaller with tables full of plants."

"There are some of those behind all that foliage. But Ari really wanted a place she could come and relax. She walks the path or sits by the fountain when she needs to think."

"I didn't realize the floral business paid so well."

"Her ex makes big bucks. She got a pretty sizeable chunk of change in the divorce and used it to buy this. As much as he cheated on her, she should've gotten everything." Man, he needed to let that go. It really wasn't any of his business. "Feel free to look around, but be careful what you touch. Toxic plants, remember?"

She dropped her hand from the leaf as though it'd burned her. "I'd forgotten. Thanks."

Moving forward on the path, she stopped to admire the fountain for a second before skirting around it and disappearing from sight.

While he'd expected Paul to follow her, the man didn't move.

He turned and looked at Paul to find him staring the direction Lana had gone.

Huh. Did Paul even realize how often he did that?

As if hearing his thoughts, Paul blinked and turned to him. "This is an impressive set-up she's got here."

"Yeah." He nodded his head the way Lana had gone. "It's also a good place to propose."

Paul's eyes narrowed slightly. "I'll be sure to remind you of that when we get Araceli back."

Message received loud and clear. *Stay out of my business.*

Dimitrios fought to keep from grinning. Too bad for Paul he didn't always listen to the messages he received, especially when it had a negative impact on someone he loved.

"Nice try, but Ari and I aren't even dating." Although he certainly knew her well enough.

"So where does she do these experiments?" The words sounded slightly hoarse. Paul looked around the greenhouse, as if expecting a lab to magically materialize.

Okay. He'd let it go. For now, anyway. "Her lab is at the other end of the greenhouse but she keeps it locked. We'll have to wait for Celeste to come with the key."

"I'm here." Celeste pulled the door to the shop closed behind her and approached.

Uh-oh. How much of their conversation had she heard?

Well, Celeste had no filter. If she'd heard them talking about proposals, she'd probably ask him outright about it.

"I locked the door and put the back in thirty minutes sign out."

"Thanks." Well, Celeste didn't look like she was dying to ask him about proposing to Araceli. Nor did she have that look he'd seen on her many times before, the one that reminded him of a dog with a treat. Maybe she hadn't heard anything other than him mentioning the key. He gestured toward the back. "I need something from Ari's workshop."

"Huh-uh." Celeste crossed her arms over her generous chest and cocked a curvy hip. "I ain't openin' nothing until you tell me what's going on. Where's Ari? And why have the cops been by several times lookin' for you?"

"Short version? We've been hiding from the guys who killed Mike but they found us and now they have Ari." The words ran over themselves in an attempt to flee his mouth.

Celeste stared at him.

Had she not understood what he'd told her?

"So Ari's been…"

"Kidnapped. Yeah."

Celeste buried both hands in her curls. Her jaw moved but nothing came out. A tear slowly leaked from the corner of her eye. "My poor sister. Taken by killers."

"She's your sister?" Paul eyed Celeste carefully.

"Not by blood, obviously. But there's more than one kind of sisterhood." She smacked Dimitrios' arm. "What are you doing here? You should be trying to save her!"

He winced and rubbed his arm. Had she not seen the bruises coating both arms? "I am trying to save her. That's why I need in her lab."

"What's in the lab?"

Celeste's attention drifted past him momentarily and he turned to find Lana returning. He swiveled back to Celeste. "That Peruvian Violet serum Ari's been working on."

Black eyes locked on him. "And what're you gonna do with that?"

"Get Ari back. The kidnappers are going to call any time to set up a meet. "

"If she told you about the serum, she probably told you she only tested it once. It might not do what you need it to do."

"It's about to be tested a lot more rigorously."

"Don't you got something better in all that fancy EMT stuff you use?"

They were wasting time. "Not that I can get my hands on right now. Ari said the serum is a fast acting paralytic. That's what I need."

Celeste still didn't look convinced and he fought the urge to take the key by force.

The longer they stayed here, the greater the chance Jim and Courtney would find him. They needed to get moving. "Celeste. Please. Time is running out and that serum might save Araceli's life."

Seconds ticked. Finally, she gave a single nod.

"Come on." She led them through the greenhouse, stopping outside a solid door on the other end of the room. "I still say there's a better way. Like the police. Isn't this a job for the cops?"

"Lana's a US Marshal."

Celeste whipped around and stared at Lana, her jaw slack.

"And Paul has..." He caught himself seconds before he felt an elbow to his back. The elbow hit high enough he knew it came from Paul.

Ouch. Figured the guy would connect with his ribs. "Paul has similar expertise."

Celeste shook her head. "Whaddya know. Never woulda guessed that one."

Turning back to the door, she pushed the key into the lock and stepped inside. An alarm panel next to the door beeped. She punched in a code and the beeping stopped.

Had Araceli always had her lab alarmed? Or was it something new?

He'd never noticed it before today.

Then again, it'd probably been at least a year since he'd set foot in here. Araceli kept this part of her life pretty private.

Celeste went straight to some shelving on the far side of the room. Containers lined the shelves, small labels on each one. A second later, she pulled a clear box from the shelf and handed it to him. "This is all she's got right now."

The box contained four small containers filled with a milky liquid that resembled melted butter. "How many doses is this?"

"Depends." Celeste looked at him. "Someone your size? Probably three doses per container. Your sister's size, now that'd be more like four doses."

"How much did Ari use when she tested it?"

" 'Bout one cc, but I'm guessin' these thugs who got her are closer to your size than hers–"

Hers? He jerked his head around. "She tested this on herself?"

"Who else would she have tested it on?" Celeste arched an eyebrow. "You know how she feels about animal testing."

"So she used an untested product on herself?" Okay. As soon as he got her back, they were going to have a serious talk about this whole self-testing thing. "What if something had gone wrong?"

"She had me here, just in case."

"So, what? So you could watch her die?"

Celeste's hands landed on her hips. "It was lab tested. Only thing left was to try it out. Now you wanna know how to use it or not?"

Yeah, it wasn't Celeste's fault Ari was reckless with her own health. "Sorry."

"I was sayin' that I'd use two cc's on guys your size. If they're smaller, go with one."

"So what happened when Ari," He swallowed the burning lump blocking his throat, "Tested this?"

"It caused immediate full paralysis of the body for about fifteen minutes, then gradually wore off. She said she could hear and see what was goin' on, but couldn't react to it in any way."

Fifteen minutes. It might not buy him all the time he'd need to free her, but it'd have to do. "And she said there were no lingering effects?"

"Some tingling. And her tummy was upset the rest of the day. But other than that, none."

"And if I give them too much?"

"Probably some vomiting. Maybe a headache or something, but you'd have to give 'em a lot to kill them. Stick with the two cc's and you'll be fine."

Good. So he wasn't going to give someone a heart attack or something. "Does she keep syringes here?"

Celeste brushed past him and opened a cupboard beneath a well-lit workbench. The box she handed him had at least a dozen empty syringes inside.

Now as long as they didn't come up against more than a dozen men, they'd be okay. "Thanks Celeste. This helps."

She offered a curt nod. "You bring my girl home in one piece."

⁂

The phone rang.

Dimitrios jerked. The burner phone. It had to be them. "Hello."

"Listen up." Same gruff voice he recognized all too well. "You got one shot to save your girlfriend, you hear me?"

His gut clenched and his fingers tightened on the phone. "I'm listening."

"Where are you now?"

"Oregon."

"Twenty-four hours. We'll call you. Be in Vegas. With everything Regan left you."

Buy time. That's what Lana had told him. "That's too soon. I can't be there by then."

"That's your problem. Figure it out."

Lana waved at him from the back. "Talk to her!"

Her words were hissed so low, he almost didn't hear them.

His throat closed and he swallowed hard to open it. "I want to talk to her."

"You don't get to make demands."

Yeah, well he was sick to death of taking them. "Look, either I talk to her or I'm going to the FBI. I won't give you these files for a bo–"

His voice failed.

He couldn't say it. Couldn't consider that Araceli might be nothing more than a cold body by now.

Heavy breathing told him the man hadn't hung up. "Just a minute."

It worked? His heart beat double time.

The sounds of movement came through the line. Doors opening and closing. Muted voices.

It felt like hours before a female voice came on. "M-Mitri?"

The voice contained more fear than he'd ever heard in it before, but he'd know that voice anywhere. "Ari! Are you okay?"

"Yeah–"

More movement.

"That's enough." The gruff voice replaced Araceli's. "You talked to her. Vegas. Twenty-four hours. We'll call you."

The line died.

Lana stared at him. Even Paul kept shifting his attention between him and the road.

He didn't want to tell her. While he needed her help, he wanted to keep her far away from Bobby.

But she'd heard the conversation and wouldn't leave it alone until she knew everything.

He could lie. Tell her that the meet was set in Portland or something.

She'd never buy it. Besides, no matter how much he hated to admit it, he couldn't do this without her expertise. "They want me in Vegas by this time tomorrow."

"That's doable." She pulled out her phone. "Let me check out our flight options."

A few minutes later, she set her phone aside. "Okay. Change of plans. We'll head straight to Portland. I booked us on a nonstop flight leaving tomorrow morning at nine."

Nine a.m.? That was cutting it too close. "There wasn't anything sooner?"

"There was a red-eye tonight, but we all need some rest. Facing down Bobby when we're this ragged would be suicide."

"I don't think we have a choice." Why hadn't she talked to him before booking that flight? He'd have to get the flight information and call the airlines. Maybe he could change to the other flight.

"It's almost two now so we should have until at least one tomorrow. The flight lands in Vegas about eleven a.m. We'll be okay."

He hoped she was right. Somehow he doubted Bobby would be very understanding.

"Mitri, relax." She placed a hand on his arm. "I've been dealing with guys like this my whole career. Right now, you two are at an impasse. He has something you want and you have something he wants. There's a balance of power and as long as that exists, he can't do anything to Araceli. Now when you meet up with him, the balance shifts. Especially if it's on his home turf, which I'm guessing is what he'll shoot for. My job is to maintain that balance so he can't kill you both and cover it up."

Kill you both. The words echoed in his head.

That was what Bobby had planned, wasn't it? There was zero chance Bobby intended to let them walk away.

Did he even have a shot at getting Ari out of this alive? "Thanks for the optimism."

"Optimism gets people killed. In a situation like this, you need realism. And the reality is that once Bobby has those files, both you and Araceli are expendable."

"So how do you plan to make us not expendable?"

"I can't." She sat back. "That's why we need to leverage those files to get the meet in a public place. Not even Bobby could kill you two in a public location without someone noticing."

Unless it was a public location Bobby owned.

Couldn't Bobby frame it so it looked like he'd killed them in self-defense? It'd be especially easy if he had cops on his payroll.

Good thing he had a US Marshal on his side.

Even if Lana couldn't save his life, she could make sure Bobby paid for his crimes.

Maybe there was no happy ending here. Maybe the best they could hope for was justice.

Nineteen

Dimitrios dumped his bag by one of the beds in the room they'd rented for the night while Paul claimed the other.

Lana set her bag next to a sofa on the other side of a small partition. What a joke. That partition would offer her very little privacy. Plus, that sofa couldn't be terribly comfortable.

"You sure you don't want to get a second room? I'll cover it."

Lana shook her head. "This is fine. Besides, it's only for one night."

He should override her and rent another room. Once it was done, she'd have to take it.

It wasn't the right move for his finances, but it was the right move for her. This whole mess had already put his finances in the hole.

What was another hundred or so dollars, anyway?

He turned for the door, but Lana sidestepped into his way. "It's fine. Just don't hog the bathroom, okay?"

It'd be easy to get by her. Heck, he could pick her up and move her out of his way without breaking a sweat. But if she was so insistent, maybe he should let it go. "Don't worry. I don't have to look my best to take down mobsters."

She smiled. "Then we're good."

"These are queen beds. They'll sleep two." Although being in the same room with her and Paul sharing a bed felt incredibly awkward.

"You see that sofa? It's just my size." She grabbed her tote bag, phone, and one of the keys. "I'm headed down to the business center to send this stuff off to Barker. We can grab dinner once I'm done."

The door clicked shut softly behind her.

Dimitrios returned to his bed and unzipped his bag. "I feel like a third wheel here."

Paul pulled a shirt from his bag and shook it to get out the wrinkles. "How so?"

"You, her, a hotel… do the math."

Paul shook his head. "It's not like that with us."

So Lana had said. While he didn't believe she'd lie to him, he still had a hard time believing this. "I don't get it. I mean, you guys are practically engaged, for crying out loud."

"It's not God's way, dude." Paul sat on the edge of the mattress and assessed him. "We both wanna do this right and God says it waits until marriage."

"I don't know how you do it." It felt wrong discussing his sister's love life, but his mouth refused to stop flapping. "I mean, I've seen the way you look at her."

"I'm not saying it's easy." Paul sighed. "But God promises blessings for those who obey, so I hold to that promise and tell myself that some things are worth the wait."

"Well, I don't see what the big deal is." Although hadn't Mike said basically the same thing to him on more than one occasion?

"It's God's way. I've spent most of my life doing things my own way. Doing things God's way has been…" Paul looked like he was struggling to find the words. "I don't know how to describe it. It's not always the easiest way. In fact, it's often not the easiest. But there's this peace about it. God loves me and I want to do things His way, even when it's hard."

Not rules. Freedom.

Lana's words from a few days ago echoed in his head.

How many times had Mike told him something similar? How many times had his parents? And now Cy was on board, too.

All of these people around him were smart, thinking people. Could there be something he was missing here?

Well, he'd given God a chance to prove Himself and so far, nothing.

Until God showed him otherwise, he'd continue to do things his own way. Because God's way had resulted in Mike's death and Araceli's abduction, neither of which seemed so good to him.

ꟷ ꟷ ꟷ ꟷ ꟷ

Had Vegas always been this garish? Or was it just the circumstances for his visit this time?

Dimitrios watched the neon signs slip by outside the window of their rental car as he navigated down the main drag.

He hadn't been to Vegas in years, not since that bachelor party for his buddy Luis a few years back.

And honestly, he didn't remember a whole lot about that trip.

Even in winter, tourists crammed the chilly streets, moving from one elaborate resort to the next.

"It should be coming up on our right pretty soon." Lana glanced up from her phone.

He nodded, returning his attention to the road. Why she'd booked them in one of the resorts, he didn't know. If all went according to plan, they'd meet up with Bobby's guys this afternoon, trade the file for Araceli, and fly out of town before the sun went down.

However Lana had insisted they needed a home base.

Might be for the best. As long as the resort wasn't one Bobby owned. She'd made the reservations under Paul's name, just in case, but those guys had already proven that they knew who Paul was. If they were watching for any sign that Dimitrios was in town, Paul's was one of the names they'd likely check.

His stomach growled, the sound loud in the confined space.

Paul lightly punched his shoulder. "I'm with you, dude."

"I could use some food, too." Lana pointed to a black sign with red lettering over a skull and crossbones. "That's it."

"Black Sails?" Paul ducked his head to look out the front windshield. "You chose a pirate resort?"

Lana shrugged. "It was one of the best deals. Besides, who doesn't like pirates?"

"Legitimate sea merchants?"

Angling her head, Lana shot Paul a slanted-eyed look. "I meant among us landlubbers."

Dimitrios pulled the car into the crescent shaped loading zone in front of the resort.

A man with a weathered black hat, black pants, heavy boots, and red ruffled shirt hurried up to the passenger side, simultaneously opening the passenger and back doors. A wooden sword hung from a scabbard at his hip. "Aye. Welcome aboard the finest ship in the desert, mateys."

Dimitrios killed the engine and popped the trunk before stepping from the vehicle.

"Ahoy, there. Do ye wish to board?" The pirate's nametag identified him as Saltwater Sal.

"You got it." Dimitrios handed over the keys, as well as a five dollar tip.

"Yo ho. And it's a fine day for sailin', too." The pirate tore a vehicle claim ticket at the perforated edge and handed half to Dimitrios. "Would ye like assistance with yer gear?"

What, all three duffel bags? Dimitrios shook his head. "I think we can manage."

Pointing through the glass double doors, Sal gave a black-toothed grin. "The captain's at the wheel. He'll direct ye to yer cabins. Enjoy yer stay or walk the plank."

Corny. Yet Dimitrios noticed that both Lana and Paul smiled at the antics.

Well, if this helped lighten their mood, then good. He didn't think he'd smile again until they found Araceli alive, but that didn't mean everyone else needed to be so somber.

Lana led the way into the lobby.

Shiny blue tile shimmered under their feet and a chandelier that looked to be made of a hundred antique liquor bottles glowed above their heads. The ceiling in the lobby was at least four stories tall, with sweeping staircases on either side of the room. Straight ahead of them was a round check-in desk, which looked like the hull of a ship except that the rich, highly polished wood was too pristine to have ever spent a day at sea. The circular counter had to be twenty feet in diameter and had eight computer monitors draped in glittering nets and sparkling seaweed.

Mounted in the center of the check-in desk area was a large wheel. A seven-foot tall statue of a bearded man with a plumed hat, scraggly beard, and eyepatch stood behind the wheel, his frozen eyes locked on some distant horizon.

Lana skirted a polished anchor that was almost as tall as she was, dodged the hull of a boat that angled up from the tile like a ship on its way down, and stepped up to the counter. Paul stopped beside her, resting his elbows on the gleaming wood, but Dimitrios hung back.

It didn't take three of them to check in.

Besides, two men and a woman sharing a room might arouse suspicion.

Then again, this was Vegas, not Lincoln City. They probably wouldn't give it a second thought.

The woman checking them in had her hair piled atop her head and wore a scarlet jacket over a white blouse cut low enough to show off her black lace bra. He noticed that Paul kept his attention focused on Lana, not the woman.

Good for him. If he'd caught Paul checking out some other woman, he would've had a serious talk with his sister.

The scent of food wafted toward him.

Ugh. He was famished.

He didn't know what he was smelling, probably some combination of foods, but it smelled delicious. Behind the registration desk, through the cascading water of a massive fountain, he could see half a dozen stairs leading up to another ship, only this ship had chairs and tables and people eating.

Man, they could not get checked in soon enough.

He looked away. No point in making himself even hungrier than he was. Off to his right, the clang of slot machines and clamor of voices carried on a wave of cigarette smoke from the casino. Well, if there was one thing that could stamp down his appetite, it was the stench of cigarettes.

Lana and Paul joined him a few minutes later.

Handing him a key, Lana nodded toward the elevator tucked away beside the stairs to their left. "We're on the seventh floor."

Room 721 contained two queen beds. A loveseat and single chair sat in front of the window.

He nodded at the loveseat. "Tell me you aren't planning to sleep on that."

"If I need to." She set her bag on the floor beneath the window. "Once we make the trade, we'll reassess. Maybe the four of us will leave town tonight or maybe Ari and I will get another room."

Once. He liked that she hadn't said "if," even though they were all thinking it.

They headed down to the restaurant. The restaurant was long and narrow, assuring a good view of the lobby from almost any seat. An aquarium dominated the entire back wall, even going up and around a doorway that likely led to the kitchen.

The hostess, a woman in a shimmering green split skirt and seashell bikini top, flashed them a smile as they approached. "Three?"

Lana smiled back. "Unless there's some great party going on that we should join."

Right. Coming from her, that was so absurd it was almost laughable.

The hostess did laugh. "If you find one, let me know, okay? My shift's done in an hour." She winked at Dimitrios.

Sure. 'Cause he was looking for a mermaid a good fifteen years younger than himself.

The hostess stopped by a table in the middle of the room and gestured for them to have a seat.

"I'm sorry to be a bother." Lana pointed to a table in the corner by the aquarium. "But is that table free?"

The hostess stared at her like she'd asked to dive into the fish tank but her smile never wavered. "Sure thing. Just thought you'd like to be in the middle of the action."

Seconds later they were seated at the corner booth, Paul and Lana with their backs to the wall. He chose the seat closest to the fish tank and angled his chair so he could see the restaurant and lobby.

Paranoia was contagious.

Then again, right now they had good reason to be paranoid.

Another mermaid, this one in purple, approached the table and took their orders. She glided away, swinging her hips like a fish moving through water.

Lana looked at him. "You have the phone, right?"

Did she think he was an idiot? "Of course I have it."

"Remember, insist on a public location. They'll probably push for a private place, but they aren't the only ones holding the cards here. Negotiate. Keep the balance of power."

Easy for her to say. It wasn't Paul's life on the line.

"You know she's right." Paul stared at him.

Dang it. His face must've given him away again. Good thing he wasn't at the poker tables right now because, evidently, he couldn't hide a thing.

"From my, uh, professional background, I completely agree with everything she said. They'll threaten to kill her, but they won't as long as you have that file."

"Got it." He ran his gaze around the restaurant before looking back at them. "Can we drop it now?"

He'd have to live it soon enough. The last thing he wanted to do was dwell on it now.

The server approached with their drinks, halting further conversation.

Just as well. It was time to change the subject anyway.

As the server left, Dimitrios turned to Lana. "You haven't heard anything on those files yet?"

"No, but it was so late by the time I sent them over that they probably didn't get started until today. I plan to call Barker after we eat to see what they have so far."

Whatever they had, it wouldn't be enough. Not unless it put Bobby away for life.

Their food arrived and conversation ceased as they all ate. The grilled steak sandwich was good, but his fries had a hint of fishy flavor, like they used the same oil to fry fish and French fries.

Okay. If they ate here again, he'd avoid anything fried unless he wanted it to taste like seafood.

He had a mouthful of steak when the phone on the table beside him rang.

Lana's salad-topped fork stopped halfway to her mouth and Paul set his hamburger down.

No one said a word. Dimitrios chomped a few times before swallowing a bite that really should have been chewed more.

He accepted the call.

"Hello." His voice sounded more frog-like than human. He cleared his throat and waited.

"Where you at?" Good old gruff voice. No time for pleasantries.

"I'm here."

"Be in your car driving east at seven p.m. We'll call then with further directions. Come alone."

What, so they could direct him to a grave in the middle of

the desert? Not a chance. "No."

The silence on the other end deafened him.

Had he made a mistake? He was doing what Lana had recommended, but what if Araceli paid for his decision? He couldn't live with that.

"What do you mean, no?" Hostility laced the words.

"No blind meets. Or calls with further directions. We meet on neutral ground in a public place. No home advantage for either of us."

"You don't get to set the terms."

He pulled in a deep breath. "Actually, I do. There's some pretty damaging evidence in this file. I know your boss doesn't want to see it made public."

"You forgetting we still got your girl? Maybe I oughta ship her back to you in pieces."

No! He couldn't let them hurt her!

Lana's words from earlier rang in his mind.

Hollow threats, that's all they were. They couldn't hurt Araceli, not as long as he held the files. "You touch her and you'll see this stuff on the evening news. I'll drive across state lines and hand it to someone in the FBI and then you'll be dealing with them."

"You signed her death warrant."

His breath escaped him. Had he killed the woman he loved?

No. He wouldn't believe that. Couldn't believe it. Because if Ari was gone, they might as well kill him, too.

The man was bluffing. He had to be. Dimitrios refused to consider any other possibility. "I bet that guy on that national evening news program would be really interested in the video of the shooting. Maybe I'll send him a quick email and attach it. How long do you think it'll take him to call me back once he sees what I have?"

The man's breathing grew heavier. "Keep the phone close."

The line went dead.

Had he won? Or was the man going to make good on his threat to kill Araceli?

"Well?" Lana's voice snagged his attention.

He relayed the conversation.

Lana stared at him. Hopefully absorbing every word and figuring out their next move.

After several seconds, a grim smiled crossed her face. "This is good. You're talking to one of Bobby's men, not Bobby himself. The fact that he ended the call without setting up anything definitive tells me that he had to talk to Bobby before proceeding."

He hoped she was right. He couldn't think about the alternative.

The phone rang again. He snatched it up and accepted the call. "You ready to work with me now?"

"Mr. Lykos." Not gruff voice. The smooth voice sounded cultured, almost like a politician.

"Who is this?"

"You seem like a smart man. I bet you can figure it out."

Bobby. It was the only option that made sense.

The man spoke with an air of authority that gruff voice had lacked. He spoke as a man used to having his every command obeyed immediately.

Bobby didn't wait for him to reply. "You have taken a lot of my valuable time lately and I don't like having my time wasted. The warehouse at the corner of Crane and Industrial. The sign by the door says Harrington Industries. If I see anyone but you, my guys start cutting your lady friend."

A warehouse? No way. "Like I told your guy, a public place–"

"This is not a negotiation." Bobby's voice remained calm and steady. "Seven p.m. Do not keep me waiting."

The line went dead.

What had just happened?

He'd failed to get the meeting in a high visibility location, that's what had happened. Instead, it was in some warehouse, likely owned by Bobby, so there'd be no record when Bobby shot him and stuffed his body into a trunk.

As long as it was only him, he could deal with that. The danger was that Araceli, Lana, and Paul might end up as collateral damage.

Twenty

"Your brother was right."

Lana watched the foot traffic drift by, making sure no one moved close enough to hear her end of the conversation.

She approached the round fountain on the far end of the lobby and sat on the cold, hard bench encircling it. Two other fountains dotted the area, a large one in the center and another smaller one on the casino side of the lobby.

"About?"

Papers rustled in the background. Barker's voice held a distracted note. "This is big. We've got senators, state representatives, police, and media personalities on this list. If this is a list of people involved in Carpelli's illegal activities, then this goes higher than I expected."

That was still a pretty gray "if." Nothing definitively said that the names on the spreadsheet were people on the take.

It'd never hold up in court, not on its own.

But if they could get to a few of those people and convince them to flip, then they might be able to bring the whole empire crashing down on Bobby's head.

That would be satisfying.

She looked back at the restaurant, where Paul and Mitri were finishing their meals. After the call from Bobby, her appetite had all but vanished and she'd left the table to call Barker for an update.

"So what's next?"

Barker paused. "I have to hand it off to the right agency. This isn't my jurisdiction."

She'd expected as much. "Who are you giving it to?"

"The FBI field office in Vegas. We've cross-referenced all the names and came up with one FBI agent, but only one. I'm going to go over his head to the SAC."

The special agent in charge. Well, that was better, anyway.

Hopefully the SAC wasn't in on it, too.

Listen to her. Now she sounded as paranoid as Dimitrios.

Besides, the fact that Barker had seen the files, not to mention would retain copies, should ensure that whomever he gave it to remained on the case. It couldn't get swept under the rug, not now that so many people were involved.

"Did you find out any more information on Bobby Carpelli?"

"Alex is taking a look right now, but this isn't our case." The words contained a hint of warning.

"I know. And I appreciate the time you've invested in looking into it." Barker had already put himself out there more than he should have.

"Well, I can't have you getting yourself killed now, can I?" An unusual gruffness ruffled Barker's words. "But I need to get everyone back on our own workload."

"Of course. Can you give me the contact information for the SAC once you hand everything over?"

"I'll do that."

In spite of what he'd told her, there was one more favor she had to ask. "One last thing. Can you find information on Harrington Industries? They own a warehouse on Crane and Industrial."

"I'll get someone on that. You thinking it'll tie back to your guy?"

"Let's just say I won't be surprised if the owner's first name is Robert." The meeting this evening was inevitable, but it'd be nice to go into it armed with as much information as she could get between now and then.

"I'll call you back as soon as we get something. Oh, and Tanner. You're cleared. Just thought you'd want to know."

They'd investigated the shooting already? That was fast.

Of course, it helped that her neighbor saw and backed up the whole thing.

The dead man's face lodged in her mind again.

With everything that had happened the last few days, she'd managed to stomp it down, but it was back now. "Did you ID the victim?"

"Owen Smith. Low-level thug from Las Vegas. He had a string of arrests, mostly small-time stuff, but had always gotten off."

Unlikely for a low-level thug. It sounded like he'd had some high-level help. "No ties to organized crime or anyone named Bobby?"

"Nothing that jumped out, but I don't have the jurisdiction or manpower to do a more thorough investigation."

He was right. This wasn't his fight.

Frankly, she was lucky he'd done so much already.

"I know. Thank you, sir. I appreciate your help on this."

His voice roughened. "We take care of our own. I'll look into that company and call you back."

The call ended and she lowered the phone.

At least she'd been reinstated.

Now all she had to do was keep everyone alive long enough to return to her job.

At the large fountain about thirty feet away from her, several giggly co-eds tossed coins into the water.

Make a wish.

It'd be nice if it was that simple.

But she didn't need a wishing fountain. She had Someone much more powerful on her side.

Okay, Lord. I need Your help here. I can't do this alone.

"Hey."

She jumped.

Paul held up his hands as he approached. "Sorry. It's not often I get the drop on you."

"You shouldn't have now. I need to stay vigilant." She sighed as he sat beside her. "But I was asking God for help."

"Always a good place to start."

His hand gently rubbed between her shoulder blades. Tension eased from her stiff muscles. "I was watching those girls throw coins into the fountain and thinking how much time and effort we waste trying to do things on our own. I mean, seriously. They can't really think that'll work."

He glanced at the fountain behind them. "Probably not. Doesn't stop people from trying though, does it?"

She followed his gaze. Hundreds of coins of all sizes and values piled on the bottom. "No."

A coin splashed down in front of her.

She watched the penny sink to the bottom before turning to Paul, a smile curling her lips. "And what did you wish for?"

His eyes searched her face. "God's blessing. And your favor."

Movement drew her attention down. Something shiny came between her and Paul, caught between his thumb and forefinger.

Light glinted off the diamond.

Diamond.

She stared at the ring. Platinum, with thin vine-like bands encircled a modest, multi-faceted diamond that glittered like shattered glass.

The lobby around them faded, the noise little more than a whisper in the background.

"I've imagined this a million times in nearly as many settings." He never took his eyes from hers, not even to look down at the ring between them. "I thought everything had to be perfect. Memorable. As special as you are. But this whole thing has reminded me that God doesn't promise us tomorrow."

Her lungs strained to draw air.

Was this really happening? Here? Now? After all this time?

Sure she'd thought about it, wondered... but she'd still not been prepared for...

"Ha-have you been carrying that the whole time?"

A soft smile creased his cheeks. "For months, actually. I kept thinking the right moment would come along and I wanted to be ready."

"A-at church? And the home?"

"And at dinner. At your folks' place. You name it, it's been there."

Her mind swirled. Words ran together in unintelligible fragments.

"Sooo," strain marked the lines around his eyes. "Will you marry me?"

"Yes." The word slid out on a sigh. She leaned forward, her lips meeting his with an intensity that surprised her.

He made a small noise.

Oh! His split lip!

Pulling back, she looked at the face just inches from her own and brought her thumb up to gently caress his lip. "I'm sorry. I forgot."

"Worth it to hear you say yes." His breath warmed her face.

"Yes, absolutely, yes."

His grin reminded her of a young boy's but there was nothing juvenile as he leaned in and kissed her gently. When he pulled back, he held up the ring. "Shall we make it official?"

She offered her hand. He slid the ring on, the too-big band moving up and down her finger with ease.

"Guess we'll have to get that sized." A hint of disappointment lined the words.

Staring at the ring for a second, she barely noticed the sizing issue. "I don't care. I love it."

A finger slid down her cheek. "Just so you know, I don't think I can handle a long engagement."

Heat rushed up her neck and her ears warmed. "I don't need one. I've known you long enough to be sure about this."

"I saw a chapel up the street. I think they even have an Elvis impersonator to officiate."

She laughed. "It's tempting."

"I'm only half-teasing."

She shook her head. "I know. And I love you for it. But we've waited this long, so let's do it right. In a church, before God and family and friends."

"I knew you'd say that." He took her hand and held it like it was made of glass. "After all, your dad has to marry us."

"And mom would be so disappointed if she didn't get to do all that mother-of-the-bride stuff."

"Oh, sure." Dimitrios' voice came from her right. "You both take off and stiff me with the bill."

Without releasing Paul's hand, she angled her body to watch her brother approach.

His eyes latched onto her hand before shooting up to her face. A slow smile spread. "Well, it's about freaking time."

In spite of the severity of their situation or the danger Araceli was in, she couldn't seem to stop smiling. "Just keep it quiet for now, okay? If mom and dad find out you heard about it first, there won't be a wedding because I'll be dead."

"Hey, if there's one person in this family that knows how to keep his mouth shut, it's me." Dimitrios clapped Paul on the back. "Yep, there's a spine back there after all."

With his face the color of a raspberry, Paul grinned. "Shut up."

Her phone rang.

She checked the caller ID before accepting Alex's call. "What's up?"

"Barker asked me to let you know that Harrington Industries' current owner is Mitzi Harrington but she's only leasing the space. The warehouse is owned by Carpelli LLC."

Carpelli. So there were clear ties to Bobby after all. "I'm guessing Harrington is in on Carpelli's illegal activities?"

"No solid proof of it, but Barker agrees. He's on the phone with the Vegas FBI now."

"Good. Do you have any information on Harrington?"

"Sure do." Papers rustled on Alex's end of the line. "She's third generation to run the company, which primarily focuses on printing, but also has some manufacturing interests."

"What kind of printing?"

"All kinds. Ads, coupons, independent newspapers, restaurant menus, even billboards. And before you ask, the manufacturing products center on parts for slot machines."

Interesting. Even more interesting was that Harrington didn't mind Bobby using the warehouse whenever he wanted. "Keep me posted?"

"You know it." Alex hesitated. "And I shouldn't have to say it, but be careful, okay?"

"Always."

"No, I mean it. A normal person's definition of careful, not yours."

So she'd had a few brushes with death before. It didn't mean she wasn't careful. "I'll be fine. I have both Paul and Mitri to help me."

"Paul's there?" Surprise tinted Alex's words.

If she was surprised at Paul's presence, she'd probably pass out if told the other news.

Lana bit the words back. First her parents, then the Lykos family, then Alex.

Still, she couldn't wait to tell her closest friend about the ring that slid loosely around on her finger. "Yeah. And he's armed."

A sigh filtered across the line. "I feel better already. Tell him that if anything happens to you, I will hunt him down."

"I'm sure he's terrified." Lana ended the call and slid her phone into her pocket.

"They find something?"

"Yes. The warehouse is…"

A prickly feeling crawled up Lana's neck.

She slowly surveyed the surrounding area, but saw nothing unusual. Still, the feeling lingered. "Let's head back to the room. I'll fill you both in there."

ꟷ ꟷ ꟷ ꟷ ꟷ

"Yeah, he's here." Nicky turned to look out the window as the elevator doors slid closed on Lykos.

"Alone?" Bobby's voice sliced into his ear.

"No. He brought his sister and that Van Horn guy with him." Van Horn was moving pretty good for a guy who'd been shot.

Next time he'd make sure Van Horn couldn't move at all.

Bobby's breath hissed in a snake-like fashion. "Keep an eye on them. I want to know if they leave the hotel."

"Do my best, but there're lots of ways outta here."

"Just keep me posted." The line went dead.

Nicky pocketed his phone. Good thing Bobby had thought to check for Van Horn's name, too. He didn't know how that Craig guy did it, but the man could find pretty much anything that was on a computer.

Then again, they all had their strengths.

Craig's was with a computer and his was with his gun and his fists.

And a blade. He was pretty good with one of those, too.

Once they had those files, he'd put all of them to good use. Maybe kill Lykos' friends with his knife and bare hands, then put a bullet in Lykos' brain.

Well, the chicks with his bare hands.

That Van Horn dude might put up too much of a fight to be worth the trouble. He'd kill Van Horn with a bullet to the heart.

Either way, this thing ended with four bodies in the desert.

₪ ₪ ₪ ₪ ₪

"This guy makes the news a lot."

Dimitrios watched Paul scroll on his phone.

"Good news or bad?" Lana shifted her attention from the laptop to Paul, who sat on the sofa beside her.

"Good, I guess. Let's see, lots of things about different shows or acts at his casino. A few charity events. Some social gossip junk. Something about a business merger. That kind of thing."

Dimitrios wasn't really surprised. He hadn't come up with anything different when he'd done his search before. "Nothing that ties him to anything criminal?"

"Nope. On paper, this guy looks golden."

Figured. It'd be that much harder to make any kind of accusations stick.

Hopefully the evidence Regan had left would be enough to sway things, though.

"Ditto for Harrington." Dimitrios set Araceli's phone aside. "Nothing looks shady about her, either. She makes the local tabloids a lot and has been seen with Bobby at social events, but nothing that would label her as a criminal."

Except maybe poor taste in men.

Although from what Regan's roommate Annabelle had said, Harrington was in good company. Sounded like half the female population of Vegas wanted time with Bobby.

Paul rubbed his neck. "What're the odds that she doesn't know Bobby is using her warehouse for a meet tonight?"

"Seems unlikely." Lana shook her head. "No matter how clean she looks on paper, I'm betting she knows a lot more than we do about Bobby's activities."

"So if he owns a casino, why wouldn't he set up the meet there?" That would be the ultimate home turf and busy enough that no one would notice a few extra people coming and going.

"If I had to guess," Paul looked at him, "I'd say security. Casinos are loaded with cameras and security personnel, most of whom probably aren't aware of Bobby's less legitimate businesses. It'd be harder to erase video footage of us being there and even harder to control who saw us."

That made sense.

"My news isn't much better." Lana relaxed back against the sofa cushions. "The warehouse appears to be in the middle of an industrial district. What do you want to bet that area is deserted at that time of night?"

Paul draped an arm across the sofa behind Lana. "Almost guaranteed."

Great. So not only were they walking into a trap, there'd be no one around to hear them die.

If that was the case, there'd be one death, not three. "I'm going alone. I won't have your deaths on me."

"Nice try, but I'm not sitting this out."

Sitting there beside Paul, she looked so... right. If he hadn't told her the meet location, he'd figure out a way to ditch her, but she knew where he was going.

"They told me to come alone."

"Standard line." Light reflected in her dark eyes. "We leave now. Scope out the place so that we at least know what we're up against tonight."

Definitely a good plan. Maybe she could give him some ideas for when he broke in later. If she couldn't, Paul could.

Huh. He never thought he'd be asking his future brother-in-law to help him commit a crime.

He pushed up from his chair. "Let's get going."

"Not out the front."

Strange. Even for her. He arched an eyebrow. "Why not?"

Hesitation.

Never a good sign.

"I felt something weird. Like someone was watching us."

Could Bobby have eyes here, too? Maybe he even owned this resort. They hadn't taken the time to track all his properties.

Whatever the case, he trusted Lana's instincts. "The valet's out front, though."

"I know. I think if we split up and alter our appearances, maybe exit through some side doors and come around, we should be okay." She shook her head slowly. "I'm probably being overly paranoid."

"As long as you don't suggest tinfoil hats, I can deal with that." His comment earned a hint of a smile.

"Not tinfoil, but you still have that baseball hat?"

"In my suitcase."

"And I brought a hoodie." Paul had hardly removed his eyes from Lana during the whole exchange. He didn't know Paul well enough to read his expression. Was Paul as worried about the outcome as he was?

Somehow he had to find a way to ditch Lana and Paul.

It was bad enough that they were here in Vegas with him. Taking them to the meet was much too dangerous.

Twenty One

A horn blared. Dimitrios started, twisting around in time to see the semi driver offer a one-fingered wave to a little black sports car.

Classy.

A glance at Lana found her focus locked on the warehouse across the street. As his should be.

Was Araceli inside? What kind of warehouse was it?

It looked remarkably similar to all the others surrounding it. Dull gray concrete walls, very few windows, multi-door loading bay. But unlike all the other warehouses in the area, no trucks lingered around this warehouse.

In fact, it almost looked deserted.

Except for the heavy steel door that looked like it could withstand an explosion. A floodlight was mounted above the door and a small keypad next to the door presumably granted access to anyone privileged enough to possess a code.

After driving around the block a few times, Lana had insisted on parking the car two blocks away and coming in on foot.

It'd made sense at the time. But after standing in the alley across the street for the last ten minutes, he was wishing they had parked somewhere within eyesight so they could keep watch comfortably.

Besides, didn't they look suspicious?

Not that anyone seemed to have noticed them.

He couldn't take the silence anymore. "What do you think?"

"It's not going to be easy to get in unnoticed. I see at least three cameras covering this side of the building. I bet if we checked the other sides we'd see more of the same. They're not about to let anyone get the drop on them."

Yeah, well he wasn't about to let them get away with killing Mike and kidnapping Araceli.

"Paul, could you hack the system?"

"Well, yeah–"

Lana shot him a look.

"I mean, nooo." He leaned against the concrete wall. "I could probably do it if I had the proper equipment. Which I don't. Besides, we need to do things the right way. The legal way."

Seriously? "Because they've been doing things legally?"

"That's what separates us from them." Lana returned to watching the warehouse. "Even though our reasons are good, if we break the law there can still be legal consequences."

Which was another reason he had to ditch them and go it alone.

He couldn't have them getting arrested because of him. Especially since an arrest would cost Lana her career.

"So how would you get in?"

She looked at him. "With a warrant and a group of law enforcement professionals."

Not helpful. "Paul? In the old days? Hypothetically, of course."

"Maybe the roof. After hacking the security system, which we can't do."

"See?" Lana turned from her surveillance to give Dimitrios her attention. "Not a valid option."

That's what *she* thought. With the right equipment, how was scaling a building any different than climbing a mountain?

Too bad he couldn't get Paul to hack the security system

for him.

Well, he'd take his chances. If they saw him, he had the serum. Hopefully they wouldn't come at him in a big group. He couldn't drug people that quickly.

The idea rooted in his mind.

If he could find a decent sporting goods store, he might be able to get the gear he needed to pull this off.

But first he had to get rid of his sister.

Playing along was the only way he'd be able to manage that. As long as she thought there was a chance he'd do exactly what he was planning to do, she'd likely stick closer than his shadow. If he could convince her he was on board with *her* plan though, maybe he could slip away when her guard was down.

"So if we can't get in, what's your plan?"

Lana looked around, like she was afraid someone might overhear. "Let's head back to the car."

As soon as the doors were closed, she spoke again. "Let me talk to the FBI. With the evidence we have, plus the burner phone and the meet set up for later, we should have enough to convince them to set up a sting."

Right.

Because law enforcement moved so fast. They'd execute the sting in two weeks when Araceli's body turned up in some parking garage.

Play along.

"Then I guess we better get back to the pirate ship so you can give them a call."

The drive back felt like it took forever. After finding a parking spot on the street a short distance from their hotel, they headed up to the room.

"Can I borrow your laptop?"

Lana cast a sideways glance at him. "Sure. Just let me unlock it."

After punching in her password, she slid the computer over to him. A quick search and his plan solidified.

There was a sporting goods store three miles away, kind of in the direction he needed to go.

Now to sneak out of here.

Lana was on the phone, so she wouldn't pay much attention to what he was doing. It seemed unlikely Paul would try to stop him, especially if he came up with a believable cover.

"I'm gonna run down to the restaurant and get a pizza to go. Want anything else?"

Paul glanced up from his phone. "Nah, that sounds good."

"Okay. Let Lana know I'll be back soon."

He grabbed his wallet, glanced at Paul, then at Lana, and snuck the car keys into his pocket.

Good thing he'd opted to leave the serum and syringes in the trunk earlier.

As the elevator descended to the lobby, he expected someone to stop him. How, he didn't know. But he wouldn't be too surprised to find Lana rappelling down the shaft and dropping through the hatch above his head.

The doors slid open.

He stepped into the lobby and headed down a hallway to the side exit they'd used earlier. The door banged closed behind him.

It was almost too easy.

Well, he better enjoy it now, because the rest of the night was going to be much trickier.

That took way too long.

Lana ended the call and looked at the display on her phone.

Thirty three minutes. Seriously.

And what did she have to show for it? A big fat nothing.

Dimitrios wasn't in sight, but Paul looked up from the

sofa. Sighing, she sank down beside him.

He placed his arm along the back of the sofa, his fingers softly massaging the base of her neck. "You're sure tense."

He turned her around so her back was to him and kneaded the muscles.

The knots slowly eased. Almost of its own accord, her body relaxed under his gentle fingers.

A sigh leaked from her. "Dealing with the FBI will do that to you."

"Don't I know it." His tone was grim. No doubt remembering his own experiences with the FBI last year, experiences that had almost cost him his life. "Did you get them on board?"

"No." The word hung between them for a few seconds. "They haven't had time to completely process the information Barker sent over, but I was assured they're working on it."

"What about Araceli? They know the trade is supposed to happen tonight, right?"

"They need proof. I guess that list has a few judges' names on it. Even if they go to another judge, they need more than hearsay to get a warrant."

"You saw them take Araceli. That wasn't good enough for them?"

"I didn't actually see them. I know there were people in my house and that Araceli and the baby were gone when they left, but I didn't see them force her into the van. More importantly, I have no proof that they work for Bobby."

Honestly, doing it Dimitrios' way would sure be easier right now.

But she'd meant what she said. If they stooped to operating at Bobby's level, it made them no better than Bobby.

God, please help me.

"Sooo..." Paul drew her against him, wrapping an arm loosely around her waist. His breath moved her hair, tickling her ear. "Not to change the subject, but how about this wedding?"

The last of her tension dispersed as she rested her back against his chest and let him support her. "Honestly, I'd love something small and simple. Maybe only family, a few close friends, and the kids from the home."

"I didn't know that was an option. You know, with your dad being a pastor and all."

It did complicate things a little. The church would love to be there to celebrate with them. As much as she cared about the people in the body, many of whom had watched her grow up, she wasn't sure she wanted something that big. "It's still our day. What would you like?"

"I don't care. As long as you're there, that's all that matters to me."

The rhythmic rise and fall of his chest behind her back was soothing. Not only could she close her eyes and sleep right now, but she could get used to this.

"That and it being soon." A laugh rumbled through the chest beneath her.

"Is April too far away?"

"Well, it is four months." She felt him rest his head on top of hers, his voice close to her ear. "But I've waited for you for years. What's another few months?"

"It does take some time to plan a wedding. Even a simple one."

Silence descended, but she didn't need words. It felt so good to simply be held, especially in light of all that had happened the last few days.

Thank you, God.

Paul was one of the few men who could understand her work without being a part of it. More than that, he could deal with the stress and fallout when things didn't go well. He'd proven that already.

Now, if they could only save Araceli. And all make it out unscathed. Too bad Mitri was a bit of a loose cannon right now.

She understood, but it made her job, the job of keeping

everyone alive, much harder.

Where was Mitri, anyway? It'd been quite a while since she saw him.

"Did Mitri tell you where he was going?" Her question sounded loud in the quiet room.

"Something about grabbing dinner downstairs. He said he'd order a pizza and bring it back up here."

Made sense. They certainly wouldn't have time to eat later.

She looked at the clock beside the bed. It'd been twenty minutes since she'd gotten off the phone with the FBI. While she hadn't seen him leave, she didn't remember seeing him the entire time she'd been on the phone. "How long ago was that?"

"I don't know. Right after you called the FBI, I think."

He'd been gone almost an hour.

Alarms blared in her head. She bolted upright.

Something was wrong. She could feel it. Every last instinct screamed at her.

Had Bobby's guys snagged him?

Think. Think. That meet was set up for later. What would be the point of grabbing Mitri? It was a high risk move when he was going to come to them on his own.

It made more sense that he had chosen to disappear.

Her eyes shot to the top of the dresser, where she'd last seen the car keys.

Gone. No sign of his wallet either.

No!

She snagged her phone from the table and brought up Araceli's number. The other end rang four times before going to voice mail.

Maybe he couldn't answer. She punched in a text and waited.

No response.

Oh, Mitri. What have you done?

She scrambled off the sofa and snagged her shoes. "He's

going solo. And he's going to get himself killed."

* * * * *

The industrial district was creepy after dark.

A chill chased up Dimitrios' back as he surveyed the deserted streets. Semi-trailers hovered like specters, casting shadows big enough to hide an army.

Man, he could probably be shot for simply being in this part of town after dark.

Although that would require another living being, something he had yet to see.

Nothing moved. Heck, he'd even welcome a rat. Just so he knew something lived in this neighborhood.

The newly purchased backpack filled with equally new supplies dug into his back, one of the prongs on the grappling hook poking his spine. He shifted the load and zeroed in on the warehouse.

His watch showed that it was a little after six. Almost an hour early. With any luck, he'd surprise them.

A dark SUV was parked at the base of the stairs leading to the keypad-entry door. He hoped that meant they were already here. More than that, he hoped they had Araceli with them.

Okay. Now to see if he could get the drop on them.

The alley he hid in was one block up from the warehouse, far enough that the cameras shouldn't see him cross the street. Shooting a glance up and down the street, he raced across, ducking into another alley.

He stopped and listened, waiting for a slamming door, shouting, someone to yell his name, any indication that he'd been seen.

Nothing.

A minute ticked by. Then another.

Still no sound except the distant rumble of traffic a few blocks away.

He eased down the alley, keeping his back to the wall of a meat packing warehouse. Shadows welcomed him like an old friend.

No sign of any cameras here. But there was a fire escape.

Stopping beneath it, he set his backpack on the ground and rummaged inside, pulling out the grappling hook and climbing rope he'd purchased at the sporting goods store earlier.

He tossed the hook up, caught the lowest rung on the ladder, and pulled it down.

Pain shot through his ribcage.

He ground his teeth. Better get used to it because it was only going to get worse.

The ladder clattered to the blacktop, echoing between the buildings like a barrage of gunfire at midnight.

If anyone was outside right now, there was no way they wouldn't have heard that.

He freed the hook and scaled the ladder. It rattled back up as he stepped onto the metal grated landing of the fire escape.

He pressed his back to the wall and listened.

No sound of anyone coming.

But they wouldn't necessarily announce their presence, especially not if they were armed.

Get to the roof. Before anyone entered the alley and saw him.

He ran up the stairs, trying to be quick but quiet, failing at both. At least there were only four flights of stairs to the roof. He pulled himself over the edge and collapsed on the roof, his heart exploding in his chest and his breath coming in short, frozen puffs.

The cold burned his lungs.

He listened, but all he could hear was the thundering of his heart and the wheezing of his breaths.

Still, if someone was climbing that metal escape, he'd hear them. It wasn't possible to stay quiet. He'd learned that truth firsthand.

Minutes passed. His breathing evened out and his heart slowed.

How was he doing on time? He checked his watch. 6:23. Not bad.

The note he'd left Lana gave him until 7:10.

Hopefully she'd find the car. He'd purposely parked it in the same place they'd left it earlier.

What would he do if she didn't find it? If she didn't find the car and the note, he wouldn't have the backup he was counting on her to bring.

He'd truly be on his own.

Well, he couldn't worry about that now. For now, he needed to get to Araceli.

He pushed up and crossed the roof, looking down on the building next door. Bobby's building, rented to Harrington Industries. The place where he'd trade the files in his backpack for Araceli.

And hopefully not die in the process.

You're not ready to die.

The words, spoken in Mike's voice, flooded his mind. How many times had Mike said that to him? Too many to count. And usually on the heels of a conversation about God.

He pushed the memories aside.

There was too much to do in a very short time. He couldn't get caught up in the past.

He studied the roof across from him. The building he stood on was a story taller than Bobby's warehouse, giving him a clear view of the roof.

The nearly full moon cast a ghostly glow across the area.

A door rose from an enclosure at one corner of the roof. A floodlight above the door and the camera beside it promised that they would see him coming.

Could he cover the camera with the black drawstring bag he'd purchased without being seen?

Depended upon how vigilant the security guards were.

It didn't matter. He'd come too far to turn back now.

If they saw him coming, then they saw him coming. He couldn't do anything about that. All he could do was be ready to use those syringes.

Man, did he hope they performed like Celeste and Araceli had promised.

Now to see if he could snag something with this grappling hook.

He checked the knot securing the rope to the hook, then wound up and released.

Pain ripped up his core. The breath vanished from his lungs. Man. Those guys did a number on him. Normally throwing one of these things wouldn't have bothered him.

He forced Araceli's face into his mind. If he could save her, it'd be worth the pain.

The first toss missed the building all together.

The second one hit the roof but didn't catch anything.

In fact, there wasn't much to catch on. Just the edge of the building. The structure with the door was too far away. And the fire escape was on the opposite side of the roof.

He threw again. And again. And again.

This was hopeless.

He wrapped an arm around his throbbing midsection and doubled over. Was there a better way to get into that building?

Maybe he could jump it. If he got a really good running start, he might make it.

He surveyed the distance.

Too risky.

There was probably ten feet between the buildings. Gravity was a harsh reality and a fall from this height, onto asphalt, would be fatal.

Trying to catch the edge of the building was still his best chance.

Maybe his only one.

He heaved in a deep breath and threw the hook again. It landed on the roof. He slowly drew it back.

The hook scraped across the roof, bumped the stone edge, and caught.

What?

He pulled on the rope.

It held.

He pulled harder.

It still held.

Yes! Finally something was going right.

Now to find something to tie the rope to on this building.

The fire escape on the other side looked like the most solid choice.

The rope barely stretched to it. He secured it with a knot, then walked back to the other edge of the roof and stared at the rope stretching across open space.

Just like climbing a mountain.

Except he had no one spotting him.

He sucked in a deep breath, put on the backpack, and sat on the edge of the roof, his legs dangling over open space.

Now for the real test.

Would the grappling hook hold under his weight?

He grabbed the rope and slid off the edge.

The rope sagged, but held firm.

Going hand over hand, he dangled above the alley below.

Waves of agony radiated from his core. Even breathing was a chore as each breath shot pain through his body.

Only a little further. He could do this.

He had no other choice.

In spite of the cold, sweat trickled between his shoulder blades. More dripped down his forehead, running into his eyes.

He blinked rapidly.

Almost there…

His legs bumped the concrete wall.

One hand slapped the roof's ledge, his fingers hunting for a handhold. There.

He dug his fingers in, then let go of the rope with his

other hand and searched for another handhold.

Muscles burned as he pulled his body up. His shoes scraped against the wall, providing little relief to his aching arms. His chest cleared the edge.

Pivoting his hips, he swung his right leg up, his foot smacking the ledge.

A groan escaped him. He pushed through the pain and pulled his body up inch by painful inch.

He rolled.

The roof was hard beneath him, but he didn't think anything had ever felt better. He'd made it.

Muscles quaked. His stomach rolled like a roller coaster and for a minute he thought he was going to spew the six ibuprofen he'd swallowed earlier across the roof.

He waited a few minutes for his stomach to settle and his muscles to calm, then pushed to his knees.

Time? 6:45.

That had put him significantly behind schedule.

He pulled the black bag from his backpack and skirted the edge of the roof, approaching the camera from behind.

The angled roof on the structure made it easy to climb up. Dropping to his stomach, he looked over the edge of the roof and slipped the bag over the camera.

Okay. Now to see how well he had retained Paul's lock-picking instructions.

The floodlight clicked on as he approached the door. Funny. The light was a security measure but now it actually helped him see what he was doing.

No deadbolt. Surprising, but helpful.

It took several tries, and probably four times as long as it would've taken Paul, but the knob finally clicked.

He swapped his tools with several syringes, stuffing a few of the cable ties he'd picked up into his pockets.

Well, this was as ready as he was going to get.

He swung the door open and stepped inside enemy territory.

Twenty Two

Florescent lights buzzed above his head. Dimitrios glanced around the stairwell as he eased the rooftop door closed behind him.

It was pretty narrow. Worse, there wasn't any place to hide. If someone came at him, he'd have to take them head on.

He looked at the ceiling.

No sign of cameras in here.

Slightly shocking, but he'd take whatever advantage he could get.

He scrambled down the stairs, his shoes squeaking on the concrete. At least they weren't metal or he'd be making enough noise to wake the dead.

Although he wasn't sure it mattered.

That door was sure to have been alarmed. No doubt they already knew someone had broken in.

It wouldn't take a genius to figure out it was him.

A door banged from below him.

He froze.

Footsteps pounded. How many?

He couldn't tell.

It sounded like more than one person.

He eased down to the bottom of the flight he currently stood on and stopped two steps up, plastering his back against the wall.

With any luck, those guys would come barreling around

the corner.

He pulled four syringes from his back pocket and removed the protective caps. Three went in his left hand, one in his right.

The footsteps drew closer. Heavy breathing accompanied them.

These guys weren't going for stealth.

Movement!

A man burst around the corner.

He stabbed the syringe into the man's neck and depressed the plunger.

The man's eyes widened and he jerked his gun hand up. Dimitrios drove his fist down on the man's arm, connecting solidly with the radius.

Not enough force to break bone, but a spasm twitched the man's hand and the gun clattered to the floor.

The man's legs buckled.

Good. The serum was taking effect.

He pushed the man backward, right into another armed man.

As the two fell, Dimitrios dove, driving the syringe into the second man's neck.

The man fought, but with the weight of the first man on him, couldn't get the leverage to fight effectively.

The gun slid from the second man's fingers.

Silence shrouded him, dominating the space as though it contained a distinct personality.

Neither man moved. Their eyes were open, mouths slack.

They looked dead.

It was creepy, really.

He touched their necks. A pulse beat back, steady and strong.

Good. The last thing he wanted was to have to perform life-saving techniques on them.

After putting the protective caps back on the two unused syringes, he removed some of the zip ties from his pocket and bound their hands behind their backs. Next he bound their feet, then connected the two. Lastly, he removed a roll of duct tape from his bag and ripped off two pieces, putting them firmly over the men's mouths.

Now if the serum wore off before he was ready for it to, these guys couldn't come to the aid of their friends.

A radio squawked from one of the men's belts.

"Conner? Patten? Report."

He snatched the two-way radio. What did Conner or Patten sound like?

Wait. He studied the men in front of him. Yeah. That first guy had been at Lana's. And he'd had a bit of a whiny voice.

He could work with that.

"False alarm." The fewer words, the better.

No response.

Did they know?

After another agonizing second, the radio crackled again. "Roger that."

Phew. They'd bought it.

Or maybe they were playing him while more men headed this way.

He needed to get out of this stairwell.

The radio was a gift, though. At least he'd be able to hear them talking. Assuming they used it.

He continued down the stairs, pausing at each corner. Now that he knew how easy it was to ambush someone, no point in being foolish.

No doors led out of the stairwell, not until he reached the main level.

He put his hand on the door handle, stood off to the side, and eased it open a crack.

When the door didn't fly toward him, he inched it open a little further.

A hallway yawned in front of him.

He stepped through the doors and looked up and down the hall. To his left, a single occupancy bathroom and a janitor's closet. To his right, a short hallway that turned sharply to the left.

How many guys were there in this place? He needed to level the playing field as much as possible.

Maybe he could trap them all in the stairwell. It beat taking them on one-by-one.

He studied the door. No good. It had a crash bar but no handle, so he couldn't wedge it closed.

Okay then. Time to see what he was up against.

He slipped down the hallway and peered around the corner. The hallway spilled into a large, open warehouse.

Wrapped pallets lined one wall. Large machines dotted the center of the room. A forklift waited idly to his right.

A glass-walled office dominated the space directly across from him. Half a dozen monitors showed images of the street, loading dock, main door, and warehouse floor.

Four guys hung out inside.

He slipped back. He couldn't take them all. Not at the same time.

With that camera watching the interior of the warehouse, he also couldn't leave this hallway. So how could he get one or two of those guys to come to him?

He needed a ruse.

Maybe that camera he covered up?

He knelt down, keeping his attention on the security office, and pulled out the radio.

Now for the whiny voice again. "Can't get this camera working. Can one of you come take a look?"

The men in the security office looked at each other. One guy shook his head while another spoke into the radio. "I'm on my way."

The radio guy rose from his chair and headed for the door.

Okay. One guy. It leveled the playing field a little.

Dimitrios retreated to the janitor's closet and stepped inside, leaving the door cracked slightly. It was barely enough for him to see the entrance to the stairwell.

Heavy footfalls echoed up the hallway, accompanied by some unintelligible mumbling.

He pulled out a syringe and removed the cap.

The footsteps drew closer. A shadow crept across the floor.

A man filled his line of sight.

He pushed the door open and launched himself at the man, jabbing the needle into the man's neck.

"Hey!" The man's voice echoed down the hallway even as his legs gave out.

The radio crackled to life. "Anthony?"

Should he pretend to be Anthony? What would happen if Anthony didn't respond?

There were 3 guys in that office. One of them would stay put to watch the monitors, no question, but the other two might come.

He could handle two guys.

Pulling zip ties from his pocket, he lashed Anthony's hands and feet together.

Static sparked from the radio. "Anthony. Everything okay?"

He dragged Anthony into the stairwell, leaving him a few feet inside the opening, then stepped back into the hallway.

Footsteps pounded from the direction of the warehouse.

He slipped back into the janitor's closet and pulled out two more syringes.

Three down, three to go. And then he'd go after Bobby.

⁂

"Stop!" The seat belt cut into Lana's shoulder as Paul slammed the brakes.

Okay, maybe she should've been a little less dramatic.

"That's the car." She pointed to a parking lot on their left, the same one they'd parked in earlier that day.

Sitting alone under a streetlight was the rental Dimitrios had driven off in earlier.

She clenched her jaw. When she got her hands on him….

Paul turned their new rental car into the lot and pulled up alongside.

The car was empty.

Not that she'd expected to find him sitting there waiting. No, she knew exactly what he was doing. Breaking into that warehouse on his own.

Cavalier behavior that would end with someone's death. Likely his.

Thoughts swirled. Had he left the car here purposefully? So she'd find something inside? Or had it simply been a convenient option?

She opened the door and approached the vehicle. The doors were all locked, but she could see a note on the dash with her name on it.

Why would he lock the doors?

The answer came to her before the question finished forming. Because he knew she was with someone who could pick a lock.

But how could he know that for certain?

Didn't matter. She needed inside that vehicle. And if Mitri was expecting them to break in, he probably hadn't armed the alarm, either.

She turned back to Paul. The driver's window was already down.

"Feel like picking a lock?" Well. That was something she'd never imagined asking her fiancé.

His eyebrows jumped but he quickly recovered. "Sure."

After putting the window up, he turned off the engine and climbed out. She watched him work. It took longer than breaking a window, but much less time than it would've taken her.

He opened the door a few seconds later and handed her the note.

It was written on a notepad with the hotel's logo on one side. Obviously took it from their room, which meant he'd been planning this all along.

If he lived through the encounter with Bobby, he might not survive her.

She flipped the paper over and read it aloud.

"Lana. Sorry to do it this way, but I couldn't risk you and Paul. I've got a plan and I'm inside. I'll call you by 7:10. If you haven't heard from me by then, something's wrong and you should call in the cavalry. See you later."

7:10.

She glanced at her watch.

It was 7:03 now.

"What do you want to do?" Paul's voice sounded loud in the empty night.

Wait? Or go in?

If she waited until after 7:10, she could make a good case for her entry. The certainty that someone inside was in peril should stand up in court.

But Mitri could be dead by then.

He might already be dead.

It was only five minutes away. She sighed. "Let's get to the warehouse. We'll wait until after 7:10."

Paul locked both vehicles, then they slipped across the street and into the closest alley.

As much as she hated that Paul was involved, right now it felt really good to know he had her back.

Chills chased each other around her body. Partly from the cold, but not entirely.

Death hovered over the neighborhood. Which was ridiculous. Besides, there had to be life for death to occur and so far, she and Paul were the only living people she'd seen.

They stopped in the alley across the street from the warehouse and watched the front of the building. Two vehicles, one a black SUV and one a luxury sedan, parked in front of the loading doors.

People were definitely here.

She checked her phone. No missed calls. Still two minutes to go, though.

The phone wasn't going to ring.

She knew it in her gut, just like she'd known they were being watched earlier.

One unanswered question lingered in her mind. She might as well get the truth while they waited. "So how'd Mitri know you could pick that lock?"

Even though she'd whispered, her voice still seemed way too loud.

"Lucky guess?"

While the explanation was logical, his tone gave him away. She stared at him.

Paul shifted. "I, uh, might've shown him how to pick a lock."

He *what*? This whole mess was his fault! If Paul hadn't shown him how to get inside, Mitri wouldn't have been able to go off on his own like this. "How could you do that?"

"I told him no at first, but then he asked what I'd do if it were you." Paul lifted his hands in a helpless gesture. "I couldn't say no then. If it was you in there, there's nothing I wouldn't do."

She fought to hang onto the anger, but found it slipping away faster than evidence in a rainstorm.

Dimitrios had known exactly what buttons to push to get Paul's help.

This wasn't Paul's fault. Even though he'd provided the means, the blame still rested solely upon Dimitrios' big shoulders.

"Are you mad?" It was too dark to see Paul's expression clearly, but hesitation marked the words.

"Furious." She kept her tone dry. "He would've done this with or without your help. At least this way he might've made it inside without drawing a lot of attention. Where was I when you taught him the finer points of breaking and entering?"

"Running. In Lincoln City."

Figured. Mitri had intentionally waited until she wasn't around.

She looked at her phone again. 7:13. Still no phone call.

Grrr.

What should she do?

She had no proof Mitri was in trouble, only his unfulfilled promise to call. She couldn't even concretely prove that he was in that warehouse.

While she could go up and push the buzzer by the door, those men knew who she was. She'd be setting herself up to be used as a pawn.

Or worse, they'd shoot her.

But she didn't see another way in.

She handed Paul her phone. "Okay, here's the plan. You wait here. I'll go ring the buzzer. When they take me at gunpoint, call the FBI. It's the last call–"

"Yeah, not gonna happen."

Naturally he'd push back. "If you have a better idea, I'd love to hear it, but we're out of time."

"I'll go. You call for backup."

If he thought she'd agree to that, he didn't know her nearly as well as she thought he did. "No. I'm the one with the training."

"And I'm the one with the background. I'm used to dealing with jerks like this."

"So am I." She sighed. "Paul, please. You know me. I can talk my way through impossible situations."

"You can't talk your way out of a bullet."

"By now they probably know I'm law enforcement. They're going to see me as leverage so they'll be less likely to shoot me."

"Less likely, but not guaranteed."

"We don't have any guarantees right now. But face it. We're up against a group of thugs. Who are they going to view as more of a threat? Me or you?"

The answer was so obvious that neither of them voiced it. A six-foot-one solidly built man or a five-foot-four petite woman?

Although if they really knew her, they'd take her more seriously.

He pulled her into his arms. "I can't lose you."

The words were whispered into her hair, his breath warm on the top of her head. "You won't. God's numbered my days, remember? I don't think that number is up today. But if we don't act now, we might lose Mitri and I can't handle that. Please. Just trust me."

His arms tightened briefly and he pressed a kiss against her head. "Go. And come back alive."

Cold closed around her as his arms dropped. "When you call, be sure to say that I'm a US Marshal who needs immediate assistance."

"Okay. But if they take too long, I'm coming in after you."

As much as she wanted to argue, she knew it wouldn't do any good.

She turned and hurried across the street, a prayer on her tongue.

Please, Lord. Don't make me a liar. Protect me and Mitri. And get us all out of this warehouse alive.

Shadows reached for him. A few more feet and he'd see who he was up against.

Two men crossed into his vision. Only two.

Dimitrios threw the door open and lunged, a syringe in each hand. He jammed the needle into the men's necks simultaneously.

The serum flowed into their bodies and their weapons clattered to the floor.

Sweat dripped into his eyes as the men collapsed. Whether from exertion or stress, he didn't know. All he knew was that the clock still ticked.

He dropped to his knees beside the men and secured their hands and feet.

No point in dragging them into the stairwell.

Which was good. Those ibuprofen had taken the edge off the pain, but after the physical toil of this last hour, his whole body throbbed.

That last dude wasn't likely to come after him. No, he'd have to bring the fight to whoever might be left. Hopefully there was only the one guy, but there could've been someone else he hadn't seen.

And there was still Bobby. Somewhere.

"Hey!"

He started as the radio squawked.

"Someone's here! It's… it's… that chick who shot Smitty!"

Chick? Had to be Lana. What was she doing?

He looked at his watch.

Dang it. He was late.

She wasn't supposed to arrive until after he'd subdued everyone. Now she was walking right into the line of fire.

He had to get to Bobby.

These guys didn't do anything without Bobby's approval. They certainly wouldn't shoot a US Marshal unless Bobby told them to.

The only way to protect Lana was to head straight to the source.

At least now the last security guy would be distracted.

He raced down the short hallway, skidding to a stop at the entrance to the warehouse.

The last remaining guard approached the exterior door. The security room was empty.

So where was Bobby?

He scanned the walls. There must be an office, a storage room, heck, a company break room. Someplace where Bobby was holed up with Araceli.

There!

On the wall to his left, drawn mini blinds covered a large window. Light filtered around and through them.

No time to waste on indecision.

He sprinted toward the door, pausing for a second before throwing it open.

A desk took up the center of the room. A man with carefully styled brown hair looked up as he burst inside. Wire-rimmed glasses, smooth face, pressed shirt.

This was Bobby?

The man looked more like a politician than a mobster. Not even the leather jacket he wore could harden the soft appearance.

If his sudden entrance surprised the man, he didn't show it. Instead, he rose slowly, a gun appearing in his hands as if by magic. "How did you get past my men?"

Dimitrios' gaze bounced around the room. Empty except for the two of them. "Where's Araceli?"

"You didn't really think I'd bring her here, did you?"

"We had an agreement!"

"Please. Like I would trust you to uphold your end. Now. Where are my men?"

"Tied up." Think, think! He had to find Araceli. "So now what? Do you call someone to bring her?"

"No. Now I shoot you, take my file, then dispose of her."

There had to be a way out of this! Maybe if he could stall long enough, Lana would be able to do something. "But you said–"

"Get real." Bobby shrugged his shoulders. "Don't you know the Vegas motto? The house always wins."

"I wouldn't count on that." Dimitrios swallowed hard. His chest was tight and his muscles begged to move, but he forced himself to remain still. "I brought a *copy* of the file. The original is with a friend, a friend who has instructions to deliver it to the cops if he doesn't see me and Araceli by eight tonight."

Bobby stared at him for a long second. "I don't believe

you." The tone was cold, but lacked conviction.

"I've got it right here." Dimitrios jerked his thumb toward his backpack. "I can show you."

A curt nod answered. "No sudden movements or tricks. I've got a hair trigger aimed at your head and I'm an excellent shot."

Shrugging off the backpack, Dimitrios knelt beside it. His mind whirled. He needed to get that gun away.

Or incapacitate the gun hand.

The serum was the obvious answer but he couldn't use it. Not until he got Araceli's location.

Hmmm.

What would happen if he injected a little, maybe half a cc, directly into Bobby's gun hand?

He had no doubt it would paralyze the hand, but would it spread further than he wanted it to?

Well, if it did, he'd at least have time to tie Bobby up and gain the upper hand.

Now the only question remaining was if he could do it before Bobby could get a shot off.

He pulled out the manila envelope containing the copies and used it to conceal the syringe he grabbed with his other hand. He rose and advanced toward the desk.

"Slowly."

The caution stalled his steps for a heartbeat.

Extending the file, he edged forward, thumbing the cap off the syringe as he moved closer.

He dropped the file on the desk.

Bobby's gaze flicked down to it.

Now!

Twisting aside, Dimitrios sprung forward, thrusting the needle into Bobby's gun hand and pushing the plunger.

"Aaah!" Bobby's holler mingled with the blast from his gun, both echoing in the confined space.

The bullet shattered the window, but missed him.

Dimitrios pulled the syringe out and jumped back.

A spasm flexed Bobby's hand. The gun clattered to the desk.

Dimitrios charged, his fingers curling around the weapon's grip.

"What did you do to me?" Bobby's words shook. Whether from rage, fear, or pain, Dimitrios couldn't tell, although if the reddening of Bobby's face was any indication, rage was the primary driver.

"Poison." A bit of an exaggeration, but who cared? He leveled the gun at Bobby. "Now unless–"

A crash came from the warehouse.

Uh-oh. He'd forgotten about the other guy. And Lana.

Bang!

The sound reverberated. It took a second to register, but when it did, his stomach clenched.

That was a gunshot!

Twenty Three

Lana hit the buzzer again.

Come on.

They were in there. She knew it. So why weren't they coming after her?

Maybe Mitri had met with success. If he'd incapacitated all of Bobby's guys, that might explain why no one was responding.

Or it might mean that Bobby's guys were busy beating the pulp out of Mitri. Heavens knew they'd tried that before.

Either way, she had to get in there.

She stepped back and looked around.

Okay, so this was a contingency she hadn't planned on. Now what?

Pretend to pick the lock? She didn't think she could actually do it, but maybe if they saw her messing with it, they'd open the door.

The door flew open. She jumped back, narrowly avoiding the swing of solid steel.

A gun filled her vision.

She swallowed hard.

It was all well and good to talk a tough game, but it was a little different to look down the barrel of a gun. One wrong twitch and it'd all be over.

"You!" The man behind the gun spit the word at her. Narrowed eyes glared out of a crimson face. His jaw repeatedly clenched and unclenched. "You killed my nephew!"

The roar of the words echoed in the still night.

Nephew? The body on her driveway clicked into her mind like a bad photograph.

Uh-oh. She hadn't banked on a family connection.

Although she should have. Wasn't that the way things went with the mob?

She straightened and jutted her chin forward. "I'm here to see Bobby."

"Oh, you'll see 'im all right. He'll be the last thing you see 'fore I put a bullet in you." He waved her inside. "Move."

She edged through the door, keeping her gaze focused on the gun.

Okay, God. I might need even more help than I'd thought.

The door slammed closed.

Hopefully Paul was on the phone with the FBI right now. From the look on this guy's face, she didn't have more than a few minutes.

Using the gun to point, he motioned her forward.

She flicked her eyes across the warehouse. Pallets loaded down with boxes. A forklift. Some large machinery.

If they got close enough to any of those things, she might be able to use them to her advantage.

A crack in the floor caught the toe of her shoe. She stumbled.

A hand closed around her arm, squeezing like a vise, and jerked her up to almost eye level. "No funny business."

Spittle splatted her face.

He tossed her to the ground.

A gunshot echoed in the warehouse. Somewhere behind her, glass shattered.

Had she been shot?

No. No pain.

Mitri? She had to get to him!

The man towering over her looked toward some point on

the far side of the room.

It was now or never.

Pushing into a crouch, she launched herself at his legs.

He flailed backward, throwing his arms to the side to try to catch his balance.

She went at him again, this time connecting her shoulder with his solar plexus.

The momentum drove them against a partially loaded pallet. A stack of boxes went flying as the man crashed into it.

She curled her fingers around his gun hand, driving the weapon up.

Bang!

The blast echoed in her ears as the recoil jolted down her arm. At least the recoil was the only effect she'd felt from that shot.

The bullet went wild, pinging off metal somewhere.

The man roared, his breath hot and rancid against her face. He pushed against her hold, slowly bringing the gun down.

No way could she outmuscle him.

She drove her knee up as hard as she could.

A gasp, then a moan, confirmed she'd hit her target. The man curled over. His grip on the gun loosened and she twisted it away from his fingers.

Her gaze danced around the room. Where was everyone? Why hadn't anyone come running at the sound of the gunshot?

Scooting backward a few steps, she leveled the gun at him. "Take me to Bobby."

The man moaned, his knees connecting with the concrete beneath their feet.

It didn't look like she was going to get anything from him.

She dug her handcuffs out and forced his arms behind his back, looping the chain around one of the slats on the pallet. It wouldn't be the most comfortable, but she really wasn't concerned with his comfort.

Okay, now to find Bobby. And hopefully Mitri and Araceli.

ꙮ ꙮ ꙮ ꙮ ꙮ

What should he do? Half of him wanted to check on Lana, but the rest of him wanted to force a location out of Bobby.

He couldn't do both.

Or could he?

He waved the gun toward the door. "You're going to tell your guy to stand down. Go."

Bobby didn't remove his focus from his paralyzed hand. "What did you do to me?"

"You oughta be more concerned about what I'm *going* to do to you if you don't cooperate. Now move!" Jerking his head toward the door, he shifted to his left so he could keep both Bobby and the door in his line of sight.

"You're a dead man, you know that?" With his right hand hanging limp, Bobby hardly looked like a menace. "My guys will kill you before you can blink."

"What guys?"

Lana's voice came from the doorway as she stepped into sight.

No visible blood. Her color looked good and the gun in her hand was steady.

The bullet hadn't hit her.

Tension seeped from him. Man, what a relief. Now he could focus on Ari.

"You good?" The question was directed at Lana, even as he narrowed his eyes on Bobby.

"Yes. The guy out there, not so much."

Was he dead? She didn't elaborate and now wasn't the time to ask.

He focused all his attention on Bobby. "You're out of options. Where. Is. Araceli?"

Bobby pressed his lips together.

If he knew Lana, the FBI was on its way now. He had to get Bobby talking before they showed up.

But Bobby wouldn't be one to respond to forceful tactics.

Maybe if he played it cool.

He shrugged. "Suit yourself. I've got all night. You, on the other hand, have poison flowing through your body."

Bobby's eyes flicked down to his hand before returning to Dimitrios.

Was that a crack in the tough façade? "Did you know that a drop of the Peruvian Violet can kill a horse? Yeah, me neither, but Araceli is an expert on poisonous plants. She's been perfecting this particular poison. I know, whacked hobby, right?"

"Liar." Bobby tried to cross his arms over his chest, but the paralyzed hand hung like an anchor. Planting his good hand on the desk in front of him, he leaned forward. "You should work on your poker face."

He'd show him a poker face. "Can you feel it moving through your body? I'm sure it's moved up your arm already. By now your stomach's probably a little unsettled. Your legs should be getting weak soon. You might even feel like you need to take a leak."

Surely if he threw enough symptoms at the man, one or two of them would stick.

Bobby's Adam's apple jumped. His face lightened a shade and the hand braced against the desk wobbled.

"'Course, I could give you the antidote." Dimitrios pulled a fresh syringe from his pocket and held it up for Bobby to see. "Got it right here."

Silence.

He stuffed the syringe back in his pocket and held up the one he'd already injected in Bobby. "Or maybe I'll give you the rest of this. Hope you've settled your affairs with God, man, 'cause you're headed His way pretty soon."

"You're crazy." Bobby's attention shifted to Lana. "You're a cop. Aren't you going to stop him?"

"As far as I'm concerned, you were dead when I arrived. That gun makes a pretty good case for self-defense, don't you think?"

Bobby's snort sounded weak. "No one will ever buy that. This is my warehouse!"

"That you ordered him to come to. The recording we made of your call earlier is compelling."

Dang. That would've been smart. Why hadn't he thought to record that call earlier? It would've provided irrefutable evidence!

At least Bobby didn't know Lana was bluffing.

And Lana's poker face was excellent.

He made a show of checking his watch. "Ooh. Almost five minutes. I don't think anyone's survived beyond ten. Pretty soon you'll lose control of your bladder. Then your legs will give out. Your heart will stop pumping blood, but only after your lung muscles fail. I think suffocation is a particularly unpleasant way to die, don't you?"

Bobby collapsed in the chair, his body shaking like a twig in a hurricane. "Fine. I'll tell you. Just give me that antidote!"

"First, the location."

"34151 Broadway Blvd. Penthouse. It's Mitzi Harrington's place." The words spilled out. He gestured with his good hand. "Now, hurry!"

"How many guys do you have there?"

"None! Just Harrington!" He writhed in the chair. "The antidote. Please!"

Wouldn't his men be surprised to hear him begging?

Served him right. How many people had begged him for mercy but received none?

He looked at Lana, who had a gun trained on Bobby. "You got this?"

"Mitri, wait for the FBI. They should be here soon."

"Araceli might not have that kind of time. You have the address. Send them after me."

He brushed by her.

"Wait! You promised me the antidote!" Bobby's frantic cries followed him.

He ignored them.

"Relax. You'll be fine in a few minutes." Lana's voice came from behind his back.

Bummer. She should've made Bobby sweat it out. It would have been small punishment for all he'd done.

"Wha–what do you mean?"

"Peruvian Violet is a paralytic. Lasts a few minutes, but then wears off."

The silence lasted for three steps before Bobby's roar echoed through the warehouse. "I'm gonna kill you! All of you! You hear me, Lykos? You're a dead man!"

Yeah, he'd heard that before.

He jogged across the warehouse.

Movement drew his attention. A man jerked toward him, but the handcuffs securing him to a partially full pallet kept him from getting very far.

So Lana hadn't killed the man.

Good. He didn't want her to have that on her conscience. One body was enough for this week.

The door flew open and Paul burst in, gun leveled his direction.

The weapon slowly lowered as Paul registered no threats. "Where's Lana?"

"Covering Bobby." Dimitrios pointed to the office. "Another set of eyes might be good."

Paul broke into an awkward jog, heavily favoring his injured leg, as he passed Dimitrios.

Perfect. Now there was no one to stop him.

The night air bit at his skin as he stepped outside. Leaving the door open, he jumped off the landing, hit the ground, and raced down the block. By the time he reached the car, his breath came in wheezing gasps.

His lungs sure didn't like the cold.

Of course, with the injuries he'd sustained, he'd probably

be wheezing in ninety degree heat.

He started the car and cranked the heater, then opened the map app on Araceli's phone and punched in the address.

The past hour crashed over him while he waited for the app to load the address.

He'd broken into a secured warehouse.

Overcome five mob guys and a mob boss.

With flower serum, no less.

He'd gotten Araceli's location and gotten away without Lana stopping him.

Most importantly, no one had been hurt. Well, not seriously, anyway.

You did pray about it.

Where the thought came from, he wasn't sure, but it lodged in his mind. It was true. He'd asked God to prove Himself by bringing him through this alive.

So far, so good.

But they weren't in the clear yet.

The phone dinged. He looked down at the display.

The location was ten miles away.

Ten miles!

He had to get moving.

As he reached to turn on the headlights, three SUVs whipped down the street in front of him, emergency lights a silent blur as they streaked toward the warehouse.

That was an FBI motorcade if he'd ever seen one.

At least they hadn't seen him. If they had, he wouldn't be going anywhere.

Sure, the FBI would get to Harrington's place to rescue Araceli. Eventually. But he didn't trust them to act as quickly as they might need to.

That was up to him. Only him.

He turned on the lights, shifted into drive, and peeled out of the parking lot.

Hold on, Ari. I'm on my way.

ꟼ ꟼ ꟼ ꟼ ꟼ

The engine pinged softly as Dimitrios inspected the high-rise across the street. The building was at least a dozen stories tall. Light glowed from many of the windows on the upper floors, but blazed through the glass enclosed lobby straight ahead of him.

A manned security booth in the middle of the lobby discouraged access from anyone who shouldn't be there.

Well, he couldn't let that stop him.

Did the security guys know Bobby? If Bobby was a regular, then maybe saying he worked for Bobby would be enough to buy him access.

It was the only play he could think of.

He'd left his climbing equipment behind, so scaling the building wasn't an option.

Besides, someone would likely see him and phone it in. Residential was a little different than industrial.

He stepped into the darkness and hurried across the street.

The two guards at the booth looked up as he burst inside.

He flashed a grin. "Brrr. Good night to be inside, huh?"

The guards stared at him, faces impassive. The short, stocky guy on the left gave a quick dip of his chin. "What room?"

"Penthouse. Bobby sent me to collect something from Ms. Harrington."

The two exchanged a look.

So. They did know about Bobby.

"Let me call up to her."

No surprise there. The bigger question was whether or not she'd let him up.

The guard picked up the phone. Seconds dragged. He replaced it. "No answer."

"She didn't leave." The other guard muttered.

The first guard shot his partner a warning look before

facing Dimitrios head-on. "Sorry. You're not on the list."

Dimitrios pulled Araceli's phone from his pocket. "I better call Bobby. He's not gonna be happy that you wouldn't let me up there. You don't cross a Carpelli."

The guards exchanged another look.

Come on, guys. Don't call my bluff.

He had no idea what he'd do if they did. Fake a phone call and leave, probably. But that still left him with the issue of Araceli being upstairs and him being down here.

He could feel their speculation as he pretended to scroll through the contacts.

Would his split lip, bruised jaw, and swollen cheekbone work in his favor?

Or would it convince them that he was nothing but trouble?

The first guard tugged at his collar. "Well, uh, Bobby's on the list. I suppose we could make an exception. You know, since he sent you."

Wow. That worked?

He lowered the phone. "I know he'd appreciate it. He's most anxious for his… package."

The stocky guard moved out from behind the station. "Yeah, well, uh, Bobby's always welcome here. Guess that'd include people who work for him."

How often did Bobby come here?

He wasn't sure he even wanted to know the purpose behind Bobby's visits. Whatever the frequency and reason for them, these men knew Bobby.

And knew enough to be scared of him.

The guard put a key into a keyhole next to the elevator, then pushed the up button. The doors dinged softly and slid open. The guard stepped inside, slid his ID badge, and hit the button for the penthouse before stepping back out.

Dimitrios offered a solemn nod as the doors slid closed.

The elevator glided up.

Man, that was close.

He wracked his memory while the elevator ascended. What had Lana said about this Harrington woman?

An heiress. Ran the family business. Yeah, that's right. Some kind of publishing outfit or something. And wasn't there something about slot machines?

He probably should've paid better attention.

The elevator slid to a stop and the doors dinged.

Didn't matter who or what she was. After the guys he'd taken down in the last hour, he could handle one rich, spoiled heiress.

Assuming Bobby had been telling the truth about none of his guys being here.

He resisted the urge to pull out a syringe.

There were likely cameras covering the hallway. If those guards were watching - and he'd bet money they were - he didn't need to give them a reason to come up after him.

A short hallway stretched in front of him. A single door waited at the end.

He strode up to it like he imagined one of Bobby's goons would and pushed the doorbell.

Chimes echoed inside.

Then nothing.

She had to be here, right? Bobby wouldn't have left Ari alone in an unguarded apartment.

"Yes?"

He jumped as a woman's voice, soft and refined, came from a discreet speaker on the wall next to his head.

Wait. There was a tiny camera beside it.

He looked straight at the camera. "Bobby sent me for the woman."

A pause. "I don't know what you're talking about."

Could Bobby have played him?

No. The guards downstairs knew Bobby and were scared, so this was definitely the right place.

What was Bobby's end game where Araceli was concerned? He certainly hadn't planned to let her go.

But how much would Harrington know?

Enough. Bobby wouldn't have left Araceli here if Harrington was in the dark about what was going on.

"Said something about taking her for a long drive in the desert."

The pause felt longer this time. Then the door clicked. "Come in."

He pushed the door open, stepping into a softly lit room.

A cream colored leather sofa and two matching chairs stretched in front of a glass wall with ornate French doors set in the middle. An outdoor patio ran the length of the room. Even in the dark, he could see the outline of a hot tub and lush foliage, turning the patio into a desert oasis.

"You're not one of Bobby's men."

He whirled toward the voice.

A slender woman sat on a barstool, one elbow leaning on the counter. Her short black skirt revealed toned and shapely legs, and the lacy v-neck top dipped into generous cleavage. Her straight blonde hair brushed her shoulders, framing a face that had a pinched, narrow appearance.

So. Bobby didn't come here for the view from the patio.

Get it together!

He tore his eyes away from those legs and looked at her face.

That she had noticed his reaction was evident in the smug curl of her lips. That it was exactly the response she intended was obvious in the way she slowly rose from the stool and sashayed closer, swinging her properly proportioned hips as if to some silent rhythm.

"I, uh, I'm new. Bobby lost a guy in Florida so he called me in."

She stopped barely out of arm's reach and put one hand alongside her neck, fingers touching her chin. "Obviously."

"Bobby, uh, Bobby sent me to get the woman. Said he wants to erase all the evidence, you know?"

A perfectly shaped eyebrow arched over eyes the color of

frozen mountain lakes. "Did he?"

"Uh, yeah."

"Well, then. Let me go get her."

Harrington turned and moved toward the kitchen, her bare feet padding silently along the carpet.

A hallway stretched beyond it. That must be where she was holding Araceli.

She reached under the bar and whirled, a small pistol in her hands. "See, here's my issue. Bobby said he'd come personally."

"He, uh, got caught up in something."

Her thin lips pressed into a narrow line. "I know Bobby. He'd call and tell me he was sending someone."

"No time."

"Or he'd send Nicky, who knows better than to stare at someone who is way out of his league."

What an arrogant little… he bit back the words.

"Now. Who are you really?"

Keep pretending? Or level and hope she was more logical than Bobby had been?

Not likely. They were cast in the same mold, these two.

"Let me guess." Her words were crisp, containing a sharp edge. "Dimitrios Lykos? Here to rescue your little girlfriend?"

Okay. Obviously Bobby had told her everything.

Or at least enough to make her a full accomplice after the fact.

No point in pretending any longer. "Bobby's been arrested. His whole operation is going down. You really want to go down with him?"

She laughed, the sound high and tinny, like a broken windshield tinkling to the asphalt. "You truly have no idea who you're up against, do you? No one can touch Bobby Carpelli. They never have and never will."

"Until now." He stuffed his hands in his pocket, his fingers curling around a syringe.

Her light blue eyes turned to ice. "Don't count on it. Once

we get rid of you and your girlfriend, life will get back to normal."

Was she crazy? "The guards saw me come up here. You let me in. It's all on camera. You really think you can convince everyone I was never here?"

"I don't have to convince them of anything. You came up here under false pretenses and attacked me. I had to defend myself. Believe me when I tell you I can sell that story easily."

Trouble was, he did believe it.

No doubt everyone else would, too. She'd sell it all too well. "What about Araceli?"

"What about her? As you said, Bobby will take her for a drive in the desert. I'm guessing she'll never be found."

He pushed the cap off the syringe with his thumb and slowly drew his hands from his pocket, shielding the syringe from Harrington's sight.

So far, she hadn't racked the slide on the gun, so it wouldn't be ready to fire.

Unless a round was already in the chamber, in which case he'd be dead before he could move.

"The FBI's on their way here now. It's over."

"Let them come. Without a warrant they'll never make it inside the door."

"They don't need a warrant if they believe someone is in danger. My sister is at the warehouse with Bobby right now. She'll convince them."

She shook her head. "You really are naïve, aren't you? She'll end up in an interrogation room for hours."

"She's a US Marshal."

The words dropped like the bomb he'd intended.

Harrington's eyes narrowed. Pink rushed up her neck and into her cheeks. Her gun hand shook.

She racked the slide and cupped her other hand around the pistol. "Then we'd better get this over with quickly."

Move!

He dove as the weapon exploded.

Somewhere behind him glass shattered, but at least the bullet had missed him.

He pushed into a crouch and launched himself at Harrington.

Pounding came from somewhere in the apartment. The sound mingled with a woman's voice, muffled but recognizable. Ari!

Swinging around, Harrington sighted on him.

The blast echoed through the suite.

Something smacked into him. Pain ripped through his torso.

He'd been shot!

Twenty Four

Keep going. He had to inject her before she could get off another shot, one that would end him.

He drove the needle into her bare thigh and shoved down the plunger.

A scream shattered his eardrums.

Another gunshot detonated.

His ears rang, but no fresh pain accompanied the shot.

Thank God she'd missed.

Harrington crumpled to the floor, the gun tumbling from her china white fingers. Her deep red lips parted slightly and her eyes stared like the eyes of the dead, but her chest rose and fell steadily.

He'd done it. He'd beaten Bobby. Taken down Harrington. Finished Mike's mission.

Ari was safe. So was his family. And Lana and Paul.

Pain pulsed through his core.

Okay, so he hadn't come through unscathed. Better him than anyone else.

He sank to his knees and looked down. Blood oozed down his pants. He couldn't see the wound because of his jacket.

The fact that he registered the pain was a good sign. Shock was the enemy when it came to trauma.

The pounding from somewhere in the suite intensified.

Ari.

He struggled to his feet, wrapping an arm about his stomach. Wobbly legs carried him to the hall beyond the kitchen.

The pounding grew louder.

Several doors led off the hallway. They were all open except for the one at the end.

He trudged toward it.

Wave after wave of pain assaulted him. Black threatened the edges of his vision. His stomach rebelled and he dry heaved.

Stop and assess the wound! his mind screamed at him, but his heart moved him forward. More than anything, he needed to see Araceli for himself. Know she was okay.

How would he open the door?

He'd left his backpack in the car so he didn't have anything with him to pick the lock.

Hinges were on the inside so he couldn't lift the pins and remove the door. Could he bust the door down?

With a gunshot wound in his abdomen? Not likely.

He leaned heavily against the wall. They'd always said that abdomen wounds were among the most painful, but he hadn't known just how bad it would be.

Until today.

Next time he'd have a little more sympathy for people with trauma to their trunk.

"Is someone out there? Let me out!"

Araceli's words were clearer as he reached the door. He put a hand on the door, leaving bright red smears that marred the white paint. "Ari?"

"Mitri?" Sniffling reached through the hollow-core door. "Is that you?"

"Yeah. I don't know where the key is."

Surely Harrington would keep it close by, though. After all, she'd want easy access.

He looked into the room to his right and flicked on the lights. A king-sized bed dominated one wall, the covers in disarray. Black end tables adorned both sides of the bed and a flat screen TV was mounted on the wall.

No other surfaces. And no sign of a key.

Might be in one of the drawers on the end tables but he didn't have the energy to walk across the room to check.

Banging sounded from the apartment behind him. Men's voices.

"Ms. Harrington? Everything okay in there?"

The guards. One of the downstairs neighbors must've called in the gunshots.

What would the guards do when they came in and found her paralyzed? It probably wouldn't be pretty. He better find that key and get Ari out now.

He looked in the room on his left.

There! On the desk, just inside the doorway, a silver key waited. He snagged it, leaving more DNA behind, and returned to the locked door.

The key scraped in the lock.

The door flew open and Araceli burst out, flinging her arms around his neck.

"I thought they were going to kill me and I'd never see you again and then there were the gunshots and I was so scared!" The words ran faster than the tears he could feel soaking his neck and shirt.

"Ms. Harrington?" The pounding at the front door increased.

His legs shuddered. Seconds later, his knees buckled.

A gasp slipped from Araceli as he hit the floor. "Mitri!"

"We're coming in!"

The words from the front door were background noise at best. His heartbeat pounded in his ears.

Assess the wound.

He lifted his head and looked down, his fingers gently probing the area. Ugh. He dry-heaved again and his breathing shallowed.

Freakin' jacket. He couldn't see the wound.

"You were shot?" Ari's voice broke. He looked up as she dropped beside him, wiping tears from her cheeks. "What can I do?"

At least her voice was stronger that time.

"Need to get this jacket off." His fingers fumbled with the zipper but refused to do what his brain told them.

Araceli grabbed the zipper pull and jerked down, then peeled the jacket back.

She may as well have poured acid on the wound.

"Aagh!" The cry flew out before he could stop it.

"I'm sorry!"

He sucked in deep breaths. "Not your fault."

Okay, now maybe he could see what he was dealing with.

The blood centered below his rib cage.

Gritting his teeth, he pulled up his shirt. Congealed blood marked a leaking hole.

So many organs in that area. Had anything been hit? Intestines? Stomach? Liver? Was the bullet still inside?

Araceli sniffled. "What do you need me to do?"

What could they do? He should know.

Nothing came to mind.

The fogginess in his head scared him. Shock was setting in. He'd lost a lot of blood.

Moving around sure hadn't helped, but at least Ari was safe.

"Mitri!" She leaned close to his face. "What can I do?"

Bleeding. Stop the blood loss. "Compress. Slow the bleeding."

She jerked away and disappeared from sight.

Sounds of movement came from the living area. Harrington! She couldn't possibly be moving around yet, could she?

"Hands up! Now!"

A man's voice. Not Harrington.

Who?

The guard.

"I said hands up!"

"He's bleeding." Irritation lined Araceli's words.

He sensed her kneeling beside him, then felt pressure on the wound. It didn't hurt. Which was both blessing and curse.

Footsteps pounded from the living room.

"FBI! Drop the weapon!"

A sigh collapsed his chest. Reinforcements had arrived. He'd have to thank Lana for that one.

His eyes drifted closed. Voices receded in the wave of invading darkness.

ꟗ ꟗ ꟗ ꟗ ꟗ

Beep. Beep. Beep.

Would someone please kill that blasted alarm clock?

He tried to make his arm move, but it felt like stone. His eyelids weren't any lighter.

Wait. He knew that sound.

And it wasn't an alarm.

The beeping sped up.

It was a heart monitor.

Memories crashed into his mind, running over each other for prominence. Bobby. His men. Harrington. The serum. Araceli and Lana and Paul and the FBI.

The gunshot.

He wrenched his eyes open, only to pinch them closed against the light. As he opened them again, the hospital room came into focus.

It wasn't as bright in here as he'd originally thought.

A TV was mounted on the light gray wall in front of him. Pictures of the Vegas strip graced the wall on either side.

Light filtered through the drawn mini blinds covering the window. Next to the window, Araceli sat sideways in a padded chair, her legs drawn up, her arms crossed over them, her cheek resting on top. Her closed eyes and the small frown that curled her lips downward evidenced that her dreams weren't good.

Then again, after all she'd been through the last few days, how could they be?

If that wasn't enough to cause a frown, the position she slept in would be. She'd probably wake up with more aches than she could count.

Blood splotches marred the front of her pink shirt.

Was she hurt? He hadn't noticed the blood when he'd freed her from the bathroom. Then again, he hadn't been in any condition to notice much of anything.

But if she was hurt, shouldn't she be in a hospital bed, too?

The truth stampeded through his mind.

It was his blood. Probably there from when he'd held her after she ran out of her temporary prison.

Movement from his other side brought his head around.

Lana sat in a matching padded chair, positioned close to the door. Unlike Araceli, her bloodshot eyes were open. Dark circles pooled beneath them, testifying to a sleepless night.

Too busy staying in full-on defend mode, no doubt.

No sign of Paul. He'd like to think the man was smarter than these two women, but he wasn't that stupid. Knowing Paul, he'd probably stepped out to get some breakfast.

Someone had to make sure Lana ate, after all.

She pushed out of the chair and approached his bed, keeping her voice low. "How're you feeling?"

Good question. He really didn't feel anything. Except tired.

He didn't have to look at his chart to know they had some pretty good painkillers pumping through the IV drip in his arm.

"Alive." He studied her. "You look awful."

"You're one to talk. I've seen corpses with more color than you right now."

Yeah, yeah. He looked at the chair she'd vacated. "At least you had a decent place to sit. Beats the plastic chairs in our hospital."

"See if you can say the same thing after sitting in one for hours." She crossed her arms over her chest. "And I can't believe you went and got yourself shot. After all the lectures you gave *me* on being careful?"

"Not much fun being the one sitting beside the bed, is it?"

"Not much fun being the one in it, either." A smile formed, making her look less like a member of the undead.

The sparring took the edge off the fuzziness. "How long was I out?"

"A few hours."

She looked pointedly at the clock on the wall, which showed it was a little after nine. In the morning. A few hours? He'd lost the whole night.

Lana didn't wait for him to reply. "With all the privacy laws, they wouldn't tell me much, but I did overhear that they didn't do surgery and that the bullet exited through your back."

A through and through. Good. Usually meant less internal trauma than if the bullet bounced around inside.

"You're not going to be rappelling down buildings any time soon," she tossed a narrow-eyed glare at him, "but I bet you'll be back to normal before you know it."

Rappelling down buildings… "Bobby? They got him?"

"Yes. And possibly one of the dirty agents. They got there and this guy starts arresting me and Paul. He didn't want to see the evidence and didn't care about my badge. Praise God the SAC himself responded to Paul's call."

"And Harrington?"

"They got her, too. She's trying to claim self-defense, but it's not going to fly. I suspect she'll be charged as an accessory."

Paul strode back in, carrying two large coffee cups. While rumpled, he didn't look as haggard as Lana.

At least someone was smart enough to get some sleep.

"Dude, welcome back to the living. If I'd known you were

going to be awake..." He shrugged before handing one of the coffees to Lana.

"That's okay. Probably against doctor's orders anyway."

Lana took the coffee and sipped it. "Just what I needed. Thanks."

"Sure thing." Paul stared at Lana's hand. "Uh, where's the ring?"

Following his gaze, they all looked at Lana's bare hand. Lana frowned. "It was right there. The last time I saw it was before going into the warehouse. I must've lost it in the scuffle."

Uh-oh. If she lost it in the warehouse, would she ever get it back?

Paul swallowed. "Uh, o-okay."

A small chuckled escaped her and she put a hand on his chest. "Relax. I'm just messing with you. It's in my luggage at the hotel. I didn't want to take the chance it really would fall off."

His eyes narrowed. "Dirty trick, Tanner." Laughter lingered beneath the words.

"Well, that's what you get for giving my brother tips on breaking and entering."

"Did I hear something about a ring?" Araceli's voice drew Dimitrios' attention to the other side of the room.

She uncurled from the chair and stretched as a yawn overtook her.

Coming around to where Paul and Lana stood, she looked at the two of them. "Is there something I should know?"

"Yeah. I finally got sick of carrying a diamond in my pocket." Paul put an arm around Lana's shoulders and pressed a kiss into her hair.

A small squeal slipped from Araceli, who quickly slapped a hand over her own mouth. She let it drop a second later. "Congratulations. I'm happy for you."

Women. Sheesh. It was just a ring.

There were far more important things to discuss right

now. "Ari. What happened? Did they hurt you?"

Her hand briefly brushed some bruising on her cheek. "Not really. Mostly they left me alone."

Yeah, that bruising didn't look like they'd left her alone. "So what's with that bruise?"

"Bobby told me to hand over Joseph." Her chin went in the air. "I refused."

"Where is Joseph?" He'd seen no evidence of the baby at Harrington's. Nor was there any sign of him here.

Araceli deflated. "I–I don't know. I haven't seen him since Bobby took him. The day I got there."

"CPS has him." Lana interjected. "I asked the SAC when I called him about an hour ago. They found him with a nanny at Bobby's estate when they raided it."

"CPS?" Tears leaked from Araceli's eyes. "That's no place for a baby. Can't I take care of him?"

Lana shook her head slowly. "They won't release him until they sort everything out."

"But I have that legal document Mike left! That should be good enough. I could adopt him."

"These things are always a little more complicated than that." Lana studied her. "You'd adopt him if you could? Even though single parenthood is hard?"

A firm nod answered the question. "I'd figure it out. I've always wanted kids, but my ex never did. I guess in some ways it's a good thing because then I'd have to deal with him, but it's still hard."

Dimitrios followed her shaking hand as she wiped the tears off her cheeks.

So that was the story. He'd always wondered, but had told himself if wasn't any of his business. Which, really, it still wasn't. Not for now, anyway.

Too bad, though. She'd be a great mom.

What would it be like if she adopted Joseph?

And why did he imagine himself rounding out the family picture forming in his mind?

Their voices faded and his eyes felt heavy.

Exhaustion saturated him like a sudden rainstorm.

Lana was right. It was no fun being in the bed, either.

"Looks like Mitri needs some rest."

His eyelids jerked at the sound of Lana's voice. He blinked to find all three of them staring at him. "Huh? Sorry."

Darkness clouded his vision once again and he startled at a light kiss on his forehead. He ripped his eyes open to find Araceli only inches from his face.

If he had the energy, he'd kiss her right now, but he couldn't seem to make his body move.

"Thank you." Her whisper felt like a caress. "Rest. I'll be back later."

He wanted to tell her to stay, but his voice had vanished. Vaguely aware of the three of them walking out the door, he succumbed to the black oblivion.

Twenty Five

"Help me..." Araceli's voice, strained, beckoned him through the dark.

Where was she?

A blood trail, illuminated by a narrow beam of light like from a flashlight, summoned him forward.

He followed the blood.

Not drops. More like a river.

He kept moving forward. And almost tripped over her body on the floor of the warehouse.

Too much blood. Coating her chest, her hands. More gushed from a deep puncture wound on top of her head.

She reached out for him, but he couldn't grasp her hand.

He jerked awake.

Ari!

The hospital room came into focus.

Only a nightmare.

Gulping air like an addict, he worked to slow his breathing. His heart pounded in his chest, each beat pulsing pain throughout his body.

It felt like whatever drugs they'd given him earlier had long since worn off.

Worse than the pain was the anxiety lacing his mind.

He needed to see Ari. Needed to know she was okay.

He'd had her phone in his pocket when all this had happened. Had she taken it back? He could call her, knew her number even.

Chill.

Ari was fine. She was with Lana. Hopefully at the hotel getting some sleep.

"Good. You're awake."

Dimitrios turned toward the voice and found a white-coated doctor walking into the room. The man appeared to be a few years older than he was, with short-cropped white-blond hair and a bulbous nose.

"I'm Dr. Abbee." The doctor approached and offered a warm, firm handshake. "How are you feeling?"

"Never better." He'd been shot. How did the doc think he was feeling?

Abbee arched an eyebrow but said nothing.

Dang it. The doctor didn't need, or deserve, his sarcasm. "Sorry. Honestly, somewhere between being glad I'm alive to wishing I was dead."

"I figure if you can be sarcastic, you're on the mend." Abbee reached for his chart. "Where's your pain level? On a scale of one to ten, with one–"

"Nine."

"I think we can help you with that." Abbee made some adjustments to the IV.

"So what's the damage?" With all the organs down there, it seemed impossible that the bullet hadn't hit his stomach or kidney or something.

"Not as bad as it could've been." Abbee replaced the chart and studied Dimitrios with an intensity that made him shift. "The bullet nicked your liver but otherwise went in and came out clean. I think the Big Man was watching out for you, my friend."

For a clean shot, should he really be this tired? "How much blood did I lose?"

Abbee blinked. "Just under three pints. You can thank your liver for that."

Three. That was pretty significant. Yet not too surprising

given that the bullet had impacted his liver. "But no arterial damage?"

"No. Obviously, you did lose quite a bit of blood, but nothing a transfusion didn't fix." Abbee assessed him. "You ask some interesting questions. Do you have medical training?"

"I'm an EMT."

"That explains it. You're asking some of the same questions I would if our positions were reversed." The doctor replaced his chart. "I opted for a nonsurgical fix to stop the bleeding, but with a liver injury we'll be keeping a close eye on it for a day or two."

Nonsurgical. That should help with recovery time. As long as he didn't overdo it.

The doctor left the room and Dimitrios relaxed against the pillows.

No serious or permanent damage. That was a relief.

The Big Man was watching out for you. Abbee's words echoed in his head.

God.

He'd challenged God to prove Himself by helping him to save Araceli.

It could be a coincidence. He rejected the thought almost as quickly as it formed. Could he really buy that it was only a coincidence that he and everyone he loved had made it out of this alive?

Getting shot aside, a lot of things had sure gone right during this whole mess.

Ditching Lana had been easy. Getting into the warehouse not too bad. Even drugging Bobby's guys was simpler than expected. Then there was getting into Harrington's penthouse, freeing Araceli, and not getting arrested amidst it all.

But was it God?

Yes.

The answer resonated inside his head like a voice. In him, yet not his own.

Weird. Even weirder was that he knew it was God talking.

Had God been speaking to him all this time and he'd just been too stubborn to listen? He knew his family and Mike would answer with a resounding yes.

So. If he believed that God was there and had helped him, where did that leave him?

Years of being forced to go to church and Sunday school as a kid had embedded the fact that there was no neutral ground when it came to believing in God.

You picked a side.

God or… not God. Heaven or hell.

If that bullet had killed him, what would've happened?

According to everyone he loved most, he would've gone to hell.

Did he even believe in hell?

Well, if he believed in heaven, which he did, then didn't there have to be an opposite? It was the balance found everywhere in nature. Where there was light, there had to be darkness. Where there was evil, there had to be good. Where there was hate, there had to be love. If there was heaven, there had to be someplace for those who didn't go to heaven. Hell.

And if heaven was the ultimate in perfection, didn't it make sense that hell would be, well, not?

Funny how years of Bible lessons could come flooding back.

God wanted his heart. Not physically, of course, but the very core of who he was.

God wanted him to give up control.

Man, that was a scary thing. If he gave God himself, what would God do? What if God made him do something horrible, like move to Africa, live in a tent, and become a monk?

Trust.

The word resonated through his head in that same his-but-not-his voice from earlier.

The tubes coming out of him, the heart monitor beside him, and the pain pulsing through him served as a poignant reminder that he had very little control over this life anyway.

Okay, God, you want me? Here I am.

Prayers he'd heard over and over when he was growing up jumbled together inside his head.

He was a sinner.

God was perfect.

His sin put him at odds with a holy God, but God loved him anyway.

He couldn't save himself, so God sent Jesus, who lived a perfect life, took the punishment for sin on Himself, and offered forgiveness to sinners.

All he had to do was believe and surrender.

God, I do believe. I choose You. Do what You want with me.

No flash of light or thunder answered him. Yet he felt a gentle whisper, accompanied by peace.

No more striving. Or fighting. Or running.

It'd taken him years and he had a lot to learn, but he'd finally found purpose.

ଲ ଲ ଲ ଲ ଲ

Her smell teased his senses, pulling him from a light nap.

Was he dreaming?

Voices in the distance, squeaking shoes in the hall. From somewhere nearby, a TV rumbled.

Yet the soft, floral scent that reminded him of Araceli's greenhouse remained.

He forced his eyes open.

His face was angled away from the door, but his eyes locked on Araceli, sitting a few feet away, scrolling through something on her phone.

Gone were her bloodstained clothes, replaced by a deep blue sweater and long flowing skirt. Her hair looked damp. She must've gone back to the hotel while he'd been out of it. Makeup almost hid the bruising he'd seen earlier. A hint of shine on her lips caught the sunlight filtering through the window.

He couldn't look away.

What would it be like to kiss her again?

Would she welcome it? Would she even let him?

Maybe he should pray about it. That's what Mike would've done, had done where Regan was concerned. On more than one occasion.

God.

He paused. It felt weird, yet he didn't feel like he was addressing the air.

God, you know what I want. Can I–

Araceli looked up. Her smile creased the corners of her eyes. "I didn't know you were awake."

"I haven't been for long." The words were raspy. He cleared his throat. "I just woke up."

Lame. Why couldn't he tell her what he really wanted to say?

"You should've said something."

"I was talking to God." Funny how that could feel both natural and foreign at the same time.

Araceli's lips parted and her eyebrows almost met her hairline. "You were… since when?"

"Since God accepted my challenge and proved He was there."

She scooted her chair closer. "This sounds like a story I have to hear."

Naturally she'd want to hear it.

By the time he finished, tears glistened in her eyes. She grabbed his hand in both of hers and held it in a mini-hug. "You have no idea how long I've prayed for this. Mike, too. He'd be thrilled."

"Well, one day I guess I'll get to tell him."

She lowered his hand to her lap, but didn't let go.

Did she realize she was still holding it? He sure hoped so.

She sighed. "Looks like Joseph will get his happy ending, too."

Hmmm. *She* didn't sound particularly happy. Happy for Joseph, but not for her? "What's going on?"

"Regan's parents are going to raise him. I guess they're flying in tomorrow."

Man. That had to hurt. She'd really poured herself into that kid. "I'm sorry."

Her chin quivered slightly. "I know it's the best thing for him. Them, too. But it's hard."

"We could always just make our own." Aw, crud. Had he really said that?

She dropped his hand as though simply holding it could bring his words to life.

Yep, he'd said it out loud.

Maybe he could claim the drugs were making him crazy.

Flames licked up his neck, engulfing his face.

Araceli's lips parted, her eyes practically bulging.

Now what? Laugh it off? Or level with her?

"I didn't mean to say that." He sighed. "But, Ari. You have to know… I mean, since seventh grade…"

Gee, that was really eloquent.

Could he blubber any more? It was no wonder she stared at him like he'd lost his mind.

Maybe he had.

"I love you." The words exploded from him. "I always have."

Shut up!

He clamped his lips together. Araceli's face had paled a shade and she stared at him. Her mouth moved a little, but no words came out.

Of course. She'd been kidnapped, beat up, threatened, and now he came and vomited his feelings in the worst possible way.

He clenched his teeth and turned to look at the door.

Maybe a nurse would come in and save him from this hell of his own making.

He could always fake a heart attack.

Hopefully he hadn't killed their friendship by dumping his feelings like that. Would she buy a claim of sleep talking?

Movement flashed before his eyes as her hand came along his jaw and gently turned his face back.

Her lips melted onto his.

The hospital room faded. All he could think about was her.

How many times had he dreamed about this since he'd first crossed that line at Lana's?

He buried the fingers of his untethered hand in her hair. If he could stand up and hold her, he would. But at the moment, he'd probably pass out.

Not to mention he was wearing a hospital gown.

Yeah, real manly.

She slowly broke the kiss and pulled back a few inches, her gaze moving across his face. "Do you have any idea how long I've waited to hear you say that?"

Really? He swallowed the acorn lodged in his throat. "You mean all this time we could've–"

"No." She eased back into the chair. "I would've said no. As long as you didn't believe in God. But now…" A shaky breath eased from her. "God's timing is perfect, you know?"

So he'd heard. "God really would've been a breaking point?"

She wiped tears from her cheeks. "Yeah. I compromised before. With Aaron. And look where it got me."

How could she even begin to compare him to her ex? "I'm not Aaron. I would never do that to you."

"I know. But the point is that the Bible tells Christians to only marry other Christians for a reason. I know firsthand how much being with a nonbeliever drags my own faith down. I love God too much to walk that path again."

Okay, that made more sense. At least he hadn't told her how he felt before, when she would've rejected him.

Thanks, God.

"So." Man, this was not how he'd envisioned having this

conversation. "I wish I had a ring so I could do this thing right."

Suddenly she was in his face again, her lips brushing his. "I don't need a ring. Just ask."

"Will you marry me?"

"Yes." The word came out on a breath that he felt more than heard.

The next kiss lasted even longer.

As she pulled back, his gaze lingered on her face. Those high cheekbones, black eyes, full lips, beautiful smile. It was hard to believe, especially after all this time, but he'd get to look at it every single day for the rest of his life.

This may not have been how he would've planned to have this conversation, but Araceli was right about one thing. God's timing was perfect. In every way.

* * * * *

"Huh. Looks like there's a spine back there after all."

Dimitrios shook his head at Paul's words. Yeah, he'd deserved that. "Well, at least I didn't carry a ring around for months."

"No, you just waited twenty years."

Araceli laughed, her cheeks the color of the hibiscus planted beside her front porch. She squeezed his hand. "Yes, but that twenty years is why I can say yes without even going on a single date. We know each other so well."

She did know him. In some aspects, better than his own family.

"Although," she looked him straight in the eye, "A girl could get old waiting for you Lykos men to open up about their feelings."

"Amen to that. But the problem isn't only with the guys." Paul's comment earned him a faux glare from Lana.

"Watch it buster or that ring might disappear for good." Lana held up her hand and looked pointedly at the ring sliding down her finger.

"Oooh, scary."

Dimitrios angled a look at Lana. "Yeah, well we're probably going to beat you to the altar. We're planning a four-week engagement."

Paul gently elbowed Lana. "We better move it up. Can't have them beating us."

"Like it's a competition?" Lana looked at Araceli. "Can you really put together a wedding in that timeframe?"

Araceli nodded. "I've had the big, fancy wedding once. This time, I want something small and simple. If it weren't for premarital counseling with my pastor, I could put this together by next week."

Next week? As much as he was looking forward to being married to her, he'd rather not be wheeled down the aisle. "Four weeks gives me time to regain my strength, too. I can't be passing out in the middle of the ceremony, right?"

A throat cleared.

Dimitrios looked toward the doorway to find a man standing there. The gray suit and polished shoes screamed FBI.

Figured. No one had been by to take his statement yet.

Kind of surprising since it'd been almost twenty-four hours since he'd been admitted.

Then again, the doctor might've ordered the FBI to stay away until he'd recovered a little.

The man walked into the room and approached the bed, extending a hand. "Dimitrios Lykos? Agent Flynn."

"I figured you'd get around to me sooner or later."

Flynn frowned. "It would've been sooner, but a few people," his eyes slanted toward Lana, "were adamant that you recovered some first."

Lana held up her hands. "Hey, the doctor agreed."

"Believe me. I know." Flynn pulled out a small notepad and pen, followed by a mini recorder. Hitting a button on the recorder, he set it on the table next to the bed, then stated

Dimitrios' name, the date, time, and location. "So I've heard several other accounts of what happened, but you seem to be at the center of it. Why don't you give me your side?"

Funny how law enforcement officials worded their orders in the form of a question.

They probably learned that technique on day one at the academy.

He recapped everything that had happened. Flynn didn't interrupt, not even to ask questions. Every now and then he'd jot something on the notepad, but he let Dimitrios simply tell his story.

Once he finished, Flynn glanced at his notes before looking back up. "So to make sure I understand, you didn't call the police because…?"

"Bobby's connections. I didn't know who to trust. Besides, they told me not to and they had Ari."

"So instead of going through proper legal channels, you broke into a warehouse, and a penthouse, and used a relatively untested toxin to drug half a dozen people?"

When he put it that way, it sounded pretty bad. "I was told to come to the warehouse and Harrington let me into her penthouse."

"Under false pretenses."

Why did this suddenly feel more like an interrogation? "I still didn't break in. Besides, *she* shot *me*."

"She's claiming self-defense. You lied to gain access, then came at her with a syringe."

"After she started shooting. I tried to convince her to surrender first."

Flynn lowered his notebook. "You realize that I could arrest you right now. Charge you with breaking and entering and assault?"

His mouth dried out.

Man, this was bad.

Sure, he'd always realized it could come to this, but hadn't really expected that it would.

Now he was going to jail. In Nevada, no less. Ari couldn't even visit him, not that he'd blame her for not wanting to.

"Agent Flynn." Lana's voice sounded slightly amused. "How many murders have you linked to Carpelli's organization?"

Flynn paused for a beat too long. "I don't know what you're talking about."

"I know of at least 3. Plus 4 more," she gestured to the people in the room, "who would have joined that number if Bobby had his way. How many others?"

A grudging respect lit his eyes. "We're still piecing it together. So far, at least two dozen."

"Two dozen people dead. And you've been investigating Bobby for how long? A year? Two? More?"

He grunted. "Try almost five."

"And in the space of forty-eight hours, my brother has given you enough to not only arrest him, but to ensure that he's not going anywhere for a very long time. Sure, his methods were unconventional, and not something I'd recommend be repeated," she shot him a firm look, "ever, but they worked. Are you really going to bring charges against the guy who gift wrapped Bobby Carpelli?"

Flynn stared at her. "It's the DA's call, not mine." He snatched up the recorder and turned it off. "But between us, I don't think you have anything to worry about. The DA is so excited about Bobby, that I'm sure he'll drop any charges in exchange for your testimony."

"You'll have it." The words scraped from Dimitrios' suddenly very dry throat.

Flynn stuffed his notebook and recorder back into his jacket pocket. "I'll need all of you to stick around town for a few days. Just until we can clear a little of this up. Take in a show or two. You all look like you could use a vacation."

That was the truest thing Flynn had said since walking into the room. Maybe they would, as soon as the hospital released him.

As Flynn walked out, a yawn overtook Dimitrios.

That had drained him more than he'd thought.

"Looks like we better let you get some rest." Araceli's words were soft.

He wanted to disagree, but that would require effort. "I hate being so wiped."

"It'll get better soon." Lana rose from her chair. "Trust me on that one."

It was terrible that she knew that from experience.

Araceli pressed a kiss to his cheek. He turned his head for a real one.

As she headed for the door, he fought to keep his eyes open until she was out of sight.

His eyes drifted closed. Sleep crowded in, his mind wrapping around a simple prayer of thanks.

⁂

"That's good news. Thank you for keeping me informed."

Dimitrios watched as Lana ended the call. It'd been a long three days, only one of which he'd been out of the hospital, since they'd heard from Agent Flynn, but the call had finally come.

Now to find out if he was headed to a Nevada state prison or could go home to his life.

The hotel room he was sharing with Paul shrunk around him, but wouldn't be nearly as small as the cell he'd share with some thug named Bruno if the DA came after him.

Lana looked at the group. "The DA's not bringing charges."

Thank God. The sigh that exploded from him caused ghosts of pain in his torso.

"But he wants all of us to know that we'll likely be called back to testify when this goes to trial."

"Bobby's taking it to trial?" Araceli sounded as incredulous as he felt.

Lana nodded. "For now, yes. He's denying everything. Even though Harrington turned on him as part of a plea deal, he still seems to think he can beat this."

Amazing. "The man's got an ego the size of his casino."

"Evidently." She perched on the arm of the chair Paul lounged in. "It could change in the upcoming months, although I suspect he's a gambling man. He'll probably play the odds."

Probably. According to Bobby, the house always won.

Paul looked up at her. "I'm a little surprised he told you all that."

"Me, too." She shrugged. "Must be a professional courtesy."

Paul rubbed her leg. "Well, I'm hungry. Feel like walking down to the restaurant for some lunch?"

"Sure. Then we'll book our plane tickets home." She looked at Dimitrios and Araceli. "You guys coming?"

"Save us a place. We'll catch up."

Araceli turned questioning eyes on him as they left the room. "What's up?"

He stared at her.

The bruise running along her jaw had deepened into a rich plum that not even makeup could hide. He gently brushed his finger along it. "I'm sorry."

Her eyebrows jumped. "For this? It's not your fault."

"I didn't protect you."

"If I recall, you were kind of tied up."

"Still. I should have–"

"Mitri." Her hand rested on his chest. "Let it go."

He picked up her hand and kissed it. "Mike would've been stoked."

"That I got beat up?"

"No. About us."

"Mike? He knew?"

"For years." He massaged her hand with his thumb.

"And here I thought he couldn't keep a secret." She shook

her head slowly. "But you know what he'd really have been excited about? That you finally stopped running from God."

She was right. Mike had preached at him enough over the years.

"Will you help me plan Mike's funeral when we get back?" Surely the police had released the body by now, especially since the killer was behind bars.

Tears glistened in her eyes. "Of course."

Mike's dying words drifted through his mind. God's timing. He wished Mike's death hadn't been part of God's timing, but he could see how God had used it.

Out of the ashes of Mike's murder, he'd found love and salvation. He may be new at the whole God thing, but something told him that only God could take a situation that started so deadly and bring something so good from it.

From death, God had brought deliverance.

Dedication & Acknowledgements

This book is dedicated to the One who is the Author of my life, your life, and the life of every person who ever has and ever will live. His stories may not play out the way we expect and might be full of twists and turns that keep us guessing, but as Dimitrios learned, His plans are always right and good.

A huge thank you also goes out to my sample readers: Linda, Janet, and Del. This story would not happen without your insight, editorial skills, and wise suggestions - not to mention encouragement and support. You are more important to me than you know.

Finally, thank you to YOU, the reader. I am so grateful that you joined me on this journey and hope God touched you somewhere along the way. For those of you who have left positive reviews of past books (or plan to do so for this one), I offer an extra special thanks. And to everyone who has shared your story with me via a review, email, or facebook, I just want you to know how much I love hearing what God has done and is doing in your life. Thank you for including me in the journey.

A note from the author

Thank you for joining me on Dimitrios' adventure! From his first on-page appearance in Deadly Alliances, I knew he had a story to tell.

Originally, I had placed his story as the second book in the Deadly Alliances series, but felt compelled to cut it - until God led me to use it as the conclusion. I can tell you that it fits so much better here than it did as the second book in the series. I love how God's plans work so much better than our own.

These last few years, I've been struck by how different God's plans are than our own. You may be familiar with Isaiah 55:9 - "As the heavens are higher than the earth, so are My ways higher than your ways and My thoughts than your thoughts."

I think we're often surprised when God's ways don't line up with ours, but scripture reveals that we really shouldn't be. When you're standing on a high building or mountain, you see the surrounding area so much more clearly than when you're on the ground in the middle of it. In the same way, God sees not only where we're at, but where we've been and where we're going. His viewpoint reveals so much more than our limited vision can possibly see.

That's one reason it's so critical for us to do things according to His ways. No, it's not easy. In fact, it's often very difficult. But God promises that obedience is always worth the cost.

I love the verses Lana quoted to Dimitrios from Isaiah

48:17-18. The Lord knows what is best for us and longs for us to walk in His ways.

Not only are God's ways right, His timing is perfect. So often, we want to rush things and get impatient when God doesn't act in our timeline. But we can't rush God.

I think back on the times in my life where He hasn't acted when I wanted Him to - and the blessing I now have because He didn't do what I wanted when I wanted it. Sometimes my desires changed; other times He gave me my desires in His perfect time.

It feels a little bittersweet to say good-bye to Lana and her friends, but I think it's time (pun intended!) They've had enough drama and trauma for a lifetime, don't you think? I hope you enjoyed the Deadly Alliances series. If you did, would you consider writing a review? Reviews can help other readers decide if a story - or series - is worth taking the time to read.

The Deadly Alliances series may be ending, but I'm eager to introduce you to Zander. He's a violent crimes detective in San Francisco who is jaded, damaged, tragically flawed, and isn't sure he believes in God, but that's okay. God will use him anyway. You'll find a sneak peek at the end of this book so keep reading. His story, tentatively titled *Silent is the Grave*, will be ready in 2018.

I've also included a peek at *Shadow of the Storm*, a stand-alone novel that takes you into the mind of someone who doesn't even know who she is! Stormy awakens with no memories, overhearing two men plotting her murder. She must stay a step ahead of her would-be killers while she tries to unravel the mystery of what happened to her. *Shadow of the Storm* is available now.

My other project for this year is *Undone: a life application journey through the book of Isaiah*. This project is near to my heart, for it takes the amazing book of prophecy and focuses on how it is relevant to us today. God has taught me so much through the prophets and I'm anxious to share that with anyone who might seek to learn with me. *Undone* is designed as an interactive Bible study and should be available in the fall of 2017. If you've followed any of my facebook posts and enjoyed that, you might like *Undone* - it's written in a very similar fashion.

Speaking of new books, would you like to receive notification when a new book is released? Join my mailing list! Visit candlesutton.com today to sign up for my monthly mailing list "Keep Me In Suspense!" In it, you'll receive updates on my current work-in-progress, an inspirational thought, and suggestions on other good Christian books you might enjoy. You'll also receive email notification when a new Candle Sutton book is available.

Thank you again for reading. I'd love to hear from you. Feel free to reach out to me on facebook at facebook.com/candlesutton or email me at candle.sutton@outlook.com.

I pray you seek the Lord's face as you wait for His perfect timing and the unfolding of His sovereign plans.

Excerpt from Shadow of the Storm

One

"You're gonna dump her off the bridge?"

The man's words penetrate the fog in my head. The ground beneath me bounces. I try to open my eyes, but they're heavy. Too heavy.

"You got a better idea? With any luck, they'll rule it a suicide."

A different voice, still male. This voice is deeper, more guttural, than the one that woke me.

"Why not just shoot her and be done with it?" It's the first voice. Slightly high-pitched and a little whiny.

"Because bullets can be traced, you fool!"

"Use her gun."

"I don't have it."

Somehow I know they're talking about me. And they're going to kill me if I don't do something to stop it.

Why would they want to kill me?

Silence descends.

Pain stabs behind my eyes. Between that and the jackhammer pounding in my head, it's a miracle I can hear anything.

But I *can* hear things.

There's water. Rain, maybe.

Yes. Rain. And a rapid swish-swishing sound that I think is windshield wipers. Tires hum on pavement.

I'm in a car.

The fog slips away. Clarity sharpens my thoughts, which

click through my head like a slide show.

Two men. Maybe more. Maybe not.

Hopefully not. I don't know how many guys I can take on at once.

Assuming I can take on any of them.

I force my eyes open. At first, all I see is darkness, but then the darkness forms into shapes.

A few feet from my face is a small purse with rhinestones on it. A blue duffel bag rests beside it. Beyond them is the back of a seat.

I lift my head a few inches off the rough carpet scratching my cheek.

It looks like I'm in the back of some kind of vehicle. An SUV, I think.

Lightning flashes outside and I jerk.

A chunk of hair falls into my face.

I try to push it aside, but my hands are trapped behind my back.

Metal cuts into my wrists.

So I'm not just trapped. I'm handcuffed.

This night keeps getting better and better, doesn't it?

"What bridge?" Whiny voice breaks the silence.

A horn blares, preventing me from hearing the response, but it doesn't matter what bridge. What matters is that I'll be dead if they succeed.

Instinct silences me. I don't know how I fit into this mess, why I'm handcuffed, or even if I'm really the one those guys intend to kill. The fact that I'm handcuffed in the back of a vehicle overhearing plans of murder doesn't bode well for my survival.

Okay, first problem. Get out of these handcuffs.

Simple, right?

I lay my head back on the carpet and ease my hands down my backside, around my hips, and toward my feet. My heels catch on the metal.

My fingers trace the shoes. Smooth finish. Long, pointy

heel.

I got all dressed up for something tonight. And I'm betting it didn't include being kidnapped and murdered.

Pushing the shoes off my nylon-covered feet, I slide the handcuffs around my heels.

Huh. The slick surface of the nylons comes in handy for something.

Okay. So the handcuffs are in front of me. Now what?

They feel a little loose. Maybe I can slip free. I flex and twist my hands. The metal chafes the skin but I can't get the restraints over my thumbs.

Dislocate your thumbs.

The thought flashes through my mind like the lightning that occasionally illuminates the vehicle.

Dislocate my thumb? Who even thinks such a thing?

The crazier thing is that I know how to do it. Just like I know it'll work.

I clench my teeth and press my face against the carpet beneath me to muffle any noise I might make. Drawing a deep breath, I do it. Everything in me wants to cry out, but the only noise is the pop of the joint dislocating. As loud as it seems to me, I don't think there was any way that the men up front could have heard it.

Fire races through my hand. I force air in and out in measured breaths.

The pain fades to a dull throb and I slip my hands from the cuffs.

Turning my face into the carpet again, I push my thumbs back into the socket. This time, a small gasp does escape, but I doubt they heard me above the road and storm noise.

Now to find a way out of here.

Before we reach the bridge or wherever it is that these guys plan to kill me.

I twist to look at the rear door.

Good, it has a handle. So all I have to do is open the door and make a break for it. And hopefully not break my legs or neck in the process.

There's no telling how fast we're going. Having broken bones will make me that much easier for these guys to subdue.

But I have to try.

I will not just sit here and let them kill me. If they want me dead, they're going to have to work for it.

The car jerks.

I slide forward several inches as the squeal of tires on soaked asphalt fills the vehicle. The horn blares and gruff voice releases a string of choice words questioning the intelligence of the driver who cut him off.

We're almost at a complete stop. It's now or never.

I scoop up my shoes, the purse, and the strap for the duffel bag in one hand and reach for the handle with the other.

Please don't be locked.

The latch releases and I thrust the door out. The dome light pops on.

Behind me, I hear the men yelling, which spurs me to move faster. I stumble out the back, my feet splashing in a puddle.

I need to get out of here.

Headlights approach.

A door slams.

Run, run!

I race across the street. A horn blasts from somewhere to my left, but I don't know if it's the guys who're after me or someone else.

Frankly, I don't care.

My feet hit the sidewalk and I angle for the closest alley.

Little pieces of rock or glass, maybe both, prick the soles of my feet, but I can't put on my shoes. There's no way I can run in stilettos.

The blackness of the alley swallows me.

Rain pelts my face, the water running into my eyes. The

deluge plasters my hair to my head and makes my dress cling to me.

Shivers rock my body. My limbs feel sluggish, but the dumpsters flashing by tell me I'm moving quickly.

I drape the strap of the duffel bag across my body.

The action slows me down for a second, but it frees one of my hands. If those guys catch up to me, I need to be able to fight.

Footsteps echo behind me.

A sharp crack splits the night, followed a second later by an exploding brick a foot away from my head.

Although it wasn't an explosion. It was a gunshot.

Those men are shooting at me! I don't know how I know, but I do.

Another gunshot. The bullet pings off the dumpster I just passed.

The dark of night is probably the only thing saving me right now. Even so, I'm an easy target.

I weave back and forth, trying to be as erratic as possible.

Are the footsteps drawing nearer? I risk a glance.

A dark shape lumbers closer. Only one.

Where is the other guy?

Doesn't matter. I can't let him catch me.

I push myself to go faster. A cross street is up ahead. Maybe there will be someone there who can help me.

I burst out of the alley.

The street's deserted.

Where the heck am I? Shouldn't there be someone around? Someone other than these guys who want me dead?

There's no time to consider the question.

I race across the street.

Another gunshot sounds as I enter the alley, another brick showers me in dust.

There's an intersection ahead. Looks like another alley. I make a sharp right into it.

Too sharp.

It occurs to me seconds too late. My feet slide out from under me and I go down, landing in a large puddle.

Pain vibrates up my arms but I can't dwell on it. I have to keep moving.

I push myself to my feet and press forward.

Ragged breathing echoes between the buildings. Dang. That fall cost me valuable seconds. He's getting closer!

Tears blur my vision. I blink them away and they mingle with the rain running down my face.

This is pointless. He's going to catch me. Then he's going to kill me. So why fight it?

Because I don't want to die, that's why. I can't give up.

A meaty hand clamps on my shoulder and jerks me to a stop.

I scream.

Excerpt from Silent is the Grave

Prologue

Wednesday was a bad day to die.

Yet, not five feet from Monica, two eyes stared sightlessly from a face mashed against the cold tile. Blood pooled under the pale cheek and slightly parted lips seemed to beckon for help. Fragile white-blonde hair splayed across the floor, soaking up the blood like an addict getting her fix.

Monica clenched a shaking fist in front of her mouth as her vision swirled. Tears broke free from her lashes and raced down her face.

Jessie! Gone!

What would she do without Jessie?

The tread of heavy shoes trapped oxygen in her throat.

Jessie may be gone, but the killer was still here.

Two blue-clad legs filled her vision, close enough to touch. Not that she wanted to. Some kind of cargo pants. Atop tan suede work boots.

Monica shrank back against the wall.

Willed the man not to look under the counter behind him.

The man knelt next to Jessie's body, his back to her. She wanted to scream at him to get away, that he'd done enough damage already, but really what more could he do? Jessie was dead.

Short, spiky, light brown hair.

A neck that wasn't as white as Jessie's but clearly indicated the man's ethnicity.

Biceps as big as Jessie's neck. Which he probably could've snapped one-handed if he hadn't had the knife.

A navy shirt that perfectly matched the pants coated a back at least twice the size of hers. Some kind of emblem on the sleeve, but the angle was wrong for her to really see it.

A uniform. Who was he? A cop? Firefighter? Paramedic?

Hard to say. But she knew one thing. She couldn't trust any of them.

The boots clomped across the kitchen. A door slammed.

Silence.

Was he really gone? Or trying to draw out any potential witnesses?

From somewhere in the building, a voice called out. People were here. Sooner or later they'd come into the kitchen and find Jessie.

Find her.

She had to get outta here! Before the cops showed.

Monica scrambled from beneath the counter. Her shoes slipped twice in the blood invading the floor and she almost fell on Jessie's body.

Vaulting the body, she raced into the supply closet a few feet away. Boxes were stacked beneath the room's single window, providing a ladder for her escape.

She scrambled on top of them, felt them sag beneath her weight.

Movement from the kitchen behind her. A gasp. A scream.

She unlatched the window and pushed out the screen.

"Is someone there?" A woman's voice.

Footsteps in the kitchen. Approaching.

Monica hefted herself onto the narrow windowsill and angled her body through the opening that was barely large enough for her to slide through.

Behind her, the boxes crashed to the floor.

Trash-littered asphalt rushed up to meet her. Pain jolted through her shoulder as she landed hard on her right side.

Her arm numbed. She rolled to her stomach and pushed herself up.

Her bag, her bag. Where was her bag?

She glanced around. No sign of it.

She'd left it inside. Under the counter by Jessie's body.

The air in her chest solidified. Everything she owned was in that bag!

But she couldn't go back for it. Not now anyway. Maybe not ever.

Time to disappear. Just as she had when she'd left home over two years ago.

She ran.

"Hello? Wait!" The same woman's voice, vaguely familiar, came from behind her.

But instead of stopping, it spurred her to move faster. It was probably one of the staff or volunteers at the shelter, but it didn't matter.

No one could be trusted.

The one lesson life had drilled into her time and again rang true. She was better off alone.

One

"Hey, kid. Hot call."

Detective Alejandro Salinas pushed back his chair, holding in the words threatening to rip his partner to shreds. How many times did he have to ask Morgan not to call him kid? Salinas, Zander… heck, even Alejandro would be better than kid.

And nobody called him Alejandro but his Madre.

But if the last eighteen months were any indicator, the nickname wasn't going anywhere anytime soon.

"What've we got?"

Detective Max Morgan slid a glance Zander's direction as they headed for the exit. "Homicide. Some kid at the San Francisco Youth Center."

A kid. Dang.

It didn't get much worse than that. Especially one who was already in a pretty bad situation.

"Witnesses?"

"None that have come forward."

Figured. No one ever saw anything.

Morgan settled his solid frame behind the wheel of the unmarked sedan and cranked the engine. "You still volunteering at that place?"

"A few times a week." Zander's thought ricocheted to the youth center and the boys he'd been working with there. He'd built a few solid connections and had even earned a little street cred with some of the boys.

Man, did he hope it wasn't one of them.

That was a horrible thing to think. A kid was dead either way.

"What do you do there, anyway?" Morgan pressed the accelerator through a yellow light.

"Soccer, basketball, football–"

"A shrimp like you?" Morgan grinned.

"You've only got an inch on me, man." An inch and probably about fifty pounds. Not all of it muscle. "I also help 'em with homework. You know, show 'em they've got options outside of gangs."

Didn't always work, but at least he could say he was trying to do something about the gang problem.

"Well, maybe your connections will help us out on this one."

"Maybe." He doubted it, though. Street kids stuck together.

They'd find out soon enough. Lights flashed from the curb up ahead.

Unlike most days, there weren't any kids hanging out in front of the building. No surprise there. Those kids avoided authority figures like cats avoided water.

Morgan jerked the vehicle to a stop in front of the hotel-turned-youth-center.

They climbed the wide stone steps of the historic building and pushed through the solid, double doors.

Hardwood floors in need of a good polish stretched before them. A stairway hugged the wall to their left. At the top of the stairs, several kids watched with guarded expressions.

Zander caught the eye of one of the boys, a fourteen-year-old with good skills on the basketball court, and nodded. The boy returned the nod.

A good sign, especially if the kid saw anything.

"So you know where the kitchen's at in this place?"

Zander turned at Morgan's question. "Sure do."

Ah, for once he got to lead. Didn't happen often. Morgan was the senior detective and made sure everyone knew it.

Zander led the way down a wide hallway, stopping outside a set of double doors about halfway down. Yellow police tape blocked the doors, which were closed.

Pushing the doors inward, he ducked beneath the tape. Morgan followed on his heels.

White tile gleamed in front of him. Massive stainless steel appliances gave the room an industrial look. An island dominated the center of the room.

Three uniformed officers clustered on the far side of the island.

Morgan brushed past him and headed for them.

Yeah. Zander figured his taking the lead would be short-lived.

He followed.

The body came into view as he rounded the island.

A girl sprawled on the floor in a lake of blood. Might've been as young as fourteen. Certainly no older than eighteen. Light blonde hair, skin that would've been pale in life but was ghost-like in death, blue eyes that were almost translucent.

The thoughts clicked into his mind.

Smears marred the blood around her. Footprints led toward a door. He peeked inside.

A pantry. The room's one window, small and set high in the wall, hung open.

He turned his attention to the footprints.

Tiny. Most likely a youth or woman. Maybe the perp. Or maybe a witness. Whoever it was, that person hadn't stuck around to talk to the police.

No sign of a weapon, either. The perp must have taken it.

Murmuring reached him. He looked up to find two women outside the kitchen's second set of doors. Rectangular tables and chairs dotted the room behind them.

He recognized the older woman as Betty Chambers, the woman who ran the center with her husband Bill. Betty shook like the Golden Gate in an earthquake.

No wonder.

Sure, the kids here got in some trouble, but he couldn't recall a murder ever happening here before.

The other woman was closer to his age. Curls the color of a freshly-minted penny brushed her shoulders and her slim body had curves in all the right places. Even from here he could see her high cheekbones, narrow nose, and pointed chin, all of which gave her face an angular and sharp edge, but somehow fit her perfectly.

He'd never seen her before. Too bad, too. She was smokin' hot. Not supermodel material, but more like the girl next door. He'd always had a thing for the girl next door.

Sick. Here he was standing over a dead girl checking out the hot chick. There was something fundamentally wrong with that.

He forced his attention back to the scene.

Being careful to avoid the blood, he knelt next to the body.

The girl was on her side, her neck twisted at an angle that would've been uncomfortable for the living. Blood-streaked arms stretched out in front of her, possibly in a defensive stance, for all the good it had done her. A tight denim skirt barely covered her hips, exposing shockingly white, twig-like legs.

Blood congealed across her chest, but there was too much of it to get a clear visual of the wound.

Marks on her arms drew his attention.

Scars. Most of them looked older. They told the tragic story of bouts of cutting and possible suicide attempts.

Poor kid never had a chance.

One thing was noticeably absent. Track marks. Didn't mean she wasn't using, though.

He glanced up at the responding officers. "Prostitute?"

The officer shrugged. "No one's saying."

Of course not. Why make this easy? "No witnesses?"

"Nope." The officer's gaze followed the bloody smears

leading to the pantry. "At least none that we found."

"That our vic's?" Morgan's voice came from behind Zander.

Zander twisted, following Morgan's gaze. A grimy pink floral backpack rested on the floor a few feet away, a police marker positioned beside it.

The responding officer shrugged. "Not sure. The volunteer who found the body said she saw a girl fleeing the scene."

"Who found the body?"

The officer's lips stretched in a wide smile. "The hottie."

So. The unknown redhead was first on the scene. He allowed his gaze to wander to her again.

Morgan drew himself up to his full six-foot height and puffed out his chest. "Better let me handle this one, kid."

As expected.

He followed Morgan to the dining room where the women waited.

Betty's splotchy face turned toward him as they approached.

"Oh, Zander!" Betty's voice wobbled. "I'm so glad it's you!"

A liver-spotted hand reached for him. He caught it and gently rubbed the back of her hand. "I'm sorry this happened, Betty."

She sniffled. "It's just so horrible. I don't know who could do this."

"That's what we're here to find out, ma'am." Morgan's voice drew Betty's attention. "Detective Morgan. Looks like you already know Salinas."

At least Morgan hadn't called him kid.

"Oh, yes. Zander's such a blessing to us here."

Oh, yeah. A real saint. Zander released Betty's hand and pushed to his feet. "Morgan, this is Betty Chambers. She and her husband manage this place."

He shifted to look at the redhead who stood silently at

Betty's side. "I'm afraid I don't know who you are."

A faint smile worked at the redhead's lips. "Elly Levi. I help out around here."

Unusual accent. Soft, cultured voice.

But it was her eyes that commanded attention. Purple. Seriously purple. Like the color of that Iris plant he'd bought his Madre on her birthday.

Must be colored contacts or something. He'd never seen that color before.

"Betty?" A man's voice echoed in the main hall.

Zander recognized Bill's rough voice from that single word.

Betty's head jerked around and her body twitched as if to move toward him. Anxious eyes searched out Zander's, the question in them evident.

"Go on. We'll talk to Ms. Levi while you fill him in."

The smile Betty offered was hesitant. So were her movements as she rose unsteadily to her feet. Elly supported her elbow until Betty's legs stabilized.

As Betty dodged tables and chairs on her way toward the main hall, Morgan refocused on Elly. "Ms. Levi–"

"Please. It's Elly. I'm not that formal."

"All right. Elly, I understand you found the body." Morgan's voice had the consistency of melted butter. "That must've been a shock."

"It was. Poor Jessie." Tears flooded her eyes, making them sparkle like the amethyst necklace Laura had thrown at Zander's head when she'd stormed out the door two years ago.

"Walk us through what happened."

As Morgan asked the questions, Zander studied her face. For someone who had just found a body, she didn't seem all that shaken. Sure, tears glistened in those violet eyes, but her voice was serene and her movements controlled.

"Betty and I were coming in to get lunch going." She pushed her curls back from her face, tucking them behind her ears.

Yeah, those curls begged to be touched.

He reigned the thought in.

Not that he'd touch them. Now or ever. Women brought him nothing but trouble.

Women. Trouble. He needed to keep those two words together, no matter how much he wished things were different.

And now he was missing the conversation. He tuned back in.

"…she was already dead. I heard a noise in the pantry and went to check it out. She was in the alley by the time I got there."

"You know who she was?" In direct conflict with his smooth tone, Morgan's questions came hard and fast, with an intensity that tended to make people uncomfortable.

Didn't seem to bother Elly, though. She offered a single nod. "Monica. She and Jessie were always together and it looked like her from the back."

"Monica got a last name?"

Elly lifted her shoulders in a slight shrug. "I'm sure she does, but I don't know it. I'd been trying to get close to those girls, but they don't trust easily. Monica may not even be her real name."

Swell. It was the answer he'd expected, but it didn't make his job any easier.

Zander shifted his weight, his eyes never leaving her face. "Did you ever see anyone fighting with Jessie? Hear anyone threaten her?"

"No. She didn't interact much with the other kids. Except Monica. It's so sad." Elly shook her head slowly. "At least she went quickly."

What?

He studied her closely. She was serious. How could she possibly know that? The ME hadn't even examined the vic to see how she'd died or how long it had taken. A human could bleed out in a matter of minutes, but until the autopsy was complete, they wouldn't know that for certain.

So how could Elly know her death had come quickly?

Unless she knew more than she was saying.

She *was* awfully calm. Too calm.

Could she have something to do with whatever happened here today?

Made in the USA
Monee, IL
29 November 2020

50013417R00194